Come midday, Matt was e‾ ‾‾‾‾
strutting in the shallows of or‾ ‾‾‾
to check that a clump of nea‾ ‾‾‾
Matt and she could have lunc‾ ‾‾‾

A few minutes later Matt h‾‾‾ ‾‾‾‾ ‾‾‾ ‾‾‾‾. ‾‾ ‾‾‾‾ something draw tight inside his chest. His senses jarred, caught off guard. He spun round, shaking himself out of the back-pack which contained their lunch and tore through the arrow-weed of the bank with spontaneous drilled aggression, all his senses alert. He lay prone in the grass at the edge of the copse of shady trees where he had heard Danielle cry out from, his pistol extended in a double-handed combat grip, searching the ground before him with his aim.

'Look, flame lilies!' she cried out again. She turned to see if he was coming and was abruptly checked by the barrel of the pistol pointed in her direction.

T. J. LINDSAY

The Shadow

SPHERE BOOKS LIMITED

A SPHERE BOOK

First published in Great Britain by Michael Joseph Ltd 1988
Published by Sphere Books Ltd 1990

Reproduced, printed and bound in Great Britain by
Cox & Wyman Ltd, Reading

ISBN 0 7474 0132 2

Sphere Books Ltd
A Division of
Macdonald & Co (Publishers) Ltd
Orbit House, 1 New Fetter Lane,
London EC4A 1AR
A member of Maxwell Macmillan Pergamon Publishing Corporation

kana mumvuri womunhu waenda ava mudzimu

When the shadow of a person has gone he has become a spirit

– African saying

November

The wheat had been harvested, it wasn't yet the right time to plant the maize, and it was Sunday. But even then, on Matiziro Farm you took your moments of leisure with the guilty feeling that you should really be working. Danielle Nel saw how her husband was instinctively checking the land about him, reminding himself to do this or that on his return, before they had barely started down river into the sanctuary of the valley for a picnic lunch.

He saw her smiling at him, and knew she knew what had been going through his mind.

'OK, I'll forget about the farm for a while and relax.'

She hugged him close against the vaporous chill coming off the river as they walked. The rising mist, raw in their throats, was caught in the light of early morning.

Their four Ridgeback dogs ran excitedly about, sniffing out every new scent, and from time to time brushing warmly against their legs.

Matthew Nel had explored the river so often in his youth, that every slight variation of its course had found a permanent place in his mind. Now, at a time of no-rain, it was little more than a long trail of countless pools threaded together by the slow trickle of a stream, but the mist gave the illusion of an ethereal depth.

Matt felt good. He always felt that way in the valley, especially at that time of the morning.

'If God is ever to be found I don't know where or when exactly, but I know it'll be in Africa, and I know it'll be in the early morning,' he said.

1

'I know where in Africa,' she smiled.

He laughed. It was as if the country was not being mauled by an embittered guerrilla war.

When the sun clasped the earth in its warm embrace, the river pools became enamelled with it.

Danielle removed her T-shirt, exposing her breasts to the sun for an all-over tan.

The river valley revealed itself before her, and all the while there could be those who were watching them from the dense undergrowth of the opposite bank.

Suddenly, Matt pulled her down into the bushes, a finger over his mouth signalling silence. Danielle, alarmed, searched the opposite bank in the direction of his gaze.

After a few moments she tugged his arm and when he turned to her she asked in a whisper, 'What's wrong?'

He gestured with his chin in the appropriate direction.

And then she saw them, baby guinea fowl in the grass close by.

Come midday, Matt was engrossed in watching black cranes strutting in the shallows of one of the river pools. Danielle went off to check that a clump of nearby trees wasn't invaded by ants so Matt and she could have lunch in the shade.

A few minutes later Matt heard her cry out. He felt something draw tight inside his chest. His senses jarred, caught off guard. He spun round, shaking himself out of the back-pack which contained their lunch and tore through the arrow-weed of the bank with spontaneous drilled aggression, all his senses alert. He lay prone in the grass at the edge of the copse of shady trees where he had heard Danielle cry out from, his pistol extended in a double-handed combat grip, searching the ground before him with his aim.

'Look, flame lilies!' she cried out again. She turned to see if he was coming and was abruptly checked by the barrel of the pistol pointed in her direction.

He caught her words at the same time he saw her. The air held in his lungs escaped raggedly. In embarrassment his hands dropped down and he looked at the weapon. He had not consciously known that he had drawn it from its holster. He shook his head.

'Flame lilies,' she said apologetically, and she pointed to a blaze of wild flowers, each like an exquisite flame on its long fragile stem, a startling display of beauty that made the land around seem harsh by comparison. Matt's automatic reaction of aggression brought back to him the reality of a land ravaged, bleeding, made ugly by war.

Danielle cradled his head against her breast, stroking his hair, comforting him.

He shrugged her off. Without saying anything, Matt went back to where he had dropped the back-pack, making safe the pistol in his hands. He felt his hands trembling. He shied away from the fear that he had felt. He could not mistake its writhing in his body. He chastened himself, he should have known, the dogs had not barked.

When he returned to her he was smiling, but Danielle saw that his smile was merely a mask to hide his real feelings.

By an unvoiced agreement, the incident was permitted to pass without verbal dissection.

He threw a stick into a nearby river pool for the dogs to chase.

She laid out a picnic cloth in the shade.

He settled down with her to a crusty loaf, cheese and glasses of red wine.

The dogs joined them too, wandering across the picnic cloth and shaking the river water from their fur.

Matt laughed; animals always had the effect of stabilising him when he felt uneasy about things.

Danielle lay back, looking up at the sky and the few fleecy white clouds that changed shape above her. She was thinking about what had taken place. Matt acted as if he had dismissed it, but she knew that he had only pushed it down from the surface to a place inside him. If one was deliberately looking for it, as she was, one would have seen a flicker of intense combustion that on consuming itself died in a glaze of despondency.

Matt knew she had come to recognise it, that chink in his emotional armour.

The quietness between them was filled by the sound of birds and insects, the rippling of the river and the breathing of the wind.

The sky and the clouds were suddenly blocked from Danielle's vision by his face above her.

He ran his eyes over her body. Every curve and hollow expressed an inviting womanhood. Her long legs were a golden brown against the light khaki cloth of her shorts which were moulded to the shape of her hips and pelvis, and her firm breasts pushing up.

She gently traced the outline of his jaw with a finger.

3

He tasted her mouth on his. Her tongue tickled and quivered.

They made love beneath the trees, beside the river, in the afternoon; broad daylight, out there in the open. It wasn't what they had intended but it was the way it turned out – thrust after thrust, and the pain of the rough ground against her back beneath the picnic cloth.

Afterwards, they lay there for some time, her silky hair spread about her head on his chest, her mouth soft against his throat.

The slow flow of the river continued. A bewhiskered barbel came to the surface in the quiet water of one of the pools and then was gone. They watched the ripples widen where the fish had been.

With the farmhouse in view once again, they followed the last stretch of the river back, accompanied by a flight of spur-winged geese and a burning African sunset. The sky was warm with colour, the earth beginning to cool. The lines between light and shadow were as sharp as if they had been painted.

But there was little the war around them had not scarred. Politically the country was in a mess. The black nationalists had resorted to waging guerrilla warfare to attain what they wanted, and what they ostensibly wanted was black rule. Matt sympathised with a lot of their grievances but not with the violence they saw as the means to obtaining what they wanted, and not with their Communist backers. Nevertheless he had gone on to the defensive rather than the offensive, hoping that he and Danielle could hold out until a just political solution could be negotiated. As a result, the farmhouse had taken on the bristling appearance of a small fortress guarded by its own militia whom Matt had trained in security and the use of weapons.

Twin security fences, three metres high with barbed-wire overhangs and floodlights had sprouted up around the house, grounds and kitchen garden, sandwiching a strip of raw earth impregnated with anti-personnel mines. The farmhands' *kraal*, too, was fenced off and guarded. Old plough-shares set in concrete, packed with explosive and scrap iron, dotted the cleared area outside the perimeter fence like buttons for a steel vest. Walls were swollen with sandbags. Chicken-wire grenade screens sealed the windows, as if some huge mutant spider had spun its webs there. Grass and creepers concealed bunkers that pushed up out of the ground where once there had been beds of gladioli.

Danielle thought idly how, along with the sunset, the blaze of

4

golden honeysuckle and crimson bougainvillaea made the verandah look as if it was on fire.

Blue sky surrendered to grey, another day ended, its night began.

After dinner on the verandah, she sat close to Matt on one side of the table, stroking her wineglass with her fingers and looking out into the night where the river went about its mysterious business in the dark. A soft warm breeze glided down and mingled familiarly with them. She drank in a long breath caressingly.

The burning candles cast a flickering glow over them, bringing with its light a feeling of comfort.

She clasped his hand which rested on the table in hers.

Matt remained silent, as if recollecting something from the past, and feeling the softness of her hand in his. Then, looking out over the river valley nestling there in the night, he said, 'There's beauty here, Danielle.'

When they came back the following day from checking on the calves and the ploughing of the fields, they found James Creasely waiting for them. He was head of the police Special Branch in the district and had been in charge of apprehending the murderers of Matt's father and brother, four years before.

It had happened right at the beginning of the overt hostilities. Being fully conversant with several of the black African languages, Matt's father and brother had gone unarmed with the commanding officer of the district police to a group of dissidents at the border end of the valley, to find out what their grievances were and report back to the government with the aim of trying to resolve them. But they had been betrayed and were hacked to death with pangas. The dissidents' grievances brooked no compromise.

Matt, together with his closest friend from childhood, Jan 'Red' van Rensburg, from Spitskop, the neighbouring farm, had volunteered to hunt the murderers down himself. They had captured them. The murderers had stood trial and had been hanged.

Since then, the political problems in the country hadn't resolved themselves, but had dragged on without much change for four years, and Matt had worked with James on several occasions when his help was asked for.

Danielle, on the other hand, really only knew James by reputation. He had only been to the farm a couple of times and, accompanying Matt, she had met him a couple of times in town.

She prepared dinner.

Matt sat with James on the verandah with a couple of beers and talked.

Danielle couldn't hear what they were talking about, yet she felt uneasy. She couldn't explain her feeling, neither could she dismiss it.

At the table they talked about casual things, this and that – nothing to suggest her feeling of being ill at ease. But she noticed that Matt was biting the ends of his moustache from time to time, a habit that he fell into only when he was nervous about something. When she put the dinner on the table she placed James's plate in front of him with a loud clatter. She could not help feeling cold towards James, could not help feeling that something which would prove detrimental to her relationship with Matt had been agreed on. She didn't know what it was; she didn't know if it was really anything at all, but she didn't desist.

James couldn't have helped being aware of her coldness towards him either, but he said nothing about it, simply enduring it as if there was a reason for it, which didn't make her feel any easier.

When James left it was late at night.

Matt was acting as if he was uneasily trying to find a way to tell her something he knew she wouldn't like. She knew then that things had definitely changed.

'He's talked you into something, hasn't he?' She threw the question at him disappointedly. 'He's so good with statistics he'll have you accepting anything. He's talked you into working with him even more against the guerrillas, hasn't he?'

She waited for him to react. He didn't.

'Tell me,' she demanded.

'He hasn't talked me into anything. I'd already decided,' he said in a voice that was deliberately calm against the fury in hers.

Danielle heard the words but didn't want to believe them. His eyes showed a quality both tender and unreachable.

'You're already doing more than your bit. You've done your military service, you do your annual call-up camps, and you offer voluntary occasional help to the police when they need it. But you've also got a farm to run, people depending on you here. What more does James expect?'

She didn't mention it, but Matt knew she was thinking of his father and brother who had died in their attempts to resolve the conflict, that she didn't want to see him going the same way.

6

About to speak, Matt raised an arm in support; it felt heavy. He felt suddenly overcome with weariness, and let the arm drop again without saying anything.

A heavy silence followed.

'Well, at least tell me what it's all about,' she pleaded at last.

'I'll let you know this once,' he agreed, 'but please don't ask me anything about it again. For security reasons I won't be able to tell you.'

Stilled and ashen-faced, she looked at him, expecting the worst.

'As you know, the political situation between the government and the black nationalists has reached a new stalemate. Neither side is prepared to compromise. The smouldering guerrilla situation is getting worse. The conventional forces of the police, army and airforce are faced with the particular difficulty of trying to locate the guerrillas once they are in the country. The guerrillas perform hit-and-run raids, then conceal their weapons and disperse amongst the *kraals*, living and working quite normally with the people. James has asked me for my help in the district on a more regular basis.

'You know I'd like nothing more than to just farm, but for the farm and its people, and for the people of the valley in general it's necessary for me to offer what assistance I can. But don't worry, I won't be involved in any real danger,' he lied to make it easier on her. 'The professional soldiers will be there for that.' He knew his words sounded hollow.

Danielle felt words of objection welling up inside her, but somehow all she said was, 'When?'

'Three days,' he answered.

'For how long?'

'I don't know. As long as it takes.'

All the other words she could think of somehow never reached her mouth.

He took her in his arms. She held him tightly.

The following day began with a gloomy morning. The wind coming off the river and the dam was cold. The sky was a soaked grey blanket. The water was murky grey. The weather weighed oppressively on Danielle. She felt it changed the way she viewed the valley, either a cause of her depression or a symptom of it. The wind faltered, appeared to have withdrawn, and then came back even

7

stronger than before. It chilled the trees and shook their numbed branches. It reminded her of the great oak tree outside her home near the city when she was a child. The wind had torn the yellow rusty leaves off their branches; and then one morning, the last leaf had hung desolate.

She looked for the wild animals that always abounded at the river. To have seen them would have cheered her, but it was a miserable day and they knew better than to come out in it, she thought.

Then she saw a black crane, but not with his family, alone. Her depression shifted deeper.

Looking up at the sombre clouds, she felt she knew what it must be like to live under water. The thought made her check her breathing lest her lungs filled with liquid and not air.

Slowly, bit by bit, the war was claiming more of Matt's life, and, in consequence, her own. It seemed so unfair because it was not of the making of either of them. If only they could be left alone, she thought.

She trembled. She felt the wind on her neck like the rasping of a serpent's breath. She spun round. There was nothing there but the river. The tranquillity of the scene she observed seemed to be mocking her.

The dogs moved into her frame of vision and sniffed at something at the water's edge.

She was scared; scared for Matt, and herself; they were too much part of the same thing to be regarded separately. The time of unthreatened, voluntarily controlled togetherness, a time of certainty in so far as knowing where each stood in relation to the other, was perhaps past. She could not prevent tears forming in her eyes. She quickly wiped them away, turning to go back up to the farmhouse. No . . . it was not over yet . . . it was not over yet . . . they still had three days.

Matt had left her to go out alone in the early morning. He had felt that she wanted to be by herself for a while. Now he watched her come back in. She nestled in the warmth beside him once again. He had needed time to think just as she had. The war loomed over the valley and the farm and he could not evade it. An uneasy sensation made him feel hollow.

He looked at Danielle beside him and offered a warm smile. She smiled back uncertainly and snuggled closer.

They lay in bed longer than usual.

8

It was 7.00 a.m. when a vehicle drove up outside. The dogs barked. Matt made no effort to get up.

With an overwhelming desire to remain in bed with Matt and let whoever it was go away, Danielle reached for her dressing gown, slipped into it and went out to see who the visitor was. It was an action in which she seemed to lose part of her strength.

The voice of a man came through to Matt as he lay in bed unmoving. It was the voice of a young man.

'Good morning, Mrs Nel, I wonder if I may speak to your husband please.'

The 'Mrs Nel' and 'husband' parts registered in the back of Matt's mind. He eventually recognised the voice as that of a policeman who had recently arrived at the outpost in the valley. He heard Danielle invite the man in. Reluctantly, he got out of bed.

The young policeman greeted him cheerily.

Matt gave a slight nod of his head.

'An urgent message for you, sir. I got here as soon as possible.'

'You don't have to call me sir.'

Matt took the folded note.

There was something about the man that reminded Matt of himself when he was a few years younger. The man was probably nineteen years old. The naïve freshness that he saw disturbed him.

The young policeman looked about the room as Matt read the message; he stared at Danielle.

Matt reprimanded him for his familiarity. The young policeman quickly averted his eyes.

Matt made no attempt at cordiality and although he reproached himself, his manner did not change.

The message was from James. Matt decoded it. It was short and to the point. He read it with mute disfavour. He wrote his reply on the bottom of the teleprint scroll, tore it off, handed it to the man and requested that it be transmitted immediately.

The man departed.

Matt went through to the shower-room. He did not know how to face Danielle. Nothing could be said that would ameliorate the fact that the war was about to take an even bigger bite out of their relationship.

Danielle knew that it was James Creasely who had sent the telex. She sat on the bed with her knees drawn up to her chin in what she

9

knew to be a defensive posture. A sense of foreboding rose within her. She had to follow him into the shower-room to find out what had transpired.

Matt saw her coming in the mirror. He continued shaving.

Without saying anything she waited for him to tell her.

He broke down first. 'Our three days are up', he said. 'I'm wanted out there this afternoon.'

There was a very difficult silence. They were imprisoned by it.

She felt herself slipping away. The present had suddenly become untenable. She took off her dressing gown, stepped into the shower and adjusted the taps. She could cry in there without him knowing.

Matt was getting things he would need in the bush ready when she came out, a towel wrapped around her, and feeling more composed. Looking at him, she shifted her balance slightly for the earth had seemed to tilt beneath her feet.

They made love once again.

His withdrawal from her was like the abrupt severance of an umbilical cord; she felt cold; moving on the periphery of a dark bottomless void.

Who could know what lay ahead of them from that moment on?

His rifle came out of the firearms cabinet. It was a symbol of hate, its appearance invoked the presence of a harsh soulless world.

War. It had come in a little more from outside and its shadow had fallen a little more upon them. Like an illegal abortionist it had no respect for life, it got deep inside and piece by piece scraped the life out of people.

She felt cold. She felt empty. She wanted to hide. And outside was the valley and the river's drifting shape.

The basis of Matiziro Farm's economy was cattle, with maize grown in the summer and irrigated wheat in the winter. In most things the farm was self-sufficient.

They had a small dairy herd, a few sheep, a few goats, pigs, chickens, water fowl, fish in the dam, a large vegetable garden, a citrus orchard, deciduous fruit trees for fresh or dried fruit and preserves. Daily they baked their own bread from their own ground wheat. They made their own butter and cheese. They made their own dried, smoked and pre-cooked meats, hams and sausages for storage in case of hard times. And from wild game in the untamed bush area they obtained venison.

A senior farmhand was in charge of each of the farm's separate enterprises, reporting directly to Matt when he was there and to Danielle in his absence, the longest of which was usually his thirty-day annual military commitment. In many ways the farm ran itself – but every able-bodied hand was needed to keep the momentum going. Matt had the vision for its future, and no matter how hard Danielle tried she could never communicate with the farmhands and the livestock in quite the same way as he could.

The days passed since Matt's departure and each day Danielle watched for his return. It was silly really, she knew, for there was no telling how long he would be away this time. It would have been better, she thought, if she simply expected him when she saw him.

On his annual camps she knew well in advance exactly what day he would leave and what day he would return, and so both had been able to plan accordingly. Now things were different.

Matt was still away when !Kai, the farm's resident tracker and gamesman, also the oldest member of the farm, advised her of damage to the fence on the farm's northern boundary. So with !Kai she picked up a couple of the other farmhands, loaded the fencing equipment in the back of the Land Rover with the four dogs, drove out there, saw to the necessary repairs, and started on her way back to the farmhouse.

The gently sloping land enclosed by Horseshoe Ridge, in the bend of the river, where Matiziro and Spitskop Farms sheltered, acted as a natural trap to mineral sediment washed down from the hill's upper slopes with the rains. It was, perhaps, some of the most fertile land in the district. Not that you'd think so now, apart from the frayed patches of green that survived along the river, not in the dry months, especially since the rains had not broken. It was a harsh dryness, countless shades of brown.

With the sun blazing languidly at its zenith, hanging there with no visible signs of moving, !Kai had hiss-clicked with his tongue: 'Tt . . . tt . . . tt! Each time the rains have come they have not even laid the dust.' Tension in the weather reflected itself as tension within himself – he was more concerned about the lack of rain than the bush war.

!Kai told her how there was a new lion cub and plenty of new impala offspring in the bush of Matiziro, how they needed the rain.

As she reflected on these things, Danielle could see the cattle were

11

sheltering in the shade of trees by the track. The cattle had proved themselves capable of surviving by themselves, even in the worst drought. Well adapted to their African environment over many generations, they browsed on the leaves of bushes and trees on the *veld* as well as grazing on grass, and were mostly resistant to local pests and diseases which foreign imported breeds succumbed to. Africa was for Africans. But, as !Kai had pointed out, they still needed what he called 'a father's guidance'.

Enough said.

Matt was out in the bush somewhere.

Danielle drove up from the valley on the dirt track that would lead to the farmhouse at the top of its *koppie*.

Suddenly, she realised that she was still on the farm's isolated dirt roads later than was prudent; it was dusk, a time that presented the most favourable conditions for an ambush.

The fourth day of the ambush seemed longer than all other days anywhere. It was almost as if time had succumbed to the oppressive heat.

Elephant grass, bleached by the flat white glare of the sun, matted the earth's crust like hair on a cow's hide, coarse and unmoving. It was difficult to believe that the monotonous sky had ever known change.

They were wedged between the sun and the earth in a dry ravine. Like a seared gash that had healed badly, it scarred the belly of the valley which lay close to the border.

Their rocky cover, streaked with the reds and oranges and yellows of desiccated lichens, came between them and the yearned-for warmth of the early sun, but, disparagingly, left them exposed to its merciless rays as it journeyed westwards; the harsh thorn scrub that broke the outline of their bodies with wispy shadows was of scant protection against the sun's ferocity.

Matt had tried to think of streets, of jostling people, of fountains, of cool restaurants. He tried to think of Danielle, but the bush forced itself upon him. Its every sound, tumescent, violated his private thoughts.

His head reeled. He felt nauseous. A sick phlegm lumped sorely in his throat. His stomach knotted in empty contractions. He itched everywhere at once; in his hair, beneath his jacket, inside his *velskoene* – brushed-leather bush shoes – wherever he could not scratch. Sand grated across his eyes, eyes that wanted to sleep. His tongue was swollen drily in his mouth. He wondered if he could ever talk again; he rubbed his jaw to try to make it work. He tilted his head towards his chest to flex the muscles of his neck. He noticed that his shirt front was mottled with dark patches of greasy sweat. Dust coated him. It embedded itself in the weave of the cloth. He could feel the sweat and the dust mingle to form something live that wriggled down the back of his neck, and then dried almost immediately on his skin in the heat, leaving a skeleton of dirt.

His world had contracted to less than a hundred paces of bush, growing up towards him, around him.

Every movement was contemplated and controlled like that of a chameleon – each limb moved in slow deliberation so as not to draw attention to itself. To defecate a man had to dig a small hole beside him, perform his natural bodily requirement, slowly, muscle by muscle, cover the hole with sand, slowly and all without a sound or the slightest obvious movement.

Concealed jerry cans of drinking water, hot during the day, tepid at night, were almost empty.

Acting on information received, they were waiting in ambush for a weapons resupply guerrilla section. It was to be a simple ambush operation acting on A1 classified information, eliminating an entire section of guerrillas who dared to wreak terror on the people and their property in the valley.

Waiting.

Always waiting.

Time passed; days fragmented into hours, hours into minutes. Every second crawled by painfully.

Each long day darkened into an even longer night.

Pictures flashed on the surface of his mind at random, creating the illusion of change. But there was no change. Each day was the same as the last, and threatened to be just the same as the next.

Waiting softened a man's brain. No action. No talking. Nothing.

The enemy had not entered the ambush. Thousands of insects had. One had to learn to ignore them. The more one scratched, the more irritating it became . . . the more irritating it became, the more one scratched . . .

Matt looked out towards the Claymores; he couldn't see them but their positions were engraved on his memory. Every time he thought about those anti-personnel mines he expected something to go wrong

13

with them; some animal to knock the bloody things over; a thunder storm to trigger the bloody things off. Animal? They had urinated at each end of the trail to discourage game from using it. As for a thunder storm? It would have taken a miracle. But it didn't prevent him from thinking about it. It was forty-two degrees centigrade in the shade, no more than an opaque form of sunlight. There wasn't so much as a breath's vapour in the sky, an empty powder blue.

He turned his head slowly towards the man concealed in the undergrowth a few paces to his left. Andrew 'Andy' King. A professional member of James's staff. Here, however, Matt was in command. But that was on paper. That was for a different world. Out here they never heard their own name nor voiced that of another. Neither did they see an insignia of rank. Talking revealed the whereabouts of a target. Names and ranks identified that target. No one in his right mind would want to be a target! All communications were reduced to silent signals.

Andy, a tall man, his height now stretched out on the ground, was motionless, wilting there. His rifle was propped up on its magazine as if it were a tuberose root seeking sustenance from the soil. He turned. He caught Matt's gaze, and of all things, smiled. Sweat ran in streaks off the camouflage cream on his unshaven face. *Mupani* bees, *bocha* – he called them 'kaffir-budgies' – collected in worrisome clouds, settling on his skin, seeking moisture in each orifice of his head. Matt expected him at any moment to commit himself to that futile swatting action, the '*mupani* salute'. But he didn't. Matt could see in his expression his fight against the infuriating desire, calling on every vestige of his self-control. Kill one *mupani* bee and all its relatives come to its funeral, Matt thought.

Mupani. Turpentine wood. It thrived where other trees could not even germinate. The leaves hung down, closed, during the heat of the day to reduce surface area exposure to the sun and thus reduce water loss; and, as a consequence, denied shade. But even if the trees offered no shade at that time of day they presented food for game that chomped the scented leaves. The seed of the tree, in its turn, stuck to the hooves of the game that were attracted to it by the leaves, and in this way would be dispersed throughout the *veld*. Worms also fed on the wood. Matt pined for the nutty flavour of those very same worms, gutted and sun-dried.

The tree was a world within a world, the same world that Man would come along to and chop down for firewood!

14

It was strange what the mind dwelt on in the bush when all that was considered 'civilised' was denied one.

Matt switched his thoughts back to the *mupani* bees. Not edible. A damn nuisance.

Waiting.

Matt, looking at the others, thought how they had concealed themselves as best they could in the bush, and in turn, he thought of !Kai and how, if the old man had been there, he wouldn't have been observable in the undergrowth even if it was known beforehand where he was going to conceal himself. Matt thought how they were poor imitators in comparison.

!Kai had taught him most of what he knew about the bush.

!Kai was, for want of a better term, a bushman, but in fact owned up to no national or linguistic self-awareness to which a label could be applied. He saw himself neither as a bushman (in English), *San* (in Cape: 'Hottentot'), *boschjesman* (in Dutch), *boesman* (in Afrikaans), *baroa* or *Masarwa* (in Tswana), *mandionerepi* (in Karanga), or any other label that outsiders chose to give him. The band of people to which he belonged had been known only by the name of the prominent feature of the locality in which it had lived. The feature was none other than Matiziro – Place of Refuge – a prominence of tumbled-down rock like an ancient temple or fortress in the uncleared bush area of the Nel farm which had taken its name.

When Matt's grandfather had staked his farm it had been right in the path of the migratory trail of a band of five of !Kai's family who passed back and forth following the seasonal migration of the game between summer and winter, when there were mosquitoes and no mosquitoes. These were the ochre-brown bushmen, survivors of first the black military raiders who were bent on possessing the land, killing the men and enslaving the women and children; and then the whites.

The villages and farms of the black and white people had increasingly partitioned the land, precluding !Kai's right of access until he appeared no more than a trespasser on the lands his people had hunted and foraged since time immemorial, long before the coming of black and white.

In order to survive, he found he had to become absorbed into the new order, and so sought employment with Matt's father. But he never forgot the old world and the old ways.

!Kai came to be an invaluable advisor as to the state of the game, where they were, how many, of births, deaths, of water and forage availability, and when others had failed to find them, the tracking of cattle that had strayed, as well as keeping stock-thieves and game poachers at bay.

The black people of the farm, in awe of him, described him as *Muzivisisi*. The description fitted like a wart hog in its hole – The One Who Knows – whilst in his own language his name !Kai was the appellation for a springbok.

Matt and he would speak together in his mother tongue, a dialect of the *San* bushmen group of languages, the language of a people who were an endangered species – like the tsesebe antelope, white rhino, cheetah . . . Even when others were present, because of its rarity, it was a private language for all but an exclusive initiated few, like a code.

If he had been there, the little old man would be staring out at the world from behind his wispy beard and high crinkled cheeks – The One Who Knows – wise in his silence, waiting with the endless patience of Africa itself; like a cobra, unperturbed by any lame distractions, striking only at the moment of absolute necessity, and then only with absolute commitment.

On the far side of Andy was Jan 'Red' van Rensburg, Matt's first white friend, from the neighbouring farm, Spitskop, the other half of the land encompassed by Horseshoe Ridge. His other early childhood playmates, apart from his elder brother, had been the dark-skinned herdboys and other children of the farmhands.

Red, at heart a gentle giant of a man, looked on unflinchingly into the bush.

Matt fingered the battery and the detonation leads, gazing fixedly to the front once more. The light multi-strand twin cables disappeared ahead of him. Three R1-M1 Claymore anti-personnel mines were linked up in series covering the game trail that cut through the ravine. The convex explosive face of each was packed with a delivery of 700 steel ball-bearings. Multiple *Cordtex* initiation. Ten grammes PETN per metre. With an explosive rate of almost 7,000 metres per second.

He had laid the mines in the pre-dawn darkness of the first day, four days – or was it weeks? – ago. Stem of grass on top, legs of the mine manoeuvred, the stem of grass aimed at the midriff of a man at thirty paces. He had placed them ten paces apart so that their fragmentation patterns would overlap, covering almost one hundred paces of the trail with total effectiveness. Beyond that, with a spread of sixty degrees they were dangerous up to 250 paces.

Behind rock cover, outside the perimeter of the concussion area, they waited. After a while, in the stillness and silence, a man began trying to see and hear things that weren't there. Listening to nothing but the bush growing around him did things to a man's mind.

They tried to rest in turns, for two hours in every three during the day, and six hours in nine during the night. In that way they hoped to avoid overstress and eye strain, to sleep.

All communications were silent, hand signals or tugs on lengths of dull green string linking each other, precluding unnecessary movement in attracting one another's attention when waking one another up, when changing watch or in emergencies.

Despite his exhaustion, Matt found it difficult to sleep. The idea of detachment in that sort of situation was disturbing. Closing one's eyes was bad enough, how more so the complete alienation of sleep?

It could happen at any moment.

The sun had finally dropped to the western escarpment. Shadows reached out mockingly. For a drawn-out eternity they would never seem to touch, then would miraculously fuse into darkness. He knew.

The fourth day of the ambush was coming to a close.

Suddenly, Matt's skin tightened with an animal instinctive awareness of danger. As if to confirm his feeling, a large kudu bull suddenly materialised from the bush and bounded through the long grass. Painstakingly, Matt studied the terrain, taking small areas of it in at a time. He was thinking that perhaps the kudu had got wind of their scent, the urine of the trail, then he saw them. A single file of men appeared in the ravine, momentarily silhouetted against a ridge of skeleton grass, pale, drawn of its moisture. They were armed to the teeth and coming along the trail.

Daylight was fading. Shadows stretched taut.

His hands automatically sought the battery and the leads as he had done so often before. He felt the comfort of rifle steel against his skin. He felt the tug on the string secured with a quick-release knot to his belt. He looked swiftly to each of the others in turn. Their eyes momentarily gripped each other's across the space that separated them. He held the exposed copper end of the wire, tracing the empty terminal of the battery with his other hand without taking his eyes from the boundary where the file of men had merged with their surrounds. Apart from the sway of grass in the ravine it looked as if nothing but the wind had been there to disturb it.

Once again they were waiting, as if everything was suspended on the held breath. But it was not. The pulse of blood, insect movement, carried on around them. Where once everything had appeared to be still, now everything appeared to be moving. They had to distinguish between human movement and the ethereal movement of shadow.

Unexpectedly, a shadowy form on the path silently crossed Matt's vision, entering his contracted world, the 'killing ground' segmented into 'arcs of responsibility'.

Christ! Lead scout . . . ahead of the others . . . must have missed him, thought Matt.

He couldn't make out the features, the face. It was getting difficult to make out anything in the fading light. He could discern nothing more than a moving silhouette.

He became absolutely conscious. All his faculties bore down on the present. Adrenalin coursed through his veins bringing awareness to stiffened limbs. He prayed that when his brain barked out orders his body would be capable of obeying.

While lying there, the most he had been able to do was callisthenic exercise, muscle acting against muscle, no abrupt movement.

The expanding darkness pressed down on him.

Surprise. An ephemeral factor. One false move now, the rasping of cloth on a bush, the clink of metal, and the endless torment of the last four days would be worthless, eliminated as simply as the evacuation of a man's bowels into a latrine.

Matt counted in time with the paces of the lead scout who was now out of sight. There was a gap of approximately thirty paces. He would be approaching the perimeter. As the distance increased, Matt felt his heart sink in his chest. Where were the others?

Then the line of men appeared in close formation, no more than five paces separating each one, each in comfortable sight and sound of the man in front. Their progress was laboured and weary. Laden with bulging back-packs, heads bent tiredly, eyes down, they mechanically followed the game trail that presented itself as the easiest route through the ravine. A man stumbled under the burden he was carrying, almost fell. Had he seen them? No. He recovered and was walking on again.

They were dressed in military shades of green and brown,

camouflage in a land where deviation from the natural order of animal and plant stood out like fire.

One of the guerrillas spoke. Matt went cold. But it was just a clip of unsuspecting conversation. Warmth returned to his body.

The lead scout would be almost out of the killing ground. Matt had to decide. Two seconds. Everything seemed closer than it was in the fading light. His eyes strained to discern differentiation in the deepening shadows, his vision blurred in the impending darkness.

He touched the bare wire to the open battery terminal. The circuit was complete. Almost 7,000 metres per second. A flash of intense light. The Claymores detonated in a simultaneous explosion, 2,100 steel balls reaped everything in their path: grass, bushes, trees . . . men.

The past four days, in which Matt had come to suspect that the falling of darkness possessed sound, had given way to something that was louder than sound, jarring his brain in his skull. It hung in the air around him.

In the sudden darkness that followed the blinding fire of the explosion, eyes, even though they had been closed against the light, had to adjust; pupils dilated enormously.

A spreading wall of steel scythed across the trail concentrated at the level of a man's torso.

There was no return fire. A man screamed thinly.

They moved forward swiftly, searching. The low scrub trees and bushes were lacerated. Raw pink and yellow furrows marred the bark of their scraggy trunks. Within the concussion area the ground was scorched and flattened.

Sources had indicated that there would be eight guerrillas. Andy's lips were moving in silent count. He moved towards a body to confirm its death. The body was curled up on its side. The body moved. Matt, who was closest, observed that it was just the escape of gas from the stomach, but immediately two shots from Red's rifle, double-tapped, cracked close past Andy. They entered the skull of the dead guerrilla neatly, but ripped the back off in their tumbling exit. Andy spun round, eyes searching for a target, his finger tense on the trigger of his rifle. Matt hastily gave the thumbs up, all clear, the all-OK sign to prevent a shoot-out between each other, defusing a potentially dangerous situation. Red gestured apologetically. Andy gave a little jump of mock fright, which made Red smile, before turning back to the task in hand. They continued the sweep.

They found a light blood spoor. The man was found dead fifty paces or so back towards the border. Four. Andy indicated the number with his fingers to Matt. Matt confirmed with a nod of his head.

Three had escaped, including the lead scout. How anyone could have escaped unscathed was beyond Matt – but they had. He readily picked up the lead scout's spoor. There were clear boot impressions in the powdery earth of the game trail; signs of cracked heels worn down on the inner edge, and two small holes in the ground, no doubt from two slightly protruding nails in the heel. He followed the spoor for a short way. As it headed back towards the border, and as the light was fading all the time, he didn't give chase. For the same reason, he didn't follow the spoor of the other two who had escaped either.

The count left one injured survivor. They returned to him.

The man was spreadeagled on his back in the bush, tossed aside by the blast. His battle fatigues were saturated with blood. It was impossible to tell at a glance where he had been hit. Matt was helped by Andy to unhook the man's arms from the cumbersome back-pack. It was heavy. A TMA-3 Yugoslavian anti-vehicular mine protruded through a torn flap. It was a mass of TNT moulded like a big cheese with cloth handles and three nipple detonators.

They carefully peeled the man's sticky clinging shirt from his chest. They found another one beneath. Infiltrators wore two or three sets of clothing; discarding the top camouflage uniform they would merge with the local populace like rain in a swollen river.

There were wounds in the neck, limbs and upper chest, but nothing to suggest the traumatic loss of blood and severe state of physiological shock. Andy wiped back congealing clots, ignoring in his haste the man's frequent cries. In one of the pouches of the combat jacket a thirty-round AK magazine had been struck. Bullets had exploded, blowing a hole the size of a clenched fist in the man's abdomen. Andy pocketed the magazine. Chromed it would make a nice souvenir bottle-opener. Matt guessed what Andy was thinking.

They ripped away the second shirt. Evisceration. Mass perfor-ations of the gastro-intestinal tract. Contaminating bowel content engulfed the wound. The certainty of peritonitis alone, though secondary to all else, made their efforts seem futile. They continued. Matt struggled to enter collapsed vein after collapsed vein with the needle for a drip, finally going into the sub-clavian vein straight through the chest wall. He put the drip on to free-flow, fully open, snapped the neck off the ampoule of morphine he wore around his neck and injected the man with its invaluable contents. A strip of plaster was stuck to the man's forehead with the time, amount and type of narcotic administered. He squeezed the Ringer's Lactate drip bag as tight as it would allow to hasten the flow of fluid into the man's body.

The man's gut was sluiced with the sterile Ringer's Lactate. The loose intestines were secured on the abdomen with a soaked bandage pad, and another drip, hung above the man on the branch of a thorn bush, was left leaking against dehydration of the intestinal tissue.

It was then that Matt realised the man had sustained a fracture of the pelvic girdle. He felt carefully along the two haunch bones supplying sockets for the thigh bones, and at the bottom of the spine. That was where the break was, in line with the abdominal injury.

Andy broke off the ampoule of morphine around his neck and handed it to Matt. Matt shot that into muscle as well.

It was impossible to avoid movement of broken bone. Slowly and as gently as possible they tried to bring the lower limbs in line with each other. It caused the man too much pain, so they stopped. The morphine would take time to work, time Matt didn't think the man had, and even if he did have the time Matt suspected that any amount of morphine wouldn't be enough.

Andy set about splinting the lower extremities together. He applied padding and overlapping bandages around the pelvis and hips. It was while padding the thighs that the man urinated. Matt felt the body-hot dark stain spread on the trouser leg.

'No!' Andy warned hoarsely, gripping the man fiercely by the shoulders, but the word merely seemed to act as a cue for the releasing of restraint altogether.

It was the first spoken word since they had moved into position. The first word in ninety-two hours. Its sound gave Matt the impression that all speech was disjointed and that it had just taken silence to prove it so.

Andy shook his head. The bladder, once emptied, ceased to act as a cushion between the fractured ends of bone. The man screamed. Matt could almost feel the abrasive grating of damaged bone. It set his teeth on edge. There was nothing that could be done for the pain. The optimum dose of morphine had been exceeded, there would be little gain in further narcotic, only an exponential increase in undesirable side-effects: respiratory inhibition, nausea, vomiting, even chemically increased psychological depression. The administration of more morphine would more than likely ensure his death.

Sweat ran off them. They continued cleaning, patching, bandaging. The man died before a second drip had emptied.

The kiss of life couldn't revive him. Artificially oxygenated blood just leaked out of him with cardiac compression. He was bleeding heavily inside.

'Five,' said Andy flatly, his tone of loss signifying thwarted professionalism rather than compassion. No survivor, no information, no finding the ones that had escaped.

That was all.

They had suffered four days that had seemed to fuse with eternity, just to touch a bare wire to a battery terminal, fill five men full of holes, fire two needless shots, then to try and save the life of a man whose injuries they had just inflicted.

It was night. A petrified silence hung in the darkness, louder than the explosion. It was as if tumultuous noise had always been part of the natural order.

They cleared the killing ground, heaping the dead bodies together. It was difficult to read the symbols of terrorism into bodies stripped of their life and tools of destruction, the malignant hatred and brutality, the indifference to right and wrong that had been their spirit. They seemed like any other dead bodies, saints or sinners alike.

Matt studied the small arsenal of rifles, hand grenades and land mines. AKs (Kalashnikov assault rifles), SKSs (Siminov semi-automatic carbines) and a PKM (which could be referred to as a 'Please Kill Many' light machine-gun), were still in their packing grease.

'Only the brand spanking newest for our super-gooks,' said Andy.

There were hand grenades from China, mortars and land mines from Yugoslavia, and military clothing from Ethiopia. There was a Degtyarev heavy machine-gun, Soviet, DSHK model 38. It was complete with tripod for use in an anti-aircraft role. It weighed thirty-six kilograms.

'Rotor'll be pleased that this thing's out of circulation,' said Andy.

'Yeah,' said Matt.

'With all that weight no wonder they chose the easy route,' said Andy. 'That'll teach the buggers.'

'Some lesson,' said Matt.

They moved off the trail.

For a time, Matt had forgotten how physically uncomfortable, how tired, thirsty and hungry he was. The awareness suddenly came surging back. Unexpectedly, he was intensely aware of his bone-weary exhaustion. It invaded the whole of his being. Everything around him seemed to lean oppressively over him.

He could hear the familiar whopping sound of Rotor's helicopter and those of the others in formation some time before he could see them, caught by the first thin rays of dawn, travelling low over the tree line, following the light rind of the horizon. He looked out towards their shapes, like growing dragonflies in the air. Dragon and damsel, among the fastest fliers in the insect world, flying backwards, catching other insects on the wing, mating in flight.

The sound was even more satisfying than the ecstatic moans of a woman making love. There was nothing more beautiful at that moment in life for Matt than the beating of those rotors in the sky.

Early in the morning Danielle attended to the small queue of patients that had gathered outside the farm's clinic.

It was she who had founded the clinic. It had been her first real contribution to the farm when she had married Matt and come to live there. As she kept up her registration as nurse, she served the farm population as their introduction to Western-style health education, hygiene and nutrition. She spent most of her time dispensing powdered milk for infants, contraceptives, tablets for constipation, diarrhoea or malaria, and attended to innumerable cuts, insect stings and even the occasional snake bite, but she had also helped to deliver several babies since she had been there, and referred a number of serious complaints to the doctors at the hospital.

Her achievement in gaining the trust of the farmhands was no small one, especially since they were part of a society in which traditional remedies, with their emphasis on an understanding of the role of good and evil in all circumstances of health, were the preferred ones. She had to work hand-in-hand with the local *nyanga* (tribal herbalist) and *svikiro* (spirit medium).

When her last patient had gone, she drove out to the cattle dip, not forgetting to take the Uzi machine-pistol that Matt insisted she keep with her at all times. Wherever she went, whatever she did, it was always knocking uncomfortably at her side, the sling rubbing raw the skin on her shoulder. It had become a part of her, a part she would have preferred to have had amputated.

She inspected the cattle for diseases and bush wounds as they went through the crush to receive their weekly dipping against external parasites.

By late afternoon, as she drove back to the farmhouse, she was tired and dusty and her muscles ached from having got involved in the physical work with the farmhands as Matt would have done had he been there, leading by example rather than from behind with the boot.

On the way, she stopped to look in on the farm's general building. The dogs leapt out after her once again, her own personal body-guard. Two of the dogs were her own, while the other two were Matt's, although they always accompanied her when he was away. Their light wheaten-coloured coats, with a ridge of reverse hair along the back, made them look a little lion-like; they were from the oldest African hunting-dog stock, their ancestors having perhaps hunted lion.

They followed her about through store rooms for seed, fertiliser, insecticides and herbicides, to the well-ventilated and dust-free paint-room, the fuel and oil section, the machinery section and the workshop.

She exchanged a little banter with the men working there before they finished off for the day.

To Danielle, the workshop had a powerful masculine appeal that spoke vicariously to her of Matt. She could sense his presence there even when he was away.

She sat down at the small writing desk in the small office partitioned off from the work area by a glass-panelled wooden wall and door. There were bookshelves of vehicle log-books, machinery records and manuals, a first-aid box on the wall, an old black telephone on the desk, an electric fan on the filing cabinet, a large grey one just like the one in the main office up at the house. She noticed even the neatly sharpened pencils, points up in an empty mug. She sighed, got up, and went back into the main work area. It was expansive enough to accommodate tractors and combine harvesters. The smaller hand-held hoeing implements hung from the tie beams in the roof out of the way.

The repairs, service and lubricating section was immediately outside the office, with its two vehicle pits, each with a shielded electric lamp hanging at its point on the white glaze-tiled walls, and carpeted with fresh wood planings. Red fire extinguishers hung on the wall close by and red buckets of sand on a rail. One complete end of the building opened up smoothly on well-oiled runners and rollers to reveal the fuel pump and air compressor under their roof outside, and beyond were the fields and the bush.

In the roof above were opaque skylights and in the walls long rows of windows let the day in, but even so, flicking a panel of switches blindingly illuminated the entire workshop with fluorescent light. The Nels had enabled that small miracle too, caused it to happen.

In contrast, the smithy with its forge was barely lit at all; but that too had its purpose, enabling the whites, yellows, oranges and reds of glowing irons to be easily discernible, showing the correct working temperatures of the heated metals.

Matt was so meticulous about everything.

There were shelves of spare parts. Each vehicle had its own shelf painted in its own colour. The lids of old fruit-preserve jars had been fastened to the under surface of the shelves for the jars to be screwed on or off as required. They contained nuts and bolts, nails and screws, washers and ball-bearings, American, British and continental, each in their respective sizes. Every tool had its place as to type and function, their outlines painted on hanging boards so they could not be muddled up or misplaced: pliers – tapered, saw, side-cutting, fencing; screwdrivers – point, star and countersink; valve grinders; ring-squeezers; torque wrenches; easy-outs; braces and bits . . .

The guerrilla war threatened everything: the farm, its people, its livestock, everything.

But, as !Kai said, everything was subject to seasons, and the war was just another season; seasons came and seasons went.

Once the men had left, she locked up the workshop and resumed her journey to the house. One of the farm militia, grinning widely, hastened to open the gate as she approached. The dogs barked at him playfully.

'*Masikati*, madam?' the militiaman enquired in greeting.

'*Masikati!*' she returned.

'*Maswera here?*'

'*Maswera maswerawo.*'

'*Ndaswera.*'

'*Taswera . . .*'

As she drove up the long curved jacaranda-lined driveway,

honking geese – a living alarm system – scurried from the vehicle's path. The dogs barked at them too.

Danielle climbed out of the mine-proofed Land Rover with its armour plating, conveyor-belt-padded floor, roll-bar, tyres filled with high pressure water, and twin AK sub-machine-guns concealed in the back and pointing to either side, activated by a solenoid on the dashboard where the cigarette-lighter used to be.

She walked along the flower-lined gravel pathway to the verandah and sat down on the swing chair there. Looking at the security fences, sandbags and grenade screens she suddenly experienced an intense emotional invasion of her consciousness, like a revelation from outside herself. Behind the wire and the sandbags it was still the same farm; through her feelings for Matt it was part of her just as it had always been part of him. It was the same farm, only wearing a temporary mask, for surely it must be only temporary?

She looked past the fences down the *koppie* into the valley at the dam with its shrunken banks, and the long necklace of pools – all that remained of the river – sparkling with myriad reflections of the sun; where striped frogs sunbathed on the stems of reeds, and Rouen and Khaki Campbell ducks and teal played in the shallows round the duckhouse island. Now that it was the cool of the evening a flight of wild white-faced ducks flew in V-formation across the water, as they did every evening, even as the water shrank from day to day.

The excavation for the clay used in the bricks which formed the farm buildings was now an extension of the dam; one of its sides comprised part of the nearside bank. In the course of centuries, fine gravel had been eroded from the slopes of the *koppie* on which the house had been built, and deposited there to form the clay and sand at its foot. The farm had risen from the virgin bush of its very earth and entirely through the industry and sweat of one family, with their own hands and out of their own lives. The fine gravel that had been eroded from the slopes of the *koppie* had been placed back up there – albeit in the form of the house.

'Never let anyone else do anything for you if you can do it yourself.' Danielle could hear the words as if coming from the lips of the oil paintings of Matt's grandfather and father in the study. 'Africa is not for the weak, only the strong,' Matt's grandfather had apparently summed up the continent. To know more about the grandfather and father was to know more about Matt, thought Danielle; to be acquainted with the driving force that had formed and guided him. It was in the construction of the farm, particularly in the smallest detail, that Matt's grandfather and father were to be found; in every planted tree of every wood, in every field cleared of bush, in every brick of every building.

His grandfather, the founder of the farm, had died when Matt was still a boy. His father and elder brother had died before he was even twenty-one. But there had been time enough for him to have learnt from each.

From his grandfather, Matt had discovered that the earliest a boy learnt to be a man, to stand on his own two feet, the better. Of his grandfather Matt had told Danielle how he remembered strength and gentleness in one form.

From his father Matt had learnt the value of fair judgement, to receive and give reward and punishment where it was due. His father had passed on what he knew of life and farming in Africa through everyday experience to both his sons without prejudice.

From his elder brother Matt had learnt camaraderie and brotherly affection. Together they had had great plans for the farm and the future. They shared something of intrinsic value, a natural affinity and love for the land and its peoples.

The male Nel standards for one another had been high, and in their closeness they had been strong as a family.

The 10,000-hectare farm was to have been divided between father and the two sons. Matt, like his brother, was to have been allotted his one-third share of the land when he turned twenty-one. Each was to build his own homestead when he found a wife. At the time of his death, Matt's brother had been engaged to Red's sister. Father and brother had helped him mark out the foundation for the new homestead, but no walls had ever gone up.

The brothers had decided between them to commit a small part of their land to maize and cattle, but in principle to concentrate on managing the land about Matiziro *Koppie* as a game sanctuary, conserving what they could of the true Africa. Instead, Matt now had the entire farm to look after by himself and it was a daunting prospect for him to cope as well as his grandfather and father had done.

The notion had been instilled in Matt from the earliest age that specialisation was for insects. Man had to be a universal agent: an architect, a builder, a stonemason, a plumber, an electrician, an engineer, grow his own food, make his own bread, be friend, husband and midwife.

27

And it showed in every facet of the farm, the utterly clean order and practicality of it all. There were no unknown elements in its constitution. All factors had been taken into consideration; everything fitted together like it was intended to be that way by nature. The buildings seemed to fit in naturally in terms of function, position, availability of sunlight, prevailing winds winter and summer; the smells of the fowl run in the wet months, and pigsty all year round, were carried away from the farmhouse by the wind; and the mill, with its white grain dust, was positioned on the lee; the principal rooms of the house were splashed with sun from season to season through one window or another; the verandahs received the benefit of breezes during the summer yet were free of draughts during the winter.

Feeling Matt would soon be home again, Danielle looked out over the gardens about the farmhouse, the green freshly mown lawns and plants in full flower, a festival of colour, and she couldn't help smiling at the beauty of it.

She went from the verandah into the house.

She felt like someone to talk to, but Maruva, who could usually be found working somewhere in the house, had gone off early that day.

Once behind the coolness of the thick double brick walls and under the terra-cotta tile roof that had insulated the house against the day's heat, she sighed involuntarily. She went through to the bathroom en suite to the main bedroom, removed the Uzi machine-pistol and its sling that cut into her shoulder, and placed it beside the bath. She ran the water steaming, despite the almost unbearable heat of the afternoon. She needed to soak away the accumulated dust and muscle aches of the day.

As she undressed, she stared at the weapon's black blunt-nosed form; or rather, it seemed to compel her to stare. Ugly, she thought. As near as she could come to hating anything, she hated it.

It was ironical, she thought, that she enjoyed going down to the makeshift fire-arms range Matt had built on the far side of the dam; it offered the opportunity of being with him during part of a day when otherwise he would have been busy elsewhere on the farm.

Her mind returned to the weapon as she stepped into the therapeutic heat of the bath. She did not believe she could shoot a man. She felt guilty that they should have to kill chickens and sheep and cattle for food.

28

The weapon was hard, cold, impersonal. There was no soul in a gun. It was a soulless, bloodless thing.

She didn't let on to Matt that she would never be able to use it for the purpose it was intended – killing. It was more preventive than anything else for her; like contraception – or was that the wrong analogy? She shuddered at the thought of armed men raping the fair country.

After dinner by herself, she made sure the radio battery was charged, the doors were locked and her Uzi magazine was loaded. Then she went to bed early and read for a while before going to sleep.

It was shortly after three in the morning when she was startled awake by the sound of the dogs barking, the geese honking and voices at the gate.

Much as she would have liked to have seen herself react differently she found herself frightened and much as she wanted them to, her limbs wouldn't respond to her desire to move. Time seemed to rush on as she lay frozen in bed. Then miraculously, able to summon a little courage, though trembling a little, she found herself clambering out of bed and fumbling for the Uzi Matt insisted she keep behind her pillow when retiring for the night.

It was then that she heard Matt's voice and heard the sound of the Land Rover starting up by the gate. She thought how, while she had still been asleep, he must have stopped to talk to the militia guards there and turned the engine off so as not to disturb her unduly. She heard the sound of the Land Rover driving on up to the house.

'Hello, love.' He kissed her when he came in and found her waiting for him there at the door. 'Go back to sleep. I'll see you later in the morning,' he whispered, and went straight to the guest room. He looked absolutely worn out, and was filthy.

When she looked in on him a little later she found him spread-eagled on the bed in a drugged slumber. He had not even climbed out of his soiled clothes. His *velskoene* were still on his feet. Thick streaky camouflage cream was still on his face and arms. He reeked of animal sweat and the hot smell of gun oil.

Later during the day, when she looked in on him again, he was still asleep. She desperately wanted to kiss him but could not bring herself to do so, not right then, the feeders and the carrion of the African bush swept into presence with stomach-lurching force. The flowered light bedcover was marked with grease and dirt. She stared

29

at the chain of bone he wore like a choker around his neck; he never took it off, not even when they made love. He had said nothing more about it than that !Kai had given it to him when he was a young boy. He had told nobody more than that.

Matt woke up as she stood looking at him. It took him several minutes to come round, as if he had undergone an operation which had required a general anaesthetic. Danielle's image came to him and he felt at peace, not experiencing the need of the past few days to struggle against his drowsy state. He allowed it to pass in its own unhurried way.

'Welcome back,' she smiled. 'You've been asleep for the best part of fourteen hours.'

'Why didn't you wake me?'

She smiled knowingly.

He sat up and studied her. 'You're real!' he said, and pulled her to him, against the harsh several days growth of stubble on his face, not noticing her resistance.

'Matt!' she exclaimed, serving to remind him of his physical state.

He looked down at his filthy clothes and body, then apologised by kissing her again, which made both of them laugh.

He spent almost an hour in the shower, the water jets stinging his body like acupuncture needles. When he came out, a towel around his waist, steam billowing into the bedroom, he smelt of coal-tar soap and peppermint toothpaste; he had shaved, and combed his hair.

Danielle looked into the bathroom and let out a moan. Clothes were hung everywhere, there were grease and dirt marks on the walls and towels, there was a shaving tide-mark around the inner rim of the sink, the floor was swamped with water. Matt grinned angelically. He kissed her again. This time she kissed and kissed him, only breaking off reluctantly.

'Get dressed, and have a good meal, lunch is in the oven. Meanwhile I'll clean up here,' Danielle insisted.

He knew from past experience that it was futile to argue with her about such things. As he dressed in the bedroom and she cleaned up the bathroom, he conducted a conversation through the open connecting door.

Maruva interrupted them. 'Eat your food while it is still hot,' she commanded Matt firmly.

'Ah! My mother hen, I have missed you so!' Matt responded, hugging her affectionately.

'Silly boy,' she waved him away. 'Eat your food. Do you expect a woman to labour all day behind the hot stove for you to eat cold food? If so, you may forever eat raw cold food, for these two women . . .'

'You too a man cannot argue with,' Matt cut her feigned tirade off.

'Leave women's work to women,' Maruva ordered, immediately fussing about the bathroom helping Danielle.

Maruva was !Kai's wife. She was jolly and rotund with the flat primitive features of the land-working tribeswoman, adorned with a garish bright caftan-like cotton dress.

The black African woman bloomed ephemerally, was deflowered, bore buds . . . and there were petals no more. Nature, eminently practical, saw no use for superficial decoration once the role of procreation had been fulfilled. But deep inside, the beauty of a mother's passionate and protective love for her progeny endured.

The bond between Maruva and Matt was far more than the mothering instinct common to the breast of every woman. She had been present at Matt's birth on the farm when his father had taken him from between the legs of his mother. When his blood-mother had died, it was Maruva who had mothered him as if he was one of her own children. Maruva herself had been unable to bear any further children after the birth of her second son nine years before. Secured with a *chari* (shawl), his ear pressed against her broad back, the crying baby Matthew Nel had been comforted by the beat of her great heart as she worked, the pulse of Africa itself.

His father had never remarried, so Maruva had looked after his house. When his father had died Maruva had continued to look after the house just as she had always done.

Danielle, whom Maruva endearingly called *Mwanangu* (my child), found herself too being sheltered under the voluminous warm wing of that loving black woman.

Matt had once told Danielle that he had never known his grandmother as she had died before he was born, and that he could not consciously remember much about his mother as she had died after a long illness when he was still young. He said how they therefore comprised no more than impressions made up of photographs and the emotions of others – love, respect and sadness – while he had always known Maruva as flesh and blood.

The dogs were barking excitedly, playing in and out of the rooms of the house. Their master was back. The big house resounded with life once more.

Passing the kitchen there was the usual mouth-watering warm smell of fresh bread. As far back as Matt could remember it had been one of Maruva's roles to bake bread daily in the huge wood range stove.

As was the usual occurrence on homecoming occasions after a while away from the farm, Danielle and Matt sat down at the verandah table together and chatted about things as he ate.

She didn't ask him about the past few days, and he didn't tell her.

He read over the entries she had made in the farm's journal, and together they discussed them.

Finally he asked, 'Any other problems?'

'Nothing that eventually couldn't be solved.'

He smiled. 'You're a marvel,' and he kissed her.

'I'd prefer it if you were here,' she said.

'I know how you feel about it,' he said, and kissed her again. 'How's the wheat? Not too much in the way of weeds, I hope.'

'No.'

'And how's our Daisy doing?'

'Much better, she'll be able to go back to the dairy in a couple of days.'

'I really don't know what we all did without you,' he said, turning to Maruva who had come in. 'Do you, my mother hen?'

Maruva laughed and said how they'd spent most of the time trying to tame one Matthew Nel – and how they had been unsuccessful.

Matt laughed in turn and pushing back his chair rose from the table. 'Excuse me, ladies, have work to catch up on,' he said. 'See you later.' And then strode off, the dogs in pursuit.

Danielle thought how, as certain as the seasons, Matt would go off to see !Kai. They would talk about this animal and that animal, these trees and those trees, the river here and the river there, about the wind and the dryness, about the damage to the fence, about stray cattle that had been lost and found.

Neither had been to university, neither had formal degrees, yet there was no university that could have offered them a better education than the land. They had imbibed knowledge of nature with their first mouthfuls of milk as infants, and had not stopped learning since – though their liquid nutriment had changed! They'd swill back beer, smoke tobacco and talk about the land in a way few others could; not about domesticity or agriculture or herding, about butter-making or poultry care, the things she knew of, but about the

32

elements, about animal personalities, about tracking, about stories of the earth and animals and the hunt.

Then Matt would go and see the other senior farmhands and discuss the things of relevance to them.

It was late when Matt eventually came back to the farmhouse, and Danielle was toying with her hair at the dressing-table mirror preparing for bed when he came in. He encircled her waist from behind, his face buried in the flowing softness of her shampooed hair that had been brushed until it shone.

'Mmm, you smell like a herbal-scented forest.' He audibly breathed in the freshness.

'You smell better than you did,' she laughed, turning in his arms to face him, and kiss him gently on the mouth. 'I missed you,' she confessed.

He lifted her up in his arms and took her to the bed. 'We'll see how much,' he told her.

'Matt, you'll smudge my make-up,' she protested playfully.

He looked down at her face, a natural complexion and beauty that had little need of cosmetics, and smiled.

She was soft and yielding beneath him, wanting him as much as he did her.

Because of the war, all the farms in the valley were in contact with one another by radio, and with the police, there being dawn and dusk check-in times to ensure that everyone and everything were all right.

When a priority radio call from James, a few days after Matt's return, suddenly intruded into the tranquillity of her home, Danielle felt her heart involuntarily palpitate. Matt was out in the fields at the time arranging the maize planting. There had been light rain the day before and Matt hoped it wasn't another false start to the rainy season. She called him up on his vehicle radio, knowing that he always ensured that it was within earshot when he was out working. He answered the radio and immediately came on up to the house. Neither he nor she knew what had been so urgent for James to contact him, only that he should be ready to go out again for a few days.

It had just turned dark when James arrived at the farm with Andy and two armoured troop carriers bristling with heavily armed escort, having already picked Red up en route.

Desperately trying to control her emotions, Danielle stood with

Matt by the front door and watched the lumbering camouflage-painted vehicles turn around in the driveway, their big double wheels flattening part of the flower bed she had recently planted with seedlings.

James, Red and Andy poked their heads up from the turret hatches of their respective vehicles and called out to Matt and herself in greeting. She called back in a buoyant voice, but it wasn't the way she was feeling.

'Come on or they'll be old men and hardly worth chasing by the time we get there,' called out James, the engines revving.

Matt kissed her. She held on to his hand as he was about to pull away. 'Please be careful Matt,' she implored.

'I will,' he said.

'Promise?'

'I promise,' he said, kissed her again and turned to join James in the cab of the front vehicle. The vehicles were already moving off as he climbed in.

Danielle walked abreast of them to the gate and, waving, called out, 'Keep your powder dry, boys,' attempting a brave smile. She received waves, smiles and whistles in return. It was as if the men were simply going off for an away rugby match.

Before long, the convoy had left the farm access road and vehicle was chasing vehicle like hunter and hunted along a dirt road that led to a distant part of the valley.

James wasted no time in briefing Matt. 'The steel mill train's been derailed,' he said.

'Locstat? Location statistic?' enquired Matt.

James pointed out the map co-ordinates to him. Matt took a map out of his trouser-leg pocket, refolded it to suit his purpose and put an 'x' in the relevant place.

'When?' he asked, as he studied the map.

'Less than an hour ago.'

'Casualties?'

'Nine, crewmen and machine-gun guard. No survivors.'

There was a respectful moment of silence.

'Military engineers say they had just checked the line for explosives ahead of the train when they heard an almighty bang, heard the sound of rending steel and saw smoke and dust rising a few kilometres behind them where the train was. Understandably, they baulked a little because they thought they'd missed something in their clearing operations. When they started back, though, they heard small-arms fire, single shots, three of them. When they arrived at the scene they found all the crewmen and guards dead. Three who had seemingly survived the derailment had been shot. When they found the site of the explosion they found evidence that it was command detonated. Whoever did this one is a hell of a cool customer. He had been watching them from the bushes as they passed,' James told him.

Matt asked a few more questions then settled back in his seat. What other questions he had could only be answered by observation of the scene itself.

He found himself vacantly looking through the wing mirror at the dust trail that glowed red in the tail-lights to the vehicle in which Red and Andy were travelling behind. He could see the headlights winding and dipping back there with the bearing of the road. The familiar features of Horseshoe Ridge had receded into darkness, merging with the impersonal dark forms of the night.

The vehicles passed through the old tsetse fly gates that once indicated the Health Department's boundary fence, preventing flies and infected, but immune, game from entering the unsprayed areas and bringing the menace of sleeping sickness to humans or *nagana* to cattle. All transport between the two areas used to be sprayed to kill the flies that might have hitched a ride.

Shortly afterwards, the vehicles turned on to a rutted track clearly intended for slow-moving ox-carts not fast-moving motorised transport.

James lit his pipe.

Matt took a couple of cigarettes from a crumpled pack, lit them both and handed one to the driver. The driver thanked him. The man's dark face, glistening with a sheen of sweat in the luminous green light of the dashboard, seemed to hang in mid-air. He stared fixedly through the thick bullet-proof windscreen at the path cutting the bush in front of them, searching for disturbances on its surface that would suggest the presence of a land mine.

Matt saw shadows in the far reaches of the headlamps.

The pressure of the driver's foot on the accelerator faltered. Eyes strained into the night.

'Goats,' said Matt.

'Goats,' said James.

'Yes, *ishe*,' the driver agreed, and accelerated once more.

35

They did not stop for the goats to cross. It could be the initiation of an ambush. Matt felt the soft thuds against the heavy metal underbelly of the troop-carrier as they drove through the herd. There was no guerrilla rifle fire.

They moved away from the valley into open country, Africa's primitive heritage, bushland remotely punctuated by the kraal-lines of tribal chiefs; people who were part of the land around them; a people to whom everything was to be reached by walking, unaware of continents and oceans, of climbing cities with high-rise car-parks; where, without having to grow the grain, prepare it and bake it, bread in non-bio-degradable cellophane wrappers appeared miraculously on shelves in hypermarkets.

It was a raw land, a land without pretence. It was a land of a natural order with a natural god. And it was Matt's backyard.

He fought back the sleep that threatened to overpower him. He concentrated on the vehicle escort's casual banter pitched above the loud clatter of heavy armour plating as it rocked and jolted over the worn ground, the curious unperturbed banter of men born to war in Africa, for not since the coming of black and white had peace ever been known there.

Matt found himself thinking about how the maize planting would go while he was away, and whether he'd get back in time to help finish it, along with the cowpeas. He thought how every day he was away would mean some ten to fifteen hectares he could have personally planted. The farm was so much a part of him, he thought about it often. He preferred to be nowhere better than on the farm.

Instead, he once more picked up the map lying open on his lap, and studied the pencilled markings that had previously darkened it. Each mark was dated, and represented a guerrilla sighting or incident.

They intercepted the railway at an old disused siding. The sky glowed ominously in the distance with a rosy hue, as if they were about to go over the curve of the earth and see the sun still setting there.

It was a bush fire.

'The engineers said the explosion must have started it,' said James.

The dirt track ran parallel to the line for several kilometres. They followed it then swung off into the undergrowth, dodging trees, and drove along the steel line for a short distance. The tail-end wreckage of the derailed train loomed up out of the dark. The carnage of metal stretched far beyond the light of the vehicles' headlamps.

A stiff breeze had swept a fire through the bush to the far end of a deep cutting. Matt noticed the direction of the wind – it was from the south-east; smoke curled upwards, as black and as heavy as storm clouds, shielding the hills there.

James told the drivers to turn off the vehicle lights, and when their eyes had adjusted to the darkness to move on a reasonable distance further, in case an enemy was still present and able to mark their positions for an attack.

After a while it was quite possible to see in the diffuse anaemic light of the full moon.

An Engineers sergeant appeared ahead of them, his men at guard in the bush about him.

James leapt to the ground from the front cab with Matt and gestured for the escort to de-bus and take up positions of defence with the engineers around the vehicles.

'Evening, sir,' the sergeant greeted James in a gruff voice.

'I notice you left off the "good", ' said James, and shook hands.

'Yes sir,' said the sergeant and grunted in greeting to Matt, Red and Andy.

James surveyed what could immediately be seen of the train wreckage in the moonlight, standing with his legs apart, his feet firmly planted on the ground; neatly pressed trousers with sharp creases, shirt and tie with immaculate Windsor knot, cream Cashmere cardigan, cleanly shaven, not a hair on his carefully groomed pate out of place. And, finishing off the picture, his pipe firmly clenched between his teeth.

Never compromises his dress-code even in the bush, thought Matt.

He remembered the first time he had met James. James had offered his condolences over the deaths of his father and brother and extended his right hand as a mark of sincerity. His handshake had been firm. Matt tended to judge a man by the firmness of his handshake. He had an instinctive mistrust of limp-wristed men.

James tapped out the bowl of his pipe on the heel of a slightly dusty, but well polished, fine leather shoe. He blew the remnants of tobacco out, and ran a pipe-cleaner through the stem a couple of times before pushing the pipe into his shirt top pocket.

'Well, show us what you've got please, sergeant,' said James.

The sergeant led the way into the cutting.

They followed, literally stepping in his footsteps, diminishing the chance of stepping on any anti-personnel device left behind by the guerrillas, and so as not to disturb unduly whatever ground evidence there might be.

Despite a limp from an old war injury in his right leg, James moved with the agility of a rock rabbit around and past the overturned trucks and their payload in the moonlit darkness, his age deceptive.

The gradient of the cutting sloped away to the south, the steep batter of its sides twice the height of a man. Bush on both sides had been blackened by fire.

The strong smell of burning filled Matt's nostrils.

The point of detonation was a short distance inside the cutting entrance. Ragged craters revealed that explosions had occurred at two joints of the track. Explosives seemed to have been placed, slightly apart, each side of each rail so that their detonation had the effect of shearing away two entire unwelded thirty-metre curved sections.

'Forty-five kilograms per metre, solid steel, clipped as if it were light-gauge wire,' commented James.

The steel mill train had been making the same trip for as long as Matt could remember. It passed through the valley not far from the farm. As rumbustious youths, his brother, Red and he would ride out on horseback from the concealment of the bush at a bend and incline and board the train without being seen by driver or guardsman, like train robbers in the old cowboy movies. They would then enjoy a free journey to the border, sunning themselves in one of the open wagons, and enjoying illicit cigarettes and brandy.

He looked to Red and saw that seeing the crippled train was a nostalgic experience for Red too.

The train was a multiple unit of three massive DE6 locomotives hauling forty-five trucks of high-grade steel.

'It would have built up a combined 6,000 brake horse-power as it dropped in altitude on its run from the steelworks,' James said. 'Even on level track, if set rolling at its average speed it would have taken over five kilometers for it to have stopped unaided.'

Matt noticed that as the train had entered the cutting it had been on a steep downward slope. The explosion had set it askew. Its leading end had gouged, with the awesome momentum of its gross dead weight, into the earth and rock embankments that had imprisoned it.

'With over ninety tonnes a loco and 100 tonnes a truck fully laden, the train was an almost 4,800-tonne missile propelled at over fifty kilometres an hour,' said James, to whom figures and calculations were second nature, and acquisition of the knowledge of all things within his area of jurisdiction regarded a necessity.

Matt saw how the front locomotive had become nothing more than the scoop of a gigantic grader, ploughing the rails, sleepers and granite-chip ballast before it.

He traced the detonation leads up on to the bank, into a cluster of boulders sheltered by trees. He found an ordinary nine-volt lantern battery there. It was difficult to believe that what had happened to the train had its initial source in such a small innocuous household object. Matt was uncomfortably aware that the battery was the same make as the one he had used in the Claymore ambush earlier that month.

Flashing his penlight near to the battery and the leads, Matt observed bootprints. Adjusting the angle of his torch to cast the most opportune shadow, he saw that the prints were the same as those he had observed on the dust of the game path after that same ambush in the valley. The prints had belonged to the lead scout. There were the same cracked heels worn down on the inner edges, and two small holes caused by slightly protruding nails in the left heel.

'At least one of these gooks escaped the Claymore ambush,' he told the others. 'Perhaps the commander in both cases.'

'If so, one has to admire his ability,' said James. Then turning to the sergeant, he said, 'Wouldn't you say, Sergeant?'

'Yes, sir, he's no slack-arse who did this, sir.'

'On clearing the line, how far ahead were you?'

'About 3.5 Ks, sir.'

'That means a gap of about 4.25 minutes,' thought James aloud. 'So bearing in mind about 0.75 Ks of track before you would have been out of sight from where the explosives had been set, and the one K of track before the train would have had that point visual, the gook who did this would have had little less than 2.25 minutes, while out of sight of both you and the train, to run the cable out, conceal it, lay the charges, plug them with detonators, skimmy back up the bank, and be snug behind the battery terminal with the leads in his hands.'

39

There was no hesitation in James's calculation. 'Any longer,' he said in summation, 'and he'd have been up on the cow-catcher.' Then looking at the wreckage of the train in apparent horror, he shook his head. James appreciated anything done well – even this.

Matt flashed his penlight torch about him once more. He found two half-burnt matches in the grass by the battery terminals. The grass there had burnt a little and then gone out. There were more matches further along near to where the fire had caught hold and been fanned on in the direction the wind had been blowing.

'It looks as if the fire was started deliberately; perhaps to thwart the return of the engineers and any chance of an immediate follow-up,' he said.

A body lay on the ground in the cutting several paces further on.

Matt examined it. Black African male adult. The bridge of the man's nose revealed that he was accustomed to wearing spectacles. Matt looked around him. He found the thick railway-issue protective lenses ground into the earth by the heel of a boot. One bullet had been fired – into the head. The hair about the entry wound was scorched from the muzzle flash of a weapon, fired from a range of no more than a few centimetres.

'AP mines? Booby traps?' Matt queried the sergeant with a gesture around him.

'It got too dark to tell,' said the sergeant.

'We'll know if we step on something,' James said, with a characteristic hint of a smile playing on his lips.

Matt shone his penlight with its thin beam over the area around the shot man. Something glinted in the grass at the edge of the track. Squatting on his haunches, he cautiously swept aside the sharp bladed grass with the back of his hand. He found a single expended cartridge case. 7.62 mm intermediate. He poked a stick into the open end of it, lifted it up and studied it. It bore a triangular ejection smudge mark near the edge of the cartridge base.

'RPD,' he said without looking up. It was a Communist-bloc manufactured weapon capable of spitting out ten rounds per second.

Matt recalled how the lead scout who had escaped the Claymore ambush had been armed with that particular type of light machine-gun.

He checked the cartridge serial number. Russian origin.

James took a small plastic bag from one of his pockets and Matt put the cartridge case in. James took possession of it for ballistic tracing, to determine if there were any other crimes the weapon had been involved in; and perhaps fragments of finger prints could be lifted from it.

Matt moved on to check the second body. It had been battered to death in the derailment, not shot. He checked the next four bodies where they lay scattered about in various places on the cutting, around the train. Two others had been shot – but like the first, just once each. He found the two cartridge cases and James took possession of them as well. There had been no wastage of valuable ammunition, the others must have already been dead when the guerrilla commander checked them.

James checked the soldiers' dog tags and workmen's cards of the crewmen. Matt could visualise James's mind photostatting them, number, rank and name. James never needed to write down things like that immediately, he just remembered.

Right at the front, the lead locomotive, crushed into and on to itself, leaned at an angle with the embankment. The last body was mangled in there.

The sergeant stood quietly, staring vacantly, as if partly blaming himself for what had happened.

Matt handed him a cigarette. The sergeant thanked him.

Matt noticed that there was blood on James's clean Cashmere cardigan. It looked incongruous, as James's tailored and groomed appearance looked incongruous in the middle of the bush. But the next day he would be just as immaculate as he had always been. Every man has his own particular magic, Matt thought.

Each locomotive contained some 2,000 to 3,000 litres of diesel. Fortunately the direction of the wind from the front had kept the fire from there. A considerable quantity of oil had drained from a fracture in the vast twelve-cylinder engine of the crippled locomotive.

Having seen everything there was to see, they started walking back towards the vehicles.

'I'll set up base and attend to matters here, you push on,' James said, and turned to Matt for agreement. Matt nodded.

Other than alert the railway authorities and get a crane there to clear the line as soon as possible, photographs had to be taken, bodies finger-printed and bagged, reports written, and arrangements made for whatever support Matt, Red and Andy needed once they were on follow-up.

'Nice negotiations we're having for a peaceful settlement to this débâcle of a civil war,' James said sarcastically.

Matt knew James well enough to translate the words bluntly as, 'Fucking politicians.'

One of the troop-carriers became the centre of operations. A number of maps were taped up in sequence on the armour plate of the nearside. A TR-48 'big means' radio was set up on the bonnet, a 'sputnik' aerial cast into the overhead branches of a tree.

By torchlight, James marked the maps with the locstats of security force elements in the immediate and outlying areas as they were passed to him over the air.

Andy and Red sat with their backs propped up against the front nearside wheel, smoking contentedly while waiting.

Matt wondered what impression of the guerrillas !Kai would have gained from the clues available, what assessment he would have made of his quarry, of strengths and weaknesses. He was concerned that he had observed no obvious weaknesses. He seemed to be up against a formidable opponent.

Finally, he turned back to James. 'I think he'll head west,' he said. 'The land's relatively accessible there. Initially he'll probably rely on speed to put as much distance between his section and the railway line as possible, and then go to ground somewhere in here,' and he indicated an inhabited region.

James circled the area immediately west of their current position on the map. A tract of land the size of a large city. They would be looking for men, who, even lying down with arms and legs stretched out to the fullest extent, would at most only encompass an area of four square metres, in almost 650 million square metres of wild bush, tortured ravines and dying or skeleton rivers. There were no streets, no printed sign-posts, no door numbers.

Where there were no people it was the earth, the plant and animal life, that would speak in their place. If one only watched and listened, camouflage disappeared and the guerrillas would be revealed naked and vulnerable in their seeming security. But if Matt missed the signs where the guerrilla commander led his section out of the bush, they could conceal their arms and to all appearances vanish anywhere amongst hundreds of thousands of people – and there would be no immediate way of distinguishing them from the everyday subsistence farmers except through information filtering back to them eventually via the sources of James's office.

42

The railway was the divisional boundary of two regions. To the east was rugged and inhospitable terrain. Matt remembered it with little affection. He suspected that part of his assessment that the guerrilla commander would head in the opposite direction was founded on hope; probably the bigger part.

Since they didn't need daylight to see their way across the burnt *veld*, it being easily discernible in the light of the full moon, and so as not to waste time, Matt took a chance and moved directly across the burnt region in the direction he reasoned the guerrilla commander would have gone, the direction the wind had blown the fire. Where the fire had been, all trace of the enemy's movement would have been destroyed so there was no point in searching there. The shoulder-high grass had been transformed to a lifeless ash that puffed up in grey-white clouds as they crossed it. Charred stalks crunched underfoot.

Fire not only obliterated spoor and hindered pursuers but would also have compelled the guerrillas to have moved quickly ahead of it, or risk roasting in the flames.

The wind that had fanned the flames earlier had died down, leaving the fire to burn itself out in the distant foothills. As the furthest point the fire had reached was only smouldering then, Matt felt that he would easily be able to pass on through it.

They reached the north-west perimeter where he expected to find the spoor, in total darkness after the moon had set. It proved difficult and dangerous to move about. They moved off a short distance into the unburnt bush to rest and wait out the night.

They drew straws to determine the order of guard. Matt drew last watch. Three hours before then, he thought to himself; all too brief. He sank into a fitful sleep.

When the sun was beginning to show on the horizon shortly after 0500 hours and the usual long false dawn, Matt stood up and brushed off the ants crawling on his legs. He shattered the transient blissful repose of Red and Andy hugging the ground. A foot restrained the hand of each that automatically sought the trigger of the rifle each embraced.

Matt mentally made a note to ensure that he could not be taken off guard like that – that he should sleep more lightly, become more subconsciously aware, even with his eyes closed. If !Kai could do it, it could be done, he thought, and if it could be done it meant a better chance of staying alive.

It was a hazy morning in pastel shades creased with gunbarrel blue. At first, the sun appeared to have no warmth, dissipating in light rather than heat across the void, another empty sky, but as it rose to clear the treeline it began to push aside the early morning chill. The bush awakened around them with the fragile sound of almost imperceptible movement.

Matt felt his rifle as an inert weight heavy in his arms. He was not fooled by the sun's gentle deception, enticing all manner of living things out into the open. He knew it for what it was, a vicious, fiery, flagrant orb that had played that same ruse many times before. He wanted to curl up somewhere out of its reach and sleep some more.

He moved back to the perimeter of the burnt area and cross-grained along it, not moving with the expected line-of-flight but against it, hoping to cut across the spoor, across the 'grain', as with fibres in wood.

When he did cut across the spoor it was easily observable, unconcealed like that of wild game, far easier to find than if it had been calculatingly disguised.

He stood for a while scanning the ground in front of him in a 180-degree arc with his eyes. There was a shine on the grass where it had been disturbed. The stems were crushed and bent forward, reflecting the sunlight. The guerrillas had left a trail like a snail's slime, glistening.

He dropped to his haunches, squatting on the heels of his feet. The sun, at its present low angle, cast deep shadows, tending to outline the ground spoor to the eye. Indistinctly depressed areas in the dust, and scuff marks on the harder ground confirmed the passing of a number of men, but he could not immediately determine how many. At least six, he decided, perhaps as many as ten.

The land ahead was open; only sparse savanna-type tree cover and isolated granite *koppies* broke its monotony. They fell into a broad arrow-head formation, spacing irregular; natural vegetation didn't grow geometrically! Matt took the point, staying with the spoor. Red and Andy went out on the flanks. The spoor ran north-west through gently swelling country. The pace was fast and constant.

As Matt followed disturbed grass, broken twigs, scuffed earth, he considered what the guerrilla commander had been doing for the spoor to have appeared how it was. He envisioned that at first, prior to sunset and once the train had been derailed, he had clearly been concerned with speed, but once under cover of darkness and well clear of the railway line, he had settled down to an easier pace. He had moved on through the night, making abrupt course changes westwards. He had kept away from the scrub paths, favouring the open ground where it was difficult to follow.

The spoor, laid at night, traversed many open areas, not keeping to vegetation cover that would have offered shade and concealment during the day.

The sun seared against Matt's unprotected flesh. The saw-edged grass slashed his skin. Sweat made the hairline cuts sting. The heat pounded against his head.

They pushed on through the heat of the day. Periodically they would sink quietly to the ground and remain there, motionless, for some time, listening, watching. Strained eyes tired the mind.

Occasionally Red would relieve him of the intense concentration necessary to stay on the spoor. But even when seconding, one's eyes leapt ahead and around the spoor. It was essential to remain aware of changes in the terrain, and even more importantly, changes in the movement and tactics of the quarry. There was much to be learnt about an enemy before ever coming face to face with him: his decisions, endurance, discipline, his knowledge of bush lore; in effect, it was an on-going analysis of his personality.

Dead leaves, their exposed surfaces bleached by the sun, swept over revealing their darker ventral sides, were indicative of movement, but in order to learn of direction there was the continual need for confirmation with ground and aerial spoor.

Occasionally the tracks led directly into the sun, offering the most favourable combination of shadow and shine. Matt's progress was swift in those places.

Frequently he related the line-of-flight to the terrain and obstacles as recorded on the maps. That way they by-passed time-consuming areas.

He felt the bush with the bare skin of his arms and legs, not de-sensitised by cumbersome clothing, determining routes that offered least resistance to the movement of Man. They made their way through buffalo-thorn, the 'wait-a-bit' tree, slowed down, snagged, stopped. Moving on again. That was where the guerrillas had rested, concealed in the heart of the thicket.

A timid breeze nervously dabbed at the heat. The heat mocked it. Valuable moisture drawn from their bodies stained their clothing in dark patches.

Conserving water, they cautiously used the little they carried; a quick gargle and swallow during the heat of the day to ease parched mouths and throats; a few small sips after sunset, only drinking freely when they were sure of refilling. That was a !Kai dictum.

When they lost the spoor again, the countless time they had done so, the dying African sun was throbbing red, big and perfectly round on the horizon. It looked as if it was within walking distance. The guerrilla commander had got his section to engage furtively in anti-tracking: carrying each other, walking backwards, rock-hopping, sweeping the grass back behind them as they moved through it.

The usual wild game of the bush did not conceal their spoor which, as !Kai had shown Matt when a boy, meant that he had not strayed off the man-scent on to that of some other animal. But as much as Matt, through !Kai's teaching, was able to see something positive in even this disappointing observation, it didn't prevent Andy from gesturing obscenely.

Wearily, they adopted the lost-spoor procedure once more.

Their 360-degree observations progressively worked further afield. Matt eventually came across what seemed to be evidence of shoes having been worn back to front or of the men having walked backwards; for in sandy soil the heel of the foot always left a deeper impression than the ball of the foot. He knew they had relocated the spoor, but it was too dark to continue. Once again they had clung on.

Matt sat with his back propped against a *musasa* tree, ignoring the gnarled bark that dug through the clinging damp of his sweatshirt. No longer stretching on the move, his weary muscles cramped tightly. His joints stiffened in the evening air that was beginning to cool. He swished a little water around in his mouth and gulped it down. His dust-sore throat remained dry. With his knife he opened a can of meat and vegetables from his jacket's rear pouch. He ate the contents cold. When he had finished he punctured the empty can several times with his knife to aid its degeneration and buried it in the soil.

He sat motionless, gazing into the dark, his rifle cradled across his thighs. Another day had seen its end. Another night was beginning. *Wishu . . . wishu . . . wishu . . . wishu . . .* the fore-wings of crickets grated in the grass. The dark and the African bush closed in on him. It was night in Africa – a time when a man was left alone to the universe and to his thoughts.

His mind, for no reason in particular, threw a scene of his

46

childhood before his eyes. He saw himself as a boy aged six on the farm. He had sneaked from his room at night with his brother and gone down to the farm *kraal* to listen to the tales of the elders as they sat round an open fire passing a calabash of *doro* – the seven-day beer. From the sun's sinking behind the hills to when darkness once more relinquished its hold on the land, many calabash gourds of the freshly brewed African beer were consumed. Polite exchanges of conversation developed into staunch debate. Men's opinions sounded against men's opinions. Men's heads sounded against men's heads.

!Kai did not fight. But !Kai too, towards morning, was flushed with beer, with excitement, and Matt and his brother were there to see him dance, dance with the instinctive rhythm of Africa, the vibration of her First People. '*Gudu, gudu, gudu . . .*' !Kai barked, not simply imitating the alarmed call of the baboon, but dancing himself into a trance-like state he became the baboon; just as he became the eland, the blue wildebeest, the zebra, the giraffe; with his head, his hands, his legs, his feet . . . his whole body . . . his entire being. The animals of the *veld* and he shared a common essence.

And we, *murume ozavatema* and *murungu* (blackman and whiteman) with our 'possession equals nine-tenths of the law', have succeeded in nothing but shattering that precious harmony, that equilibrium between man and beast, thought Matt sadly, his conscious mind intruding harshly upon gentle recollection, which seemed more real, more present.

If the land belongs to anyone besides God, besides Nature, thought Matt, it belongs to the First People, !Kai's people.

It's odd, he thought then, that !Kai should so calmly tolerate the black people, live amongst them, have married one of them, a people who were direct descendants of those who, having seldom remained in one place for more than a single generation of tiring the land, had invaded his people's natural paradise, killing and oppressing, limiting them to desert areas where others were unable to survive; a people who had pillaged, raped and enslaved.

Africa then was a continent of continual migration; great movements of insect and animal life. But !Kai's people had arrived from no other place. They had sprung up with the first bushes. They were part of the land; and yet they were deprived of it by barbarous usurpers, besotted with greed. The blacks and the whites ('whose knees could not be seen') all called the land their own. And it was his grandfather who had fenced it! It was he, Matthew Nel, who now occupied it, and right at that very movement was intent on defending it with his very life if he had to! It was not the impulse of something simple and pure as hunger, it was a purposefully acquired sentiment, complex and debased. Why the hell was he thinking about such things? He shoved the painful thoughts away from him, but they didn't go far.

!Kai had long since put down his bow, and his arrow-heads dipped in the poison compound of *n'gwa* grubs, roots and the glands of selected reptiles. It had suddenly occurred to Matt that he had never heard of !Kai killing a man. In fact he had never seen him become even angry. !Kai always preferred to part company rather than argue; argument invariably ended in conflict. He only killed in order to eat, not out of some mental perversity, and then he was always strangely perturbed and repentant, never faltering in his profound respect for his fellow creatures.

Matt marvelled at the sudden revelation. It seemed to him he had been blind to these facts before. Why was it that he was so powerfully aware of them now? He stared into the darkness. How it all fitted together he had no idea. He sat there toying with this anomalous puzzle for some time but could come to no understanding.

He could so easily recall the smell of wood smoke, the beer and the harsh *shoro* tobacco from the past. Unable to keep his eyes open, Matthew Nel, the six-year-old boy, had drifted off into a sleep filled with a fantasy of images, sounds and smells. !Kai would carry him back to the house with his brother.

Matt's father, Geus Nel, had come to respect !Kai, and !Kai in turn had come to call Geus Nel *Mutongi wakangwara* – The One Who Judges Wisely. That had been a significant event since for !Kai labels were not simply lifeless words but the symbolic flowers that suggested the quality of a plant's roots. A greater understanding had developed into friendship.

Matt used to believe that no one ever knew that his brother and he had the habit of escaping from the house to the farm *kraal* at nights. Only when he was older did he find out that his father knew of every occasion. He found out too that !Kai always watched over them. That his father knew also, and considered !Kai's guardian mentorship with satisfaction.

!Kai had adopted them, not so much in word as in deed. One day he had shown them the *hwiza shava* (the large red locust) and told them a story about how they destroyed a man's crops, how they shielded the sun and ate everything that a man had grown in a season. It proved to be the first of many lessons. Matt remembered the stories of the hunt, told with that hint of dribble that found its way from the corner of his mouth into the sparse hair of his beard in the excitement of the telling. Clouds of red acrid dust driven by tens of thousands of sharp flying hooves across the sun-baked plains, burning in nostrils and throat like snuff. The beautiful people – the antelope – colouring the ground as far as the eye could see. The large multi-variate herds brought together by drought, otherwise spreading far and wide with the rains and the consequential rebirth of the bush. The black-and-white clown-like face of the roan with his tufted ears and mane of stiff hair. The long face of the blue wildebeest with its ears sticking out good-naturedly at the sides. The zigzagging little steenbok. The impala leaping high and far, across several bushes at a time. The largest and the smallest side by side: Mhofu the magnificent eland, one hundred times the weight of Ndundu the shy, charming blue duiker. That harmless creature was forced to retreat into the forest areas, to live in ones and twos, where, by the curious way of Nature, the tsetse fly alone would protect it – for there, neither Man nor his cattle could follow without risking sleeping sickness or *nagana*. Grysbok and bushbuck were chased into the shelter of thick bush fast shrinking before the onslaught of Man. And the graceful waterbuck, by a perversion of fate, was marked with a white target ring, to be shot in the buttocks by an amused hunter. !Kai's stories were a great spoken literature; Matt heard many of them, and with each telling he hungered for more.

As irony and the perversity of Man would have it, while Matt and his brother were steeping themselves in the ways of the black man and the ancient mysteries, crafts and bush lore of !Kai's ancestors, the two sons of !Kai and Maruva wished nothing more than to have the things that white men had, dress like them, talk like them, live like them. And as irony would compound it, Matt's father sent them to a school.

What it meant was that in time, Po and Kut began to look down on the menial positions and 'lack of education' of their parents. They saw the tradition and skills of the bushman as dying ways that would have no place in the Africa of the future with the bush, the true Africa, shrinking before Man's agricultural rape, and the forever land-guzzling expansion of the cities.

So, at the first opportunity Po and Kut got on leaving school, they migrated to the Big City. In the city they foresook their ancestry and reached out for what the strongest tribal group of the day, the Whites, had to offer – civilisation. They tried hard to become civilised, but in the process succeeded only in inheriting some of its worst traits – alcoholism and crime. Matt himself had had to bail them out several times, but it wasn't a solution – Nature was against them.

Matt and his brother, meanwhile, spent much of their spare time with !Kai roaming the as yet uncleared bush areas of the farm. They observed everything he did. !Kai seldom talked when out in the bush, but would draw their attention to things of interest, a plant here, the effect of weather there, a bird call from somewhere else. They tracked down lost or stolen cattle with him – and with Africa always being a hungry place, farms had continually to contend with stock thieves and game poachers, though as time wore on and the recovery rate and imprisonment of the offenders at Matiziro Farm approached 100 per cent, there were no longer any cattle stolen and few attempts at poaching.

They would record the species and number of wild inhabitants of the farm, following the spoor of lion, leopard, cheetah, rhino, hyena, jackal . . .

At nights they would search out nocturnal movers and hunters, or would relax by a watch fire with venison steaks spitting fat on the coals, and recount stories.

Sometimes Red would come with them, and they would test one another's prowess at hunting, tracking, finding water and grubbing for food.

They would learn about trees, bushes, grasses, flowers, what was good for thirst, for nutriment or for its medicinal value. They would learn about animal calls, what they meant, whether they could be recognised as warnings of approaching danger, or could be imitated as personal signals from one to the other.

Sometimes they would be out in the rain, sometimes at night, other times in the winter dark-morning cold, or in the summer midday heat. Sometimes they would have no water, no food or no rifle.

Never was the bush to be taken for granted. Sometimes, when they erred !Kai would say something like 'The lion will feast well this day.' You always had to remember in the bush that you were a potential meal for something else. Wild animals gave no second chances. If you failed to observe the signs it could be an omission that proved fatal. You had to remember that in the bush there were always other animals stronger than yourself. The only chance you had was to be alert and mindful.

Sometimes they would follow !Kai, and even as frail as he looked they would find themselves unable to keep up with him. He wouldn't stop to help them unless they absolutely needed it. When he had seen their true limit, though, he would tend to them and say, 'What gives way first? If it is your muscles we must strengthen them. If it is your mind we must strengthen it.'

!Kai was an old man now, yet he still paid particular interest to Matt, as a master would do in watching over the progress of a disciple.

Matt thought about these things, and he thought also how it had been survival in the bush !Kai had imparted to him, and now he needed it more than ever.

Matt slept. But his dreams were troubled.

The following afternoon they reached the first of the *kraals* in the *kraal*-line that extended through the Badza Range; hills that reminded one of the shape of a hoeing implement made from a club root and hammer-flattened metal digger.

The spoor skirted the *rapoko* grass and *rukweza* (finger-millet) fields and sugar-cane patch near the huts. They broke off lengths of the old remaining 'sweet-stick', chewing the inner pulp and drawing on the energy-giving juice as their quarry had done before them. But unlike their quarry, they pocketed the chewed pith and cane debris, not throwing it on the ground as they walked.

The debris trail suggested the guerrilla commander's confidence in having shaken off any pursuers. Matt followed at a brisk trot until the debris petered out.

The spoor changed once again towards evening. The guerrilla commander had adopted the ruse of walking on tip-toes and swinging from left to right, leaving prints similar to those of cattle. It would have thrown off a common soldier, but Matt was quick to see that they lacked the clear sharp edges of the bovine hoof. He wondered what !Kai would have made of it. He could visualise him squinting his eyes thoughtfully before etching the outline of a *kraal* hut on the ground. Yes! The guerrilla commander was mingling his spoor with existing cattle spoor, which might well mean he was intending to go to ground in the *kraal* from which the cattle had come, without leaving an obvious trail to it.

It was dark when they reached the *kraal*. The central yard within the thorn tree and brushwood barricade of the outer fence, hard swept to keep it free of weeds, showed palely against the dark shadows of the huts.

Dark figures were silhouetted by the glowing embers of a fire outside the central hut. The clank of a bucket, the thud of a log thrown on the fire, the drowsy murmur of voices carried softly in the still night air. The shrill of the crickets was at one with the darkness.

They watched and they listened. There was no sign of the guerrillas.

There was no sign of any dogs either; it made Matt curious.

He slipped away into the night. From the perimeter fence he watched and listened, and cautiously scanned the darkness about him, his eyes moving from shadow to shadow, shadows that seemed to gain life the more he stared. He tried to rest his eyes now and again but they jerked open with each new sound magnified by the night. The metal of his rifle was cold. The ground was shedding the day's warmth. Sweat and dirt had emulsified on his skin, drawn tight by the effects of the sun. It plastered scratches by thorn bush, grass and rock.

Overhead the Orion constellation showed prominently in the star-smattered sky. The tip of the mythical hunter's misty knife, tucked in his belt, seemed to point directly towards Matt as if he were a threat along with Taurus the charging bull. Faithfully accompanying the hunter were his two dogs, and there crouching at his feet was a hare . . . there above Matt in that cosmic hunt.

In the *kraal* there were two men: the *kraal* head and his brother, both old. It was the *kraal* head who was responsible for his family, who allocated land, who determined trivial disputes, who referred greater problems to the headman, and in turn to the chief. There was the *kraal* head's mother and there was his wife. The children of the *kraal* were away. There were seven other relatives by blood or marriage.

By observing the *kraal* layout and the number of huts, Matt deduced there were perhaps eighteen to twenty inhabitants who commonly stayed there.

Still he heard and saw no dogs at the *kraal*. He was unhappy about that. Didn't every *kraal* have dogs? To flush out *dassie* and birds from the thick bush for the young herdboys to strike down with their *knobkerrie* (throwing sticks) and take home for the pot . . . to keep the *kraal* clean of rodents . . . and to warn of the presence of intruders? But then, perhaps the dogs were out with the young boys.

Matt heard the *ambuya* (the mother of the *kraal* head) ask of her son what such men could be, these *vakomana* (boys of the bush) who sent young children out with the animals of the night. Her son grew anxious with her speech. He was frightened by something. A presence that was not Matt's, not Red's, not Andy's, close by perhaps?

!Kai, illiterate, not able to write things down in order to record them for posterity, had the phenomenal capacity to remember speeches word perfect, a capacity that literate people tend to lose – a capacity that Matt had difficulty with now.

He returned to Red and Andy with nothing but a slight rustle of grass to announce his arrival. He was satisfied with the course of events, but he didn't let the feeling reflect on his face. Success was expected of them. Besides, it was premature, anything could happen.

'*Pasi nerunyoka,*' he mouthed and gesticulated soundlessly. 'Down with the venereal disease.' They understood the association with the guerrillas, for they smiled.

The children of the *kraal* were the eyes and ears of the guerrillas. They were the *mujibas*, the young unmarried males, the recruiting ground for ancillary guerrilla forces. They would have been instructed to warn of any security force presence. They would search for spoor whilst out herding cattle during the day, and check features that could be used as observation posts. Matt looked at the dark swell of the hilltops around him where the *mujibas* would be. Somewhere within their cordon was the guerrillas' transit camp.

They settled down to wait out the night.

Even with close companions around him, Matt felt that it was a distinctly lonely feeling sitting there in vast Africa, between the tropics, south of the equator, on the revolving mass of the world, in the unbounded emptiness of space, its stars so far apart and so far away, their meaning as yet unknown and death so close at hand.

With painful slowness the night grew lighter as they sat there. The pole and *daga* (mud, straw and dung) huts with their close-thatched conical rooves became more discernible. Matt could see the rich earthy red of the clay walls.

Smoke filtered through the thatched roof of one of the huts, identifying it as that of the wife; it whispered against the dawn sky. Matt could smell it in the air.

The *kraal* had been built in the half-moon recess of the hills, above the pre-dawn river mists, overlooking the cattle pen. He could see the slope of the land on which the crops were planted without contour ridging. Each year the rains would wash away more and more of the precious top-soil that was needed for growth down into the river, a mere stream now, silted up and barely replenished. Extensive soil erosion had eaten away its banks. Cattle had been allowed to over-graze the surrounding grass to bare ground void of vegetation. It was vegetation that held the surface soil together, protected it against blistering and cracking in the sun, against being battered by the explosive impact of raindrops, prevented it being scarred by run-off rivulets and channels; it was vegetation, the silent unpaid worker that had done all those things, yet had been allowed to die and with no ceremony being paid to it. The dry earth, the dry earth void of vegetation, cried out for rain that now would come and whip its bare back.

Poor subsistence farmers sorely needed ploughs and agricultural education, thought Matt, and all they got was an over-abundance of foreign military hardware and ideological advice.

A cock crowed.

The cattle were restless in their pens. The damp smell of dung, moist with the early morning dew, was fresh and familiar in Matt's nostrils.

The ridges of the hills were burnished with the first touch of the morning sun.

A young black African woman, the wife, came out of the cooking-hut and washed pots in a drum of water. When she had finished she adjusted the position of the baby in the baby sling on her back, wrapping a length of printed cloth more securely about her. Balancing a large pot of *sadza*, the staple diet of stiff maize porridge steaming in the early morning, on her head, enough for eight perhaps ten hungry men, she picked up a rusty five-litre tin, filled it with water, and followed a path that led across the fields and into the bush.

They followed the woman like wild cats, silent.

54

A while later they let the woman go back empty-handed past where they had concealed themselves.

They moved on a little in the direction she had been, when suddenly a man rose unexpectedly from the bush to their right, and picked up the food and water the woman had left. Matt froze immediately. He had been following a path that was soon to circle back upon itself within full view of the guerrillas. He wouldn't have noticed the man if it hadn't been for his movement.

At that moment, the only sound was that of a distant clinking of metal on metal. It came from behind them, somewhere in the direction they had come from the night before.

Matt identified it as the sound from a cowbell, the cow languidly grazing. He paid no further attention to it. His attention was once again focused entirely on the area where the man had been, and the area beyond.

They found the camp. It was deserted, although it had been occupied only moments before. The occupants had been in the middle of eating. There was a bowl of relish that added variety to an otherwise monotonous diet of *sadza*, and there was meat and *mohwa* (African wild spinach, known in the cities as 'poor man's spinach'), with a hand-rolled ball of *sadza* dunked in the bowl and left there, a sign of sudden departure, Matt decided, rather than a slight of manners. There was a thirty-round AK magazine with rounds on the ground beside it. Somebody had been in the process of loading it. There were two clips of small-arms ammunition for an SKS self-loading rifle. Perhaps the rounds were being removed from the clips to load the magazine?

There were eight simple A-frame *musasa* shelters, constructed out of the branches of the tree of that name, and grass that blended in with their natural surrounds; difficult to see until you almost stumbled upon them. They were just high enough for a man to slide beneath and sleep, shielded from the early morning dew.

The guerrillas had 'bombshelled'; individual tracks radiated out in a 180-degree arc at the rear of the camp.

Had the woman realised that she was being followed and so advised the guerrillas? If so, why had they commenced eating regardless?

Had their approach been observed by the man in the rocks, or perhaps by another? If so, why, with superiority of numbers and firepower, and with the element of surprise on his side had a guerrilla

55

commander of the calibre he obviously was, not committed them to a fire-fight?

Matt's mind struggled for an explanation.

They went to the *kraal*.

The occupants seemed to be going about their everyday business as normal, as if nothing untoward had been going on there.

Andy was first over the fence into the *kraal*, rolling quietly underneath the grain hut which was supported above ground on poles to protect its contents from damp and vermin.

Covering the doors to the huts, which were all on the west side against the prevailing wind, Andy watched over them.

Matt and Red called on the occupants to come out of the huts, and herded them into the central yard.

They checked no-one was hiding in the huts. Matt crashed through the door of the cooking-hut. The door flopped back on its leather-thong hinges. The internal darkness was split by a shaft of sunlight. There was movement. He threw himself instinctively to one side. A startled chicken fluttered squawking past him into the open. Matt's eyes darted swiftly about the hut, observing. There were the clay- and straw-plastered walls, the compacted and levelled clay and dung floor, the moulded central depression for the fire, the three hearth stones positioned there, the shelf on which the wife had placed her clay cooking-pots, and there was the fixed bench on which no one but her husband was permitted to sit. Matt saw all these things, and the drinking gourd and ladle, the dried strips of meat and bundles of maize suspended on fibre strings from the poles, the cross-poles that supported the thatch, seeds dried and stored ready for planting. His rifle followed his scrutiny from the clay and cattle-dung floor to the thatched roof.

'Where is the key?' Red demanded of the *kraal* occupants outside.

'We do not know where it is,' came the reply, which was immediately followed by the sound of splintering wood.

It had been known for a guerrilla to sleep inside a hut with the door secured from the outside by a padlock to make it appear no one was inside, and to avoid a search for weapons of war. Security forces, on being told that the key was lost and not wishing to damage the meagre property of poor peasants, left it alone accepting what they had been told – only to be raked in the back with copper-jacketed lead from the hut as they were leaving.

Back outside, Matt saw Red come out of the neighbouring hut

through the shattered door, pull a swale of thatch from the roof, light it and set fire to the hut.

The cattle, still in the pen, became agitated when they caught the smell of the smoke. Matt stopped suddenly. He asked the *kraal* head how many cattle he had. The *kraal* head told him. Matt counted the cattle in the pen. They were all there. None of the cattle had been released to graze. Of course, the children were away from the *kraal*, there was no one there to herd them. He recalled the sound of the cow-bell they had heard on the approach to the guerrilla camp. Damn fool for not recognising it earlier, he cursed himself, none of the cattle were wearing bells.

He pointed out the observation to Red and Andy.

'Sonofabitch,' said Red.

'Warning signal,' said Andy.

The explanation had struck them as suddenly and plainly as it had Matt.

'*Mujibas* must be using cowbells to warn the gooks of any security force presence in the vicinity,' continued Andy. 'One of the little bastards must have seen us or come across our tracks.'

Red nodded in agreement.

There was the sudden cracking of gunfire. Rounds that the guerrillas had concealed in the thatch of the now blazing hut began to explode.

They discovered grenades amongst the maize in the grain hut.

Red found a mound of fresh earth not far from the *kraal*. 'Arms cache?' he queried. 'You,' he commanded one of the *kraal* occupants, 'dig.' If there was a booby-trap he didn't want to be the one to detonate it. The man dug, and the bodies of two dogs were unearthed, their throats cut.

'Somebody didn't like being barked at!' Andy commented.

The occupants of the *kraal* lay stretched out on their stomachs in the yard in quiet submission; their upturned faces expressionless, like unworked clay; their eyes glazed with indifference, unresponsive, wasting not the slightest amount of emotion on something they would get nothing in return from; feeling towards their antagonists as they would have felt towards a bush fire or a swarm of locusts. These were insensitive things that simply happened and a man achieved nothing in kicking against.

Matt sucked in a great gulp of air. Caught in the middle of a desperate and callous conflict, the tribespeople supported those they feared the most. The barrel spoke louder than the word. The security forces didn't kill indiscriminately, they didn't kill women and children. They would go away and leave them shortly to continue as before, but the *magandanga* – savage men, the guerrillas – were always with them; they never left them alone.

From one of his annual military call-ups Matt remembered a nine-year-old orphan picking his nose nervously as he had spoken to him. 'Freedom fighters came to our village,' the boy said. 'They gave me sweets. I told them what they wanted to know. When they went my family was dead.'

Matt pointed to a baby clutched in the arms of the *kraal* head's wife. It cried with the increased tightness of her grasp. Red was a big man but he had difficulty restraining the woman's newly acquired strength in the defence of her child. Met with resistance, Red's somewhat simple expression turned sour. The muscles of his neck stood out like knotted cords. The woman clearly became terrified of him. Red finally wrenched the child from her, forcing her to relinquish her grip against her utmost will.

Matt scratched a line on the ground.

'When the shadow of the tree,' he said, gesturing to the stunted *musasa* in full view of them all, 'touches this line' – he scratched the line deeper – 'and you have not told me that which I wish to know, I will kill this child.'

He went behind a hut with the child, out of their view, and waited.

Shadow crossed the line. No one had come forward.

Confronted by the random violence of endless conflict, the tribespeople owed their allegiance to the certainty and reality of violence, not lame threats.

Matt fired.

The baby flopped back.

Silence.

Then one solitary gasp of unsuccessfully suppressed emotion came from the mother.

When the baby was dragged by one arm and dropped remorselessly in front of the shocked assembly, the mother, seeing the reality of the event, screamed and broke down in uncontrollable sobbing. The harrowing ululating wail of the women that then commenced was disturbingly incessant.

Unwavering, Matt came forward once again and pointed to the second youngest child. Red grabbed hold of the terrified girl. She and her crying mother clung together as if inseparably bonded, fingernails digging into each other's flesh.

The tormented *kraal* head scratched furtively at his face, pock-marked by a disease suffered in early childhood. When he lifted his head all his family was beseeching him.

'*Mira*,' he finally uttered. 'Stop.' Defeat and fear sounded in his voice and showed in his eyes. Defeat and fear at what was happening to his family and at having to 'finger' the guerrillas. Besides, the guerrillas forced every family to send at least one of its members across the border for training. Perhaps there was a son!

Andy took the man away from the *kraal*. The man would tell him everything he knew about the guerrillas. He would probably not know much except that guerrillas were forced upon his hospitality, staying at and near his *kraal*. But he would be able to identify the chairman of the local guerrilla cell. It was the chairman who was responsible for ensuring his people's support of guerrilla infiltration and operation in the area, and as such was familiar with the system of transit and base camps, would know which *kraals* were responsible for each camp, *kraals* to which the guerrillas would turn for information, shelter, food, supplies and women.

Meanwhile, Matt went to the baby's still form. Unknown to the inhabitants of the *kraal*, before the child had been dragged in front of them, it had been smeared with blood, Matt's blood. It could have been chicken blood, but rather than risk the *kraal* inhabitants making associations between the catching of a chicken and the blood on the child, with the help of Andy, Matt had insisted on drawing a couple of syringes of blood from his own arm.

Then having assessed the baby's weight, he had intravenously injected it with the acceptable quantity of a bottled solution which contained in part, thiopental-sodium – a short-acting barbiturate – and d-tubocurarine chloride – a neuro-muscular blocking agent. The baby had been unconscious in seconds. The striated muscles of the limbs and body were paralysed, while the smooth muscles of lungs, heart and other vital organs continued functioning normally. Just as the eyes and mouth had closed, the crying having ceased, Matt had squeezed the trigger of his rifle; the barrel had been pointing harmlessly skyward.

Now he injected the seemingly dead child with the neostigmine antidote which allowed normal muscle activity to resume. The child's breathing was sound. He slapped it. It cried. Matt had risked the child's life, but the black African baby was a hardy survivor in the worst of conditions. That the population had multiplied four-fold since Matt's grandfather had first stepped foot on the farm ought to say something for the baby's resilience. It would have no more than a hangover. He carried it down to the river and washed off the congealed blood. When he handed the child back to its mother she wept and laughed alternately, not knowing which to do. She would not stop thanking him.

'We have no quarrel with you,' he said.

In the days that were to follow, James and Andy would work with the *kraal* head. They would try and ascertain who exactly the guerrillas were, who were their contact men in the district, and where they were likely to be found. It would take time. They were prepared to be patient.

December

Back on the farm, the maize plants and cowpeas were beginning to push their way above the surface of the soil. Matt's frustration at waiting for the rains to come, and watching the dam dry up, was over. The wet season finally broke with an almighty thunderstorm.

Massive cumulo-nimbus, as dark and as heavy as a giant iron anvil hundreds of metres high, filled the sky that had been no more than an empty space above the farm for weeks. The wind tore leaves off the trees which tossed their heads and thrashed their limbs as if in a fusion of the emotions of delight and abjection.

Matt loved a healthy storm with the same intensity that he detested incessant, insipid drizzle. And this first storm, heralding the summer rains, he loved more than any other. A storm was a stirring thing, alive, a magnanimous display of Nature's uncowering strength, whereas drizzle seemed to be the symptom of a tired, weak and ailing sky.

A single bolt of lightning burnt a long white scar through the clouds and died in the waters of the dam. The wind swept in gusts across the porch where Matt and Danielle were sitting after an early dinner. Danielle was filled with an endearing almost childlike excitement. Her hand clutched his.

Deep blue shadows lay across the trees. There was a heavy smell of earth and plants. There was silence and then a crash of thunder that shook the ground.

Matt looked out across the valley. There was no usual silhouette of the hills against the sky; the sky was merely a continuation of the land's black form. The wind slashed blindly at the trees. Huge drops of rain splattered across the porch, beat on the roof.

They went inside.

Matt built a log fire in the great stone ingle-nook fireplace of the study. Shadows jumped in the sudden light of the flames.

They sat before the fire on the huge lionskin rug with its tussled jet-black mane; its fur was sleek and shiny, the mouth of the magnificent head set open. Then her face was before him, the taste of her lips on his, the scent of her warm body. He parted the light silk wrap of her robe.

She was naked beneath it. She tilted her head back as his lips caressed her neck and shoulders. She made a slight movement and the robe fell to the floor. The leaping fire burnished her body with red gold. She arched back in his embrace, felt his warmth against her bare skin. The skin of her breasts and about her pelvis was tinged a delicate pink-brown from sunbathing in the nude and skinny-dipping.

A sheet of lightning momentarily illuminated the room with its stark brightness. Thunder quickly followed, the earth trembled. Rain showered from the leaves of the trees and off the eaves of the roof. The curtains flapped wildly in the wind that came through the open windows. The air was fresh with the smell of nature.

Danielle leaned against him waiting for the next thunder crash, her mouth against his chest. The thunder came, and it brought them tight together. She drew a breath and raised her eyes to his face.

'Will you still love me when I'm old?' she asked plaintively.

He cupped her head in his hands and kissed her firmly.

She was grateful to him for replying that way. His action, the thunder and the rain spoke for him. There was no need for words.

She let both him and the storm have their way.

The flickering shadows of their love played on the walls in the glowing light of the fire. She ground her pelvis hungrily at him. She felt his need but was dominated by her own. The curtains flapping in the wind, and the rain outside, mingled with the sounds of their love.

The heavy dark cloud passed and was gone.

Matt worked dawn-to-dusk days throughout the first three weeks of December, attending to the dipping and dosing of the cattle, weed cultivating, and fertilising the young maize plants when they were shin high.

He often worked into the night repairing machines and equipment, all so that he could catch up on time lost while he had been out in the bush and take a few days off over Christmas. On a few of those nights Danielle worked with him in the workshop, overhauling the tractors.

'Monkey-wrench please, nurse,' he would call out to her, and she would pass it to him, and he would kiss her, and together they would get covered in grease.

They would eat a take-away dinner together in the workshop office, listening to music from the portable radio there.

Much of the time, when the ground was hard enough between showers of rain, he spent out in the fields with the tractor-drawn cultivators breaking up the ground and uprooting the weeds between the rows of the young maize plants.

The young seedlings were a favourite with the birds, so he rigged up devices to scare them off until the plants were older.

She spent her time keeping the house in order, tending to the vegetable and flower gardens, her daily stints at the clinic, and holding her usual weekly get-togethers with the womenfolk of the farm, weaving, pottery-making and exchanging gossip.

Life on the farm had returned to normal, and the days passed. It would soon be Christmas.

Two days past the summer solstice it stopped raining.

Danielle made preparations for the thirty-five guests they were expecting for Christmas lunch the following day. Her parents arrived that afternoon to spend Christmas at the farm.

Matt could do no more than welcome his mother-in-law and father-in-law before he had to leave Danielle to entertain them alone, while he retired to the study with James and Andy who had come round unexpectedly with Red.

Once in the study, James let Andy start to tell Matt what had taken place since they had last been in contact with one another.

'We returned the *kraal* head to his *kraal* to see what information he could come up with. We used one of our black operatives to regularly debrief him. Well, it seems to have paid dividends. Acting on information received, we've done a considerable number of file searches and interrogations of gooks captured elsewhere in the country, and have put a patchwork account together of the events that led up to the derailment of the train. We've managed to identify the individual members of the guerrilla section concerned.'

James took over the briefing. 'The guerrilla who commanded them was none other than a sector commander who has been entrusted by the guerrilla High Command across the border with infiltration into the district through the valley.'

'And the description of the weapon he carries fits that of an RPD, right?' said Matt.

'Right,' said Andy.

'We feel that information now to hand confirms your initial suspicion that the guerrilla commander who twice escaped our net was responsible for both the weapons supply and the derailment of the train. He's of particularly high calibre – the sector commander no less. But unlike guerrillas of the same rank elsewhere in the country, who prefer to stay in the relative safety of a camp across the border, this one gets actively involved, leads by example,' James said.

'Sonofabitch,' said Red.

'He is known by the guerrilla codename "Mumvuri". And right now he's just that – a shadow. We can't find any antecedent information on him. It's almost as if, apart from his exploits as a guerrilla, he never existed.'

'Ballistics have tied the RPD which fired the cartridge cases we found at the derailment scene to five, possibly six, other incidents; of which three or four were murders and two were sabotages,' said Andy.

'Nevertheless, despite finding no background information on Mumvuri himself,' said James, 'we've found out that a guerrilla meeting is to be held as a symbolic show of strength on the day of the Western world's foremost religious holiday – Christmas – tomorrow night. We know near to which *kraal* it is to be held – but don't know where exactly. Local guerrilla cells have been instructed to ensure that as many locals as possible attend in support. Mumvuri's likely to top off the occasion with an incident or two. Before that's possible I'd like the three of us to go into the area, find out exactly where the meeting is to take place, and do what you can to disrupt things.

'We're at a disadvantage in that none of us have seen Mumvuri's face. Apparently witnesses claim we don't have a mugshot of him on criminal file. However, the *kraal* head we've been working on has agreed to identify him. I suggest you take him along. He's outside in one of the troop-carriers with our vehicle escort,' James continued.

Matt looked out of the window and saw Danielle and her mother with trays of mugs of tea, serving the men in the vehicles. He thought how Danielle would have to look after their guests over Christmas without him.

He went to tell her.

That night, a rosy glow illuminated Matt's face in the corner of the troop-carrier as he smoked a last cigarette on his way once again to a distant part of the valley.

Five kilometres east of a place called Vamasikana Vhatatu – The Three Daughters – rocks, weathered by wind and rain and balanced precariously on one another like heads on bodies, James slowed the vehicle down but kept the revs up giving the aural impression that no change in its speed had occurred. Only military vehicles were known to move on the roads at night, so a vehicle slowing down could only suggest a deployment of troops.

Matt and the others de-bussed in turn, each running behind the vehicle a short distance as equipment was passed out to them.

When all were out, they watched James drive on.

They moved on through the night to the *kraal* near which the meeting was expected to take place. A rapport had developed between them in the bush that made speech superfluous. They seemed to know what each expected of the other.

Matt found an ideal observation position and they spent some time anti-tracking in their approach to it so as not to leave too obvious a trail behind them.

Shortly after first light, 25 December, two young boys came within a short distance of their position, looking for signs that would indicate the presence of intruders, security forces. Matt spent a few anxious moments waiting to see if the boys would pick up the spoor that had inevitably been left behind, but he needn't have worried for the boys passed on by. He had purposefully not selected the apex of one of the surrounding points of high ground and now his reasons for not doing so were justified for those were the places that the *mujibas* were most interested in searching.

The guerrillas were already gravitating towards the meeting place from the surrounding area.

As the guerrillas arrived it was the informer's task to identify them to Matt and ferret out Mumvuri, using a camera with a powerful telescopic zoom lens James had provided. As each guerrilla arrived, Matt took whatever photographs he could of him. He made a note of the frame numbers relevant to each guerrilla identified.

There was much activity in the *kraal*. Food far in excess of normal requirements was being prepared. A 210-litre drum partially filled with water stood over a wood fire to boil, ready to add maize meal for the preparation of *sadza*. There were signs that an ox had been slaughtered days before and hung to drain of blood and mature before being cut up. Women stamped the last of the required grain in their hollowed out iron-wood mortars, the long wooden pestles incessantly rising and falling, bare breasts bobbing and buttocks jutting in rhythmic unison. An elderly man, seated on a stool in the sun, smoked a cob pipe. A young woman strained *doro* (African beer) through a strainer made of loosely woven bark. She sat on the ground as she worked with her legs drawn politely beneath her and to one side as was the custom. There were young children playing in the yard.

Matt reflected how as a boy out with !Kai he would try and distinguish the footprints of young black and white children from one another. Once !Kai had pointed out that children carried on their mothers' backs as babies grew up to have slightly bowed legs, causing them to walk on the outer edge of the soles of their feet. It was generally black children who were carried in this way.

Together with Red, Andy and the informant, Matt waited out the day. He watched the area round about the *kraal*, ensuring he would remember it well enough to move about in the dark. He looked for clues that would give him a clearer understanding of the guerrillas' movements and strengths. The meeting was only hours away and they had to be fully prepared for any eventuality.

Under cover of night they had slipped through the guerrillas' outer security cordon, but it was now tightening up around the meeting place and around them. They had to sit it out quietly, hope that they wouldn't be discovered, and wait for the correct time for things to happen.

Come sunset, three guerrilla sections had arrived, each with an RPD-gunner commander, but much to Matt's chagrin Mumvuri had not been identified as being among them. On the positive side, Matt had by then come to know exactly where, in the land around the *kraal*, the meeting was to take place. People were already gathering at a nearby clearing. He worked out how best to get there, where best to position themselves, and what to do once they were there.

Soon it was fully dark.

The meeting was well into its stride with political oratory interspersed by singing of political songs, when Matt signalled to the others that it was time to do what they had to.

They had made their preparations thoroughly. They moved as stealthily as possible through the darkness. There was no rattling of equipment, not even the movement of a round in a magazine, not even the slopping sound of water in a partially filled water-bottle. Before departing, Matt had tightened a screw that might have allowed the dust covers over the barrel of his rifle to rattle, that was all.

Their rifles were specially designed for sniping, fitted with silencers and image intensifiers that could magnify the light of a single star 50,000 times. They would easily be able to see a man in the dark from 100 paces.

Matt settled snuggly into position overlooking the clearing. With the informant, he, Red and Andy searched the gathering for late guerrilla arrivals, but there didn't seem to be any. He waited, hoping till the last that Mumvuri would put in an appearance.

The meeting was beginning to break up when he was forced to acknowledge that Mumvuri wasn't coming. Using sign language he instructed Red and Andy what arcs of fire they were to assume so as not to be shooting at the same targets. He was to initiate fire and the others were to follow. When he ceased fire they were to withdraw.

As would have been the case if Mumvuri had been there, they were to choose their targets from the top of the hierarchy on down. Matt made only one simple alteration – in case the informant was deceiving them about Mumvuri's not being there, they were first to eliminate all those guerrillas who were armed with RPD light machine-guns, who in any event were at least section commanders.

He turned on the image intensifier and as its electronic apparatus warmed up it emitted a high pitched whine, inaudible to human ears at a distance but easily detectable by dogs. The dogs barked. But it would be to no avail, their barking would serve as no warning. By the time the guerrillas realised that the dogs were not barking at the strange sights and smells of the many people gathered there, it would be too late.

Matt's finger flexed against the trigger guard. His mind was still locked on Mumvuri, the dark form, the shadow he had seen moving silently through the bush the month before, when through the phosphor screen of the image intensifier, as he swept the sights across to the first of the RPD-gunners, a form flared into brightness, as if by spontaneous combustion. His heart thudded. It was a late arrival. Mumvuri? Then he saw that it wasn't.

In his mind's eye he visualised the events that were irrevocably started when he squeezed the trigger, once and then twice more at two more targets as if in slow motion . . . each specially prepared bullet leaving the rifle barrel . . . each with its low grain charge so as not to crack noisily through the sound barrier . . . each with its hole drilled in the bullet head, half-filled with mercury and sealed with wax . . . the mercury thrusting forward from the bullet head on impact . . . exploding into the body . . . dispersing in small but heavy toxic globules. Matt saw each of his targets thrown around as if by an invisible force with each squeeze of the trigger of his rifle, and out of the corners of his eyes he saw other bodies falling as Red and Andy picked their targets off too.

There was no sound to indicate that death had come from the barrel of a gun. The distanced cough of silenced weapons with their suppressed muzzle flashes seemed to merge unnoticed with the sounds of panic and superstitious fear as the meeting broke up and people ran screaming in all directions.

Cho . . . icho . . . pasi nesoja . . . down with the soldiers . . . the white racist henchmen. The words of the guerrillas' political sloganeering still seemed to be in the air as Matt ceased fire, patted Red and Andy each on the shoulder to get their attention, and with the informant in tow gestured for them to withdraw.

Once they had put an acceptable distance between themselves and the target, he radioed James.

Five kilometres east of the place called Vamasikana Vhatatu they enbussed as James, driving past, slowed down, keeping the revs of the troop-carrier up as before.

Christmas day was over. Not that it had had much meaning out there. Not just then. Not that it mattered. It had just been another day, signifying that life had continued for some and not for others. And out there somewhere, Mumvuri was one of those for whom life still continued.

The bastard's got the luck of the devil, thought Matt.

By common consensus, James started debriefing them in the troop-carrier on the way back rather than wait until they got to the office. They were all eager to spend what was left of Boxing Day with their families.

But they didn't make it back home.

James was advised over the radio that the police outpost in the valley had come under small-arms and rocket fire.

A helicopter intercepted them on the way to the scene, landing on the road ahead of them. They de-bussed from the troop-carrier and proceeded faster by air.

The pilot and technician-gunner were the two other members of the team – Philip 'Rotor' Rogers and Jacob Maritz. Matt knew them both from previous occasions on which he had helped James, and from the hotel bar on Friday nights out. They greeted him warmly.

The police outpost was a small redbrick building on a rise by the river. It comprised nothing more than a charge office and sleeping quarters. It was surrounded by a security fence. A wall to protect against small-arms and rocket attacks was still under construction. There were several bullet marks on the sentry box at the gate, and a huge cavity where the window of the charge office had been, a rocket having crashed through it and detonated against the rear wall. Part of the roof had been blown off, and everything in the room destroyed.

There had been one fatality – the young policeman who had recently arrived in the valley.

James stayed on at the scene while the others set about following the guerrillas.

Matt had no difficulty in picking up the spoor as it was less than half an hour old.

Before he had gone very far though, it broke up into two pairs and a group of three. Matt chose to follow the group of three, not only because it was the largest group, but also because there was the familiar spoor of cracked heels and protruding nails which belonged to the guerrilla commander's boots who had escaped twice before, and whom Matt knew now as Mumvuri.

A short while after that the guerrilla group split yet again into two and one. Matt observed the familiar boot print with the double spoor, so he followed that.

Shortly before nightfall, Matt saw two figures making their way up the side of a hill in the distance. Matt knew he couldn't catch them before dark so he called James for Rotor to come forward with his helicopter, and tried to keep the figures in view until the helicopter arrived. It was a long shot, but it was the only chance they had.

Within ten minutes he spotted the helicopter. Over the radio, Matt guided Rotor to the point where he had last seen the figures.

Several minutes passed as the helicopter searched back and forth across the tree tops. There was the clatter of an AK assault rifle from the ground and suddenly the helicopter dropped out of sight. The solid retort of Jacob's twin MAG machine-guns followed.

Rotor came back over the radio. 'No doubt you heard the shooting. One of them took a few pot shots at us. We wouldn't have seen him if it wasn't for that. Jacob responded and I think he got him. We don't know where the other one is, we didn't see him – will have another look around.'

Matt searched for the body of the guerrilla fired on from the air. He found it.

By then it was too dark for Rotor to achieve anything by continuing to scout around. Matt fired a pencil flare to mark his position. Rotor acknowledged seeing it and the helicopter turned to come back.

Because the dead guerrilla was armed with an AK and not an RPD Matt didn't have to make any fancy deductions to suspect that it wasn't Mumvuri. Yet, with a feeling of uneasy anticipation, almost anxiety, and not taking anything to do with Mumvuri for granted, Matt checked the boots of the dead man. On finding out that they were definitely not the boots he had been hoping to find, he was left with a feeling of disappointment that surprised him, such was the cold shiver that accompanied it.

The helicopter landed.

He heard it whine down. He saw the brake drum engaged, stopping the engine after shut down, and preventing the rotors from turning in the wind. He watched Rotor climb out and come towards him. Matt lit a cigarette and drew the smoke deep into his lungs letting it work there before escaping slowly from his mouth. Rotor gave a royal wave of greeting. Matt couldn't help smiling in return. Following close behind was Jacob who barely spoke a word of English. He called out a customary 'TBFK' – which stood, as far as he was concerned, for 'Two Bloody Fucking Kool'.

'Nice work guys,' Matt congratulated them.

'Yeah,' said Red and shook hands.

'Jeez, you're a couple of jammy arses,' Andy smiled, slapping them on the back.

'After that, Jacob and I deserve a smoke, don't you think?' Rotor said, frisking Matt's pockets as he spoke.

The frisking was a usual occurrence, Matt recalled. Rotor never carried any cigarettes of his own as he was persistently trying to give up smoking.

Rotor found Matt's cigarettes, threw one to Jacob, and lit one for himself.

'Help yourself,' smiled Matt.

As they studied the dead guerrilla, Matt thought of the guerrilla commander who had once again got away. Once again he could hear himself counting off the paces in his mind as Mumvuri moved along the game trail in the dying light of that earlier evening, the month before. He saw himself allow Mumvuri to leave the killing ground in favour of waiting for the eight following guerrillas to enter it. If only he'd decided to detonate the Claymores just two seconds earlier, he thought, Mumvuri would have been dead, and all that had since followed would never have happened. There would have been no derailed train, no rocket attack on the police outpost, and no one would have died. He thought how the young policeman had been no more than nineteen years old.

Back at the police post James congratulated them, as usual not wasting words, but at least you knew that he was sincere.

He took possession of the dead guerrilla, photographed him and took finger-prints for identification.

They spent the night guarding the helicopter and what was left of the building.

At dawn, Matt searched for spoor at the spot where Mumvuri had last been seen. They found it – but lost it later and couldn't find it again. Mumvuri had over twelve hours start on them and had obviously anti-tracked for a good part of that time. They would have to wait for information to find him, or once again wait for him to make the next move. Matt had a strong hunch which it would be.

A replacement for the dead young policeman arrived that afternoon, together with an additional two men, an extra builder, and extra weapons. The builders immediately set to finishing the protective wall around the building.

Matt felt how good it would be to be back at home with Danielle.

*

71

New year's eve.

Danielle, with Maruva's help, had once again prepared a lavish dinner, her *pièce de résistance* being a stuffed de-boned chicken within a de-boned duck within a de-boned turkey with all the trimmings, cold ham and Christmas pudding with silver coins, so that Matt could make up for his Christmas away.

She invited James, Andy, Rotor, Jacob and their female partners too. She hoped that she could get to know the men with whom Matt was now spending so much of his time.

The van Rensburgs, their 'next-door neighbours', were there too as expected, no Nel get-together being complete without them.

They were at that stage of the dinner where they were trying to construct a pyramid of empty bottles at the centre of the dining-room table in a vain attempt to reach the ceiling.

'Pity about that rocket attack on the police post,' commented Oom Van to James.

'The cops needed an excuse for redecorating,' smiled Rotor.

'Not rebuilding,' interjected Oom Van.

'Rotor you're full of shit,' grinned Andy.

'Nothing like a bit of that to help something little grow,' laughed Red.

'Sorry about that young policeman though,' said Oom Van.

'And he was only just a kid,' said Tanny Van.

'Yes,' said James.

There was a respectful silence.

Matt recalled the young policeman's only visit to the farm. He remembered how he had felt that there was something about the man that reminded him of himself when he was a few years younger, how the naïve freshness that he had seen had disturbed him, how he had made no attempt at cordiality, how the man was now dead.

But, as was the propensity of people at war, it didn't take long before good-humoured badinage, born of acquired personal familiarity and high spirits, abounded again. You couldn't grieve for the dead all the time or there would be no time to live, and you couldn't grieve for everyone.

Danielle had frequently been made to laugh. Her sinuses ached with it. On yet another occasion she was forced to swallow yet another mouthful of wine to clear her throat surreptitiously, and was becoming quite light-headed.

72

Red went round to all the ladies with his own personal twig of mistletoe, from the Christmas he had missed.

'Anyone got a cigarette?' Rotor asked at that point.

The men laughed and Matt threw him his twenties-pack.

Danielle's attention alighted on Rotor. He was a man of small build, a matchbox width shorter than herself, with sandy hair and a moustache that turned up at each end of his mouth ever so slightly, giving his face an air of perpetual light-hearted mischief; a true indication of his character. He grinned affably and encircled her waist with his arm as if he had known her for years. He was, as he put it, a bachelor 'by inability', completely unable to commit himself to marriage – or any one woman for long, for that matter. To him the ideal home appeared to be one of two places: in the Hotel bar or in a helicopter. It was said that he had AVTUR (aviation turbine fuel, the ether content of which increased from time to time!) and not blood flowing through his veins. Apparently he had a different woman on his arm at almost every occasion. He was with a stunning blonde that night. Matt said that he had a reputation for being as wild with women and booze as he was in his flying exploits – that she would be wisest not to trust him in the first regard at all, the second with caution and the third with absolute abandon . . . and be careful not to place her trust in the reverse order. Danielle smiled to herself.

She turned her attention to Jacob, the blue-eyed Afrikaaner with sun-bleached hair towering above his superior officer Rotor. Every now and again someone would translate something that had been said in English for him. When forced to speak in English he described just about everything, in view of his limited English vocabulary, as TBFK. It was only when she started using the expression herself, a catch phrase that rolled so easily off the tongue, that Rotor had felt compelled to point out that in Jacob's diction the letters stood for 'Too Bloody Fucking Kool'.

On the other side of Jacob was Oom Van.

Oom Van didn't take much to small talk, but when he did his conversation was always liberally spiced with humorous anecdotes. 'I found an egg timer the other day. I thought it might help Tanny to tackle soft and hard boiled *eiers*, sorry, eggs,' he said, correcting the infiltration of Afrikaans into his conversation as he was with predominantly English-speaking people. 'It'll be *maklik*, easy, I told her. When the sand's finished, the eggs will be soft boiled. She looked at me distrustingly, you know, in that way that she has; anyhow she says she'd try it. Well, you know I waited a helluva time for the eggs, so I went to see what was holding things up. What's up, Tanny, I says, how are the eggs? "But, Love, the sand is not yet finished," she says, with that tone that matches her expression of knowing that she should never have trusted my hair-brained scheme in the first place. And there the egg timer was, boiling away merrily with the eggs.'

When they had stopped laughing, Tanny Van prodded him fondly in the side. 'You always know how to tell a story,' she accused.

'An embellishment here, a bit of stretching there,' he protested.

It was Oom Van who had called his farm Spitskop. He did so because he knew perhaps a hundred places in southern Africa called Spitskop, the irony being that there wasn't a pointed hill anywhere on his farm or within sight of it for that matter. There was a flat hill, a round hill, an anvil-shaped hill, but there was no *spitskop*! Danielle smiled happily. Her eyes alighted transitorily upon Oom Van's hands; working hands with rough creased knuckles and distended blue veins. He was over seventy yet still did a full day's work on his farm. They all knew that if a couple like Oom and Tanny Van stopped working on what they had struggled to build up all their lives, the meaning to their existence would be gone and they would die. That's the way it was; one willed to live only so long as there was meaning, and every man created that meaning for himself.

The van Rensburgs and Nels had always been like one extended family. Red was as much Matt's brother as his friend, and it was not forgotten that Matt's brother had been engaged to Red's sister. She had not taken his death easily; but in time she had met someone else, married and was now living overseas – away from the place of memories.

The all-encompassing grey-green centres of Oom Van's eyes seemed to draw Danielle's gaze into them; flashing deep within them was a bright quality, a vitality that belied his age. He smiled warmly at her and she smiled back. It was an exchange such as to suggest that she had been accepted into the family.

She looked at Matt. He was relaxed. As relaxed as one could be who had come to acquire the habit of being ready to bolt to his feet at any moment.

Red turned an empty beer bottle upside down on the table. 'Hey, barman', he called to Matt, 'you're serving empty bottles here.'

74

Matt smiled, lopped the top off another beer (using a capped full one as an opener) and threw it to Red who caught it and had it to his mouth before the froth could spill over the old yellow-wood of the table.

Red was a heavy-boned man, with a red bushy beard that bristled thickly from his face. There was dark hair with a shiny red lustre on long thick arms that seemed to stretch down to his knees, like those of an orang-utan. To women he managed to be ugly and appealing at the same time; perhaps it was because behind his external façade he radiated gentleness. Some men joked about him being a 'walking armpit', but never to his face; and besides, he took the joke well. He was not a lucid speaker, often unable to put his feelings into words. When he ran out of words he had the tendency of retreating into himself. But above all things, Red was absolutely honest, honest about himself and absolutely loyal in his personal relationships. He was simple in his needs, with faith in the old ways. For him responsibility towards family and community played a fundamental role. And it was clear he loved Matt. He would have followed Matt anywhere. Matt, in turn, was very protective of that big, simple soul.

Danielle looked at Red's wife, Suzanne, a quiet, pretty girl. She was from farming stock. Her family owned a farm nearby in the valley, so Red and Matt had known her all her life. There was a pleasant tenuity about her. They had been married in the same year as she and Matt. Matt had been instrumental in encouraging the shy Red, whose courage always seemed to fail him when it came to amorous dealings with the opposite sex, to invite her out. Danielle herself had sounded out Suzanne for Red on the topic of marriage, and Red had proposed – on bended knee, and on a moonlit night as the most romantic of traditions would have had it. Suzanne had borne him their baby daughter Sarie in their second year of marriage. The topic of her thoughts made Danielle feel a pang of sorrow, for both she and Suzanne had been pregnant together – only she had miscarried. She couldn't help being overcome by guilt. There seemed no way of escaping it; it seemed to come by association and as such was the more difficult to face up to. Fighting back her sudden change of mood that threatened to be depressive, Danielle managed a half-smile, but biting her bottom lip at her recollection of Red in his beaming proud and doting fatherhood role, carrying Sarie over one shoulder as he went about supervising things on the farm. 'The best cure for colic,' he had told her; and he must have been right, for the baby would always stop crying the moment he put her over his broad shoulder.

Danielle felt Matt take hold of one of her hands and kiss the palm. Danielle saw Andy smile at Matt and her.

'Ah! young lovers,' he said cooingly. 'I remember when I first met Elaine. It was at a coffee-bar in the big bad city – I felt her slip off her shoe and then felt her bare foot brush against my leg several times while we were sitting there. Uh huh! I thought. I felt her foot brush against my leg when she had got up and left. It turned out to be the bloody tablecloth flapping around in the wind!'

'He makes people laugh. He's crazy but he makes people laugh.' Elaine shook her head with exaggerated incomprehension.

Danielle recalled what Elaine had told her about that first meeting with Andy. He had apparently rushed from the coffee-bar and proposed to her then and there in the middle of the street. They hadn't even so much as said good morning, although they had sat at the same table having an early morning cup of coffee before going to work, as Andy had been quick to remind her. Elaine had thought him crazy, but being kind of crazy herself, as she explained, agreed to go out with him that evening to see his favourite movie, which turned out to be *The Jungle Book*. Danielle laughed anew at the thought. Andy had arrived at Elaine's flat to collect her, with a huge bunch of roses, which, as she later found out, were prize blooms he had stolen from the park. She hadn't known that he was in the police then, and it was later still before she found out he was in the Special Branch. What exactly she had expected that to imply she wasn't sure. What she did know was that he didn't mirror any of the detective and spy stereotypes she had been exposed to in books and on television. Knowing nothing about him, shorn of number, rank, name and reputation, he had been just another pedestrian on the pavement.

Danielle remembered how she had first met Matt. Having spent three years as a student nurse in the city hospital, she had been transferred to a forty-eight-bed hospital in what seemed at first to her to be a one-store backwater village far from civilisation, which you'd miss if you blinked when passing through by car. One weekend she had gone hiking with fellow nurses into the valley where she had had her first chance encounter with Matt.

The river was in full flood, and he had come hurtling past, where she stood with her friends on the bank, on water skis behind a powerful police patrol launch at full throttle at the hands of a big, slightly simple looking man with red hair. He had waved. And so she had become acquainted with the fabled, unperturbable Matt Nel; a young man defying the flooded river, wild animals, southern Africa itself for that matter.

When the boat came back he let go the tow rope and glided up to them on the bank.

They all went out together in the boat.

That night, he invited them back for drinks and dinner on his farm.

They talked about things close to each other from the start and met often after that.

She became captivated by his strength of personality, his sense of humour, his love of people, whatever their shade, his profound yet unassuming knowledge of animals and nature.

Once he had caught her staring at him. She had glanced away uncertainly, but only after realising that he had held her eyes with his own too intently, meaningfully. When he had so readily responded with affection she knew she was in love. They married after a whirlwind courtship.

'Well, a man's like a camel, he's got to have a hump,' came Andy's voice, breaking into Danielle's thoughts.

Elaine cupped her husband's face in her hands and kissed him. 'So romantic,' she sighed. 'He's got the morals of an alleycat.'

'What do you mean?' Andy countered. 'I've been moral with you several times,' and he laughed at his own joke.

Elaine turned to Danielle. 'He's strange but nice, you know what I mean?'

'Dare I ask?' she replied with a smile.

Andy King appeared to be a man who worked and played with equal tenacity. His steel-blue eyes seemed to indicate that commitment to life. They took in everything with seemingly indifferent abandon, yet one suspected there was nothing that was not appraised by a hard-worn value system that had taken many knocks in its development.

Danielle thought how, for the men there that evening, life was a question of capability, a man had to find out his limits, had to push those limits outwards, forever expanding them to that unattainable frontier. Lovers, friends, foes, those men approached them all with their utmost being.

At that moment, Danielle saw James thoughtfully studying his protégé Andy, before saying to him, 'I think now is an opportune time to disown you before you get in any deeper and need to be extricated by someone.' He was straight faced, but with an appealing smile playing at the corners of his mouth and in his eyes. Sometimes Danielle was surprised that a man of such aristocratic bearing should be involved in the job he was. He had been a professional policeman since the age of seventeen. He had joined the force when it was still doing horseback patrols in the outlying districts. His wife Alexandra, a lovely person, was a perfect match – like his tie and handkerchief, she joked. They had two teenage daughters. On the two occasions Danielle had been with Matt to call on James while they were in town, he had been found in his tastefully furnished office behind his desk studying a chess board; 'work' he had called it on the first occasion, 'relaxation' on the next. For James it was as if the two were synonymous. It was as if the answer to the guerrilla threat existed in the moves of those thirty-two pieces on those sixty-four squares. He had the tendency of reducing the war to the status of an intellectual game. Even the most obscure fragment of detail was reproduced in his mind with phenomenal speed and accuracy. Danielle thought how he was the only man she knew who could actually remember the precise colour, pattern and even design of a woman's dress at a particular meeting – as he had demonstrated that evening by reminding her what she had worn on the two occasions she had been with Matt to his office.

The grandfather clock chimed the death of the old year, the birth of the new.

Matt gave a toast – 'The Valley.'

'May she never be red,' added Andy.

'Yeah, one Red's enough,' commented Rotor.

Red swatted him.

They laughed.

Matt clasped Danielle tightly; a little too tightly she thought. He kissed her eagerly; a little too eagerly. It was the sort of intensity that expressed fear of parting or loss.

The festivities started anew, arms linked and dancing to the strains

78

of 'Auld Lang Syne-cum-Sarie Marais' from a battered family heirloom concertina in the hands of Oom Van.

The earth had commenced another orbit of the sun. It would be a very good year!

Danielle suggested to Suzanne, Alexandra and Elaine that when the men were away another time the wives should get together again. The suggestion met with unanimous approval.

Before dawn, they drove out to Matiziro *Koppie* in the bush, continuing an old Nel tradition that served to remind themselves of the farm's origins.

A cool breeze wafted over them from the rawness of the surrounding land. The tip of the horn of the moon peeped from behind scattered grey cloud that drifted up the valley. Matt found himself sobering quickly in the cool fresh air and the prospect of the *koppie* ruins around him, which with a little imagination you could envision to have been in times past the heart of a grand African empire, a temple of stone, a political and religious capital of a black monarchy; the place that was called Matiziro – Place of Refuge.

The only accessible approach to the highest point of the *koppie* presented itself as a tight zigzagging ancient passageway permitting them to pass only in single file. Enclosed by massive boulders of granite and black dolomite, it was protected by traverse after traverse like those that would have shielded warriors guarding the right of access.

Matiziro. Place of Refuge. The giant koppie dominated the surrounding countryside, from which the farm had acquired its name. Its sheer, virtually unassailable sides protruded high above the bush. It was there that warm winds, saturated with moisture from the Indian Ocean, their journey across the flat coastal plains unimpeded until forced up into the interior through the valley, relinquished their life-giving moisture. It was said that the last of the great rainmakers had been buried there, his spirit dwelling there for all time.

Breathless, they reached the pinnacle. The false dawn touched the sky, as if the sun would emerge from the dark ridge of the east at any moment, but it was a while yet before sunrise.

They joked and laughed.

Then the sun peeped over the eastern parapets.

Matt felt Danielle hug closer to him. Sitting there facing the rising sun, he was made powerfully aware of blood-red earth emblazoned by the sudden invasion of light. The stone balcony he was sitting on might well have been a sacrificial platform.

Bursting majestically into full view, the sun rose swiftly into the sky, released from its moorings of darkness to start another fiery day.

There was the pop of the cork from a bottle of sparkling wine, the clink of glasses. It was almost like a ritual consecration.

Bright little white, yellow and pink everlastings flowered in the valley with the sun gallantly riding the sky. Antelope grazed in the bush below. It made him aware of his heart beat. For a time nothing was said. It was a time of rapture, of undefiled chasteness, too easily spoiled by words.

'A very good year,' they re-affirmed.

January

It rained relentlessly for almost the entire first week of the new year. The only cessations were the short periods when fresh barrages of dark cloud moved in to relieve the spent forward assault lines.

The river flooded, the dam overflowed. Some farmers who had dry-planted their maize crop before the rains were forced to replant later at great expense. Now they could only look on in anguish as their young vulnerable crops were brutalised by the very forces they had prayed to save them.

Over the rainy nights Danielle spent time with Matt in the study. They chatted as they went over the farm records, and he even found time to add a few notes to his Bush Lore manual which he was accustomed to doing whenever he had a free moment. He had started it when a teenager to help him remember !Kai's teachings and wisdom.

During the rainy days the soggy ground presented the last opportunity for tractor-drawn cultivators to dig up weeds between the rows, for the plants would soon be too tall to allow the belly of the tractor to pass over without damaging them. Many farmers preferred to use chemical weedkillers instead of labour-intensive harrowing and cultivating; it took less time and the weeds were dealt with in one go for that year. But chemical weedkillers were expensive and Matt was concerned about the build-up of substances in the soil which might in time affect insects, birds, animals, both domestic and wild, and by affecting the water supply harm fish, frogs, ducks and other living things. Wherever there was something negative there was something positive, however, for when the plants were tall enough to prevent weeding they were also tall enough to block out the weeds from receiving sunlight.

Matt attended to catching up on work that had been neglected elsewhere on the farm.

The rain came down and !Kai smiled like a contented child at the majesty and power of Nature.

At the end of the week Matt drove the thirty-nine kilometres into town with Danielle to pick up supplies and to attend to business. Leaving her to browse through the department store, and to go and see Elaine who worked there, he went to see James.

James's office was in the CID (Criminal Investigation Department) section of the old double-storey police station. The only new additions to the police station were an outer perimeter security fence and an inner wall protecting against rocket and small-arms fire, as well as serving to control access. All complainants and unofficial visitors were searched at the gate for weapons of war. Matt was passed on through the gate to the Charge Office and on to the grille door of the Criminal Investigation Department and Special Branch offices manned by an armed plainclothes detective. Everyone in that section of the building wore plain clothes, and as they worked without jackets in the heat their shoulder harnesses with pistols in holsters could be seen.

James's office was at the end of the passage. Matt presented himself familiarly to the secretary in the outer office who advised James on the intercom, then waved Matt on through.

After all the closed gates, doors, grilles and old echoing passages with lime green paint peeling from the walls, James's office seemed somewhat innocuous and aesthetically appealing. James was sitting behind his large stinkwood desk, pencils, papers, paperweights, letter opener, everything, perfectly in place on its top, phones to the left and a fine ivory chess set to the right, the pieces positioned as in a game still to be completed. Wooden shelves lined the walls with books. There were a couple of paintings by a renowned local artist on the walls.

The only incongruous aspect of the office was an open heavy steel door to the left which led down a flight of steps to a reinforced concrete armoury that doubled as an operations bunker.

'You must have sensed something had happened,' James said to Matt on seeing him. 'A report's just come in. The *kraal* head we've been using as an informer hanged himself yesterday.'

'Damn!' exclaimed Matt.

'One of the guerrillas killed at the meeting turned out to be one of his neighbour's sons. I expect by killing himself he believed it would prevent retribution against his family.'

Matt felt how ironic it was that no retribution came, not the externally imposed kind. And it need never have come, because apart from the man's family and the team no one knew of his involvement.

The law required that a police officer should indict all persons aiding and abetting the guerrillas. James had not done so. He considered that such action, apart from being unduly callous on people who were caught in the crossfire and losers either way, meant reams of unproductive paper work and an unnecessary burden on the tax payer. Besides, the prisons were overcrowded, and by leaving known guerrilla sympathisers in the field at least some influence and control could be exerted rather than creating a vacuum to be filled by unknown elements. It was the devil-you-know syndrome. You could pull out the thorn, but not without bleeding.

'Damn,' said Matt again.

'Things aren't too rosy apart from that either,' said James. 'The entire police and army are spread thinly across the country for a few gooks giving them the run around.'

James reached to the shelf behind him for a whisky decanter and a couple of glasses. He poured a double tot by eye for each of them and pushed a glass to Matt.

'To better days,' he said.

They each drank.

'The war itself is just window dressing. The real battle is going to be lost or won by the politicians of countries far from here, and to be honest, with the bunch we've got I don't fancy our chances.' He took another swig of his whisky. 'But no matter what happens elsewhere in the country we can at least win our war in the valley.'

'With Mumvuri out there I'm not so sure,' said Matt.

'With you out there, I am sure,' said James.

It was late afternoon when Matt left James's office to pick up Danielle and head back to the farm.

★

The following day Matt examined the maize plants to determine what balance of fertiliser they needed.

The bulls were run with the cows for the first time that year, so that the cows would calve during the next spring and early summer when the grazing would be good. !Kai said how the animals in the bush were following their natural instincts too.

On Matiziro Koppie a pair of martial eagles were nesting. The rare birds had an incredibly vast area of operation. They had quickly become well known if not infamous in the district, often seen soaring high overhead, and on occasion, as much as 100 kilometres from their nest. It was not uncommon for them to be blamed for the disappearance of lambs and kid goats, which they would swoop down on from tremendous heights, quite capable of killing on impact. But !Kai protected them by not revealing to anyone other than Matt where they were nesting.

It was on Matiziro Koppie too, under a wild gardenia, believed by the black African people to keep evil away, that his grandmother had been buried, and around that one gravestone had grown the small cemetery.

That evening Matt, feeling particularly troubled, went to see !Kai. It had been a while since they had last been able to spend some time alone together, and much had happened.

!Kai lived in the *kraal* with Maruva, but in truth the only home for him was the open bush, where he spent much time, checking game and fences, and looking for lost cattle in the *veld*. Confinement to a village, to a set routine was tantamount to caging a creature of the wild.

That night, Matt sat down across the wood fire from !Kai outside his hut. Like his father before him, !Kai would have liked nothing more than never to have had to build a home of any durable kind, such things remaining strictly finite to him. But even then, as it was, he could have got up there and then and left his hut together with everything else he materially possessed and suffer no loss. His physical needs were few and simple; when he had satisfied them he was inclined to sit back in spiritual communion with his world, as he was doing then.

Flickering shadows cast by the flames deepened the lines on his face. His skin was fissured like the bark of an old *muzhanje* tree exposed to the changes of many seasons. His eyes had the dull smouldering quality of a man who had experienced just about all there was to be seen and done in southern Africa, and silently but compellingly spoke of a supreme self-knowledge, that whatever there was left could not trouble him. Looking into !Kai's eyes, Matt found himself looking back into the wild unrelenting heart of bushland, the heart of Africa itself. An entire continent's past seemed to live on in those eyes. This was an illiterate man who could not even read the hands of a clock's face, yet he instinctively knew the progression of the day by the movement of the celestial bodies, and that of the insects and animals around him; there was no need for artificial divisions of time.

!Kai, in the evening of his life, smiled at Matt from behind his wispy beard and high crinkled cheekbones, as if he knew exactly what was going through Matt's mind. He squatted there, in that timeless pose that he could hold for hours on end without tiring, buttocks resting on his heels, his loose frame bent forward as if he bore a permanent burden on his shoulders; the weight of over three-quarters of a century of survival in southern Africa, from arid unpeopled deserts to towering coastal cities.

!Kai was of an unprepossessing appearance, nothing more than a little over one and a half metres tall, slight, stringy upper body, narrow hips, lithe limbs, buttocks protruding one way and belly the other. His small and finely shaped hands and feet had a strangely aesthetic femininity about them. Alongside black or white people he looked distinctly frail. His strength was not in the capacity of muscle exertion so much as in the fact that he kept going; when he came up against something that exerted a force greater than that which his old muscles could counteract, he went round it. He yielded like grass before the wind, never resisting, simply flowing, in body and spirit, with the universe that had formed him.

They sat placidly looking out into the night, receptive to its movement and sound. From afar, near Matiziro Koppie, the rumble of a lion, the bay of a wild dog, the yelp of a hyena, and near at hand the rasp of crickets, the churr of a fiery-necked night jar, the lowing of cattle, the rustle of wind through the maize fields. Now and again one of them would adjust the logs on the fire, place another in the flames, or sweep a hand at the smoke that came his way with a change in the breeze. Sometimes !Kai would gently rescue a moth from the flames. He was like that, he was concerned even about injuring the flies that, attracted to anything that moved in the bush, would buzz around annoyingly. When he walked, each step was carefully placed to avoid standing on any insect or other living creature; and it was done instinctively, not self-consciously.

Right then, !Kai picked up, with his bare hands, a live red coal that had been thrown out of the fire on to the ground beside him, and placed it back in the fire. It was not just that the skin of his palms was toughened with callouses, but as he had once told Matt, he picked up the hot coal with his mind as well as his body.

When they spoke to each other it was with an economy of words. That which was left unsaid was understood. !Kai chose his words carefully, seldom had Matt known him to voice unconsidered thoughts. The old man nodded for a while to himself after talking and then filled a small charred hardwood pipe, shaped like a thin funnel, with a mixture of *shoro* harsh tobacco and wild leaves he had specially collected. He held a burning stick at the open end, puffed away until it was properly fired, and settled back in utter contentment once more. It was the same old procedure; he was an inveterate lover of tobacco.

Matt knew those moments when !Kai simply preferred to sit without verbal interference, and at those times he left him alone, for he would only speak if he wanted to. At other times he was brimming with mercurial vitality and light-hearted nonsense. Matt knew those times too. Now they sat in silence, once in a while uttering a few words before sitting on in silence once more.

!Kai knew very little English or Afrikaans, and his natural aversion to the two languages meant that he avoided even the few words he did know. African dialects, on the other hand, came readily to his tongue.

He laughed easily, no, hooted rather than laughed, mused Matt. When he did so his face broke into multitudes of smiling creases, revealing a mouth of gaps, a few nicotine-stained teeth that pushed from their gums in no certain order, and a flash of gold, a perfectly fashioned incisor. The gold mines. But he never liked to talk about that. Matt had a painful image of the little old man burrowing mole-like away underground into the smallest crevices where larger men could not go, billions of tonnes of rock pressing upon him, forming a two-kilometre solid barrier between him and the freedom of the bush he had known as a child.

Often the air seemed to be filled with golden rays of light when he laughed, and on his head clusters of silver-white hair glinted like coarse wire spirals of native silver in the lead-grey of argentite ore.

Matt would often translate an English or Afrikaans joke for !Kai's benefit; sometimes the old man would hoot with merriment, his ribs shaking alarmingly; then at other times, as he was doing now, he would simply shake his head sadly and grunt, 'Hao! . . . The white man is a strange being.'

It was statements such as this that made Matt wonder where he stood in terms of 'race', and now with the war, where there was so much animosity being invoked between black and white, it was a problem that concerned him deeply – for he did not see himself fighting black men but barbarism and violence which was directed against innocent people no matter what colour. !Kai did not seem to include him in the category of 'strange being' nor, by inference, the category of 'white man'. The colour of one's skin, one's eyes and hair, or one's facial features and bodily stature, seemed to be such superficial criteria for the sub-division of Man. Surely, least fundamental to the human species' function as they were, they could not be perceived essential in their own right for any world development. After all, the leopard, as the ancient African proverb proclaimed, licked all its skin, black and white!

Were child-rearing and cultural practices responsible for a man's behaviour, or was it a matter of genetic inheritance? Could one happily consider the population of black and white as two entirely separate 'races'? If the environmental conditions such as education, work, wealth, opportunities, to think of but a few factors, were reversed, would the men inside those skins simply trade places?

Matt felt that even if mankind was once racially differentiated, since all human beings were inter-fertile, it could be more than suspected, with migrations, invasions and occupations throughout history, and the natural tendencies of man and woman being as they were, that the make-up of all peoples was by now pretty well intermingled. He doubted that few, if any, peoples were zoologically uniform enough to be declared distinct sub-species.

As to psychological traits? In his dealings with people of all colours, personalities, shapes and sizes, he had experienced that individuals varied in degree along a continuum. How could one deign to establish discontinuous categories out of continuous variation? Surely it was nothing more than a matter of pure arbitrary choice. The average intelligence of the white people was exceeded by numerous black people, despite cultural and opportunity biases weighted against them. It was absurd, Matt thought, how an immoral and unintelligent white man could exalt himself above the most moral and intelligent black man. Matt doubted he would ever come to understand that.

Could one discern a relation between physical characteristics and cultural ones? Matt looked at !Kai. Appearances could be so very deceptive!

So what was this thing 'race'? And where did he, Matthew Nel, fit in? Was it a geographic determinant? Language? Tradition? Religion? Habit? Common Fate? Proximity? Or how about social values and norms? In all those respects he could surely call himself 'black African'. He was born right there in the main bedroom of the farmhouse. His ears were attuned to the melodious rich and earthy tenor of black African languages and dialects long before the grating discordance of English and Afrikaans. The ways of the black people – farming and the bush – were his earliest and still enduring education. He was nurtured on what Africa had to give. Were the colour of his skin, his eyes, his hair and the structure of his facial features to be considered as the only precluding factors? Or was it education and wealth that excluded him? Was it that he had failed to share a common history? Was it perhaps that he did not share common aims and goals? What were those aims and goals? Did they really represent a struggle of values? Perhaps it was easier to generalise and view the world in terms of stereotypes.

Matt found he was asking these questions but the more he asked, the less the biological, psychological and social concepts of his racial predicament could endure being looked into.

So who was this man Matthew Nel who couldn't even label himself with a particular 'racial' category? What did he look like to another? What conclusions would that other make from assessing the external clues of his facial features and physical status?

What did !Kai see? Matt was *Mutongi wakangwara*'s son. That was a clue. He recalled a photograph of his father taken when he was about the same age. He saw a young white man, weathered by the elements of nature to a sun-deepened brown, his tall frame deceptively thin, but tautly muscled, lean and strong boned, all spare flesh wasted from his body by the enduring toil of working the land. Most said he was the spitting image of his father.

As if !Kai had heard Matt's thoughts, he shook his head gently in amazement. 'Is one to believe that we are not of the same womb?' he asked, but clearly did not expect an answer. He took up his *mbira* with its snail-shell buzzers, and started playing softly as he was accustomed, crossing the separate rhythms of the two hands, and his singing of different notes, enfolding Matt in a web of music, as if the earth itself was singing.

February

The maize crop was flowering though many of the stands were uneven due to the storms early in the season. The male florets, appearing as tassels at the top of the stalks, were shedding pollen to be borne by the air to fertilise the female styles that formed the 'silks'.

A calf was born to one of the dairy cows. One or other of the dairy herd were always calving, so that there was always milk available for the farm all year round.

Customarily it was that time of year when Danielle and Matt could relax a little, but although Matt had been taking short cuts in farming technique to catch up on work because of his absences, there was still much to do.

One Saturday afternoon Matt was phoned by James and asked to pick up Red and meet Andy and himself at the police station in town.

When she heard, Danielle phoned Suzanne, Alexandra and Elaine, suggesting that they all see their husbands off at the station and then get together over tea at the hotel.

She drove into town with Matt, picking up Red and Suzanne on the way. They saw their husbands depart for the bush, and went with the other wives to the hotel as arranged.

Over tea and cake the wives tried to joke and laugh and pretend that they weren't affected by their husbands going off, but before long their true feelings came out, and Danielle learnt that, as wives with husbands who challenged death each time they left home, they shared certain feelings in common.

'Matt says it's nothing dangerous but I'm sure it is,' Danielle said.

'Red says the same thing, and I'm sure he's lying just to protect me,' said Suzanne.

'James has been giving me that story every time he's walked out the door to his office for the past twenty years,' said Alexandra.

'Andy swears that it's no big deal, saying that it just means he gets to climb out from behind his desk and the mountain of paperwork into the open air once in a while,' said Elaine. 'I guess our husbands are dropping us the same line for our sake, but none of us are prepared to take it.'

'Being married to 24-hour-a-day policemen, how do you cope?' Danielle asked Elaine and Alexandra.

'I take each day one at a time,' said Elaine.

'James pretends that what I don't know can't hurt me, and I play along with him,' said Alexandra. 'As times in the country are abnormal I try and make James's home life, whenever he shows up, as normal as possible.' Then, as an afterthought, she said, 'Perhaps sometimes I overcompensate,' and she offered a smile.

'Sometimes things are not easy being married to Andy, but I love him,' said Elaine. 'Besides,' she laughed, 'with things as they are in the country, there's no ready alternative, is there? No matter what man you turn to – emphasis on man here – they're mostly all in the same boat, with annual call-ups and things.'

They laughed with her.

'I guess one thing we've got on our side is that our men are survivors,' said Danielle.

When Matt arrived back at the farm four days later it was half past twelve in the afternoon. He went through the house looking for Danielle. There was the aroma of freshly baked bread as usual. But it didn't make his mouth salivate as usual because the aroma was mixed with a smell from the past few days he would prefer to forget – charred flesh. He went into the kitchen. He found Amai there and chatted with her for a while. Danielle had gone down to the dairy. He went back outside to go and see her but the midday's soporific heat and his awareness that he had barely slept in the past three days and nights suddenly came back to him and he found he could not keep his eyes open. He sloushed his face with cold water from the garden tap just off the verandah, and drank until his

91

stomach was glutted. He told himself that he would rest for a few minutes before going down to the dairy. He kicked off his shoes and pulled off his shirt on his way to the hammock slung in the shade between the two plane trees on the lawn. He lay down in the hammock and closed his eyes. The scene of a burnt-out petrol tanker and the burnt remains of the driver was still in his mind – the smell of charred flesh still in his nostrils. An RPG-7 rocket had scored a direct hit on the petrol tanker in the middle of a convoy. Two police reservists of the convoy's armed escort had also been killed by small-arms fire.

The convoy escort had taunted the guerrillas for not standing and fighting like men, calling them 'yellow-bellies'. But the tactics employed by the guerrillas against the superior numbers and firepower of the convoy had been pushed home to best advantage; the convoy had suffered serious loss of life and property while the guerrillas had escaped completely unscathed.

For three days, Matt, Red and Andy had pursued those responsible to no avail. They could find no proof that Mumvuri was involved but they all suspected it.

The guerrillas didn't seem to have rendezvoused anywhere, preferring to go to ground and regroup at random through codes and contact men, but only when it was considered safe to do so. Matt tried watching one of the suspected contacts but there were just too many suspects and the guerrillas could choose any one of them at any time – days, weeks or months later. It was just too impractical for the team to stay on watching one in preference to all the rest. Finally they were forced to give up the chase until further information received from the network of sources handled by James's office could shed new light on the perpetrators' whereabouts.

Matt thought how he had learnt one thing from !Kai from the beginning: nothing moved through the bush that didn't leave its mark, didn't affect the bush in some way. You could even tell where there was perpetual shadow – moss grew on the shaded sides of trees, and grass deprived of light turned brown, withered and died. Although he had not seen Mumvuri he knew where he had been simply by the death that he left behind.

Unable to prevent it, Matt fell into a seemingly bottomless sleep.

He felt he was awakened almost immediately.

He swore irritably, brushing off the hand that was shaking his shoulder. He raised his head stiffly and found himself looking into the anxious face of Danielle. He did not immediately know where he was. He had had the sensation in his waking moments before but this time it lingered interminably.

'I'm sorry, Matt, but there's a radio call for you,' said Danielle, pointing to the house.

Matt looked at the sun, questioning its position low on the horizon. Curiously, he couldn't tell if it was morning or evening. He looked at the watch on his wrist. It was 17.07 hours. He had been asleep almost five hours.

'It's James Creasely. He says its urgent,' advised Danielle.

Matt stretched. He ached to the root of each limb. His muscles seemed consumed with fibrositis. The sun was shrinking away from the world. In less than half an hour it would be dark. He felt an enveloping chill on his body.

He walked back to the house along the lawn, picking up his shirt, stiff with dried sweat, and pushed his bare feet back into the *velskoene* he had kicked off earlier. He stepped on to the path before the verandah steps. Tired. So tired. The crunching of gravel seemed distant beneath his feet.

He raised James's callsign on the radio.

James told him that there had been another incident, that he was heading towards the farm with Andy and a witness to act as a guide.

'I'll drive over to Red's place. Pick us up there. It'll save time,' said Matt.

He drove to Spitskop.

James picked them up, and on the way to the scene they questioned the witness.

The incident had happened the day before, but it had taken the man that long to get to the police outpost and report it. Two guerrillas had come to one of the *kraals* where Matt had been asking questions two days before. The witness, on seeing them, had hidden in the field where he was working. Those in the *kraal* were less fortunate – accused of being 'enemies of the people' for collaboration with the *masoja*, the white soldiers. They had been dragged into the yard and shot, seven of them – men, women and children. If it hadn't been for the witness there would have been no one to identify the culprits.

The witness's description of the guerrilla responsible matched that of Mumvuri. He was described as a high commander, and the description of his weapon fitted that of an RPD, the light machine-gun Mumvuri was known to favour.

It was quite dark when they arrived at the *kraal*. They chased half-wild hungry dogs away from sniffing about the corpses. Matt surveyed the scene in the light of the troop-carrier's headlamps. He studied the bodies. Hundreds of flies swarmed about them; they had been exposed to the tremendous heat of the African sun thoughout the day and a gagging smell was thick in the air; much blood had been absorbed into the ground.

The cause of their death could be taken for granted – death by severe overdose of 7.62mm intermediate sleeping tablets, Matt diagnosed wryly. Just one bullet each, but in the head that was a severe overdose.

He studied the expended cartridge cases scattered about the bodies.

'These *doppies* were not fired here,' he said at last. 'Some of them are internally tarnished, and there's soil of a different colour and granular structure to that of this area inside them. If they were here for a time as long as they look weathered, there would also have been definite impressions in the ground.'

Matt continued his observations. 'Furthermore, the ejection marks are in the centre of each case, indicating they're from an AK not an RPD, as described by the witness.'

They questioned the witness further as to what he had seen, but hiding in the field, keeping his head low, he hadn't seen the shooting, only heard it, and nor had he been able to see if one of the guerrillas had picked up any cartridge cases after the shooting and replaced them with others.

'Apart from everything else, each body has been delivered the *coup de grâce* by a single shot in the head, which has been a Mumvuri trait on at least two previous occasions.'

Matt reflected over the facts for a few moments, then concluded: 'To me it seems that the *doppies* from bullets fired here have been removed, and replaced by *doppies* fired from another weapon at another scene entirely. It's my guess that they've been deliberately placed here to confuse ballistic tracing – to prevent any connection being made between this incident and others. Mumvuri's trying to throw us off the scent by making it look as if he had nothing to do with these killings, on the premise that his weapon wasn't used here so he wasn't here either.'

They body-bagged the dead and loaded them into the troop-carrier.

That night and for the next two days they patrolled the area on foot, visiting every *kraal* they came across, looking for information. Information came but it was stale. Too much time had lapsed since the incident, giving Mumvuri ample time to make good his escape once more.

The name Mumvuri was enough to cause blood to thicken and hearts to clog, labouring to beat. While others died, he lived. The people believed that bullets turned to sweat on his chest!

The stubble left from last season's wheat and lucerne was ploughed under to allow time for it to decay in the soil, revitalising it for the next planting.

Danielle started thinking about when last she had broached the subject of children to Matt. He was adamant that he would not cause a child to be brought into their wartorn existence. He was right, of course, but that didn't make her position any easier to accept.

Two years before, she had had a miscarriage. Since then she had not managed to conceive, although Matt had gone for tests and her gynaecologist had said there was no reason why she shouldn't. Recently Matt had taken to wearing condoms. He said it was because of the war, but she felt it was because he was protecting her against protracted knowledge of her barrenness.

She did not know why she had thought about it just then; one thought had simply led to another. She had been thinking of her mother always knitting things.

She felt how the growing war was pushing Matt and her apart. It was coming between them in their day-to-day lives like an impenetrable barrier. An enemy was driving a wedge between them. She unconsciously twisted the engagement and wedding rings around her finger.

The war was fast becoming first, second and third in Matt's life. When they were together there was always the nagging awareness that he could be called away at any moment. He was a man whose fate seemed to decree that once he had fought he would have to fight until the end.

The war, the war, a barrier as insurmountable as death.

It was as if the world gained a new lease of life when he came back.

It was difficult to contemplate that it might just be a change in herself and not the world, a change in which Matt acted simply as a catalyst. It was like the change of expression on people's faces when the sun broke through the cloud after a drawn-out drizzling winter. That was how she had come to perceive her life, in terms of seasons, winter and summer, darkness banished by light.

When Matt returned from the bush again he looked weary and he moved as if weary.

'I expect you're very tired,' she said. 'Go and have a good sleep, I'll see you when you wake up.'

'I'm not tired,' he said. 'I slept last night on James's couch at the station. I was too tired to come home then.'

No, it wasn't tiredness she had seen so much as oppression.

He showered. She sat on the edge of the bath and they talked about the farm. But then Matt suddenly changed the topic of conversation.

'What's happening to the people out there is heart-breaking,' he said. 'We come, we see, and we go. The guerrillas move out while we're there then move back again when we're gone. The guerrillas play the man and not the ball.'

He stepped out of the shower and was towelling himself down when he stopped and looked at her searchingly for a few moments.

'Do you want to make love?' he asked.

It wasn't just the question, it was the way he asked it; the tone of really needing her to love him.

She received him with an intensity of passion that might have surprised her had she not known its cause – known that she really needed him too. She pulled him down on her there in the bathroom, her mouth fastened to his. Her body moved desperately under him. The hardness of his masculine body, his strength, she pulled to her; her hands exploring the muscle tone of his arms and back, and the valley of his spine sheltered between ridges of muscle. It wasn't just love; there was the relief that he had returned safely; relief from that suffocating fear under which she lived while he was away. Matt was back. Matt would take care of everything, he always did.

The liquidity of her love-making was furious; a fusion of desire, love, joy and relief that heightened the mere functioning of the senses. He tasted of steamy moss fires in bracken and fern ravines.

She felt the excitement pound right through her, her heart racing against his chest.

The perspiration of their bodies fused, filling the room with an intoxifying scent that spoke of an inseparable union of bodies, two mixtures that should never have been parted if not for some bitter accident.

March

Each day in the fields Matt checked the quality and development of the maize, pulling back a husk of leaves here and there to expose the cob and decide whether it was lacking any particular nutriment, whether he should add more fertiliser, whether they needed to be sprayed against pests or treated for disease.

Early in the month he harvested enough of the maize, when it was still green and their kernels at the milky stage, to supplement the cattle feed throughout the coming winter when grazing on the *veld* would be poor. The plants were shredded, stalks, leaves, cobs and all to fill the farm's tall cylindrical silage silo, where it was allowed to ferment partially, making the leaves more easily digestible.

Later, Matt and Danielle, with Red, Suzanne and their little girl, went into town to attend to business prior to the main maize harvesting. They arranged to meet James, Andy and their wives for a sun-downer at the hotel before going back to the farm.

James, Andy and their wives arrived without a smile.

'I'm sorry, Danielle, Suzanne, but can you make your own way back home? I'll arrange an escort for you, or if you like put you up in the hotel for you to go back in the morning,' said James, and without waiting for their answers he turned to Matt and Red, saying, 'We have to be on our way at once.'

Danielle gave James a cold stare, and taking Suzanne and the little girl Sarie by the hand, said, 'That's all right, we'll have a drink together as planned, then Suzanne and I can go back in convoy.'

'Stay with me,' said Alexandra.

'Good idea,' said Elaine. 'We can all have a night out on the town.'

It was agreed between them.

The men kissed their wives goodbye. The wives smiled meekly.

'I'm sorry,' Matt apologised to Danielle again.

'That's OK. There are more important things for you to attend to,' said Danielle, not believing she said what she did, then squeezed his hand. 'Be careful.'

Matt drove with the others to the runway where minutes later Rotor, with a military medic aboard, was flying them to the scene of the latest guerrilla incident.

From the air they looked down into a deep dip between two hills, like the cleavage between a woman's breasts. The sun was going down on the western horizon. The subdued light of the warm ly coloured sky was beautiful, and peaceful looking.

Matt thought how he had less than half an hour to piece together what had happened there. Mumvuri persistently chose to attack at last light, thwarting whatever chance there was of a follow-up and letting him escape unhindered under cover of darkness.

A dirt road crossed a tributary of the valley's river by means of a concrete causeway some three or four metres above the water level. Stranded on the causeway were two trucks with the Agricultural Department insignia on the cab doors. Dotted in the bushes, in belated defence formation were the eight survivors. One of them was flat on his back, obviously the seriously injured one a casevac had been called for.

Rotor put his helicopter down as near to the casualty as he could. James and the medic leapt out with medical bag, stretcher and a trauma board between them.

'Rotor, make a couple of orbits with me before you go, will you, so I can get a good look at the ambush site,' Matt said.

Rotor pulled back up into the air and made two slow circles.

There appeared to be no visible movement of any guerrillas preparing to launch a second attack. Observing the damage to the front vehicle and the causeway wall, Matt felt it appeared anti-tank rockets had been used.

'That thing's got a big bite,' Andy remarked of the rocket-launcher that had spat the engine out of the front vehicle and munched holes in the bridge wall.

'Once again Mumvuri's just buggered up and buggered off,' muttered Red.

'So damned un-cricket,' agreed Andy.

Matt traced the likely trajectories of the rockets, using the lie of the land as a guide to their probable firing points. He could start looking for spoor there. Meanwhile, he tried to assess the guerrillas' most likely lines-of-flight.

'OK,' he gestured downwards to Rotor, seeing the casualty being prepared ready for departure. 'That'll have to do.' He felt how the extra three or four minutes they had spent in the air had not been wasted.

By the time they landed again, James and the medic had the casualty on the trauma board and were ready to load him into the helicopter. Jacob folded up the rear bench to accommodate the stretcher, and with the medic looking after the casualty, Rotor immediately headed for the hospital in town. He would make it back just as it was turning dark.

No sooner had the helicopter gone from view than Matt and Red commenced a ground examination of the scene.

With routine precision, it not being necessary to tell each other what they were doing, James and Andy meanwhile took to questioning the survivors separately.

As soon as they could, they shared what information they had found out and were able to determine what had happened there.

Every evening two vehicles of the Department of Agriculture travelled back from the lands along a solitary dirt road to a protected village nearby where they customarily spent the night. It seemed the guerrilla commander had chosen the site with a practised eye, exploiting maximum camouflage and adaptation of the ground. The vehicles had to pass across the narrow causeway with the stream several metres below, and then had to labour slowly up the steep gradient of the opposite side, with the road veering sharply to the left. The drivers had been forced to pay careful attention to their driving at that particular point, giving little thought to anything but the short stretch of road directly ahead of them.

By reports on the volume of fire the vehicles had sustained, and the direction it had come from, Matt estimated that an entire detachment, three sections of eight to ten guerrillas each, had been employed. He found spoor and cartridge cases indicating that one section had been split into two groups of four and placed as a decoy along the incline, right along the side of the road just across the causeway. He found spoor, cartridge cases and a rocket booster which indicated that one section had taken up position in the thick bush of the west ridge. There were scorch marks in the bushes from the back blast of a rocket-launcher being fired twice. He found that the third section had moved into cover on the east ridge immediately overlooking the causeway. Matt observed that the guerrillas there would have been able to see the vehicles ahead of their dust trail and hear their engines several minutes before they entered the hazard.

As the vehicles had carefully negotiated the bridge and changed down to their lowest gear to meet the ascent, a guerrilla had apparently stepped out from cover into the middle of the road ahead. As he had knelt down with an RPG-7 rocket-launcher over his shoulder and sighted at the grille screening the engine block of the approaching lead vehicle, the decoy groups, from extremely short range, had directed a high rate of fire at both vehicles for a few short seconds, long enough to distract attention from him while he was exposed. His action had required unflinching nerves. He had had to hit first time, for in the fifteen seconds or so it would have taken him to reload and fire again amidst the hail of bullets that sought him out, he would have been dead. The rocket had struck the front of the vehicle with an explosive impact powerful enough to penetrate thirty-two centimetres of armour plating. The vehicle only had plating measuring 2 centimetres. From near maximum range for a moving target, a second rocket-launcher, though less powerful, perhaps an RPG-2, had fired twice from cover on the west ridge, missing the second vehicle each time but slamming into the causeway wall close to it. The second vehicle had not been able to go forward since the first vehicle had blocked the causeway exit, and it had not been able to reverse out the way it had come due to its cumbersome size and the damage to the causeway.

From their high but close-range positions, the section on the east ridge had shot down into the open tops of the trapped hardskin vehicles, their bullets ricocheting lethally inside the armour shells like steel peas rattling in metal pods.

With withering fire being directed from all angles, directions and ranges, the targets were helpless. No sooner had they identified one of the ambush positions than fire was directed from somewhere else, and the first groups had withdrawn in the resultant confusion.

Matt estimated that within about ninety seconds the guerrillas had withdrawn and the ambush had been over.

Once again Matt could find no evidence to indicate that Mumvuri was involved. None the less, because of the precision of the ambush he believed that only Mumvuri could have been responsible. He believed only Mumvuri would have had the audacity and guts to step in front of the oncoming armed vehicles, unflinchingly draw fire, fire a rocket and hit the centre of the grille of the lead vehicle first time.

Night came on unhesitantly. There was no hope of pursuing the guerrillas that night. They had once again timed their ambush well, to put as much time as possible between themselves and any follow-up forces.

Matt joined the others clearing the causeway in the dark. Apart from the seriously injured man who had been casevaced, there were two dead: the driver of the front vehicle and one other man in the rear of the second vehicle. They had to be moved before the vehicles could be moved. James and Andy bagged them.

The irreparably damaged front truck had its front wheel housings removed and its drive-shaft disconnected so that it could be pushed off the causeway. Matt then started to drive the other one on through, but owing to the rocket damage to the causeway it was a toss-up whether he would make it or not. The nearside wheels bit at the crumbling edges of the blast holes, while the offside body panels scraped one of the concrete buttresses.

'A condom's thickness less tyre rubber and you'd have ended up in the drink,' Andy assessed the situation.

They hitched up the damaged vehicle to the other one and together with survivors and bodies, drove on to the protected village.

Come dawn, Matt, Red and Andy spent the next two days in the bush before arriving at a *kraal* at the end of a long trail of acquired evidence and information.

Matt noticed how branches of the *mutupfo* 'never-die' tree had been planted around the huts and had grown into a living fence, borer and termite proof. The flat rocks outside the *kraal* were covered with bright green *chidemdemafuta* – 'containers of fat', the long-horned grasshoppers – drying in the sun.

Matt swallowed a couple of quinine tablets against malaria. They stuck in his throat. No amount of tepid water from his water-bottles appeared able to dislodge them. Standing in the open, looking around him at the obvious carnage that had taken place in the *kraal*, the merciless sun thudded against him. His limbs thrusting through shorts and sweatshirt were tanned a rich brown, but his face and eyes were bled of colour in the naked heat. He could envisage Mumvuri standing there. In the dark vision his flesh was incandescent, his eyes shining like candles at a satanic altar. Matt shuddered involuntarily.

In one *kraal* there was no room for two bulls!

Five people had been there at the time. Those working in the fields and herding cattle had fled. There was the old man, the *kraal* head, accused of being a sell-out for not sending a member of his family for training across the border. There were his two daughters, the eldest with her thirteen-year-old daughter, and the youngest with her ten-month-old son.

From the two women and the girl who lived to relate what had happened, Matt learnt that the guerrillas had forced the old man, with a stick tied to his penis, to go through the actions of having sexual intercourse with his thirteen-year-old granddaughter, as they looked on in riotous laughter and mockery. They had then bayonetted him where he lay exposed and humiliated on the ground. It was reported that one of the guerrillas had thrust the pig-sticker bayonet of his weapon right into the body, right up to the muzzle in the sucking wound, and having drawn it free had licked it clean of blood as a warrior might have done with his assegai almost a century before, the deceased's spirit becoming one with his spirit so that it could not harm him without harming itself. While he was still alive they had poured paraffin on him. He had taken some time to burn. The ten-month-old baby would not stop crying. One of the guerrillas snatched it from its mother and stuffed grass into its mouth. The sound of its choking had been as annoying to the man as its crying had been. He had taken hold of it by the feet and bodily swinging it around had forcibly struck its head on the ground. There were Tardieu spots – tiny haemorrhages in the eye membrane, the skin of the eyelids, face and scalp – evidence of mechanical breathing difficulty. The child had died of suffocation not the fracture of the skull.

It was what James considered 'chasing history'. No matter how much you may have wanted to there was nothing you could do to change it. Although he had stepped out of the hotel bar into the dazzling afternoon sunshine two days before, Matt felt as if he had stepped into the darkness of a nightmare.

Pasi nemapriveya. Down with sell-outs. Sell-outs? Caught in the 'cross-fire'!

The body of the *kraal* head would be rolled in a red oxhide and placed in the grave being dug near the anthill, his few pots broken (to prevent them being stolen) and placed with other symbolic items to comfort him beneath the blanket of earth that would cover him in his final sleep. Not far away, in the wet bank of the river, was the smaller hole in which the child would be delivered back to the profluence of creation, as was the custom, to be carried on by the flood with the rains. The *kraal* head's wife, comforted by her kin, stared with eyes numbed by events.

When Matt left, the young girl stood there watching him. When he looked back he could still see her. He could not help feeling that she was not simply watching, but accusing. He was leaving, but James was to stay there, awaiting others who had been contacted to come and assist the family. Matt's role, meanwhile, was to see that those who perpetrated these atrocities were accounted for. And yes, white man's intransigence was very much responsible for the conflict in the land, for oppressing the black man, but Matt could not say 'I am white therefore responsible,' or 'They are black and therefore not responsible.' He sympathised with the people's call for self-determination, but not by violence. And he was caught in the paradox of trying to prevent violence by violence.

They did not get the guerrillas that day, or in the days of fruitless search, of frustration, heat and exhaustion that followed. Eventually they were forced to return home.

The evening Matt arrived back he and Danielle sat together on the verandah rail watching the sun go down.

'When one sun sets, only then can another rise,' said Matt. Danielle nodded. But it was not the sunset Matt had been referring to. His mind was still locked on the incidents of the previous few days. Incidents from which there had been no release of the frustration, the pent-up fury inside him. One would have thought that one could get used to the reality of violence. Matt hadn't. He was only numbed by it, and when the numbness wore off, what then?

When he went in to shower Danielle sat on the edge of the bath like before to talk to him, but he didn't want to talk.

'There's nothing I can say – don't ask me to talk about it,' he said.

'OK, I understand,' she said. 'I'd prepared something for dinner in case you came back. I'll just go and pop it in the oven.'

'I don't want to eat,' he said. 'I just want to make love.'

He came out of the shower.

She didn't really know what was happening until it was too late and she had submitted. He pawed her aggressively. She felt used.

'There are things happening out there that I'm supposed to be putting a stop to, but I can't, no matter how hard I try . . . and I feel as guilty as hell,' he said at the end of it.

The following morning, while Matt ate breakfast at the table on the verandah, Danielle nibbled at her toast and stared disconsolately out towards the valley.

'I'm sorry,' he said, but he knew the apology, just feeble words, could not erase the smallest part of what had happened.

'I'd prepared a meal I thought you would like,' she said in answer.

'Yes, I know.' His voice was passive.

'It's silly of me I know,' she said quite calmly, but she was unable to maintain her composure. She shook her head and there were confused tears welling in her eyes; she stood up, wiping them with her hand in an extension of the same motion and hurried into the kitchen as if something needed her urgent attention there. She had tried not to cry, but knew as a woman that tears might help.

She remembered Matt as a person who was as sensitive and gentle as he could be tough; each in its own place. But now the toughness was turning to hardness, and he was confusing the appropriate places; allowing a hangover of the bush war to creep into his home life.

Never had a man captivated her as much as Matt had. Never had a man made her feel so much a woman, so alive, so important in a man's presence; but also, never had she been faced with the hurt that was facing her now, the prospect of the break-up of that relationship.

It was the war that was doing it, she knew; a subtle manifestation of its brutality destroying their lives from within, quietly, imperceptibly, until it was too late to defend themselves against it.

And she knew she could never live with a frighteningly ordinary man, not since she had met Matt; he had ruined her for that. The world felt so flat without him; events seemed artificial, empty. He had the power to make her feel and to be aware of her feelings.

She lived in fear. Every day he had been away the fear had multiplied. It was natural to be frightened, she told herself, it would be so easy to lose him. He could leave the farm one day, just like all the others, never to return.

Her feelings were so confused, she didn't know what to make of herself. For now too, was she to feel nervous every time he returned, not knowing what he would be like?

She could perhaps excuse him for what had happened, what was happening, understand what he was going through, not say anything more about it, shield him from her true feelings, but at the same time she had known people with no means of release, with no outlet for their feelings, all their passions and hungers bottled up inside, to fester and turn sick, and in their panic they would reach out blindly for substitutes. Or she could perhaps allow all the resentments, doubts and buried needs of the past few weeks to burst to the surface and explode at once; tell him straight out 'I need you, but not as someone who changes every time he steps out the door, coming back a different person, to rape me.'

She could have allowed herself to react in that way, to say those things, but she didn't. She excused him.

When she came back on to the verandah, Matt noticed that her eyes were dry, but the little mascara she wore was smudged. He wanted to comfort her but all the words he wanted to offer seemed hollow. He did not say anything.

They both felt caught up in something that was far bigger than themselves. There was hate, cankerous inside him. Matt was dumbfounded that he could be made to feel in such a way. Mumvuri . . . Mumvuri . . . Mumvuri . . . the name pulsed like a raging fever inside his head.

Danielle resumed her gaze into the valley. The cattle, the *veld* grass, the trees, the maize, the water of the dam, stood still. There was not the slightest movement of air. It was as if the world outside had caught its breath, concerned lest it should miss something that was about to happen inevitably, but didn't know when.

Early the following morning Danielle woke up. Looking at the alarm clock, she saw that it was 4.00 a.m. She stayed awake. Matt was asleep beside her. Outside it was still dark.

Inexplicably, she remembered how Matt had once pointed out a small hole to her in an evaporating pool of the river, at the end of winter, just before their first summer as man and wife. It had been an airvent that marked the spot where an African lungfish had burrowed deep into the mud as its water supply had disappeared around it.

Danielle thought how with that summer her world had been cast into a spin of colour like that fish must surely have seen, swimming from its gloomy mucus-lined hole into the river, brought to life by the summer rains.

But she should have known that once again cold dry winter would be waiting. Season followed season. All was transient. Continual creation and destruction were perpetuated, followed one another endlessly. As soon as one had something there existed the inevitability of losing it!

The summer rains were beginning to abate.

The cattle mating season was drawing to its conclusion.

As the maize had ripened, the silks of the cobs had gradually changed colour from a pale greenish white to pink-purple and now they were turning brown. The cobs were picked for the table, for the farmhands and their families, and for market. They were tender and full of sweet juiciness; to eat them when freshly picked was the best way, before the sugar in the kernels turned to starch and they turned tough and dry.

Veld hay was reaped. The fields for the winter wheat continued to be harrowed to rid them of weeds.

The seasons continued unchanged but life had changed for all in the valley.

April

The days passed. One month terminated and another began.

Over the first weekend of April guests came round, old friends from Danielle's student-nurse days, the Vans and Suzanne's family, James and Alexandra, Andy and Elaine, Rotor with the latest *femme fatale* on his arm, and Jacob. They all joked and drank too much, then were gone again.

The week following, Danielle went about her duties on the farm during the day while Matt went about his, but often they would find moments to do things together.

She saw to the clinic, her butter and cheese making, helped Maruva prepare cooked meats and sausages to store, saw to it that the kitchen and flower gardens were tended to.

Matt supervised the harvesting of cowpeas to be mixed with molasses or green maize for the cattle. The rest he reaped for hay as soon as the pods were filled and the first ones were ripening.

Danielle prepared a picnic basket, and had lunch on a white tablecloth spread out in the field with Matt like they used to. Around them lay the freshly mown hay to cure in the field, its heady scent in Danielle's nostrils.

In the sun in the middle of the field with Matt, Danielle felt that for her the world was warm and wonderful again.

That night, she felt Matt couldn't have been a more pleasant companion. He was sensitive and caring just as she had always remembered him. Perhaps he was making a conscious effort to make up for that lack of consideration for her feelings he had lapsed into a while back.

They shared a bottle of wine over dinner. Afterwards, her head was delightfully fuzzy, sounds and colours were mellow.

They danced on the verandah, without music except for the singing of crickets in the long grass, the frogs in the reeds of the dam, and the birds of the night. She swayed towards him so that the tips of her breasts, rising through the satiny sheen of her loose blouse, just touched his shirt front.

He drew her gently close to him and kissed her. Her tongue caressed the inside of his mouth and her head slid down his belly. Her soft and gentle eyes were filmed with the uncontrollable pain of desire. Her face was before him, her moist lips parting, then the taste of her mouth again and eyelashes.

She arched backwards allowing his hand to play beneath her blouse. She had had ample proof in the four years of their marriage that her body could make his heart beat and now with no little surprise she found herself using it to make up for her recent emotional insecurity. She desperately wanted him to ease the fear that she could again be alone. She shook back her sun-gold hair, catching the light of the candles in that typical manner of hers that she knew he loved. She saw that he had noticed it. She smiled.

'When you're away I think of you all the time,' she whispered.

Yes, he could have told her that she occupied his every thought while he was away, but there was no substitute for reality. And for him to have said that he could not afford to think of her out there, since such thoughts took the edge off a man's alertness, blunted the keenness, softened the hardness; that to survive he had to sever all links with civilisation; that out there were animals, Man the meanest of them all, who killed or would be killed; that out there was a land which acted against his every step, striving to rid itself of the irritation of mankind that crawled upon its surface, a natural defence, like anti-bodies attacking an alien toxicant in its system: for him to have told her that every time she appeared in his mind he had pushed her aside as an intrusion; for him to have said these things would have been to stab her, and to have twisted the knife in the wound.

'I love you,' he said instead.

The following morning Matt was awake before Danielle. Outside it was still dark. There was always something to run from, he thought. A man needed something to run to, a place and someone to come home to. A man needed to come home.

Danielle breathed softly against him.

Later that day Matt called Danielle up on the vehicle radio from the *veld*. 'The first autumn lamb's been born,' he told her.

The ewes were at their peak of fitness with the good grazing during the rains, able to supply bountiful lactations replete with the necessary nutrition for those first critical weeks of rapid growth and development in the vulnerable lamb's life. Only as they became progressively older and more capable to survive would the value of the grazing pasture decline proportionately, but then they would be supplement fed.

Matt went about his usual checks of the farm. Daily, he examined the tall maize stalks, stark and brittle with their well-filled cobs, heavy with ripening seed. The moisture content of the grain had to be just right for mechanical harvesting to avoid rotting when stored.

Because the winter season was dry, the maize dried naturally in the field. But he couldn't leave it in the field too long because the drier the plants, the more fragile their roots became and the plants would be blown over in the wind. Besides that, enough time had to be made available for ploughing and planting the winter wheat. The timing had to be just right.

At last he declared it was time for the harvesting to begin.

Matt loved the harvesting. It was the fulfilment of good work, good weather, good timing and good fortune. Their money was tied up in the growing crops and livestock, and in machinery and the land. The return they would get from the maize was much needed to pay off the day-to-day running expenses of the farm. When Matt's father and brother had died, Matt had been faced with having to sell the farm to overcome a huge financial crisis. For fourteen months when the estate was being wound up and all funds had been frozen, Matt had been without money. He had had to borrow heavily from the bank and from the Vans to keep things going. Then when the estate was concluded he had to surrender all the farm's financial reserves and sell off livestock and equipment to pay for death duties. Danielle had married Matt shortly after that. She had watched how hard he had worked to get out of debt. It had taken almost the entire four years of their marriage. But never did he complain, and he always allowed time for his friends and relaxation. Danielle, meanwhile, had thought how insensitive it was of the government to have saddled Matt with death taxes when his father and brother had sacrificed their lives for the country. It all boiled down to the fact that the necessary insurance had not been taken out for just such an event. Matt learnt from the omission, and made certain that such a predicament would not arise again on Matiziro Farm.

His enthusiasm for what he did inevitably rubbed off on the farmhands and they went to work eagerly, with the knowledge that at the end of each day they had done a man's meaningful work.

They had three tractor-drawn combine harvesters which they were still paying off. In three parallel lines they trundled together, one staggered behind the other to allow them to be accompanied by trucks to take the grain, and to be clear of the dust created by the others.

Together the combines cut a fifteen-row swathe through the maize fields, cutting the stalks, cobbing, husking and threshing the grain. The grain moved through the funnels extended over the open-back trucks which moved alongside. Empty cobs, leaves and stalks were cast on to the field behind from the bottom of the harvester. As the trucks were filled with grain they would drive off to the railway silos in town, where they would be weighed and graded. The cattle were allowed to graze on the residue and the stalks in the harvested fields.

Danielle watched Matt and she wished that he could be left alone, perhaps one day to realise his ambition of having sons so that together they could run the farm as a wildlife sanctuary.

Matt remembered how, when he was a boy, his father overhauled all the machinery in the slack moments of the year when other farmers were taking it easy. That way he seldom had a breakdown to repair during the busy times. He remembered all the precautions his father would take during the harvest, from drawing off half a litre or so of fuel from each of the old diesel tractors in the dark of the morning, removing water and impurities that may have settled overnight, to the refuelling in the dark of the evening, guarding against 'breathing' moisture condensation in empty or partially empty tanks when temperatures dropped. Now a man, Matt tried to pay as much attention to everything as his grandfather and father had between sunrises and sunsets past, supervising the farmhands, driving tractors with their combines, fixing faulty machinery, adjusting the combines correctly for the size of the grain here (or some would not be threshed whilst there was the danger of others being cracked), advising, even checking on jute bags and twine to keep some of the crop aside for their own milling, for poultry feed

111

and all its other uses. He paid attention even to the most seemingly insignificant detail that might otherwise have hindered the harvesting operation.

That was the way a Nel was, the way he was. He left as little as he could to chance. But there were other things beyond his control . . .

Matt, Red and Andy spent four entire days travelling on foot through the bush pursuing Mumvuri and two other guerrillas, following spoor, asking questions and checking information received via James's office. In the hunt, *kraal* after *kraal*, herdboy, wandering visitor from an adjoining district, old woman, young woman, girl, everyone they came across was questioned . . . then they crossed the hills into the dry region.

On the fifth day they reached Borehole 14. At that time of year it was only at such a borehole, sunk by the Agricultural Department, that water was to be readily found.

On seeing the carnage in one of the *kraals* that clustered round the borehole, Matt felt a cold shudder as if an invisible force of chilling evil had passed through him on its fateful journey to the darker levels of existence, and by that feeling alone he knew Mumvuri had been there.

He felt an intense need for a cigarette, to mask the sick taste that had built up in his mouth; he shielded the match with his hands as it flared and he lit one.

A woman at the *kraal* had been forced to cook and eat the severed lips and ears of her husband. But that was not all. The guerrillas had tied her husband to a tree, pinned his eyelids open with pieces of straw, and repeatedly raped his wife and daughters in front of him.

Matt looked at Red and Andy. Distress had carved its way into each of them, but none would have admitted it before the others, though all instinctively knew, without having to be told, what the others were feeling. Their attitudes were almost palpable. All of them had wives, whilst Red, the big lovable oaf, also had a child – a daughter. So all were very close to what had happened there – it could so easily have been Danielle, Suzanne or Elaine that had been subjected to this. And when James came there was his wife Alexandra and his two teenage daughters to think of too . . .

At that moment Matt felt particularly close to Red as usual, but also to the team as a whole. Over the months they had been together they had become close friends – no, more than that. They had shared experiences of an intensity they hadn't shared even with their own wives. Faced repeatedly with life-and-death situations they had to know what the others were thinking and react accordingly even before a thought was translated into action. Somehow they had come to be bonded in a relationship even closer perhaps than marriage. Matt thought how it had been when he had lost his father and brother, and how he had needed something to take their place. Oom Van and Red had always been there for him; and now he had James and Andy and Rotor and Jacob too.

'This is a beast we're chasing, Matt,' said Andy. 'In the beginning I thought it was just a man.'

Matt thought how Man, so far as he had seen, was perhaps the only beast amongst the animals.

Red, like Matt, was silent. What words could be said?

Only !Kai would have appeared immune, thought Matt. Not indifferent, but accepting the way-of-man, the strongest of them all.

Still Mumvuri lived.

The bush war had escalated as Matt had known it would but hadn't wanted to believe.

The Communist aim of world domination had been fused with the black nationalist purpose. It was becoming so that you couldn't fight the Communist threat without fighting black self-determination.

The violence and the atrocities against the innocent people in a war where no one was permitted to remain neutral were increasing. The guerrilla policy was that if you weren't with them you were against them.

Back at home Matt felt himself faced with a wall, a solid insurmountable barrier that had built itself up stone block by stone block, without him being fully aware of it, between himself and Danielle. An immovable object was what the enemy had become. In rage and fury he battered at it, trying to make an opening that he could pass through, but the wall was not visible. The result was only frustration, and the sense of futility in trying to attack something he could not see.

On the other side of that 'wall' was Danielle; but being nothing more than a mental construction it did not deflect the pounding, the hammering, the thrusting, which simply passed on through, still primed, stabbing, bruising flesh. By a process of osmosis she absorbed all his hatred and frustration. All she had to parry those lunging thrusts with was a resilient love and an unfailing faith in the real Matt.

It was almost as if he were trying to get back into the womb, away from the pain and disillusion of the world into which he had been breached.

He came at her with an animal desire, unrestrained, born of the cynical, hard-worn world of savage survival from which he had returned. He took 'woman', not seeing Danielle, his sexual appeasement primitive. His need and the angry release of tension that had built up solidly within him sought gratification at one and the same time, taking on something far more than their individual ferocities in the union. The granite monolith of his new identity collided with her soft flesh. He was stark and alone. She took him with his need, even though it filled her to bursting, and then left her empty. It was a bestial act; Danielle knew there was no attachment in it.

The night was long. She smiled and kissed and caressed, while her heart and body took a battering. There was the constant rasping of his unshaven face against her skin, the hot animal smell of his sweat. She closed her eyes but it did not shut out the pain. Tormented in his absence, she was crushed on his return.

When it was over, his heated body lay on top of her, still partly within her, but now limp and inoffensive.

He slept.

Danielle subsided into an uneasy slumber . . . to find him needing her again when he awoke.

In the early hours of morning the last wave of fury had broken over them and washed away.

That afternoon, Matt's laughter and frowns chased each other like sunshine and shadow; like the autumn sky, bright one moment and overcast the next.

The hay was dry enough to be stacked without danger of spontaneous combustion or mould. Matt attended to it.

That night, Matt felt Danielle stir beside him; warm, yielding, the pungent warmth of her body rising towards him from between the sheets, where she nestled, filling his nostrils, tantalising, beckoning. His hand cupped a breast gently, his breath quickening against her neck.

The original Matt had returned. He stood over her in the morning. He bent down to kiss her lovingly on the mouth. He arranged a bunch of self-picked wild flowers, fresh with the early morning dew, in several positions until he was satisfied she could see them comfortably from the bed. He smiled that endearing, totally disarming smile. He had been fishing down at the dam, at Termite Point, an enormous anthill now submerged, and had brought back a couple of bream for lunch. The dogs were in the bedroom jumping up on to the bed, growling and barking alternately, not knowing which to do in their excitement. They licked at her face, they left muddy paw-prints on the clean linen sheets. He did not shout at them, he did not push them away as he had done when he came in the night before, but stroked them in that rough playful manner they loved.

The tiredness, the language of worn oppression, had faded from his eyes, revealing an intense limpid blue, like sunlight viewed through water, not something you could point at; it was everywhere, dissipating light.

His touch was gentle, soothing. 'Forgive me,' he said, and kissed her again before striding off, the dogs in pursuit, to prepare the fish for lunch.

Danielle thought how he witnessed his own behaviour as if from below the surface, somehow distanced from it, as if it had a life of its own which he was not accountable for. When his head broke the surface, able to breathe freely once again, she breathed freely with him; the moods of his life governed hers, and he was governed by something else.

The seasons continued.

The maize crop yield was down on the previous year. They had to hurry to take advantage of early delivery bonuses and a moisture content as near to the acceptable limit as possible. Extra attention was paid to gleaning after the harvesters by the farmhands' wives and children, to recover some of the cobs which would otherwise have been lost.

There were good seasons and there were bad, thought Danielle, and the season of the bush war was well into yet another year.

May

Danielle looked out of the window during breakfast as she often did. Something out there troubled her. Then she suddenly knew what it was. The telephone-wire chorus lines of birds had gone. In their place had come the first warning bite of winter; nights were turning cold. !Kai said how the wild residents of Matiziro were beginning to show nervousness at the approach of the dryness and the cold.

The maize crop had been harvested and transported to the grain silos in town. That night it was the night of the beerdrink.

Come sunset, all the farmhands had gathered at the *kraal*, which, like the farmhouse, was surrounded by a double security fence and was guarded by armed militia. Wood fires were lit in the clearing at the village centre against the approaching night, and beer was already being drunk.

Danielle sat with Maruva and chatted to the women. They laughed and joked while working just as much as at play. There were the old and the young. The old could remember spending most of their life on the farm, and many of the young had been born there.

Danielle had come to know the women and their families reasonably well in the four years she had lived there. Most knew her as *nesi* – the one who looks after the sick. She was the one to whom they brought their problems, with whom they shared their crafts of clay-pot making and weaving.

Everyone on the farm had their function to fulfil no matter how old or how young. A man's meaning was in his work. The old were the receptacles of tradition, of wisdom. The young learnt their future roles in the community from their very first games.

As the sun went down the clear sky was coloured with the most beautiful oranges and reds. The men sang in the mellow harmonies only Africans could. Others chatted and joked and the sounds that filled the farm village were those of a hardworking people at leisure. They entertained one another and themselves with their own good humour and singing and storytelling and antics. No entertainment had to be specially provided for them; these were not a passive people who could be satisfied to sit back in soft chairs and allow themselves to be entertained without their active involvement. They had to be doing something – for it was in action that a man knew his own worth.

Matt, sitting with the men, exchanged anecdotes and funny tales about things that had happened in the harvesting the year before and the year before that. They could remember as many harvests as they had years of work.

These people didn't have a lot, but they had work, they had as much as they could eat, they had roofs to shelter them from the weather, wood, wives or husbands to keep them warm in winter, their children had a school to go to, they had their own plots of land in which to grow their own crops a couple of hours a day, they were protected, and in good years they received bonuses. Not all in the country could boast that it was true, but it was so on Matiziro Farm – almost like a little state in itself.

Matt had no holiday cottage at the coast, no yacht, no big bank balance to squander in living the easy life. All money earned went back into developing the farm, improving the standard of living of its people and perhaps one day having enough to be able to re-stock Matiziro with the wild animals that once lived there in profusion.

'The stomach is not made of bones. It is capable of great expansion,' Matt chided the men and grinned conspiratorially, inviting them to 'Waste no time or effort but with the drinking'; 210-litre drums of beer stood close by to be emptied. He politely wiped his lips, raised a calabash of the thick, foaming seven-day fermented beer and drank before passing it across to his neighbour.

On grills over the fires thick beef steaks spat fat and filled the air with their aroma; on a spit was a roasting calf; and in the coals were chickens and pigeons, their entrails removed, covered in clay, baking slowly. Now and again someone would take one out of the fire when the clay cracked. The feathers came away with the clay as it was peeled, and the carcass was passed from person to person, each breaking off a joint. Matt chewed on the soft ends of the bones rich in iron, then casting them to the dogs felt compelled to break out into song. The others were quick to accompany him.

> *Yebo*! A river in a valley flows
> Like Fate towards its destiny,
> A place where a man is a man
> And, sucking marrow from bones,
> Tosses them over a shoulder . . .

It was an old traditional song that had seen many renditions as the years had changed, taking on the meaning of the time, and now in the song, strange emotions were latent; but there was much joy in the singing, and one song followed another.

Danielle watched !Kai, the oldest member of the farm, who had been mentor to Matt and his brother in their youth. He sat beside Matt forming part of the circle of menfolk around the wood fire, placidly taking in the sights and the sounds of festivity about him and drinking.

In !Kai's relationship with Matt, Danielle witnessed an unassuming friendship, an innocent guilelessness that one tended to lose with childhood, yet which that little old man had somehow retained.

She remembered when Matt had been admitted to the town hospital with tick fever after his first annual month-long military committment since the wedding. !Kai would visit him dressed in what passed as his Sunday Best: ill-fitting trousers and threadbare jacket, old shoes worn down at the heel by an owner before him, and an old hat that he held a little uncertainly in his hands like some strange totem of great importance to others but of no practical purpose to himself. He was respectful of it, and careful not to offend by placing it down where it could get dirty or creased. He sat there in the same spot barely moving, with incredible patience and self-discipline, not even leaving to empty his bladder. 'Who are you waiting for?' a black nursing sister had asked. 'A son,' he had replied. Matt had told Danielle that the old man had secretly been supplying him with his own herbal remedies. 'Did you take them?' she had asked. 'Of course!' he had said.

In looking at the little old weather-brown !Kai, Danielle recalled what Matt had told her of him, and her first reaction was to feel sadness, for it was like being given a privileged glimpse of an old world order about to die out, be lost forever. The wild bush, his unfettered world, shrank daily before the onslaught of 'civilisation'. Survival for !Kai had meant coming to work on the farm, marrying into the world order of the black man, so that at least part of him would survive in his progeny. But his sons had been a major disappointment to him. They mocked what he had to give them of the old world order, and neither bushman nor blackman, they were caught in between two world orders, neither of the old nor the new.

But then again, the sadness didn't seem to have touched !Kai so badly as one might have thought. In Matt and his brother, !Kai had found two disciples to pass on what knowledge of the African bush he had come to inherit over all his years. He had found two young boys who hungered for what he knew, two boys of kindred spirit. And the fact that those two boys were white didn't seem to have bothered him, despite his natural distrust of whites, for they shared in common their love of the bush and they had been young enough to be moulded. One disciple had died, but there was still Matt.

Matt revered !Kai above all other living men. And Matt was !Kai's last hope for immortality.

Danielle thought how it was as if Matt was the only surviving fragile clay jar of a people's scrolls of their language, history, tradition and wisdom – only, in this case, the receptacle was vulnerable living flesh and blood, and the literature was a spoken one, handed down from father to son for countless generations.

Danielle thought that if Matt died, a part of !Kai as well as a part of her would die with him. She thought how Matt used regularly to add to his manual on Bush Lore. It was far from complete, but over the past few weeks Matt hadn't even opened it.

Danielle felt she had never really understood what the unusual side of Matt's upbringing meant, until recently with the growing bush war. That side of his learning was being called on more and more, simply to survive.

Danielle watched !Kai sternly consider the muddy-looking froth at the top of the calabash before cupping the lip with his mouth and tilting the beer into the open passage of his throat without pausing for air for what seemed a considerable time for such a little man. When he took his mouth away he gave a loud unrestrained burp of satisfaction that seemed once again to belie his small frame.

'You speak, old father?' called out Matt.

The others laughed delightedly.

!Kai's face cracked into a wry smile, a flash of gold tooth, his eyes set thoughtfully, then he politely wiped the rim of the calabash with the back of his right hand and passed it before sitting back with a look of contentment. The action had brought attention to him, and now someone called upon him to dance.

'Old father, will you not speak to us in the dancing?'

'Surely there are too many tales to keep inside one man!' another implored, but words appeared of little insistence.

Then the drums, carved from solid trunks of trees, patterned with burning hot iron, and stretched tightly over with hide, beat out their steady, ceaseless rhythm . . . *mutumba* . . . *mutumba* . . . *mutumba*; and a deep base *gandira* shook the earth, throbbing like a gigantic pulse, the heartbeat of a beautiful yet cruel land. Low notes, played in the centre of the big drum heads and high notes played near to the edge of the small drum heads, drove through the air. It was like an invisible force, and !Kai seemed defenceless against it. It took hold of his body. The drum rhythm was punctuated by the shrill of a whistle, the old traditional *chigufe* accompanied the foundation beat, the sound leaving the reed mouthpiece and resonating in the *muzhanje* (wild loquat) chamber with a mellow honest tone, instinctively in harmony with the vibration of the land, lending what otherwise would have resulted in missing notes of the melody, fusing with it in ethnic purity. And somewhere, encapsulating the whole, was the sound of ankle-rattles, and of small gourds of plant shot. It was music to be felt, even more than heard; music that was incomplete without physical expression.

!Kai seemed powerless in its grasp. It was assimilated by the whole of his body. As if possessed, he rose to his feet.

He told a story with his body, with gesticulations of his limbs, expressions of his face, with sounds that were the rushing of wind and the falling of rain.

As usual, when !Kai danced, Danielle was enchanted. She could not take her eyes off him. It was as if he was telling the story of Africa.

As the others grew in courage and excitement they beseeched Matt to join !Kai. '*Hovo* . . . *Hovo* . . . *Hovo* . . . ,' they called, eventually pulling him to his feet and overcoming what seemed irrepressible modesty.

Mupfura seeds, from which the yellow fleshy fruit had been sucked, were discarded on the dull red coals of the fire. They burnt brightly, like precious gems as they seemed to Danielle, lending an aura of fantasy to the night.

The men formed a ring, dancing and singing around Matt and !Kai, and no one could mistake *Hovo*, the slender mongoose, afraid of nothing, standing inquisitively on his hind legs, testing the air. The black mamba and the mongoose embraced, locked in the death act. Amidst the ululating and hand-clapping of the women, the foot-stamping *ho . . . ho . . . ho . . .* of the men, and the driving force of the music, the black mamba was killed, again and again, and the act applauded with even greater enthusiasm each subsequent time.

Finally, exhausted and teeming with sweat, Matt and !Kai stood aside and two more dancers, seized by Manyawi, the Spirit of Dance, took to the middle of the circle. Some danced vigorously, lifting their feet high and stomping the ground heavily. 'What is this, have you two club roots for feet?' called out one man. Others, unbelievably energetic, spent more time in the air than on the ground. 'What, are your feet nothing but fledgling fluff?' another man joked, and once more somebody danced with heavy footsteps thumping the ground.

Danielle was taken into the middle by Maruva, and she followed the footsteps, as was expected of her, each of which spelt out their own meaning like words to be tied together into sentences, in many ways. 'Ah! She dances like the impala,' one of the people exclaimed in admiration. 'No, like the clouds,' insisted another.

These were the children of Africa. They danced and they sang, the sweat pouring off them, and their dancing and singing was of the earth, the Mother-of-all-things.

As the night wore on, Danielle thought, as she often had in the past, how at ease Matt was with these people, and they with him. They were part of the same conception. Matt was at home there in the *kraal* as he was at the house, and she had marvelled at the fact on more than one occasion. Only now the fact seemed to perturb her. She didn't quite know why. Perhaps it was because she felt that he was becoming more at home there and less at home in the house. She had often heard from others how the bush was as familiar to Matt as the backyard of a suburban home was to a city boy, only now she knew it was more than true.

They slept at the village in the early hours of the new day, not in one of the brick buildings with running water that had been built for the farmhands, but in a hut. Matt insisted. Danielle lay with him on a sleeping mat, a *kaross* of old animal skins thrown over them against the chill of the early morning.

'*Hovo?*' She used his nickname – the Slender Mongoose – the name most of the farmhands knew him by. 'They're a snake's, aren't they?' she asked, touching the vertebrae choker around his neck. He had never told her.

'Black mamba,' he said.

'What for?'

'Goodnight,' he said.

It was a night of firsts for Danielle. It was the first time she had made love to Matt in a *kraal* hut, and the first time she knew what the bones around his neck were.

She remained awake for a long time afterwards. She thought how Matt seemed to breathe in the atmosphere of the hut, with its rough natural smells, like some life-giving elixir. His existence had always seemed to require it, but now more than ever. Many strange thoughts came to her in those wakeful hours. She couldn't help thinking how her mother always warned her as a young girl, even in the city, to iron all items of clothing against the maggot-fly larvae which would bore into the skin and incubate there. She thought about the long strip of leather that hung about the roof supports, and was reminded of Matt's bone choker and shuddered. Not so long ago the leather had been a hide, folded up with decomposing cowdung between the folds to help loosen the hair for removal. The hide had been cut into one long continuous strip ready to be cut up further into riempie. It hung there in the roof, entwined like a snake. Matt had told her how usually it would be tanned with *muunga-* or *musasa-* bark, giving it a dark reddish colour or yellow. *Muunga* had been used here, she could see. Strung up over a braying pole, it would have been twisted tight with a heavy stone weight, and left to untwist and twist again back and forth, squeezing the residue tanning water out and helping to make it pliable. Round and round . . . She thought of the black mamba bones . . . Round and round . . . Her eyelids became heavy . . . Her eyes closed.

She felt she had only just fallen asleep, exhausted, when Matt woke her, proffering a cup containing a fusion of what he called *mutiri* root, roasted and ground.

122

'Good for a hangover,' he said.

'But I haven't got a hangover,' she said.

'Better than coffee,' he said.

Bush war or no bush war, the seasonal cycle on the farm continued. It could not be slowed down or halted for Matt to come back to. What he missed he missed forever. There was always more than enough to do just to maintain things as they were, let alone improve them.

While Matt was away yet again, Danielle oversaw the sowing of alfalfa as a rotational crop in selected fields planted the previous year with wheat. Any later and germination would have been retarded during winter.

There was no end to records on the farm to keep. There were records for everything – livestock, crops, machinery, fuel, pesticides and herbicides, banking, income tax, health . . . everything. They had to be kept up to date and Danielle spent much time doing so.

When Matt came back, early each morning before the sun came up, he checked the tractors and took his turn behind the wheel along with the farmhands, ploughing under what remained of the maize stubble after the cattle had been on it, or ploughing under the green manure crops that would revitalise the soil for the winter's wheat.

For a while, Danielle watched him going back and forth across the field, leaving behind him perfectly straight furrows, a skill he had mastered in his youth on holidays from boarding school. The depth of ploughing had to be just right each season, deep enough to prevent hard pans of earth forming beneath the root systems of the crops that would be planted but not so deep as to bring infertile sub-soil to the surface and reduce the crop yield.

When she asked him if he needed a break he told her how his grandfather had first worked the land with a horse-drawn single-furrow plough.

Matt spent long hours out on the land, with the smell of the fresh ploughed earth, the *veld* and the bush, with the animals and the African minds he understood best. When ploughing there was the constant drone of the tractor engines but otherwise he was at peace.

When he moved across the *veld* either on foot or on horseback, he would instinctively check how the cattle were grazing and browsing, check that they had adequate shelter, check for the spoor of unwelcome visitors and predators that may have strayed from the

123

bush, check fences, check water availability and purity, check insects like hoppers and unwarranted infestations of caterpillars that could cause damage to crops. He would eye out the cattle to ensure they were fit and healthy, putting down salt and mineral licks where necessary. Once in a while, he would squat on his haunches and inspect the cattle droppings to ensure they were of the correct consistency, moist but firm, having broken a little on dropping to the ground. If they were too runny or too firm he would know the farmhands responsible for their supplementary feeding had the balance of dry and green feed wrong, and he would make sure it was remedied. More often than not, by quietly observing signs and symptoms Matt knew how things had been on the farm while he had been away. The farmhands saw it to be a little like magic.

Danielle went about her own business too. At half-seven in the morning she had breakfast prepared and Matt took half an hour off to eat. They talked about the farm, first attending to matters in hand by a sort of question-and-answer session with him doing all the questioning and she all the answering.

'You have your monthly meeting with the school teacher today, don't you?' he asked.

'Yes,' she said. 'He'll be coming for morning tea.'

Together with Red and Suzanne, they had hired the man to teach at the farm school, a single classroom in the village which catered for the children of both Matiziro and Spitskop farms.

'Daisy milking OK again?'

'Yes.'

'She recovered remarkably. No more problems at the dairy?'

'No, it's running as smooth as clockwork. In fact our figures are up on the same time last year.'

'Wonderful,' he said smiling at her. 'I'll have a look at them later.'

Then the question-and-answer session was over and they talked about things in general, about the country, about friends they should get in touch with, about sending a birthday present to this relative and that one. They did the things they normally did.

Finishing breakfast, Matt excused himself from the table, pushing his chair back as he stood up and reaching for his rifle close beside him. 'Won't have time for lunch,' he said. 'Have to start servicing the water pumps. If I need any spare parts I'll let you know and you can phone through to town, OK?'

She nodded. The big water pumps down at the dam had to be

ready for irrigation of the wheat crop through the dry winter, she knew, but nevertheless she was disappointed in him for not being able to come back for lunch. She was surprised at the illogicality of her reaction and felt apologetic.

He kissed her and went out.

Mid-morning, Suzanne came over for tea, and Danielle made a great fuss of her little girl.

When Danielle had been pregnant, she had made clothes for her baby, but when she had miscarried she had given the clothes to Suzanne for Sarie.

The teacher arrived and together the three of them went over plans for the school and arrangements for examiners and examinations. When the teacher had gone, Suzanne stayed on for a while.

'Matt filled a gap in my life I never quite knew was there before I met him,' Danielle told her. 'His absences bring that sense of incompleteness back stronger than ever. I'm scared of losing him. If not to the war, then because he's losing interest in me.'

'You mustn't underestimate how big a gap you've filled in Matt's life too, Danielle,' Suzanne reassured her. 'I've known him all my life. He loves this valley and its people with a passion – but no part of it greater than Matiziro and no one greater than you.'

'But he seems to be so different at times.'

'Red too – they must be going through a lot of strain.'

'How do you handle it when Red's away?'

'I worry all the time,' Suzanne said, 'but at least I have Sarie . . .' She clutched her little girl, then paused apologetically before saying, 'I'm sorry, I didn't mean it like that.'

'That's OK, I know you didn't. If only I did have a baby to care for, I feel I'd be able to cope with Matt's absences that much better. A baby would be part of him to have with me no matter what happened. When he's away I think of him all the time. When he's home I want to be with him all the time. Then I think how suffocating I must be for him.'

She bounced a giggling Sarie on her knee.

'I think I could get over the miscarriage if only I could have another baby. We've tried but I haven't managed to conceive. Matt takes it very well, he tries to defend me against any futher disappointment by saying things like he doesn't want a child to be brought into a wartorn existence, and has resorted to wearing condoms again.'

'You'll have another baby when it's the right time,' said Suzanne, and clasped Danielle's hand reassuringly.

Danielle smiled bravely, but bit her lower lip as if trying to keep tears back.

'You speak to any man or woman who grew up with Matt in the valley and they're likely to tell you how much they care about him. But it's you he chose. He needs you. You have to be strong for him.'

When Suzanne left with Sarie, Danielle went about the farm doing her chores. She thought what it meant to be a Nel; how the ducks, drakes and ducklings at the dam were not just ornamental nor just for food, but were there also to control the algae and soft vegetation that would otherwise take over; how the thick mass of grass growing on the earth walls hadn't just sprouted there nor was it there just because it looked pretty, but had been planted deliberately and with considerable effort, to prevent erosion and to offer cover and food for the ducks; how the wheat fields did not just happen to be lower in the valley than the dam but were there so as to take advantage of gravity in their irrigation; how the dam was not by chance as deep as it was with as small a surface area as it had in proportion, but had been purposefully constructed that way so as to reduce loss of water by evaporation to a minimum.

Instead of having lunch alone, she wandered down to the paddock nearest to the house. Matt ran a young bull with the senior sire there. Danielle often went there to watch the youngster's amusing antics. It bolstered her spirits.

Maruva found her there, leaning over the fence.

'His company is good for the old *sekuru*, is it not? It helps him keep young, pumps the blood in his heart for when he needs it in his . . .' and Maruva gestured with her forearm dangling between her legs.

Danielle laughed.

The bull was an important member of the farm, and so he held his head proud. On him depended the progress of the breeding stock – the accumulation of three generations of the family's efforts to establish their cattle herd.

He displayed a form as near to perfection as a living thing might be, from his glorious body and the smooth reddish-brown gloss of his hide to the handsomeness of his head, reflecting traits that were distinctly masculine.

Danielle couldn't help thinking how it seemed that all the

'important members' of the farm had something horrifyingly in common. They had all bred, beast and Man alike, simply to send their progeny off to the slaughter. She felt she could understand Matt's reticence to follow suit. It was preservation of the species that seemed to matter, not the individual.

At the milking shed, Maruva gave a chuckle and nodded approvingly when Danielle fondly stroked the soft muzzle of Daisy, the cow they had recently almost lost to illness. The prettily marked Friesland with a white star on her forehead turned her head towards Danielle as if in affection. She was the best milker, and also the most highly strung.

'You are still the one she likes to milk her; for others she does not let her milk down properly,' said Maruva and laughed merrily. 'Remember once when I dropped a bucket and she was so upset she did not let her milk down at all?'

Danielle remembered and smiled, but her mind was really in the present and not the past. She thought how the dairy cows with their docile-looking eyes and long eyelashes lived a peaceful existence of routine feeding and regular milking, each cow allotted her own stall and her own milker. It was an accountable world; how she yearned for such a world.

She thought of Matt, for her idea of an accountable world started and stopped with him.

Danielle checked up on the butter- and cheese-making, and then went to check on the chickens and pigs, while Maruva continued on her way to the *kraal*.

Looking into the valley above the dam she could see the ploughing-in of the maize harvest's stubble, and below the dam the ploughing-in of old lucerne fields and those fields that had been allowed to rest fallow, before the planting of the wheat.

Far across, she could see the *koppie* where Matt's brother had marked out the foundations for the farmhouse he had hoped to build there. Grass and bush had grown back over the clearing. The site seemed to have a mournful air of unfulfilment about it.

Thinking of Matt always having to go and sort out problems elsewhere, she wished that the farm was an island by itself. How voracious and insatiable a land it was surrounding the farm. She thought of the small Nel cemetery on Matiziro *Koppie* and inwardly winced at how the Nel family was offering up one last sacrifice.

Walking back to the farmhouse late in the afternoon to get dinner

127

ready, Danielle thought how Matt tried to secure peace for others but how he himself was deprived of it.

Matt drove up the road at that very moment, and skidded the Land Rover to a halt beside her.

'Hello, beautiful,' he called, 'may I give you a lift?'

'OK, but don't tell my husband,' she replied with a smile, climbing in and giving him a kiss. He smelt of fresh ploughed earth and cattle and a little grease from the water pumps, not an unpleasant smell. They drove up to the house.

It wasn't long before Matt was back in camouflage, and his skin darkened. Weapons and equipment were checked again and again. He glanced at Red holding a sensitive F-1 detonator gently cupped in his huge hand as he flattened the split points of the pin to ensure its free and easy release from the grenade when needed.

Red and Andy were singing.

Oh when the saints,
Oh when the saints,
Oh when the saints go marching in . . .

Matt turned and walked away to the flight line. What's happened to you, he asked himself. He found no humour in the incongruity of hymn and situation.

The three helicopters took a flight path that would intersect the river further down the valley before nightfall. Matt glanced at the others flying slightly below him in formation. He shook his head incredulously. They were nothing to look at, much the same as any men you'd expect to pass on the pavement. Those whom James in private, somewhat jokingly and somewhat seriously, had come to refer to as *vapostori*, the Apostles, not only because of their names – Matt, Jan, Andrew, Philip, James – but as his poetic spirit would have it, because of their mission 'to teach, to rule and to sanctify'.

They were away for a week following up information, and doing well until they got to a *kraal* where the intransigence of the *kraal* head there – Orwell Banana – prevented them from pursuing the latest information any further. It gave Mumvuri more than enough time to escape back across the border.

Orwell Banana consistently tried to deceive James. He swore that he knew nothing of Mumvuri, yet James had received information to the effect that he was responsible for a transit camp in his area. The information had been cross-referenced from various sources to ensure its accuracy. James's methods were tried and tested over many years. He knew well the need to validate all information, especially in a society where it was good custom to tell a man that which would please him, whether it was true or not; where it was good custom to exaggerate totally bad things so that when the true perspective was known, it always seemed by comparison to be better than it actually was.

James surreptitiously put a wad of bank notes in the mattress in the man's hut, leaving one note poking out. On leaving the *kraal*, he shook hands with the man, and thanked him most profusely in front of the others for his help.

Matt knew James. His mild manner, forever deceptive, had effectively made the man's relationship with the others in the *kraal* difficult. No doubt it would be followed up by an operative spreading a few well-placed rumours about the man's complicity with security forces. If another found the money the man would have a lot of explaining to do. Even if another didn't find the money, the man would experience difficulty in resisting spending the money he had found. But he would not be able to spend the money, new bank notes of large denomination, without arousing suspicion about its source. It was a poor subsistence farming area. There were no banks. An entire *kraal* could hope to earn little in an entire year.

It was poetic justice, as only James could administer it, not so much as grubbying a finger in the process.

As for Matt, the incident caused him to wonder what he was achieving chasing around the bush. He was beginning to feel that Mumvuri had got the better of him. If only the border didn't persistently present itself as a political obstacle preventing him from continuing the chase across it. He felt how Mumvuri had to have a base camp there to which he was continually escaping. He thought how he would have to speak to James about it.

'Well, what did you expect of a man with a name like Orwell Banana?' Andy stated on the way back home.

They waited expectantly for some mystical insight as to how to use the cue of a man's name to discern deceit in seeming innocence.

'Well what?' Red was eventually exasperated enough with waiting to ask.

'Have you ever seen a straight banana?' came Andy's reply.

'Oh shit!' Red groaned, and hurled his cap at him.

*

When Matt came back he slept eighteen hours without a break.

When he awoke he was irritable.

Danielle felt that he was grasping hold of civilisation while the bush lured him in. It was almost as if she could feel the skin tearing from the tips of his fingers, losing his hold as he clung on.

'Classic case of hurry up and bloody wait,' was all he said over breakfast.

She tried to involve him in conversation but each time she finished awkwardly, her mind only half on the point of what she had wanted to say. All she knew was that something had driven him back inside his shell. He was distant, reticent, determinedly impersonal. Once more he would not be roped into idle conversation, small talk.

He sought physical contact. It was the only language he seemed to understand. His mind was caught up in a physical world and physical action. He needed to be comforted.

Matt thought how he would soon have to go out there once again, and knowing what he was up against didn't make it a prospect to look forward to.

That night in bed, he awoke in a swamp of sweat, afraid. He became aware that Danielle's hands still grasped his shoulders, shaking him, her eyes wide with startled concern. The nightmare seemed so real, even now when recognition of familiar things around him told him he was back in the world of present reality. Why, when there was no longer any menace, was he still afraid?

The sheets were clammy, crumpled and twisted about him. He was shivering yet was burning hot, not cold.

He got up and went through to the fridge. He hooked the top off a bottle of beer and drained it without taking his mouth from the bottle. He took another one, lit a cigarette and went out on to the verandah . . . standing there, naked, staring out into the darkness. A cold breeze touched him. Out there, in the valley, the river was writhing in the dark.

His battered emotions sweated from his body. And outside, the world was touched with the depraved strokes of a mad artist's brush in a frenzy of creation; and destruction was just another form of creation!

He watched the cigarette vibrate between his fingers. Fear felt like cold water poured on his skin and in his belly.

He saw Danielle before him, momentarily caught between passing memory and the present. He was not sure in which time frame she existed; was she too merely an illusory figment of a disturbed mind? Was she too only from the past? His heart threatened to rupture in despair at the impending replay of some brutal loss that until then had been blocked from consciousness.

But she was there, soothing him, wiping away with the soft cloth of her night-shirt sweat that, despite the chilly air, exuded from the imprisoned heat of his body.

Matt saw the shadow of concern in her eyes. He stared incredulously at his cigarette. It had barely burnt half way. He stared at the bottle of beer standing on the verandah rail. Its contents had not been touched. He had relived whole chunks of his past in a matter of a couple of minutes. He suddenly became aware of the darkness that enveloped him.

He was staring at her.

'It's me, Danielle . . . It's me, Danielle,' she was saying. 'It's all right, Matt, everything's all right.' The voice was soft, soothing, comforting; and she was comforting him against her body.

He was aware now that the early morning air was cold.

Danielle. An innocent sanity amidst far flung and hopeless confusion.

She took him back inside, put clean sheets on the bed.

He clung to her, seeking the comfort of her body. Locked in life's procreative act he hid against the rawness everywhere, shying away from destruction.

At last the reality and colour of dawn touched the land through the night's impersonal darkness. He could see the duck-house island and a strip of yellow water that turned to white on the horizon. Only then did he sleep.

Reading the newspapers at lunch – late breakfast – he suddenly found that publication of all information relating to the war had been restricted. An article on some peroxide blonde with her new hat displaced the war. It's better that way, he thought.

Waiting once more for Mumvuri to make his next move, Matt returned to civilian life, but in truth he could never return, his mind was taken over more and more by Mumvuri.

Out in the fields he supervised branding the weaners of the spring calving. The following day he commenced the wheat planting.

Mumvuri was there with him in the fields. Matt tried to leave him there when he went back to the farmhouse in the evening. It didn't work, so he tried only to go back when physically exhausted, having released his pent-up energy into the land. His relationship with Danielle was safer that way.

Matt thought how sources of information quickly dried up when Mumvuri was in an area, a clear sign of the fear he instilled in the local populace. He moved randomly from one place to another to avoid surprise attacks, and was never in one place for long. He would never allow the locals to know where he had been or where he was going; he often gave false information to his own contact men, and would cancel a meeting at the last moment or simply not bother to turn up, as he had done with the planned Christmas meeting the year before. He would hold an impromptu meeting elsewhere, or none at all. He observed every letter of the time-honoured rules of guerrilla warfare: when the security forces pushed forward he pulled back, when they halted he harassed, when they avoided confrontation he attacked, when they pulled back he pushed forward. He trusted no one. He was completely ruthless and capable of any deception, any action that may win him whatever advantage, however temporary.

For Matt the entire guerrilla war had been reduced to a one-man personal crusade against one guerrilla commander. It was a battle of wits, a test of mettle that he could not bear to lose though he felt he might.

Danielle thought how Africa was like a great mortar in which men were pounded together by the pestle of war. It brought forth the essence, even as it crushed the matter.

Matt sacrificed his totality to war, but in the name of peace! How long could a man go on serving two gods, changing from one to the other like the flick of an electric switch which cast a room into darkness or into light? Men throughout history had been torn apart by such dual allegiance and left to stumble about amongst the torn remnants of their lives, beaten by an insoluble paradox. But Danielle thought how there was really no paradox. If that was what it meant to preserve one's life, a complete compromise of values, then such a life was not worth living. She realised that Matt attempted to keep hold by dealing with the two opposing aspects of his life one at a time. By creating the deception that they were completely separate, having nothing to do with one another, he dismissed whichever was not the immediate focus of his attention. He tried never to allow the war directly to raise its head in his relationship with her; he checked himself when he found it creeping into their conversation; he never talked about his experiences in the bush. But then he didn't have to. She felt his every emotion as though she had taken part in what had caused them.

At night she suddenly woke up gasping with the weight of it all.

Grey light suffused the room from outside. Shadows clung to the corners.

She felt how his mind was becoming more and more divorced from those gentle considerations on which her love for him had been founded; considerations necessary in a relationship between lovers, but the fatal dropping of one's guard between enemies. He struggled against it, and recently seemed to have gained some advantage, but had suffered a relapse.

Soil outside was the wonder of all life; in the home it was dirt. How could she tolerate such an obvious contradiction? But she had to, the analogy was so relevant to Matt.

The following week, as the helicopters cut through the bleak drizzle of the morning, Matt thought how a short time before he had been sharing a pot of hot black coffee with James, Red and Andy in the warmth of James's 'operations bunker'. They had spent the night there trying to re-evaluate the situation in the valley. Matt had brought up the issue of pursuing Mumvuri across the border, and James had promised to approach the powers-that-be on the issue, although with his lack of faith in politicians he didn't fancy the issue would be immediately resolved to the team's satisfaction. By then it was only an hour before daylight so they had decided to see darkness through with a pot of strong black coffee.

That was when the next incident report ear-marked for their attention had come through. A mission station in the valley not far from the border had apparently been 'visited' by guerrillas the afternoon before, but owing to the slightness of the information received they weren't prepared for what they saw.

As they approached at tree-top level they could see the alien mission that crumbled on the land's face like a scab which would eventually be shed. The smoke filtering upwards was almost indistinguishable from the misty drizzle. Africa seemed intent on holding her own against the advances of civilisation.

The personnel-carrying helicopters loosed their human contents and pulled up through the falling drizzle to join the gunship prowling overhead with its 20mm cannon. Systematically the helicopters conducted an aerial reconnaissance, the radius of their orbit increasing but the sound of their rotors never out of earshot.

There was a pole and *daga* construction that was still smouldering. The thatched roof had collapsed inwards. The partially burnt remains of books, blackboard, wooden desks and chairs which were piled up in the centre, suggested that it was a school-house. By the volume of books and writing material present, school seemed to have been in progress at the time the guerrillas had made their entrance. Matt thought how disruption of the school system made youths available for guerrilla recruitment!

The clinic, built of brick under asbestos, had resisted attempts to burn it. The paint on the external walls had long since become weather-stained. The interior, unpainted, had been ransacked, the few items of furniture overturned, bottles of medical supplies broken, and shelves wrenched from the walls. Fragments of glass from the shattered bottles had settled like dust. Medical reports in a pile and a number of burnt matches were on the floor.

Outside the clinic in a small clearing in the bush, the waiting area for patients, was the body of a white European man. His chest was not stabbed once but many times. Blood stained his faded garments and the white of his clerical collar. The run-off drizzle had channelled the earth of the clearing; it was coloured a faint red.

In the scrub nearby were two forms clad in long white dresses; female missionaries who had worked as nurses in the clinic and teachers in the school. The harshness of the years showed clearly on their faces. One was frail and the skin on her arms, face and neck was freckled and reddened where she had not protected it from the uncaring African sun. Her dress was thrown up in obscene suggestiveness showing white pants stitched at the seat in dark cotton. The other was a large woman, motherly looking, her eyes fixed in an accusing stare at the heavens. The inner thighs of her legs and her private parts had been burnt with molten plastic. A plastic bag which had been wrapped around a stick and set alight was still protruding from her vagina. There was a band of white skin where a wedding ring had once been on the fourth digit of her left hand. The pudgy finger was no longer attached to the hand.

God or no God, pain was the same, mused Matt.

Their life had been released into the soil of darkest Africa by the people they had come to 'save'. And in the major cities of Europe, social welfare organisations, humanitarian causes and churches had helped indirectly to kill them by making available funds that had been used to purchase the bayonets. Their despairing screams had joined all those millions of others that already wavered in the air of that vast and angry continent, Africa. For those that endured there was nothing left but the pieces of a shattered faith.

There were markings that the drizzle had not dissipated. Live rounds on the ground close by suggested that a rifle had been cleared of a stoppage. There had been no shooting. It seemed that when the rifle had jammed free-play had been made of pig-sticker bayonets. Besides, it was better to save bullets for those who could defend themselves.

Matt cut a cross-grain search to pick up the spoor. There were many tracks that led from the mission grounds in one direction.

Matt was quick to locate the tracks of a pair of small feet that led away from the mission on their own, at the opposite side. '*Musikana*,' he said, and showed with his hand the height of the young girl, careful not to point his fingers down and so inadvertently restrict the growth of the child as some would have it believed happened. He realised that he hadn't been speaking English, and that he had been gesturing as a blackman would.

They found the six- or seven-year-old girl, poorly clad, curled up in the cold drizzle trying hard to make herself unnoticeable in the undergrowth. She whimpered on seeing them, but when Red gently lifted her up and carried her back, she closed her eyes and her head drooped in the crook of his arm. He covered her with his battle-jacket which despite being saturated kept the fall of the drizzle off her.

James arrived with back-up forces. Red handed the little girl over to him to look after. She could tell them nothing. She slept.

They followed the group spoor at a run for over an hour, as though they were tracking a rogue bull elephant. The children, herded close together, carved a clear track through the bush.

Matt called Rotor forward with the helicopters. They divided up, Red and Andy forming one pair, and Matt remaining by himself. They started leapfrogging forward in kilometre jumps, following the spoor from the air. They stayed with the spoor until whoever was ahead had reported finding the spoor further on, then they were up again, and put down a kilometre further on still to check for the spoor again.

'TBFK,' Jacob said each time they relocated the spoor.

'He's quite lyrical,' Rotor said to Matt.

Another child, a young boy, was found. Dead. It seemed that he had sustained a fractured femur and being unable to walk was summarily dispensed with.

Towards evening, as the light began to falter, the drizzle settled into steady rain. The helicopter's Perspex became a distorted fish-eye lens.

'Not the best conditions to keep the helo in the air,' Matt said to Rotor in understatement. Most large birds of prey were grounded in wet weather; Rotor ensured his helicopter flew.

'Not the best conditions to be on the ground either,' Rotor commented with a grin as he watched Matt squeezing out his drenched cap, once worn to keep the sun out of his eyes, now the rain.

On the fifth hop, Matt was on the ground for some time, much longer than the previous occasions. He discovered the evidence of a miscarriage; a breach of childbirth deposited unceremoniously in the bush to be cleared away by predators. He thought of Danielle and felt a constriction in his throat. The woman had been made to press on. There was always the death of the young boy with the fractured leg as a spur.

It was apparent that Mumvuri intended the group to stay together at all costs. It would take a severe mind to prevent the column from stretching out thinly as age and strength began to segregate the individual members. There were signs that the older pupils were having to carry the younger ones who were slowing the column down. Sapling rods had been cut from young tree branches – for purposes of punishment, no doubt.

The pupils acted as potential recruits as well as porters, forced to carry supplies taken from the mission: food, medicine, blankets.

With first the rain and then the dark, Mumvuri had once again chosen his time well. He couldn't have considered, though, that a search would be conducted by air when there was minimum visibility. Even so, with time on his side, he may well have got clean away.

Matt continuously studied the terrain ahead as revealed on the map, desperately trying to determine Mumvuri's intentions, trying to put himself into his position, trying to think like him.

The elusive answer to the question 'Where's he going?' stared back at him from the map. A store stood five kilometres off the plotted line of flight, one of the few that remained open in the area.

The store had been ransacked. The mill, the central meeting point of the community, was deserted, yet there were signs of freshly milled *mapfunde* flour which some people called 'kaffir-corn'. In the *kraal* nearby, the floors of the huts had been recently swept, but the *kraal* too was deserted. Whether its occupants had been abducted or had fled there was no immediate way of knowing.

Matt heard from James over the radio that information indicated that the guerrilla bases across the border had been experiencing supply difficulties and that there was a shortage of food. In other parts of the country guerrillas had broken into stores along the border and stolen from local tribesmen.

Matt requested permission to perform a hot pursuit across the border come sunrise.

James told him that he would have to consult the Minister of Defence before coming back to him.

Matt blew on the seemingly dead fire in one of the *kraal* huts and minute cinders hidden in the grey ash glowed red. He built it up with dry twigs and branches from a pile inside, as a decoy against possible surprise attacks, while they spent the night elsewhere.

They spent the night in the store, a brick building under corrugated iron, out of the rain. There was no point in spending a miserable night and being worn out in the morning; he counted on the fact that that was exactly what Mumvuri would be doing. In war any advantage, no matter how small, could prove the deciding factor.

They mixed cans of the inevitable corned beef and baked beans in a large tin and shared it cold.

'Looks like it'll be pretty muddy in the morning,' said Rotor.

'There won't be any left in the morning,' said Red.

'Not the fucking bully and beans, mutton head!' chided Rotor.

It rained incessantly.

Matt thought of Mumvuri and the school children out in the rain.

'More will try to escape as night sets in and this rain continues,' said Red as he shovelled the mixture of cold corned beef and baked beans into his mouth.

Andy stared at him. 'How do you manage to talk with your mouth full?' he asked.

'I wait till I'm eating,' gruffed Red, unperturbed, and carried on until his tin was clean; he slapped his belly and lay back in contentment.

'That smug expression of yours reminds me of that day we first met, on that training exercise,' laughed Rotor.

A dumb grin slapped clean across Red's face.

'If you want to make Red grin all you have to do is say "That day",' laughed Rotor.

'Sonofabitch,' grinned Red again, even more widely than before.

Matt remembered how on that training exercise Andy had popped out of the bush yelling 'Fire! . . . Fire! . . .' Thinking it too good an opportunity to miss, Red had fired a full magazine round and about him, knowing full well that Andy had been referring to the ruddy great flames that were leaping out of the bush behind him.

'Your smile for the rest of the day was as rare as rocking-horse shit,' reflected Rotor of Andy.

'Sonofabitch,' said Red.

'A whole bloody cavalry of them,' Rotor added with serious afterthought.

'And you, goddamned Rotor,' Andy remonstrated, 'you throw that chopper around the sky like some goddamned drunken cowboy.'

There was no response.

'You listening to me?' Andy reprimanded.

'Yeah.'

'Then how come you got your eyes closed?'

'My ears are open,' Rotor said, and burst into laughter.

Andy turned to Matt. 'Matt, being tumbled around in that chopper did you get that furry feeling in the back of your throat as if your arse was coming through? I sure as hell did.'

There was laughter then a moment of quiet. They could hear the rain drumming loudly on the corrugated iron roof. They had had to talk above it.

'Damn cowboy,' Andy muttered again.

Rotor grinned his enigmatic grin.

Night was upon them. They could no longer see each other in the dark.

'Anyone want a smoke?' Rotor asked, fishing around in the many pockets of his flight suit.

'Yeah,' they replied in unison, all apart from Jacob who replied with a 'TBFK'.

Rotor searched around in his pocket some more then said, 'Oh! That's a bit awkward 'cos I haven't got any. I forgot I had given up smoking.'

Someone threw a bully-beef tin at him in the dark of his corner.

'Goodnight, John-boy,' he called back, knowing it was Red who had thrown the can.

'Go fuck yourself,' said Red.

Matt took a cigarette out of his twenties-pack for himself and tossed the pack to Rotor.

'Thanks, Matt,' Rotor said.

Matt lit his cigarette and threw the matches after the cigarette pack. The pack and matches made their way round the group.

'How I'd like to wake up in the morning and find a woman beside me and not the cold-arsed barrel of a rifle,' Rotor sighed.

'What you need is a wife; we'll have to find you one,' said Andy.

'Night-night,' said Rotor hastily.

Matt smoked in silence, studying the map in the light of his penlight as if reading a paperback novel. He thought how close the members of the team had become in the few months since they had been together.

He was still thinking and studying the map long after he had ground out the stub of his cigarette.

Some time later he found that he had fallen asleep. The map had fallen across his chest and his drenched clothes had partly dried on his body. It was still dark outside, drizzling and cold. It was an hour before dawn.

Rotor woke up then, and immediately saying, 'Wakey-wakey, rise and shine,' he prodded Red's peacefully sleeping form.

Red had the ability to sleep quite obliviously anywhere. 'What do you mean? It's still midnight,' grunted Red, rolling into a more comfortable position.

'Nothing like it to invigorate a man, up before sparrow's fart, quick shit, shower and shave, or slash in a puddle as the case may be, and fly out into the blue,' said Rotor.

'Blue!' exclaimed Red. 'It's fucking black out there.'

James came back over the radio then, giving them the green light to cross the border. 'But take every precaution,' he instructed. 'Under no circumstances fire on any neighbouring forces, even if they fire first.'

Red and the others immediately leapt to their feet and within minutes they were ready to go.

The drizzle had abated but the sky remained an oppressive overcast. It was miserably cold. The ground was saturated; a gelatinous clay that sucked at a man's feet, clinging to his boots.

The exhaust gases of the helicopter's heating burners were comforting to Matt in the chilly, damp dawn.

When a rind of light appeared on the horizon the three helicopters took to the air once more. The Perspex canopy of the helicopter shook with the rush of cold wind. The whine of the turbine and the throbbing of the blades through the early morning filled Matt's head. He was sitting on the edge of the front port seat, his feet dangling down out of the doorless machine, looking as if he was about to leap out, held there only by the centrifugal force of the helicopter's movement, his rifle poised in his hands expectantly. His eyes were rivetted downwards to the green bush tops and the rich red earth beaten by the rain, that sped below him.

The helicopters, in a broad V-formation, one within sight on either side and slightly below Rotor's machine, worked the sections of a grid, surveying the ground for several kilometres over the border.

The helicopter's airframe rattled against the cold air, almost as if pushing through some solid force.

Startled eland, bedraggled by the recent rain, ran in confusion, not knowing which way to flee as the helicopters cut across the sky above them, making the air vibrate with alien sound.

In the helicopter down and to the starboard, Matt saw Red drive his fist into the air – 'attack, support troops, artillery' – the signal represented. He felt a violent lurch in his stomach and the helicopter seemed to drop away from him. There was the painful whine of the tortured airframe as it plummetted downwards in a stomach-rending bank to come out level just above the tree tops. His eyes, dazed from the wrenching turn and sudden downward acceleration, took a moment to focus. Rotor was furiously indicating directly ahead of them and talking into his mouthpiece to the other pilots at the same time; his right hand on the cyclic, the index finger squeezing the microphone trigger on and off, his left hand on the collective, his feet working the pedals, continually making adjustments to the controls, his eyes all about him, aware of each plane of three-dimensional movement simultaneously.

There they were. The column was breaking up like scattered splinters of shrapnel in an explosion. Running figures were dispersing beneath heavy tree cover. The three helicopters bore down on the target. Matt could see Jacob glaring through the sights of the twin Belgian MAGs, his fingers tensing against the trigger guard, ready for a running contact. But he could not fire. It was difficult to differentiate the abductees from the abductors.

On the assumption that innocent people didn't run those that did could have been shot.

Matt saw the shadowy form of a guerrilla below the tree cover waving his rifle at the children to scatter while he made his escape in the resultant confusion. Mumvuri! Matt said to himself, and then the form vanished from view.

The ground below was obscured by overlapping flat canopies of an extensive wood of umbrella thorn, and only occasionally in the gaps could they see movement.

Matt pointed out two running figures frantically weaving in and out of the trees, just like all the others but adopting a monkey-run they were crouched almost double, in practised military fashion, offering as inconstant and small a target as possible. One of them started firing a rifle over his shoulder as he ran.

The second helicopter call-sign was on the other side of the orbit.

'Take the one to the right,' Rotor directed.

The second helicopter banked left.

Rotor lifted each of his hands in a gesture of making sure that he had not got his right and left muddled up. He hadn't, but what he had overlooked was that the other pilot, going counterwise to him at the time of the instruction had meant exactly the reverse to what had been intended.

'Your other right, shithead,' Rotor said without depressing the microphone trigger, and took the other running figure.

He manoeuvred the helicopter so close that the wheels were clipping the tree tops, and they could see the pack on the guerrilla's back with its worn game skin straps, the curved magazine of the rifle and the muzzle flashes as he fired aimlessly, too high to be of any danger to those on the ground and too low to be of any danger to those in the air. Rotor pivoted the helicopter round on its axis, Jacob lined up, fired a three-second burst, and the man was thrown violently headlong, and Rotor pulled out.

It was then that it happened.

Tat . . . tat . . . tat . . . tat . . . tat . . . tat . . .

Several bullet hits, through the flimsy engine housing panels. The revs dropped. Something vital had been hit. Rotor was instinctively ready for auto-rotation. The engine spluttered as the last drop of fuel made it to the turbine. Fuel leads severed? He floored the collective maintaining rotational speed to counteract the instant sensation of falling, counterbalancing with the pedals at the same time the disappearance of torque from the main rotor. There was no reasonable place for a landing.

'How about there?' he indicated to Matt.

'There?' queried Matt aghast, pointing to a very small and tight clearing amongst fifteen-metre-tall trees. 'The one with the split-level floor and tree garden?'

Rotor nodded.

'Perfect,' said Matt, and under his breath to himself, 'Like hell!'

Without so much as being able to circle first to check out the LZ (Landing Zone), Rotor bottomed pitch and pulled back on the cyclic to flare the disc, momentarily overlapping blades with one of the other choppers as he managed to squeeze into the clearing. The helicopter's 1,140 kilograms crashed through the gap in the trees, the rotors chopping off branch ends all the way down to the ground upwards of 300 r.p.m. It made the bullets cracking about them seem twice as many as they were; but more frightening than the bullets were the rotor blades which seemed to splinter apart.

They hit the ground with a heavy crash and sudden check of downward movement.

'Anyone hurt?' asked Rotor, after a few seconds of winded silence.

They called off their names and their casualty status. Apart from a few bruises they were all right.

'Christ!' muttered Andy considerably shaken. 'More arse than class if you ask me.'

Matt came out of the helicopter firing into the trees directly in the face of heavy fire from that direction.

Another guerrilla was shot and wounded, others had gone to ground against observation from the air.

The guerrillas withdrew in staggered movements, covering one another with scathing firepower as they did so.

Matt found places where some guerrillas had pushed mortars and other weighty objects of equipment under bushes, no doubt to lighten their burdens, intending to escape and collect them later. It could be the day after, or it could be in a month or six months, but only when it was considered safe to do so.

Matt found places where other guerrillas had discarded their camouflage clothing, and concealed their rifles in dense bushes, no doubt so as all the better to look like just plain civilians – the reluctance of security forces to fire on unarmed personnel being well known by the enemy.

One of the rough-made back-packs contained partially empty bottles of penicillin labelled 'For Veterinary Use Only'. Such bottles were freely available in any Co-op without prescription, but it was just the same as that dispensed in different bottles and under prescription by pharmacies for humans.

'Some gook's got the clap,' said Andy.

'Let's hope Mumvuri,' Red said.

The two undamaged helicopters remained in orbit, observing movement on the ground and in contact with Matt. A person moving amongst stationary objects was easily visible from the air.

Fifty-seven children were rounded up. It would be a number of days before all were accounted for, the frightened, the hungry, the injured and the slain.

There had been twelve guerrillas. Three were dead. Four bodies had fallen at the scene of the contact on being fired at from the air, but on the ground follow-up the fourth body had disappeared. One guerrilla must have fallen down and feigned death, only to scurry away at the first opportunity. Matt cursed. He couldn't help feeling that Mumvuri had been that fourth body. Even the most experienced helicopter gunner could have been fooled in the heat of combat, flying at speed and from 100 metres up darting this way and that all over the sky. If you saw something fall when you fired at it you presumed it had been hit, and you didn't have much chance of checking for a pulse or dilation of pupils.

The woodland was strewn with medical supplies and blankets, bags of mealie meal, five-litre cans of cooking oil, sugar, tea, powdered milk, paraffin, candles, soap. The children helped to collect them.

The helicopters searched far and wide for signs of the other guerrillas but to no avail. In the confusion, whenever they spotted something moving down on the ground it turned out to be one of the children or an antelope. Each time another child was located the priority lay not with the guerrillas but with the child, picking it up and ferrying it to the regrouping area.

Time was against them, darkness was not far off, and they couldn't go too deep into a foreign country without causing political problems, and without stacking the odds against them; already they had breached another nation's airspace since sunrise.

Matt thought that in all probability, on hearing the helicopters, Mumvuri would just conceal himself, stop moving and wait for them to pass. Perhaps he was holed up somewhere waiting for darkness, when he would flee without being menaced from the air. With this in mind, Matt tried to track him down on the ground, but he was continually frustrated by finding that he was following the spoor of one or other of the children. Even then, since the guerrillas had bomb-shelled, dispersing in different directions, there was no certainty any guerrilla spoor he could have found would have been that of Mumvuri.

When Matt came across the woman who had miscarried, he gave up the pursuit of Mumvuri to attend to her. She had been too scared not to go on with the guerrillas after she had lost her baby.

Together with Red, Matt chopped two sturdy young *musasa* saplings, lopped off the branches and stripped off the bark, leaving two straight stretcher poles. He got Andy's battle-jacket and together with his own pushed the poles through the inverted sleeves, buttoned the jackets up and made struts out of the stripped pliable inner bark. When they placed the woman on it and told her that they would carry her out of the forest to a helicopter by which she would be flown to hospital, she collapsed. Concerned, Matt checked her vital signs thinking that she may have died, but then decided that it was relief that had allowed her to surrender to her body's physical exhaustion and sleep.

James arrived by air that evening.

The first thing he said to Matt was, 'Well done, but we've got to get the hell back across the border because we haven't really got permission to be here. I misled you: the Minister turned our request down.'

They started transporting the children back across the border, before they could come under attack by that country's border guards, and become embroiled in a political incident. They left no irrefutable evidence that they had been there.

When the situation report would be written it would reveal that the incident had occurred well inside their own border.

Once again Mumvuri had escaped.

When Matt came in shortly before midnight, Danielle was sitting reading in the lounge.

'Still up?' he remarked. He seemed weary. It was as if mere speaking was an effort.

'I couldn't sleep,' she said, smiling uncertainly at him.

Matt wondered how many times she had waited for him to return, as she was waiting now, and he had not done so . . . never knowing if he would return at all . . . How many times she had been sleepless because of him, and he had not known?

He took her in his arms. The action triggered off the need within her for him. She pressed against him.

'Hold me tight,' she whispered. She clung to him in her fear and loneliness.

He soothed her gently, combing her hair through the fingers of one hand. Not stopping to consider his actions, he went through to the bedroom, opened a cupboard and flung a suitcase from it on to the bed. He started packing.

Danielle looked at him, crestfallen.

'Where are you going?' she eventually managed to get the words out.

'We,' he corrected her. 'Grab a few clothes, we can use the same suitcase.'

'What . . .'

He placed a finger against her lips. He didn't want there to be any questions; he didn't quite feel he could answer them. All he knew was that he needed to get away. In his mind he passed countless signposts, names, labels, he did not pause to allow them to take on meaning, the identity of rivers, the shape of towns, places. He thought how it would be better not to have a destination but one always seemed to be going somewhere.

They drove off in the Land Rover, but the furthest they made it was the narrow tarred road at the T-junction with the farm's dirt road, where Matt braked hard, went round to the back, threw the case out, cursed the bush war, cursed Africa, cursed the farm, cursed himself, and started walking back.

His father and brother wouldn't have run. He wasn't under direct orders from anybody to do anything, no one could force him to do what he was doing, but he had taken on a commitment and that meant taking it to 100 per cent, anything else wasn't good enough.

If he took so much as a day's brief respite for himself, for his relationship with Danielle, it might mean one or more deaths that he could have prevented if he had been there, and it could have been the last day for Mumvuri.

June

Danielle thought how Matt had asked her to cancel his normal annual engagements with the local Farmers' Assocation and the club. She thought how seldom he was able even to talk farming with the other farmers in the valley, which he always used to love to do over a *braai* and beers.

For Danielle, winter was a sad time, for cattle were transported to the abattoir before they lost weight with the poor grazing to come. The optimum balance of the herd had to be obtained – breeding bulls and heifers replaced the old bulls and cows.

Wearing one of Matt's enormous jerseys against her bare skin, she stood on the verandah clutching her arms about her, having a break from tending to the vegetable garden. The weather was getting colder from week to week. A bleak wind swept the farm. The red-brown earth, harrowed for a final time to ensure a weed-free seedbed, looked arid.

Danielle saw !Kai go to Matt who was out in one of the prepared fields starting the sowing of the wheat. Matt stopped the tractor and she saw them talking for a while. Then Matt turned to one of the farmhands and gestured to the tractor. The man took Matt's place behind the wheel and continued the harrowing with another of the farmhands riding 'shot-gun' with him.

Matt came up to the house.

'!Kai has just told me that there is suspicious spoor crossing the farm near the *Koppie*. I'll ask Red to meet me, and we'll go and have a look.' He went through to the radio, contacted Red and alerted James.

'I'll oversee the sowing while you're away,' she said, trying to put on her bravest face.

'I thought you might,' he said. 'Ensure you're armed and that somebody rides "shot-gun" with you at all times, and that the dogs are with you.'

She nodded.

Red arrived, greeted her, and then Matt drove off with him and !Kai towards Matiziro *Koppie*.

Danielle drove down to the wheatfields.

The farmhands needed more bags of seed and fertiliser, so she went to the seed and fertiliser stores to load up.

She remembered the previous wheat season when she had helped Matt select the best of the wheat seeds from that year's crop, helped him clean them, dry them, check that they weren't damaged, to dress them with pesticide and store them. It was those seeds that were to be this year's crop, but she had never thought then that she would be responsible for it.

She drove back down to the tractors and helped refill the planters' respective hoppers.

She was doing that when she cut a finger on a sharp corner of metal. 'Shit,' she swore, and suddenly she was protesting against the war, against Matt being endangered. And surprisingly she reacted against the effect of his continual absences on her, that she had no time for herself, no chance of following any life other than the farm. When she returned to the house in the evenings she was so tired it took a superhuman will even to shampoo a carpet or the fabric of the lounge suite, and with the dogs in and out all the time such things were necessities. There was no time any more even to prune the roses.

And as suddenly as the tirade had started it was over, and she felt guilty.

She reminded herself to ensure the wheat fields were rolled after sowing. Most farmers didn't bother, but Matt did. It would ensure good contact between seed, soil and moisture, encouraging a high rate of germination.

But she couldn't help thinking how ominous the bush was, forbidding, all-powerful. It was taking from her that which she most cared about.

*

Trees and scrub grew thickly between the tumbled granite walls of Matiziro *Koppie*. High up, looking out over the bush of wildebeest, zebra, buffalo and impala, were the gaping mouths of hollows and caves.

The *Koppie* was separated from the river by a stretch of open ground, its flatness broken only by a few *musasa* and *munhondo* trees, all that one came to expect in the smooth undulating land between *koppies* that stretched across the *veld* either side of the valley.

It was dark amongst the rocks. Matt, !Kai and Red appeared like shadows. The damp faeces of *dassie* clung to the crevices. Matt breathed in the comforting smell of the cave's interior, the vegetal smell filling his nostrils. He thought how in the *veld* legend was all about, how the *dassie*, the tail-less rock rabbit, had been too snug in his burrow to collect his tail from Mwari when the Great Being had handed them out.

He spat the saliva and dust that had gummed his lips into a patch of stinging nettle.

On the smooth walls and the domed ceiling of the cave, an ideal canvas sheltered from the vagaries of the weather, were the tales of the land's First People, !Kai's forefathers, in pictures that Matt remembered from his youth. Eternally reciting natural history they stood off the rock in bold natural earth ochres, emblazoned blood-red haematite pastes and bright yellow limonite stains in colours made of animal fat and urine. They told of jagged plains and valleys teeming with wildlife in their countless thousands, before white men, the burst of cordite and the smell of gun oil. He winced mentally even now with the knowledge. As a boy, moved by the great storyteller, he had gone in search of the great herds. He was young then and did not know that they had gone, never to return.

He remembered how !Kai had sat there nodding his head interminably, occasionally giving a grunt of satisfaction, as if partaking in the mystical communion of an exclusive brotherhood. The first time Matt had seen the paintings he had mourned the painter's demise, a sense of tragic loss that had grown with each subsequent viewing, and now threatened to overwhelm him.

He forced himself once again to resume observing the mass of milling cattle on the far side of the river. A few egrets strutted behind them, looking for insects disturbed by the cattle's hooves, and men clustered around the site of the dip on the opposite side of the river.

'There's something wrong,' said Red.

'It's the dip,' said Matt.

'Yes,' !Kai agreed.

The whitewashed walls of the dip should have shown starkly against the hard barren red clay, worn flat by thousands of cattle hooves over many years, but it could not be seen.

Matt scanned the terrain before him once more and then rose to his feet. Emerging into the direct sunlight after the dim chill interior of the cave, he immediately felt the comforting warmth on his body. His rifle followed his eyes as he looked about him, one arm held to protect his face as he moved through the high coarse grass. Things had changed since his childhood. His rifle was no longer just for the promise of grilled venison steaks over a wood fire in the open cool of an African evening.

The river was slow, and the crossing stood out high above it. The rains had come and gone. The far bank was scarred by the cloven hoofs of cattle. A gulley had been widened by their passage to water. Precious top-soil had eroded away, more and more each year. The surrounding grassland was severely over-grazed by the herds of cattle that had waited over the seasons as the tribesmen took their turns at the dip.

It was, of course, Saturday, when the draft oxen were not called on to work. The tribesmen milled about, each with their few cattle. Horseflies drew blood from the ears of cattle, dogs and men alike. Parts of the brick and concrete splash walls had been smashed and pushed into the swim-channel. Its corrugated asbestos roof sheeting had been broken up; parts of it jutted from the water. The borehole pump had been damaged, but all in all, the tank itself was intact and the creosote-treated wooden poles of the crush fence were still standing.

'Yesterday?' asked Matt.

!Kai nodded.

There was no evidence that Mumvuri had been there, but Matt felt that he had. And it unnerved him. Did Mumvuri know that it was Matt and Red who had been trying to track him down over the past few months? If so, was this incident with the cattle dip so close to their farms a warning?

'We'd better tell everybody to keep more of a look-out,' said Matt.

'Yeah,' Red agreed.

Matt felt Mumvuri knew that in destroying the tribes-people's means of existence, those people, struggling as they were for a hand-to-mouth living off the land, would do anything for peace, even support Mumvuri's cause if that was what it took to stop his killing and destruction.

The tribespeople stood around nervously. Matt could see the cattle were thirsty. It would be dangerous to allow them into the arsenic-treated water in such a condition.

'*Sekuru*, would you not like to water your cattle now? We will dip them shortly,' he advised the senior elder. It would also give them something to do while the dip was cleared. The elder nodded.

The damage to the dip was only superficial. Matt knew that if Mumvuri had intended it to be anything other than a warning he would have ensured its absolute destruction. The dip could still be used. They constructed a dredge out of branches and bark rope.

Matt radioed James to arrange for the Department of Agriculture to organise repairs, and believing that tracking was counter-productive in the heavily populated area north of the farm where the spoor led, Matt asked James to make surreptitious use of sources there.

When the Agricultural assistants arrived, having been delayed by ditches dug in the road by *mujibas*, they were able to commence dipping immediately. The elders thanked Matt and the others, but only with their eyes. Guerrillas might be listening and watching.

Was not the life of these people in their cattle? Were not cattle a man's wealth and prestige; did they not draw his plough and draw his cart, supply his milk and his meat, and manure for his crops? Did not Man sing of his cattle in all these things, and for rites of *vadzimu*, the ancestral spirits? It was so.

And it was so that Man lived on in his children, and in his children's children. For children, a man had to have a wife. For a wife, he had to have cattle for *pfuma*, the bride wealth, to compensate the bride's father. In turn, the bride's father had to have that *pfuma*, those cattle, to ensure a wife for one of his sons, to ensure the male line . . .

Thus was it not true to say that children came from cattle? Was it not true to say that cattle ensured everlasting life?

Mumvuri was not only content with taking life, he wanted souls as well!

*

Death had more than one method of attack, Danielle thought. While looking one way, it would strike you from another; so what was the point of sitting up all night keeping an eye on the front door when it could climb through any number of open windows?

A litter of piglets was born. Danielle looked after them, nursing them through the first few days of their lives, keeping them warm.

That afternoon, Oom Van drove over with Suzanne, paying her one of his visits to see if she could use any help while Matt was away.

'The only real problem is that the mechanic needs a spare part for one of the tractors. I've ordered it but the suppliers say it'll be maybe two or three months before we'll get it,' Danielle told him.

'Let's go down to the workshop and have a look. Maybe I've got a spare I can let you have.'

Together they went down to the workshop.

Oom Van chatted with the mechanic and checked the tractor.

'We're in luck,' he said. 'I have just the part. I'll take one of your farmhands when I go and he can bring it back with him. You can send me the spare part when it comes in.'

Danielle started to thank him.

'In the old days Matt's father and I used to share a tractor before we could buy one each,' he said, effectively cutting her off. 'After that it was sharing a harvester before we could buy one each. It took many years.'

They walked back to the farmhouse, chatting about the farm and the country.

When Danielle asked him how he thought the bush war was going, Oom Van replied 'The safety of a farm is directly proportional to the loyalty of its population, you know. It is my opinion that the loyalty awarded Matt has superseded even that of his father – and you know what they called him.'

Yes, Danielle knew. They had called him *Mutongi wakangwara*, the one who judges wisely.

Oom Van smiled at her. 'I know you are thinking of Matt before all else, but if there is to be any trouble here he will hear about it and be able to take the necessary precautions – as he heard from !Kai recently,' he told her, and then, 'Now I haven't come all this way just to leave without some of your Earl Grey tea and buttered scones with homemade *konfyt*,' he said. Danielle smiled at once, for he thought

.152

drinking perfume-scented tea a very curious custom that revealed her English ancestry.

Shortly after Oom Van had left, leaving Suzanne to spend the weekend, Alexandra and Elaine arrived in Elaine's flash-looking sportscar. When the geese honked, Elaine honked on the hooter right back, and there was much laughter and pleasure at seeing one another.

'We passed Oom Van on the way in. He said if we hurried we'd be in time for scones and *konfyt*, so Elaine floored the accelerator and here we are,' said Alexandra.

'You're looking marvellous, both of you,' said Danielle as the girls kissed each other in greeting. 'How I envy you townees, you're always so beautifully dressed.'

Elaine laughed, and spun around like a fashion model. 'I wore this because I thought it would fit in with you country yokels.'

'Well let's get your suitcases out of the car and we can get the party in gear,' said Suzanne.

'Suitcase?' queried Elaine, twirling around her small handbag with an impish smile. Clicking open the catch, she pulled out a flimsy silk négligé and a toothbrush. '*Voilà*, equipped for the weekend,' she said. Then turning to Danielle, she said, 'You won't mind if I wash my knickers in your basin and leave them to dry on your towel rail overnight will you?'

There was more laughter over tea and with a *taran-tara* like a trumpet the girls from town produced a couple of bottles of sherry.

That night they were in a more subdued mood.

'It's been eight months since the infamous team was formed,' said Alexandra. 'Have any of you noticed much change in your men? I've been married to James for well on twenty years and he's been a professional policeman all that time, but never before has he been so changed in such a short period. He spends less time with the children, is even a little irritated by them encroaching on his free moments. He's become less flexible, more assertive, if that's possible, even showing a tendency towards aggressiveness.'

'Yes,' Suzanne nodded.

'What, Red too?' exclaimed Danielle in disbelief.

'I don't know what's happening out there, but it seems to be changing all our lives,' said Elaine.

'I thought I was the only one it was happening to,' said Alexandra.

'Me too,' said Danielle. The sudden knowledge that there were others who shared her feelings and fears was itself almost a relief if it wasn't for the implications it had for the others.

'Well, at least we're not alone,' said Suzanne.

'We must stick together,' said Elaine.

Then, with a deft change of conversation, Elaine, who went to the city once a month as a buyer for the town's only department store, told them about her last trip and what could be bought there, the beautiful winter fashions and the 'gorgeous hunks' of men in three-piece suits.

They talked about the news in the papers, what was happening elsewhere in the world and they all agreed that things didn't seem to be quite what they used to be anywhere.

The following morning, Alexandra and Elaine found it a novelty to work on the farm, so Danielle didn't feel so guilty about entertaining them and enjoying herself at the expense of getting on with jobs that needed to be done.

On the Saturday night they knocked up dinner together.

'You're such a wonderful cook, Danielle, I envy you,' said Elaine. 'I have Andy eating frozen pre-cooked meals most nights,' she laughed.

They built a fire in the hearth and lounged in front of it, downing another couple of bottles of sherry. They confided in each other and found strength in one another. As the night wore on and more sherry was consumed, the conversation got more adventurous.

'It's during these cold nights that I miss Andy,' joked Elaine.

'Do you think we could put in a petition for a truce to be called for the duration of winter?' asked Alexandra.

Elaine took out a small bottle of expensive perfume from her bag. 'I've resorted to wearing this,' she chuckled. 'It says: "the fragrance a man cannot resist or forget . . . for the woman who understands heady romance and passion . . . but wear with caution . ." '

They laughed and joked and had fun, but suddenly the weekend was over and Danielle was left alone once more.

Matt, Red and Andy were hopping from *kraal* to *kraal* by helicopter, following up information received from James, when there was a request for a casevac. Since they were in the vicinity they picked up the call.

The casualty was a pregnant woman, unconscious and bleeding profusely from within.

'Complications giving birth, I think,' said the commandant in charge of the protected village.

As the unconscious woman was being put into the helicopter on a stretcher she was caused to roll slightly on to her side. Her dress and belly were drawn tight like the skin of a drum. A sharp edge showed clearly pressing against the inside of the womb.

Looks just like the tip of a hoof, thought Matt.

He looked around him at the large fenced-off and guarded area of consolidated huts arranged in grid lines around the administration and security keep, its earthen parapets rising above the ground at the centre of the village. There, an attempt had been made to improve living conditions and safeguard the people from guerrilla intimidation, prevent the guerrillas from sheltering amongst the people, from eating their food and from sleeping with them. But there also the people had been uprooted from the lands which had been handed down from father to son, on which their ancestors had lived and died; the protected village was an impersonal place with which they had no spiritual connection. But also in the protected village were the mothers and fathers and sisters and brothers of guerrillas. They were little more than prisoners in a holding camp, bound by a dusk-to-dawn curfew.

When the helicopter returned it was with James, dressed as usual in immaculate shirt and tie, direct from the urban portals of civilisation, making the change with particular éclat. But this time anger or something inflamed his speech.

'The woman may not make it. She gave birth . . . but not in the hospital . . . somewhere out here. The evacuated womb was stuffed with two primed 200-gramme blocks of TNT and her lower part secured by tied rags.'

They were dumbfounded.

'Lucky the chemical time-pencil that was to be used to detonate the explosive wasn't properly triggered.'

Bush war was not nice. The people who waged bush war were not nice. Matt had never heard anything so obscene in his life. It would have been ludicrous if it wasn't true. It wasn't a normal war, it breached the bounds of rationality, of bestiality. If one ever needed anything to dispel the notion that a bush war was romantic, then this was it, thought Matt.

'Shit,' exclaimed Andy and Red. 'It's unbelievable.'

Matt was silent. Mother of God, what exactly are we up against, he asked, and swallowed a lump of phlegm that had compacted at the back of his throat. It scalded his stomach.

He wanted to get drunk there and then; so much beer that it would numb his mind; so cold that it would stop the scalding in his stomach; and he knew there was no chance of it.

'You were fast in getting here,' said the commandant.

Matt thought how they hadn't been fast enough, but what he said in answer bore no relationship to what he had been thinking. 'Yeah,' was all he said.

'Thank heavens,' the man breathed in relief. 'It's all a bit much for me to take in.'

Matt was trying to figure out what was happening in his mind. Something was happening there. He was so painfully aware of his thoughts originating from some source, some place, that it frightened him. Was it too, like awareness of the heart beating, only there once it had stopped?

'God,' he found himself uttering.

'If it . . . she . . . I'm sorry . . . if . . . if it had gone off would it have caused much damage?' the man asked.

'You mean to your offices?' cut in Matt unfairly, and then, 'You wouldn't have had to worry about burying the woman.'

He was thinking of a little nondescript time-pencil with a ten-to eleven-minute delay. It was eighteen minutes flying time to the hospital. He saw a hole blown in the sky, and the helicopter dropping out of it like a fire-ball. Rotor! Jacob! He saw the charge blow the casualty section of the hospital into fragments of dust. And he blamed himself.

Wherever he looked, the unnerving statement was there; emblazoned on the bark of a tree, formed by the clouds in the sky, etched in the dust . . . like scars on the earth's face.

'He's playing God,' Matt grunted incredulously.

'What was that?' enquired James.

'Nothing,' said Matt. He turned away, signalling for the others to cut for spoor.

'Do you think they'll find them?' Matt heard the commandant ask James.

'Even if they sprouted wings?' he heard James ask in reply.

The ground outside the fences was marked by the feet of its many occupants who came out to work in the fields and herd their cattle everyday. Bare feet had left leathery imprints behind them, their non-angular outlines with smoothly bevelled edges. The women's prints were smaller than the men's, and either pigeon-toed, or with their toes splayed from carrying a weight. The role of bearer was traditionally fulfilled by women, leaving men unencumbered to ward off predators or enemies. If the guerrillas had entered the area barefoot, or wearing footwear common to the local inhabitants, such as the rubber tyre-tread sandal, the task of tracking them would be complicated.

Matt moved further and further afield; a procedure he had adopted so many times during the course of his life that it had long since passed from the stage of monotony into that of automatism, each sense sharpened to the slightest change in detail.

In the bush outside the fenced perimeter Matt seemed to sense a hand against his chest, halting him from walking on. !Kai's hand! He studied the ground but he saw nothing to arouse his suspicion. He shook his head. What was wrong? Something was wrong. He knew something was out of place although he didn't immediately know what.

He started gently prodding the ground with his knife at a forty-five degree angle.

He unearthed a PMN anti-personnel mine, otherwise named after the Black Widow, the most venomous spider in Africa, which had the tendency of eating its mate after copulation.

'You're like a bat-eared fox,' said Andy, 'only it's not insects you hear moving underground.'

Matt didn't tell the inhabitants of the village about the mine, depriving Mumvuri of the satisfaction of the fear that it would have instilled. For Mumvuri, fear was worth more than an amputee, an amputee was worth more than a kill. Matt knew.

He searched the other paths radiating from the village, but found nothing; nothing, that is, apart from the place where the woman had been induced to give birth; the tiny grave. When the tiny body was dug up it was found to have had the soft part of its skull pressed in.

There was little light left when Matt struck out into the valley with Red and Andy once more. When night fell they stopped to rest and wait it out. The darkness heavy on his sweating body, Matt forced his eyes tightly shut, clenched his teeth together and tried to make his mind conjure up the deepest nothing that he could.

Danielle came into it.

There was always comfort in Danielle, in her voice, her touch, her body. It was as if she absorbed his fears, his hurt, his torn emotion. It was as if she drew more than just a part of his body into her.

His mind seemed to have no other way of dealing with the horrors that were confronting him, but to call forth in his mind Danielle, someone he knew to be warm, caring, loving and rational. The thing that he was chasing had no reason. It could not be confronted by reason.

Once again he was haunted by the fact that if he had only detonated the Claymore ambush a couple of seconds sooner he could have dispensed with Mumvuri at the very first instance – and none of what had since followed, the deaths, the destruction, the horror, would have happened. He felt responsible, and the guilt was the same as if it had all been caused by his own hand.

With dawn gilding the land, he looked across the gentle rift of the valley. It appeared to be draining the mists away.

They found the spoor of nine men. Hard ground had been scarred by heavy boots. Further on, they confirmed the number in a region of sand *vlei* where anti-tracking had proved futile for the guerrillas.

Bordering on a vast undeveloped wildlife reserve, they located fresh spoor that indicated a large herd of buffalo had roamed in their nightly grazing through the guerrillas' night camp in which bits of security-forces-supply rubbish had been placed to confuse identification of the occupants. There was dew in the sharp-edged depressions left by the buffalo hooves and there were signs that the guerrilla section had moved hurriedly, scuffing the ground; the length of their strides had increased, running, pressure concentrated on the balls of their feet. They had vacated the area.

Matt allowed himself a grin of bitter amusement; a grain of humour that in those times may have stuck in his throat. He envisaged the dark forms of 600–700-kilogram buffalo bearing down on Mumvuri, like black phantoms in a black night. The new moon would have set by 1940 hours. There would have been no light to have shown him who his visitors were, even though he would no doubt have heard them. Shapes moving at night could be very deceptive, and were not to be trusted.

They lost the spoor later that morning when it rejoined the reserve and they could not find it again though they tried until last light.

Come daylight they relocated the spoor, but staying with it taxed Matt's ability to the fullest. The guerrillas had moved in front of a herd of cattle for some distance, their footprints being overtrodden. Then they had mingled their spoor with the locals, and seemingly vanished amongst the people.

After considerable effort Matt was able to make out the familiar boot print that he had come inextricably to link with Mumvuri.

They picked up the spoor again. It was fresh, so close ahead that Matt found his heart beating faster and faster. The spoor was following a footpath which could be seen at intermittent intervals as it cut a contour through the hills into the distance.

Matt left the footpath and went over the first hill at a run to intersect the path the other side. No one was on the path.

He repeated the performance over the next hill, estimating Mumvuri would not yet have had time to reach it.

They set up an ambush.

A man passed along the path. Not Mumvuri, just a tribesman, Matt informed himself.

They waited.

No one else came.

Matt cautioned himself to be patient. To risk compromising the hunt at this stage would have been criminal.

He waited twice as long as it would have taken anyone to have travelled the distance between the two hills. Perhaps Mumvuri had stopped somewhere en route or perhaps he had left the path.

Finally he decided that if Mumvuri wasn't going to come to him he was going to go to Mumvuri. He signalled to Red and Andy to move abreast of him as he went back along the edge of the path.

It was then that he noticed the footprints in the dust.

He turned and looked behind him. The footprints went right along the path through the middle of the ambush.

Damn! he swore to himself.

He raced along the path and caught up with the man, and giving him no explanation overbalanced him. While the tribesman was lying on his stomach with his face forced into the ground, he checked his boots.

They were easily identifiable as the ones he had come to anticipate every time there had been a guerrilla incident. They had the same cracked heels, worn down on the inner edges and the left heel with the two slightly protruding nails.

The man was not Mumvuri.

Matt could see the boots were too big for him – he could not have walked far in them without the boots chaffing. The soles of the man's feet were hardened from years of walking barefoot – he was not used to wearing boots.

Matt asked the man where he had got the boots.

The man told him that he had not stolen them, that he had been given them as a gift that morning. He took them back to the point where he had been given them. It was at the point where the guerrillas had intermingled their spoor with the locals.

The man had no idea where Mumvuri had gone.

Matt found no reason to disbelieve him. He knew only too well that nothing concerning Mumvuri could be taken for granted. Nevertheless he took the man in for further questioning by James and Andy.

He radioed James to be up-lifted.

The bush war changed from day to day. Like the waters of a great river, it was always the same yet never the same, always comprised of new parts. Matt and Danielle drifted with it like debris caught up in its flow.

Danielle felt as if she was clutching for Matt, but that he was only an emanation before her that could not be grasped, that he was somewhere else, although visibly just a caress away. When she held him it was like holding a body from which Matt had gone, an empty shell left acting out its part without him.

She went to the deep-litter hen houses to collect eggs, check the feeders and drinkers, and see how the hens were.

She went to check on the day-old chicks. They were chirping continuously, warm and snug from the cold air of the June morning in their brooder.

Danielle thought how winter was there, and she was out in it.

She went down to the pigsties to check on the enormous white sow with her sucklings, warm in their straw. She checked to see that the mother was supplying enough milk and squeezed some iron paste into the mouth of each suckling to guard against anaemia. One of the sucklings did not seem strong enough in the fight to feed itself amongst the others at its mother's teats so she bottle-fed it.

The length of the gestation period of all the domestic animals on the farm sallied through her head, from twenty-one days for the chicken, through to the duck, the turkey, the goose, the sow, the ewe. She stopped. Woman . . . how she would like to have children, but . . . the 230 days of the cow, the 340 days of the mare . . .

Many of the cows were heavy with calf, another of the sows, and one of the mares was pregnant, and chicken eggs were being incubated.

A week before, all dams and their progeny from the previous year's spring calving had been moved to a paddock where the calves would graze. When it was clear that the calves knew their own way about the paddock, the cows were moved out of earshot. She had heard their bellowing at the separation since then. That day, it had suddenly become a painful experience, even though she had witnessed the process each year before and even though she knew that all crying would cease by the following day, another weaning being over.

She went to the sheep yard, across the floors of clean brick, through the forcing pen and on into the sheep shed . . . just in time to hear the horrendous bleating of a baby Dorper lamb, and see the first knife stroke and the carotid fountain of blood. A little scream involuntarily escaped her lips. She turned and fled. But it was too late. She had seen it and she had screamed without intending to do so; the lamb, on its side, its head drawn back, and the path of the knife across its throat. She had seen it several times before, but now it was different.

The war and its pressures were wearing Matt thin. It had affected him to the point where he was openly expressing agitation before Danielle, something he had never consciously allowed to happen before.

Danielle swiftly gained a practical knowledge of his increasing moodiness. He was irritated by the smallest of annoyances at home. It was as if he could never find the equilibrium of his personality, he was always unsettled.

Their relationship seldom played a part in his conversation any more.

They were seated at the table. Danielle served dinner.

'What is it?' he asked.

'A vegetarian dish,' Danielle answered.

161

'I don't want you spending all your time in the kitchen for me,' he said.

'It's for both of us,' she countered.

'A straightforward steak and baked potatoes and a simple salad will suit me fine.'

'It's OK really, Matt, I enjoy cooking for you.'

He slammed his fist down on the table. 'Damn it, Danielle, why can't I get through to you? I don't want this rabbit food.'

'What's happened to you?' she demanded, turning back to him. 'We're not talking about food here at all, are we? We're talking about what's happening to our relationship. Your involvement in the war is destroying us.'

'What the hell are you so worked up about?' he said.

Such an inappropriate reaction and such apparent unawareness on his part had never happened before in the Nel household.

Immediately afterwards, he bowed his head and grasped his glass of beer unmoving in his hand. He withdrew into silence; but not before Danielle looked into his eyes and read the nakedness there.

He raised a shield around himself, completely locking out the outside world; and she was locked out along with all other things.

Danielle was distinctly aware of a formidable loneliness in his life that she could not satisfy. She was aware of a heart, palpitating signs of life, through solid steel plating, tender but unreachable. She felt that despite Matt's efforts to armour his emotions, the war was tearing a hole in him that he might never be able to refill. When she tried to reach out to him he retreated. He had a craving, a dire need for understanding, peace and love, but he was blocking off every channel of access to him through which he could have realised such needs – for through those channels the war too could have got to him even deeper.

Through past experience Danielle was sure Matt would not allow the problem that was bothering him to be bandied about in words, but she was wrong. It totally surprised her when he mentioned it later as he poured himself a glass of brandy and warmed it in his hand. It was not to be the subject of discussion, but at least Danielle knew what was going on in his mind.

'I have two problems and they're both big ones. They're both enemies. One is flesh and blood, and the other is in here,' and he tapped his chest, 'somewhere in the dark.' He paused. 'And I can't fight either one of them. I can only wait until they strike.' He

162

continued hesitatingly, 'If . . . if only I could pin them down like butterflies on a setting-board.'

Danielle read his eyes in conjunction with the working of his lips; he was reaching out for a hand to hold. It was the nearest he had come to stating that perhaps he couldn't cope.

It was hard to tell a person's true expression through a mask, but Danielle knew Matt well enough to detect that his expression was one of pain. His posture, the way he held his head, his manner, were all symptoms.

In the past she could share his burdens simply by being there, being his lover, confidante and friend. Now it was different.

'Your problems are my problems. We must share them,' she said.

He took a sip of his brandy and then stared for a full minute into his glass as if watching his thoughts helplessly flounder there. He smiled, but his mouth and eyes didn't smile together.

She studied him. When tired, his eyes seemed to grow unbearably old.

'It'll pass and we'll see it pass together,' she said.

She got up to pull the curtains and looked out through the wire-mesh grenade screens. The outer security fences filled her vision. She shuddered involuntarily. They seemed such frail defences against the infiltration of the outside world. The effects of war had passed on through them unimpeded to disrupt their lives. The battle would be lost or won within each individual.

A stain of darkness was on the sky. She pulled the curtains to. They were heavy, weighted at the bottom with lead and lined with shock-absorbent material. Along with the lamination on the windows they would guard against the concussion of an external explosion, prevent shrapnel and shards of glass from lacerating those inside.

When she turned to him again her mouth fastened on his.

Whereas once he would have taken the phone off the hook and revelled in the silky tightness of her body, having dreamt of it so many thousands of times in the bush that he had to remind himself it was real, as he used to tell her, seeking to draw out every moment; he didn't respond now. It was as if all his energy was involved elsewhere, and he couldn't so much as move.

Early in the pre-dawn darkness, Danielle awoke and stayed awake. Beside her Matt slept heavily. She was scared of losing him. It was difficult to believe he was there. She felt the need to check that he was still breathing. It wasn't the first time. The fact that he was with her didn't always seem real.

The morning was grey, like a great translucent shadow fluttering over the ground.

She pressed softly against him.

It wasn't properly daylight before the phone started to ring. Matt was immediately awake. He stared at it, reached across her, lifted the receiver and replaced it.

After a couple of minutes it started ringing again. He reached across her once more and this time answered it.

Danielle could clearly hear the disembodied voice of James Creasely.

'Matt . . . James . . . can you switch over to scramble?'

Matt went through to the secrephone in the study and pressed the scramble button.

Within ten minutes he was in the Land Rover, the engine revving.

Danielle stood in the drive watching until he was out of sight. Even then she remained there, listening to the diminishing sound of the engine as it grew fainter and fainter, further and further away, and then silence.

For ten days the team capitalised on the fact that for the first time they had received information that indicated where Mumvuri was going, not just where he had been. They checked every informant and every known or suspected guerrilla contactman or sympathiser in the area concerned. Finally, perseverance paid off.

There were two unattached daughters in a *kraal*. Matt felt certain that Mumvuri would have slept with one of them, but both, as expected, denied any knowledge of him.

Red pointed out the mulberry blood stains of menstruation on one of the girl's pants. Information they had on file suggested Mumvuri had a curious quirk to his otherwise bloody personality – he had a distaste for the normal female monthly function, regarding it as 'unclean'.

Matt concentrated his questioning on the other woman.

The woman eventually led them to the spot where she had lain the night before, just beyond the perimeter of the *kraal*. Matt could see where blankets had been, the grass flattened. He pictured Mumvuri mounted on the woman, thrusting away, facing out from the brightness, his eyes not having to adjust to the darkness in the event of a surprise attack from that quarter.

How many wild oats had germinated in fertile soil? How many illegitimate 'little devils' had been sired?

After that they managed to convince the father, an established contactman, as it turned out, that it was in his best interests to initiate a meeting between themselves and Mumvuri as if they were members of one of his detachments.

Mumvuri, however, sent a vanguard of three guerrillas to check the initiating party out at an arranged place and time, and things went wrong.

The three guerrillas refused to surrender, putting up such a fierce fight instead that the team, in mortal danger, were forced to kill them.

None were more distraught than Matt, James, Red and Andy – they hoped that with the capture of members who were in regular contact with Mumvuri, they were at last in with a chance of a face-to-face encounter. But it was not to be. With the death of the three guerrillas invaluable information died with them.

Once photographing, finger-printing and identification of the dead guerrillas had been completed, James spoke to Matt, Red and Andy.

'We're not to be discouraged, boys. We must make do with what we've got. Mumvuri has led the people in the district to believe that he and the guerrillas under his command are invincible, and so far the majority have had no reason to believe otherwise, having never seen a dead guerrilla. Whenever one of his men has been killed we have carted them off to the mortuary and Mumvuri has just said to the people that they have been transferred to open up a new guerrilla region elsewhere. Knowing Mumvuri's survival despite numerous contacts and being hounded by us, the people are beginning to believe that there is powerful medicine there, that it is true.' He looked at each of them in turn. 'Well, today we're going to change all that. From now on we put all dead guerrillas on display before we bury them.'

'Hear, hear,' enjoined Andy.

They tied the bodies to the bonnet and over the front wheel-housings of the troop-carrier, before driving through the *kraals* of the area in which the guerrillas had operated.

The families of the victims and those that had been terrorised could see for themselves that the guerrillas were dead. They didn't have to do or say anything, just see and know.

James was adamant that as many of the tribespeople as possible should witness the road show. But four days of that and the decomposing bodies on the scalding armour of the troop-carrier's engine and in the heat of the African sun during the middle of the day, had 'cured' a little. The smell became so bad that the driver couldn't drive and even the men behind were gagging and groaning.

Rotor was called in to cart the bodies away and to have them committed to the ground.

Rotor, backed up by Jacob, understandably didn't want the bodies in his 'nice clean machine' so they slung them in a net below, and offered the team a lift home 'in style', while the escorts accompanied the vehicles back.

On the way back, Matt said, 'Why should we have to bury them? Let their own have the spade work.'

He directed Rotor to the *kraal* where the guerrillas had last been sheltered – the parents of one of the guerrillas lived there.

At first light the helicopter, contour-flying at treetop level, approached the *kraal* into the wind. The normal eighty to ninety decibels of the turbo engine, like that of highway traffic, was so reduced by the lie of the land and the strength of the wind that audio and visual perception for anyone on the ground were barely seconds apart, giving the occupants next to no time to flee.

The helicopter hovered about fifty metres above the centre. Matt released the cord securing one side of the sling cargo net beneath the helicopter. The bodies tumbled out.

Several occupants looked up. They knew it was too late to run. Innocent people didn't run. They waited, but they were far from innocent.

Matt hoped that if Mumvuri was nearby he could see the spectacle. Matt pictured him standing unmoving, perhaps against a tree trunk to avoid being seen from the air, his RPD cocked and pointing skywards. He would not have immediately known what he saw falling earthwards. There would be no explosions as of falling bombs.

Then he would clearly see a body jab grotesquely through the thatch of one of the hut roofs. Then another would hit the hard swept ground of the *kraal* yard, the dead flesh, after days of exposure beneath the African sun, coming away from bone like that of boiled chicken.

Matt felt a knot of disgust at himself in his stomach. It showed for a brief moment in the clouded gaze of his eyes, but as quickly as it came it vanished.

Danielle had been thinking about Matt each day he had been away, but was then surprised to see him. It was late afternoon. She had heard the Land Rover, and through the window of the farm clinic had seen him climb out of the cab and go into the house.

There were a few farmhands waiting for her attention so she did not immediately go to see him. Or was that the whole reason, was she unsure of him perhaps? She dismissed the thought. Anyway, it was probably best to let him have a shower and unwind a little first.

He didn't come to see her either, although she felt sure Maruva would have told him where she was.

When she finally finished with her last patient, closed the clinic, and went over to the house, it was almost dark.

Matt was in the lounge. He was drinking whisky straight from a bottle. It looked as if he had been drinking from the time he had come in. He had not washed or changed and was sitting on the clean fabric of the big wing-backed armchair. She had cleaned the chair covers only a couple of days before.

She went over and kissed him.

'I'm so glad you're back,' she said. 'I've been thinking of you all day.'

His breath tasted sour with whisky. He merely grunted, and his mouth greedily attacked hers. He was hurting her.

'I need you,' was all he said. There was no light conservation, no eager expression of joy at being back home, being together again.

She smiled, but the smile was only skin deep.

'Let's wash up first. I'll cook you a good dinner and then we'll have the night to ourselves.'

He did not appear to have paid any attention to what she was saying. He groped at her there in the lounge, with Maruva just through the open door of the kitchen.

'Can't you wait?' she pleaded.

'Can if I have to,' he said, and pushed her down on to the carpet.

She saw the worn look on his face, the dull smouldering of his eyes.

167

She broke away, crying out, 'A woman isn't property, Matt.' And then, after a deep breath and with more control, 'You must shower, Matt, your skin is caked with dirt and you smell like a wild animal. I'm exhausted, I've been working . . .'

'Dirt!' he cut her short, mouthing the word disdainfully. 'It's natural dirt, natural sweat from a man's body . . . Smell? Smell like a wild animal do I? Well tell me just how a man is supposed to damn well smell who's had to live like a goddamned wild animal to protect his wife, to safeguard his home, because he just happens to believe in this goddamned farm, this valley.'

The words, the tone of his voice, his whole manner frightened her. She tried to speak but no words passed her lips, and anyway, she had no idea of what she intended to say. The only thing she was clearly aware of was the hurt she was feeling.

Then his voiced lowered. It was even more disconcerting.

'I come home after a long period of separation from my wife and all she does is point out my dirt, my smell, instead of looking for the man, feeling for the man who's beneath it.' He felt the words spilling from his mouth like bile but he couldn't stop them. 'You exhausted? Had a long day?' he questioned softly.

The words hung uncomfortably in the fleeting silence that followed.

'I'm sorry,' Danielle said submissively, feeling at the same time that it wasn't up to her to apologise. She was frightened. She was confused and desperately alone, wanting Matt, not the man who wore his guise standing before her.

She knew what a wild animal was capable of when provoked so when he leaned towards her she suppressed her spontaneous reaction of self-defence. She pushed down her revulsion at the hot animal smell. She closed her eyes, blacking out his image and what came uncomfortably into her mind were the events of the farm that had taken place that day – the ear-tattooing of the piglets and the castration of those males not wanted for breeding to prevent their meat becoming tainted with the strong unwanted flavour associated with the uncastrated. She felt a strong sense of revulsion. The association of the imagery was horrific.

She guided him to the bedroom.

By closing her eyes would the hurt be blackened out as well?

She felt his hunger for her body driving the blood in his loins. He came at her, thrusting his need at her, into her; he threw himself bodily into the man-snare between her legs. She was aware of the hot animal smell of the sexual act; there was no excitement in his eyes, only an appeasement of insensitive animal desire. His dull smouldering eyes were empty.

He had his way with her and rolled off.

She felt used, soiled, violated.

She was silent.

The indignity had been suffered. There would be no tears in her eyes any more; those soft 'gazelle eyes' as he used to call them, would not cry. She wept still, but no longer on the surface, never again on the surface where he could see.

It was late the night after when the phone woke him.

Once again it was the disembodied voice of James Creasely.

Matt went through to the study.

On hearing that he wasn't immediately required to go into the bush again Matt cupped his hand over the phone's mouthpiece as he exhaled in relief. James was just giving him a friendly call, to keep him abreast of events.

When Matt came back into the bedroom he said to her, 'I've become as nervous of the sound of the phone ringing as I am of rifle fire.'

June, one of the farm's busiest months for manual labour, meant that Matt spent long hours out in the fields supervising and working along with the farmhands. He guided tractor-drawn disc harrows back and forth across the fields for hours on end, acting against weeds that would compete with the next summer's crops for nutrients, water and sunlight.

Danielle took him a packed lunch, and he ate it on the tractor, not pausing for a break.

God, how he loved the land, she winced to herself, a love that at times was almost physical pain. But he was in such a constant state of tension that he no longer seemed able to benefit from it, no longer knew what it was to relax.

She felt that he must be thinking how everything he did on the farm would be done away with by the guerrillas in a single attack, so that whatever he did had to concern the war first and foremost. She thought these things and she hated herself for thinking them.

The earth's surface cooled dramatically as soon as the sun went down, and with it the air grew cold.

Matt spent long hours repairing machinery in the workshop.

He laboured without pause so that when he came back to the house his muscles were tired. The tractors were expensive, and as the workhorses of the farm had to be kept going.

There was condensation on the window panes at dawn. The lawns around the farmhouse had turned brown and crunched underfoot; growth was dormant.

Guti – low clouds – blew in from the south-east, miserable.

Late that month, Matt was dropped in the area of Borehole 23.

For the second time they knew where Mumvuri was heading – not the exact place but the area at least. In the dryness at that time of year, the only place to obtain water readily was the borehole.

There was no way the team could ambush the borehole as it was in the centre of a vast open dry-earth clearing surrounded by heavily subverted *kraals*. Mumvuri had much support amongst the people there. And even if they did ambush the borehole there was no telling when, or even *if*, Mumvuri would use it. He usually got others to fetch the water for him and leave it somewhere.

That night Matt made his way to the pump, disassembled it, poured the contents of a ten-kilogram sack of salt into the pipe, and then reassembled it, leaving no trace. It would teach the locals for associating with Mumvuri. For a while at least, they would have to travel far afield for water.

It could have been poison!

Mumvuri, meanwhile, would have to change any plans he had made for that region, and would be forced to move into one of the surrounding regions where he had less support and would therefore be more accessible once again.

Back at home one night, Matt woke up with a start, his heart racing madly. He tore the black mamba vertebrae from around his neck and threw them to the ground. He had felt as if they were not just bone but flesh that had grown back around them.

As a boy out with !Kai in the bush, he had inadvertently disturbed a black mamba and was standing in such a position as to be obstructing the path to its lair. !Kai had once told him that if anything inhibited its path it would strike; and unlike many snakes,

170

would not strike lamely as a warning – one would receive the full dose of venom.

Matt had immediately blasted it with all five twelve-bore cartridges in the automatic shot-gun he was carrying.

'Form is not to be feared. There is no Form, only Forming,' !Kai had said. 'If Snake is not Snake it will be another thing.'

Matt had nodded as if he had understood, but he hadn't. Only now was he beginning to understand what !Kai had meant.

It was !Kai who had cleaned and sunbleached the tail end vertebrae and tied them around Matt's neck, with the instruction, 'Wear them always, until the fear is no more.'

Matt had nodded obediently. It was believed that a snake's poison, its power, was contained in its bones.

Now he picked up the vertebrae, threaded them on to a short length of new fishing-line and tied them back around his neck.

July

The earth was at its furthest from the sun. It was as if the sun had retreated, getting as far away from the earth as possible and would have gone further if not bound by natural physical laws.

It was the coldest and driest month.

The tractors were out harrowing the fields for maize, cowpeas and oats. The paddocks looked lifeless. The cows and heifers with calf started receiving 'steaming-up' feed to see them through to calving and ensure there would be adequate milk.

On three occasions during those first winter nights, Matt had nightmares. One of them particularly disturbed him. Once awake he couldn't get back to sleep and had to turn on the bedside lamp to combat the dark. The nightmare went but its effect didn't.

Suddenly he had been flung back into the past. He found himself as a ten-year-old boy with his brother and !Kai, gazing for the first time into wise sightless eyes that seemed to have sunk in their sockets. They were the eyes of a man who had been born in the year of the rinderpest, when almost all the cattle throughout the land had succumbed to the disease; an old man indeed. They were the eyes of the *svikiro*, spirit medium of the valley.

The power of the *svikiro*, possessed by the great *mhondoro* (tribal guardian spirit), over the local inhabitants of the Matenga Hills was so great that nothing could be done there without his approval.

The crusty grey skin, shrunken with age over the bone-contoured head, was as seamed as a well-worked coal face, encrusted with dust and the smoke of countless watch-fires. The few teeth that remained in his head were stained the heavy yellow-brown of nicotine and blackened with rot. The sleek leopard skin, the forelegs drawn together around his waist, presented a sharp contrast of youth and age. The copper bangles, glazed baked clay beads and bones glimmered with an intensity they seemed to possess within themselves, not dependent on the sun for their light. Strings of 'lucky-beans', their black eyes staring from their gaudy red skins, were as sightless as their wearer, though his vision was said to go far beyond that capable by the senses.

That is how Matt remembered him, the grand old man. He remembered the querulous old voice unrelated to the body chanting some strange litany as old as the hills themselves, rattling from a bony, gummy mouth. The old *svikiro* visited by the *mhondoro* seemed drained of all natural being and filled with a force far greater than mere life itself. He remembered the leopard-skin clad form throwing out his arms and casting the *hakata* divining bones, with his wildebeest tail-switch twitching spasmodically in his hand as he examined the fall of the symbols – *chirume*, *kwami*, *chitokwadzima*, *nokwara*.

Then, in the nightmare, Matt found himself ten years later overlooking the vast dense forest of the *svikiro*'s domain once again. *Guti* cloud was so low it looked like grey shadow landing sombrely over the earth. In the forest was a cave high on a rocky *koppie* where the remains of past chiefs were buried. There, too, not far away was the cave of the *svikiro*.

A solitary footpath had been carved through the impeding undergrowth by faithful acolytes over almost a century. The trees that loomed and creaked overhead, even though there was no wind, seemed to bend down to watch them as they passed. Huge snakes were said to glide through the forest.

The strangely fluttering cloud robbed the ground of all but an infused grey light, and the trees dripped humidly.

No one could enter without the spirits seeing, it was said, no one could pass if the *svikiro* willed it not.

Shadows lengthened and the expansive forest filled with the sounds and movements of darkness. Night fell about them and they were wrapped in it. Moisture continued to collect and drip from the leaves of trees whose shadows loomed up into the darkness.

Matt sat down at the base of a tree, and drew his jacket about him. He had not meant to fall asleep. He was unable to defend himself against it. When he woke, it was with a start, surprised that he had been sleeping. How long he didn't know.

As he sat there a glimmer of light seemed to flicker away in the darkness, high up, like a star in the sky. But he knew that there, the giant *koppie* on which the *svikiro* lived, blocked out the sky. It would be the *svikiro*'s watch-fire.

'Do you see that light?' he asked the others.

'No,' said Red.

'No,' said Andy.

'Probably a star,' said Red.

'Hidden by cloud again,' said Andy.

'I don't see anything either,' said James.

Come first light they continued.

The ground rose jaggedly upwards and the giant *koppie*, strewn with giant rocks, protruded through the giant *muvanga* iron-wood trees, up through the *guti* and into the sunshine.

In his nightmare he found the cave of the *svikiro* high on the *koppie*. It was just as he remembered it.

The clearing in front of the cave was compacted hard with use. The floor had been harshly swept around the fireplace with its blackened hearth stones near the entrance, but not recently.

Matt sifted through the ash with is hands. There had been no fire there for a couple of days!

Inside the cave were the bodies of the *svikiro*, Matt's father and his brother, hacked to death by pangas. Blood was everywhere.

Matt and Danielle were lying in bed. It was ten o'clock at night.

Something was perpetually nibbling at Matt's nerves. He was giving nothing of himself; that which made him human, that which constituted his personality, he guarded deeply within himself, so that it would not be exposed.

She rolled her head away from him into the pillow's comfort.

'What's happening to us?' she asked, her voice plaintive. She wanted to get more from him than just words.

'What do you mean?' His voice was cold.

She moved a little further away from him.

'There's no longer any peace in you, Matt. When I hold you I can feel the aggression trembling through your body.'

Something had moved into the room and come between them; an emanation, perhaps, of a dying fire, a fire behind a brass screen.

Loving him was not always easy now. Not when he was near her. When he was away it was always the Matt that she used to know whom she thought of.

'What's happened to the Matt I fell in love with, the days that were always like a dream?' There was a sense of loss in her voice.

'Dreams are reality only when dreaming. You're awake now. Look at life around you, there's no dream-like quality in that.' His voice was quiet but somewhat callous.

'It's as if you're in love with the bush and the war, no matter how much it hurts you, and no longer with me.'

'The bush is neutral,' he said. Then, after a silence, 'Love!' he grunted, 'a four-letter word. Who knows what it even means any more?'

Danielle caught her breath.

'In a relationship with a woman,' he continued, 'someone will always get hurt. No man's safe with a woman. She can reach far across borders, and way down inside a man's belly. A woman is no different to war.' As soon as he had said it he realised he shouldn't have.

Danielle winced visibly, as if the words had been rocks. She was intent on striking back, but when she turned to face him, she found him studying her with an apologetic expression, and was caught off guard, as though her thoughts had ventured from cover further than they should have and he had detected them. She was momentarily subdued by something showing in his expression, in his eyes. He looked lost, so alone.

'What do you want?' she asked, recovering herself. 'People to point at you and say "Hey! There's Matthew Nel, the greatest hero", when you're nothing more than just another one of war's greatest casualties? Is that what you want?' There, the words were out, they were below the belt, she knew, but she had said them.

She had almost expected him to reel in agony, fury, but his voice remained quiet. His moods had fluctuated between quiet and loud so frequently of late that she never knew what to expect. It was as if he was moving through a forest, the sun filtering through the trees, barring him in light and shadow alternately as he walked.

'Anyone who believes in anything is a fighter,' he said.

Danielle had the distinct feeling that he was trying to convince himself.

He continued, 'If he isn't, his belief isn't worth pissing on.' He was using language again he wouldn't normally have to her.

They were staring, aware of division. Simultaneously, they both realised that the wall damming the tension between them had broken and they were floundering.

'In war, people break the rules of life as freely and carelessly as if they're unconscious of them, but they're not, they feel the consequences the whole time through their relationships with others, unless they cut themselves off entirely from all those that love them,' said Danielle.

'In war, life has no rules but one – to survive; by all means and any means.' The dogmatism was thick in his voice. 'Besides,' he said, 'we all have to live our own lives; I sometimes forget who's living mine.'

'You've changed so.' She felt she was breaking in two, he the one part drifting away from her.

'That's the price of doing what I have to do, what has to be done; for being the man that I am.'

'And if you destroy yourself in the process?' she asked.

'We all have to die sometime.'

'That's not what I meant.'

There was another silence.

'And what about us, Matt? What about me?' she found herself asking in a submissive voice.

'What do you want of me anyhow?' he demanded anxiously. 'Why do you still stick to me even though there's so much about me that you find at fault? Money? Is that what you're concerned about? You'll be cared for. Money's a powerful aphrodisiac, as they say. This farm, everything, will be divided between you and the Vans. You should be happy about seeing me go off into that bush out there . . .'

Danielle gasped. She slapped him across the face using all the strength that the moment had wrought. 'You can talk,' she accused bitterly. 'Sometimes I think you only married me because you were short of a regular fuck, and an employee thrown into the bargain.' The words were sharp, cruel. 'Oh no, I don't mean that,' she retracted. 'Oh God, what am I saying? I don't mean that,' she pleaded to him.

As for himself, he hadn't known what he'd been saying until the words had been out of his mouth. If he had called her a whore directly it wouldn't have had more of an effect; and a whore was what she had accused him of treating her as!

The words hooked into each other like barbs. Neither could dislodge them.

'I'm sorry,' she said, exasperated with herself, and turned away.

Matt didn't know how to say sorry, not right then. More than anything he would have liked to unsay it, all of it, but instead he only mumbled a little incoherently, 'I'm not the sort of man who is good at telling the half-truths it appears one has to tell to keep a woman believing in him; the same sort of half-truths it appears one has to tell to get a woman into bed for the first time.' He had meant it to be an apology but he heard it come out all wrong. It seemed to add to the weight of everything he had already done and said to hurt her.

He climbed out of bed and into his trousers. He knew if he stayed any longer he would only aggravate the situation further.

He did not wait for any reply to his fumbled explanation.

He was out of the door as she spoke, dragging it shut behind him, so he didn't hear what it was that she had last said.

He hated himself. He needed to get drunk. He drove the long drive of dirt road and single-tar into town.

The bar was crowded with camouflage uniforms and military insignia, raucous voices, people talking too loud; a rifle rack by the door bristled with weapons. It was stuffy with tobacco smoke, the smell of old cigarette ends, flat beer and sour breath, the thick air heavy to breathe.

He stared into the bar mirror, his fourth double whisky in his hand.

Events, the victors of us all, he thought. He found himself impotent to do anything about them.

He was angry with himself for having let the words past his lips, but he had not retracted them. He had not been able to find anything to say in his defence, for all she had said was true, all of it. He had expected such questions, and wished they hadn't come, for he did not have any suitable answers.

One can only be strong on one's own, he thought, trying to withdraw from the feelings he felt for Danielle. She was the closest person to him and the one who was getting hurt. He couldn't bear the fact that he was hurting her, and was likely to carry on doing so as long as the war lasted. But he felt powerless to change things.

'Woman's logic was never one of my strong points,' he muttered to himself in self-defence.

Who was it who had said, 'Travel alone, travel light, and never have anything you'd care about losing'?

The night before was a night they would both remember but one they would rather forget. They had known the crisis was coming, but that had not made it any easier to meet.

They both tried to pretend that the incident had never taken place. But it had, and inwardly there was no escaping it.

It was a stinking war. Danielle wished that the bush would choke itself to death.

What was it Matt had once said to her, in the beginning? 'One may bend but one must never break.' She didn't see the difference if the bending did not permit one to resume one's previous shape.

He was always aggressive now, rough, uncondescending; always alert, never relaxed, his body coiled ready to spring. There was a part of himself that he kept locked away, concealed from brutal eyes which like talons and beaks would tear him apart as they would soft raw liver. There were tender stirrings that still grew with fragile beauty in even the most unnatural environment.

She went into the study, a traditionally stern male refuge. Like the workshop, it was a place that she loved, but more than the workshop. It smelt of leather and antique wood furniture, calf-skin bound books, brandy, cigars and dogs; and there was the Bush Lore manual Matt had been working on before his involvement with the guerrilla troubles had increased.

It was a place to find the Matt she once knew.

Matt now saw no peace for anyone in the valley, and for that matter in the country, so long as the guerrillas with their tactics of violence to procure support by fear for their Marxist–Leninist policies, wreaked havoc amongst the people. He had taken it upon himself to confront the horror, to destroy it totally. It was all or nothing. Anything less was ineffectual, not worth a damn, as he had told her. She shuddered. What was there to prevent him exhibiting the very characteristics he was protesting against?

Initially, it had only been the first night of his returns that the dichotomy of his character was so evident, the transition from the bush to civilisation complete only come morning. Now that his trips

178

away had progressively lengthened and become more frequent, it seemed that his bush personality was his only one; there would be no differentiation between the two worlds; that 'other world', as she called it, overcame him, moving into her bed.

In the dark of early morning he was pacing the room yet again.

With the pain Danielle was experiencing through the dissolution of her world with him, she was concerned about the changes that were occurring in her own mental outlook. She did not hate, but she was hating. She hated the bush. The bush was untamable, cruel. It took from her. But her hate was madness, she really loved the plants, the animals, the birds – but not the overall something without a heart that the bush was. And she hated James Creasely. The disembodied voice on the telephone was synonymous with Matt's departures.

She knew deep down there was no blame to shift, yet she felt she had to blame something, someone. The bush and James Creasely acted, and seemed to allow themselves to be used so passively, as the focus of her accusations against the whole machinery of war.

When they went into town to collect supplies Matt arranged to meet the others at the hotel for lunch.

On meeting Red, James Creasely and Andy, Matt was in high spirits. All the men were. Danielle couldn't help noticing the difference between his relationship with them, and with her.

'The boys are back in town,' Andy called out, and they were laughing, uninhibitedly. 'Watch out town . . .'

Red kissed Matt with great gusto on the forehead.

Despite her knowledge of the lifetime relationship between Matt and Red, Danielle felt a guilty pang of heartbreak at being witness to that private and strangely intimate action between those two tough men.

They slapped each other, shook hands in the tribal manner, hands, thumbs, hands; and laughed; as if they hadn't seen each other for months. The contrast was so dramatic that Danielle was forced to catch her breath before she sobbed out loud.

Over lunch the men joked almost exclusively amongst themselves. From the glances the women gave her and each other Danielle could see that they too felt left out. They tried to join in but the men seemed to be sharing private jokes. To outsiders they didn't appear to be so funny. The men laughed about 'furry feelings in the back of their throats,' about 'cowboys' and 'rocking horses', and when Rotor

179

asked Matt for a cigarette they laughed at that too. It was all a little beyond Danielle and the other wives.

That evening, back at the farm, Matt studied Danielle over the dinner table with a guilty intensity. But the pupils of her eyes seemed to be full of mist, and search as he might for some indication of her inner feelings, the only image that came back at him was his own pale reflection, distant and distorted.

He saw the bags of tiredness beneath her eyes. She was wearing more make-up than she usually did.

'I have to tell you the bush war's getting worse, Danielle,' said Matt. 'Please go home to your parents until things are once again under control.'

She was taken aback by what he said.

'This is my home,' she told him. 'I won't leave it. And I won't leave you. You are wrong to ask me to.'

'It's not safe,' said Matt.

'You're doing what you believe is necessary, allow me to do what I believe is necessary.'

'I'll feel easier if you are with your parents near the city.'

'No,' stated Danielle flatly.

Matt stared at her across the table but didn't say anything further.

Danielle meanwhile felt as if the distance between them had increased, that they each stood alone and were looking at each other across a vast gap. He was no longer reaching out for her.

She had prepared a vegetable dish for herself and steak for him. Now she started to clear the table.

Matt lit a cigarette and watched her through the smoke.

Three days later, the team once again reacted to information received via James's Office that a section of guerrillas headed by Mumvuri were seen bringing arms across the border into the valley. Matt felt that he was going back in time to when he had first seen Mumvuri.

In the afternoon Matt, Red and Andy reached the point near the border where Mumvuri had been sighted, where the river fell off the escarpment.

Looking back into the valley of his birth from the border, a valley that seemed to change just because of the border line, Matt found the *mupani* and the dense *muunze* woods excited some part deep within him, and the cold metal of the AKM folding butt he carried was comforting in his hands.

As he moved through a copse of *mupfuti* trees, old woody pods crunched under his feet. He observed where numerous men carrying burdens had crunched their way before him, the newly exposed edges of broken pods lighter in colour than the outer surfaces. As a boy it had been enthralling to sit in a wood of such *mupfuti* trees and listen to the pods exploding like fireworks all about him, casting their seeds.

He observed cream-coloured raw-topped stumps, and where bark had been stripped from tree trunks; traces of the pink underbark being made into fibre cords.

Had a raft been constructed to carry across the heavy weapons? he asked himself.

Removing their trousers they knotted each leg, soaked them so that water cohesion between the weave of the cloth created an airtight bag. They swept the open waist down on the surface of the water, trapping air inside, then tied up the waist. They used their trousers like buoyant floats to help carry their radio, weapons and ancillary equipment across the river.

Matt saw by the spoor on both sides of the river how each guerrilla section had provided protection to the others, securing both banks; more than likely, only a couple of men were in the river at any one time. Strategic observation points had been posted on the high ground.

Once across, it had not been long before Matt discovered the rough-hewn raft concealed in the bushes.

The guerrilla group had progressed several kilometres away from the crossing point before breaking up into separate sections and basing up for the night. Each campsite was expertly chosen, with good fire-cover, little dead ground before it, and each man was in a carefully appointed position with all fields of fire and arcs of responsibility clearly defined.

The moon had been up all day, and now was setting with the sun. There would only be starlight to relieve the darkness.

Matt prepared to settle down for the night. He hacked sheaths of grass from places scattered apart on the hillside. It was only a while later that he noticed that someone had hacked grass in the same manner before him.

He secured a simple trip-wire attached to a tin containing small stones, across his spoor leading to his sleeping-place.

It was night in the bush, when shadows had shadows.

It was cloudless. There was nothing but cold white splinters in the void. The ground would be the coldest yet, that night. The moist cold wind penetrated the clammy layers of his clothing. The cold ground stiffened his joints in their layers of shivering flesh.

A little while later he had bedded down – and, as he found, in exactly the same place where someone else had slept. There were still signs of the remains of a grass 'blanket' trapped between the two rocks, and a small depression made in the earth for a man's hip, lying on his side. He tunnelled into the heap of straw he had cut, placed between the two rocks against the wind.

He was jarred awake by the rattle of the stones in the tin can in the early hours of the dark cold morning.

He stayed awake and alert.

He felt how a growing familiarity with the tranquillity and the constant closeness of Danielle had rendered him temporarily deaf to the solicitations of the raw wild earth about him.

Come daylight, he had not slept, and it was so warm in his straw that he had to struggle against his desire just to lie there, not wishing to expose himself to the cold elements of dawn once again.

Danielle sat up in bed, but the cold forced her back under her soft down-filled duvet.

Outside, the irrigation pipes were being moved to new parts of the wheat and alfafa fields. Though there was little visible growth of the crops on the surface, the roots were developing underground; there would be rapid growth during the spring.

Danielle thought about them, but she couldn't bring herself to go outside into the fields. She couldn't bring herself even to see the bush.

As she lay there, half in and half out of sleep, she drifted like down borne on the chilled wind. Suddenly yet another season was there; winter had crept into the room. Where had the 'good old honeymoon days' gone? The days before Matt fell headlong into the bush war? Yellow umbrella sunshade-filled days, green lawns, cool crystal clear water, the sky an empty washed blue; a light wind playing with the umbrella tassels. Days of starched white tablecloths and just as stiffly starched waiters yawning in the sun. Days of fun and sunsets. Nights of *marimba* players, enchanting rhythms of Africa throbbing through the sultry air, frosty-glass drinks, dinner by candle-light. Making love long into the early morning.

She could find nothing from the past to cling to, so distanced from the comfort of it as she was. She could feel nothing, completely deprived of all senses but the sensation of floating. She panicked, but even as she panicked she felt supported by some warm breath.

Matt hauled himself to his feet, out into the cold. It hit him like a physical, tangible force.

He found the spoor that had crossed the early-warning trip-wire. He learnt then that it had been a civet cat in its nocturnal wanderings that had kept him awake all night.

When he moved on again he was still tired.

Nests of the red-billed buffalo weaver, dominant in the area through which they were travelling, were consistently on the far side of the trees they passed; a rough indication that they were keeping to a westerly bearing. A hungry bare-faced gymnogene, flapping its wings wildly, raided a nest of fledglings as they looked on.

It set Matt to remembering once again. He was unable not to, already recollecting momentarily before he could push the recollection aside.

It was Danielle's first day at the farm after their honeymoon. Her eyes had been on his face. He had seen the movement of a tiny pulse on the side of her throat. He had felt the Adam's apple slide in his own. He had kissed her there, the pulse coming stronger against his mouth. Their lips had met. He had felt her body press against him. One hand had stroked her back whilst the other had held her head close to him. The hand had moved beneath her blouse, raising it. She had said how she had felt the soft warm breeze against her bare skin. He had taken her to the unmade mattress on the bed. He had pushed the door to with his foot. The dogs had scratched excitedly against it from the other side. Danielle had laughed shyly. Her body had moved under him; her arms and legs had tightened around him. They had tried to start a family then.

His mind returned to the bush, his eyes to the ground.

The guerrillas were now wearing a variety of common civilian footwear to mingle spoor with the locals. Nevertheless the tracks left presented a drilled formation of one type or another, a military imbuement once acquired never forgotten, difficult to disguise or alter.

The temperature, cold in July's winter, was slightly colder now than it had been a couple of nights before. For every 100 metres in height they ascended, the temperature dropped a quarter of a degree centigrade or so.

With the increasing density of the local population, Mumvuri's security network must have been increasingly effective. At a specific point, tribespeople had congregated with the guerrillas. When they had left, their steps had become shorter and their impressions deeper. They were obviously carrying heavy burdens. It seemed apparent that porters had been recruited. For the first time in a week the guerrillas had been able to transfer their loads, remove them from their shoulders and off the smalls of their backs which would have been rubbed raw of skin by then, thanks to the awkward shape of heavy equipment; pack wounds that would serve to indicate members of the guerrilla detachment once they attempted to disappear amongst the populace, acting as common civilians in the *kraals* and the fields. As good as a branding iron, thought Matt.

The recruiting of porters occurred several times. They were changed frequently to prevent them knowing the whole route, and so as not to arouse suspicion by taking them far from their own areas. It was in these terms, and not in some mathematically converted psychological quotient, that Mumvuri's personality and intelligence were to be measured.

An informant indicated where a land mine had been placed on a dirt road. There was a knot of tied grass at the edge marking it.

Matt, Red and Andy tossed a coin to see who would have the 'pleasure' of lifting the mine. Matt won, or lost, depending on your point of view.

He cut a stout forked stick from a bush, sharpened the single end, and with a coil of cord approached the mine, together with the informant as an insurance policy against it being a set-up. The man was forced to lie down on the track beside Matt, legs and arms stretched out; any attempt on his part to get up and go or to interfere would require maximum movement of limbs, and so be readily discernible.

Red and Andy watched the bush about them from a safe distance away as he worked. There was no point in them all going if the mine should go bang.

Matt lay stomach down on the surface of the track, and with his hands extended in front of him, gently brushed the surface earth to the side using the heels of his palms. With careful, unhurried movements, the dull olive sheet metal of the mine was exposed. Statistics went through Matt's mind . . . TM 46 . . . green . . . Chinese . . . but the TMH 46 will have an anti-lift facility at the base to prevent disarming, watch out for it . . . 8.7 kilograms . . . 5.5 kilograms being the main charge, and booster . . . detonating pressure approximately 180 kilograms – if you are lucky . . . less if you are not! . . .

Using his index finger, Matt cleared the earth from around the mine's circumference.

He looked momentarily at the informant. The man was sweating profusely, and not from the climatic conditions. He turned once again to the mine. He located the handle on the side and cleared the soil around it. He passed the cord through the handle and tied a slip-knot. He worked the forked stick firmly into the ground a couple of hand lengths from the land-mine's outer rim, and passed the cord over the fork.

Signalling to Red and Andy to move into cover, he hauled the informant to his feet, and played out the cord as he walked with him along the track. Fifty paces further back he instructed the man to lie flat, face down. He himself sat down, stuffed pieces of two-by-four rifle cleaning cloth in his ears and then lay on his back, keeping the cord taut and pulling it with him. The mine lifted upwards towards the fork of the stick. The road vomited dust and gravel over him. The concussion of sound hit him, leaving his ears ringing dizzily despite the bits of two-by-four.

As he reeled in the cord, walking back to check the site, the dust and smoke were beginning to settle. The mine had left a deep cavity.

'TMH 46,' Matt advised Red and Andy when they came up.

'Guessed as much,' Andy grinned.

Red looked at the frayed end of cord. 'It could get a bit short,' he laughed.

They reached a site where it appeared arms and equipment had been dumped and the porters disbanded. Only the commanders would have been involved in the actual placing of the arms. For the rest of them, and for Matt, Red and Andy, the arms could have been anywhere in an area several kilometres across.

Matt contacted James.

James arrived with troop-carrier loads of police and military personnel. A systematic sweep and search was conducted of the area. They recovered well over half a ton of weaponry a mere six kilometres from Horseshoe Ridge.

Mumvuri had spread the cache over the whole area one or two items at a time, concealed beneath the ground, in rock crevices, or at the foot of trees; places that could be remembered for their distinctiveness.

There were AKM folding butt assault rifles, a Degtyarev DP light machine-gun, PKM light machine-gun, and SG 43 Goryunov, RPG-2s and -7s, even an M-20 American rocket launcher that could be folded in half to enable easier carrying through the bush, and a Type 56 recoilless rifle weighing over eighty-five kilograms, complete with tripod. There were 60mm and 82mm mortars, with base plates and bipods. There were many rocket projectiles, 75mm shells (heat and high explosive), mortar bombs and thousands of rounds of small-arms ammunition. There were F-1 frag grenades, RGD-5 offensive frag, RG-42, and defensive stick grenades, M-60 anti-tank rifle grenades, and anti-personnel rifle grenades. And there were stacks of land-mines, box, metallic and bakelite; but the pride of the cache was the Type 56 75mm recoilless rifle – with its heat and high explosive shells.

'There are enough armaments here for Mumvuri to have controlled the future of the valley,' said James, 'but according to the inventory list we've managed to put together, there's still a quantity of small-arms ammunition, a land-mine and a recoilless rifle high explosive shell missing.'

'What we can assume is that Mumvuri is somewhere out there with them,' said Matt.

'At least that's all he's got,' said Red.

Over the next weekend that Matt was back, he and Danielle invited friends around for a long belated get-together. Danielle's old friends from her student-nurse days in the city and her nursing days in town came round, and of course the Vans, James, Alexandra and their children, Andy, Elaine, Rotor, Jacob and neighbouring farmers from the valley.

Most of the farming community seldom managed to meet each other these days, only staying in contact by phone calls and through listening to everyone respond to the morning and evening check-in calls with the police station over the community's radio network.

There was eager exchange of news, talk of the valley, the political and economic situation, and the guerrilla threat.

Matt himself talked nothing of the bush war, but conversed happily with Oom Van, Suzanne's father, Red and the other farmers from the valley about farming, about the weather, about crops, about cattle. All the farmers expressed their disappointment that Matt was no longer able to take up his seat on the valley's Farmer's Association. He caught up on recent developments, and had a chance to enjoy himself amongst people whom he liked, trusted and respected.

The children played 'open-gates' and 'touch-rugby' on the lawn, with their parents joining in.

It was a real family occasion.

Beer and conversation flowed freely amongst the men and before long they had formed two teams and were playing *bok-bok*, one team forming a scrum around one of the plane trees, the other hurling themselves at it after a run up one at a time; the scrum that remained intact was the winner.

Then, armed with a broomstick, having been forced to down a beer and been spun around by the others until quite dizzy, they each tried to hit an orange thrown on the lawn some distance away, without invariably rushing off every-which-way and ending arse-up on the lawn.

Tanny Van, renowned in the district for her cooking, had divulged to Danielle the secret recipe for *sosaties* handed down by her family from their days in the Cape. Alternate diced pieces of fat and lean salted and peppered pork and mutton were skewered, grilled over coals, and dipped in a tangy-sweet sauce of golden sautéd onions, apricots, orange leaves, curry and vinegar; and *bobotie*, minced meat with diced apple, raisins, blanched almonds, and lemon leaves, was served with yellow rice cooked with tumeric and demerara sugar, and anointed with mango chutney. There were steaks, *boerewors*, chops and chicken.

The meal was topped off with Tanny Van's famous *melk-tert*. There were *vet koek*, spiced and wined *soet koekie*, *boere beskuit*, *mosbolletjies*, *koeksusters* fried in hot fat and plunged in syrup, grid-iron crusty *rooster-koek*, homegrown crushed wheat bread, *marula* jelly and an assortment of *konfyt*.

As the evening drew to a close, the farmers who lived nearby returned to their farms. The Vans were the last to leave.

'Why don't you stay over, you're as sober as a fart!' Matt told Red.

187

'Have to see to a few things on the farm for tomorrow,' Red said. 'Some of the farm hands are waiting for me.'

Matt watched him drive off with Suzanne and Sarie, Oom and Tanny Van following behind. The other guests, who were to stay the night, waved goodbye from around the fire and shouted after them. Then the tail lights disappeared from view.

Matt pried off the caps of a few beers, using an uncapped bottle as an opener, and threw one each to the other men who were still there.

As Matt sat down, and picked up his tankard of beer, he looked over at Andy and the dogs who appeared to be in earnest conversation.

'You staring at me again?' Andy enquired of the dogs, helping himself to another piece of *boerewors* from the *braai*. 'What's wrong? Have I got your piece again?' He shared it with them, dividing it equally as was his custom.

The guests were sitting drinking, smoking and chatting when a muffled rumble washed gently across the still night.

Everyone froze, cocking their ears to the sound, but it had come and gone. They turned to each other, almost on cue.

An unaccustomed ear would have been hard pressed to identify the sound exactly for what it was, but Matt immediately recognised it. It was the sound of an explosion coming from several kilometres away.

'Biscuit tin?' Andy asked uneasily, as if hoping to be proved wrong.

Matt nodded with dread apprehension. 'Spitskop,' he said, detecting the direction the sound had come from, compensating for wind.

'The Vans,' James said, looking at his watch and observing the time they had left. It was a statement that no one else had wanted to make. None of them wanted to believe it.

The party was over.

Red's Land Rover was off the road, resting at a precarious angle to a tree.

Matt could see Suzanne's slow and ponderous breathing. As he watched it stopped. Cold jagged steel. Warm flesh so vulnerable, so easily penetrated. The cracking of cartilage joining ribs to sternum as he persisted with cardio-pulmonary resuscitation. Refused to give up. There weren't enough first-aid dressings. Danielle ripped off her cerise silk blouse, tore it into strips to staunch the bleeding. Off came her skirt as well. When neither direct pressure nor use of pressure points had stemmed the bleeding from Red's badly gashed leg, James pulled the leather belt from the trouser loops around his waist and used it as a tourniquet. It was a last resort. James was twisting the belt tighter and tighter with a stout stick. There was so much damned blood. James twisted the belt so tight that it cut into the flesh before the bleeding was halted. Trying to revive Suzanne and Sarie. Refusing to give up. All the way to the hospital. Refusing to give up but it was to no avail. And the ominous discharge coming from Red's nose and ears.

At the hospital, the baby girl Sarie and her mother Suzanne, surrounded by hospital staff, relatives and friends, but alone, where silent darkness was natural. Two crumpled ephemeral flowers. Matt remembered the flame lilies down by the river, their beauty, and it struck him then that they were poisonous, that that was how they survived!

Someone said Red was lucky.

He told that someone that Suzanne and Sarie weren't.

Someone said he was sorry about Suzanne and Sarie.

He told that someone about Red.

Matt knew instinctively that Mumvuri was responsible. They had found the missing land mine.

He couldn't help seeing a shadowy form moving silently through the bush of a dry ravine, hear himself counting off the paces, ready to touch a positive lead to a battery. But he had waited two seconds too long.

'Will you go stay with your mother and father now?' Matt asked Danielle.

'I can't,' she said. 'Not now.'

The mine-laying party had split up one by one and disappeared amongst the people.

Relentlessly, Matt and Andy, with James's unfailing back-up, followed spoor and information. Even when tired to the point of exhaustion, hungry, muscles aching unbearably, they pushed on. Knowledge of what had happened somehow made their present deprivations and pain seem trivial.

While Matt clung to the faintest scent of the guerrillas on the ground, James was flying this way and that in the air, in continual radio contact and keeping them abreast of the latest information. Scores of clandestine meetings were occurring between intelligence operatives and sources all over the valley.

Within forty-eight hours they had the name of one of the guerrillas concerned and had marked on their maps the *kraal* where he was staying, even to the extent of indicating which hut he had chosen.

At three a.m. the following morning, with eight back-up members from the Office armed with high velocity rifles, James had the *kraal* surrounded.

Matt and Andy moved in on the designated hut.

All was dark. There was no moon. Not the least man-made sound could be heard.

When Matt threw himself bodily at the light boarded door it instantly gave in to his weight.

The light of Andy's torch swiftly shone around the interior.

A man lay in bed with a woman.

Matt gagged him while Andy started securing their hands to the bedframe. Together they secured their feet.

Without a sound being made, two of James's men came in and moved out the bed with the man and woman handcuffed to it.

Matt and Andy cleared the other huts, dragging all the occupants out into the centre of the yard, where one or other of James's men took custody of them, and without hesitation commenced an in-field interrogation.

Nothing of immediate value was ascertained from the other occupants of the *kraal*. It appeared that they knew little beyond having been intimidated to house the guerrilla.

None of the other occupants were indicated as being guerrillas, and no knowledge of other guerrillas in the immediate vicinity was forthcoming.

As for the captured guerrilla, on first questioning him about the land mine Matt knew that he would not divulge anything through mere verbal persuasion, and such a man would withstand physical abuse and pain for some time, which they could ill-afford to waste. Matt hadn't run a successful farm in Africa since before the age of twenty-one without being a good judge of a man's character. Only natural fear, its core deep in the man's psyche, would unlock the man's tongue.

Matt called Rotor forward with two of his colleagues. They would fly the other Office members and their charges to town where they would continue the interrogations and decide the fate of their prisoners.

Matt, meanwhile, took the man off the bedframe, secured his hands behind his back, blindfolded him, placed a sack over the man's head and bundled him into Rotor's helicopter.

They flew to a *kraal* Matt knew in another part of the valley.

The occupant of the *kraal* took them to a large pit dug in the bush not far from the huts. The man made his living collecting and selling snakes – to be put on display, to be used in magic, or for making snakebite serum.

Matt watched the snakes writhing at one end of the pit, kept there by the collector with a long forked stick. He unlocked the handcuffs securing the man's hands and lowered him into the pit at the cleared end.

'Take the sack and blindfold off,' he commanded the man.

The man did so and on seeing where he was gave a tremulous gabble of fear and, turning, clawed above his head at the pit's edge to get out.

Matt ground the man's fingers with a shod foot.

The bite of the *boom-slang* meant a slow horrendous death, perhaps the most painful possible, over several days, as the haemolytic venom destroyed the cell walls of the body's organs, causing death by internal rupturing. The cytotoxic venom of the puff adder meant death within twenty-four hours, as it caused severe local oedema, necrosis, gastro-intestinal haemorrhages, extensive destruction of body tissue. The neurotoxic venom of the banded cobra meant death within a few hours, that of the black mamba within minutes, the poison attacked the nervous system, causing death by suffocation and paralysis . . . a bite from the black mamba and almost immediately he would be feeling palpitations of the heart, be experiencing difficulty in breathing . . . It wasn't black but an olive green-grey, darkened by age in places almost to brown, signifying the added strength of matured venom . . . his lungs and heart would collapse within minutes . . .

The collector, worried about the safety of his snakes, fretful that they might be hurt, cursed the man in the pit.

Matt milked the profusely sweating and babbling man of information like the poison sacs of a snake's fangs pressed against the rubber diaphragm of a milking-jar; the poison from which a serum could be obtained.

191

When the man hesitated before telling Matt about Mumvuri, Matt told the collector to release the snakes into the cleared area, and turned to walk away.

The neglected answer came quickly but even though Matt heard what he had wanted to hear he kept on walking.

James gave a quick questioning look in his direction, then helped the collector haul the terrified man, who had soiled his pants, from the pit – not a moment too soon.

As Matt strode back to the helicopter he was aware of what was happening behind him at the pit and of the black mamba vertebrae around his throat, aware he was trembling uncontrollably.

The information obtained took them to an old abandoned *kraal*.

In one of the huts they found a goat tethered with a steel chain, chickens in a wire-meshed cage and a bag of mealie-meal. Guerrilla sympathisers had left the food supply there perhaps a week previously judging by the age of spoor and animal droppings.

'I'm not looking forward to another long ambush,' said Andy.

Matt observed that the goat and chickens had finished their supply of water and feed. He estimated that at most they would have a three-day wait if the guerrillas wanted their food still alive and fresh when they arrived. He told Andy.

After erasing their spoor, they concealed themselves in the nearby bush.

Night came on and they were thirsty, hungry and very cold.

Day came and they were very tired, more thirsty, more hungry, and being in the shade they were still cold, although there was warm direct sunlight only a couple of paces away.

It was in the darkness just before the following dawn that Matt suddenly became aware that someone had cautiously and quietly entered the *kraal*. He alerted Andy.

He couldn't see the man, but he could hear him.

Then he saw a shadow move between the huts. He felt his blood run cold. He found himself reliving the moments before he had detonated the Claymore ambush on his first encounter with Mumvuri, waiting for the main guerrilla section to enter the killing ground. He had let Mumvuri go.

He intended not to do the same thing again now. He levelled his rifle in the general direction from which he heard the sounds of a man placing each foot carefully, as if checking the ground before committing his weight. He heard the goat bleat, heard the chickens flap about in alarm.

It was getting lighter all the time.

Matt found himself praying tentatively that the dark shadowy form in the *kraal* would soon be revealed in the light.

Then there was silence; no more movement in the *kraal*.

The man had gone.

Morning came, and in its light the *kraal* looked just the same as it had before. Matt and Andy waited expectantly. But nothing happened and the morning wore on.

The goat and the chickens could be heard moving around in the central hut.

Matt was debating with himself as to whether or not the man had silently slipped in and left with the bag of mealie-meal and perhaps a chicken or two, when movement to the right of him and on the far side of the *kraal* suddenly caught his eye. Whoever had come early in the morning had not left, he was still there. He had been there all the time, keeping the *kraal* under observation.

Matt shivered. He felt that if he had abandoned caution, so much as twitched unnecessarily, the man in the bushes would have seen him, and who knew what could have happened?

Shortly before midday another guerrilla made contact with the first, went away, and within minutes returned with a further four guerrillas chatting unconcernedly.

The guerrillas went into the *kraal*. One of them went into the hut where the goat and chickens were.

Matt saw that it was the same man who had been there in the early morning.

The man passed out the bag of mealie meal, then the chickens.

One of the men, with his back to Matt, proceeded to wring the chickens' necks. An RPD was slung over the man's back.

Matt thought they were probably quite hungry by then, and were intending to eat the chickens soon, perhaps somewhere away from the *kraal*, but didn't want the noise of the chickens to draw attention to themselves while moving through the bush to wherever they were going next.

Matt couldn't help thinking that perhaps the man with the RPD was Mumvuri.

The goat was led out of the hut at that instant.

Matt didn't intend to give the man with the RPD the slightest chance. It wasn't a sport, there was no sense of fair play. It was war. You had to take your advantages as they presented themselves.

He fired his first burst, letting the natural tendency of the rifle to rise on automatic fire and rake across the man's back, from the lower right quadrant to the upper left where the heart was.

Within the next three seconds Andy had thrown a grenade and they had both thoroughly raked the area with automatic fire.

Then there was silence.

After the smoke and dust had gone so had all but two of the guerrillas whose bodies were lying there. One of them was the man with the RPD. The goat was also dead.

Matt radioed James. He didn't dare to believe that the man with the RPD was Mumvuri.

When James arrived it was by helicopter with a witness who could identify Mumvuri.

Mumvuri?

The witness said it wasn't Mumvuri.

Matt wasn't surprised. He had gained too much of a respect for Mumvuri's ability to survive. Nonetheless he couldn't help feeling somehow cheated.

James took possession of the RPD and the bodies.

Matt picked up the spoor of one of those who had escaped. The marked dragging of the right leg suggested that the man had sustained an injury. Together with the spoor Matt found a small dark mark on a leaf. It might just have been dirt, but then again it might not have been. He removed the soil-like substance from the surface, and put it on his tongue. It tasted salty. Blood?

They went straight to the nearest *kraal*.

There in the rubbish pit they found strips of torn bloody cloth, concealed in an empty can labelled 'Whole Peeled Tomatoes'.

The man was not in the *kraal* but in such a rural village there were few secrets. The villagers assisted one another in the labour of working their fields, in times of crisis, and in times of celebration. The individual tribesman was not so much an individual as an intrinsic part of the family *kraal*, the district, the tribe, the greater whole.

They found a solitary *basha*, a branch-and-straw shelter in the bush a couple of kilometres from the *kraal*.

The injured man was not there either, but in the bush a few paces away Matt found human excrement. The man from whom it had come could be no more than a few minutes away – it was still warm. Matt examined the contents of the excrement. His examination revealed tomato seeds passed through the body's system.

James advised Matt over the radio that examination of the recovered RPD revealed that sample cartridge cases fired by it matched cartridge cases previously recovered from other scenes perpetrated by Mumvuri.

It still seemed open to conjecture whether or not Mumvuri had been killed. James promised to come back to him with further information as soon as it came to light.

A short while later, Matt found the injured man with little trouble.

At about the same time he found a nest of vicious tree ants.

Not bothering to ask questions, he stripped the man of his clothes. There on his back were the brand-like wounds from carrying heavy armaments for long distances. He pegged him down, arched over a wooden stake he had sharpened, and smeared his body, face, the whole of him, with honeycomb that the man had been eating.

The man became increasingly worried. He hadn't yet been told what was required of him.

Finally, as Matt was about to break the nest of ants over him the man pleaded, 'I will tell you anything, anything . . .'

'Not anything.' Matt told him, continuing to break up the nest over him. 'Tell me everything you know about Mumvuri.'

'Yes, yes . . . but first take these ants off me . . .' the man implored.

'You don't come off there until I find him, so you'd better tell me what I need to know. Each minute you waste could be your last.'

The man couldn't speak fast enough. As he winced and struggled, writhed and screamed, with the ants biting into him he unavoidably worked the flesh of his back on to the stake, slowly impaling himself.

Matt cringed at every pain the man felt, but he didn't raise a hand to help the man, and he didn't let his own emotional agony show. He hoped to create the impression that he just sat silent, cold and expressionless throughout it all.

The ants would go everywhere, through every orifice of the man's body: anus, penis, mouth, ears, nose to the brain. They would strip him raw with pink scars, they would chisel and dig, cut and furrow, tunnel, carry off pieces.

'Do not let me die . . . do not let me die . . .' the man pleaded in English.

'I am not God,' cut in Matt sharply in the man's mother tongue.

Although he felt he was going through his own personal hell in those moments, he remembered everything that was said.

Mumvuri had not been there.

Mumvuri had swopped weapons with the guerrilla who had been killed.

The bastard doesn't miss a trick does he? Matt spat. It was another one of Mumvuri's ploys to confuse ballistic tracing.

As they headed across country by helicopter three days later, Matt looked down upon the hills of the valley that washed in waves below, Rotor beating each crest then dropping away into the next trough.

He felt something within himself leap out, fall and disappear into a grey-white granite crest in a sea of foliage; green and brown trees, green and brown grass, grey granite, green . . . brown . . . grey . . . brown . . .

The guerrilla captive had died, but not before he had revealed information that led the team to kill every member of the land-mine-laying section, except for one – Mumvuri.

They hadn't been able to find him anywhere. It was as if he had vanished into thin air.

Something had changed that day. All of them knew it. But if one of them was able to place a finger on exactly how it had come about, and what exactly it was, he didn't say. It could perhaps have been likened to the hardening of the arteries, made impervious to the osmotic process that permitted elements to pass through from outside; moral sclerosis. Men had to build walls, against the elements and against themselves – the darker sides of their natures.

Standing on the road that joined Matiziro and Spitskop once again, Matt put together a picture of what had taken place there. The captured guerrillas had revealed Mumvuri's actions in laying the land mine.

The land mine hole had been filled in, and it was as if nothing untoward had ever taken place there, but Matt recalled the whole incident nevertheless, much as he would have liked not to have had to remember anything of the horror at all.

He saw, too, the exact point where he had commenced his search for spoor along the edges of the road.

Mumvuri had chosen to cross the farming area by night, avoiding contact with the farmsteads and the African villages on the farms alike. As he was about to cross the road he had signalled to the others to take cover, and indicated that he had heard a vehicle, by gesturing as if he were holding a steering wheel.

Matt thought how it must have been one of the farmers from the valley returning home.

The grass verges either side of the road, right up to the fences, had been cut short so that they offered no cover, and the guerrillas had had to climb over the four-strand barbed-wire fence of Spitskop Farm to get to the long grass of the *veld* and concealment.

The noise of the vehicle's engine and the lights of the vehicle passed and then faded.

Another vehicle passed shortly afterwards.

It was after that that Mumvuri had ordered the land mine they had carried from the arms cache to be brought forward.

There was nothing to show if Mumvuri had deliberately intended to mine that particular road before then and there was nothing to show that he had known Red would have to travel back along that road that night. But there was no telling exactly what Mumvuri had been thinking; he was known not to discuss his intentions or actions.

He had scouted the road for a brief while then pushed the land mine into the centre of the concrete conduit of a culvert that in summer channelled storm water under the road. The missing 75mm recoilless rifle shell followed.

Damn the recoilless rifle, that pride of Mumvuri's latest weapons supply!

Mumvuri had connected the recoilless rifle shell to the mine as a booster. The conventional booster was merely an extra 200 grammes of TNT. The shell would have been up to fifty times that, would have had the effect of a second land mine placed on top of the first, with the advantage of creating its own shrapnel.

He had trailed wires from the land mine to a battery, then to a pressure detonator that he had made from a stick. He wound the two separate strands of wire, positive and negative, around the separate split ends, then stripped the insulation off, exposing two bare contact points which he kept apart with a brittle twig that would snap under the weight of the vehicle. He concealed the stick just below the surface on the left hand track of the road, replacing the top-soil that he had carefully preserved in one pocket, to allow no change of texture or colour to be visible where he had tampered with the road. The mine had been set for a belly-blast that would detonate directly below the centre of the cab, causing maximum damage and making it somersault to increase the effect.

Mumvuri's ruthless efficiency and experience were evident in every respect: location, minimum of labour, minimum of surface disturbance, maximum impact; placed away from animal spoor, avoiding unwanted detonation by cattle or game; placed with careful consideration to tree shadow which fell across the left half of the culvert during day; the tyre tread mark that had been disturbed was re-etched with a stick to match almost exactly, any inaccuracy not observable from an approaching vehicle travelling at the speed capable in any gear above first. And Mumvuri had not made the mistake of waiting around to observe the result of his handiwork. He had pressed on quickly out of the farming area.

Just one land mine, one recoilless rifle shell and a handful of small arms ammunition was all they had missed out of the arms cache, thought Matt, but it was one land mine, one recoilless rifle shell too many, and there was a life riding on each of those small arms bullets.

Suzanne and Sarie were dead, and Red was no longer part of the team.

Mumvuri, damn fucking Mumvuri, damn you to hell, swore Matt to himself.

Matt expected he would never know if the land mine on that particular road, at that particular time, for that particular vehicle was anything more than a coincidence or not. But if it was not a coincidence then Mumvuri knew who one or more of his pursuers were, and was coming after them one by one.

Matt felt he would either never know what had been in Mumvuri's mind or would find out soon enough.

Somewhere out there was Mumvuri, the maggot from a mother's flesh, a mother who knew not who the father was, or even if it was human.

Matt, James, Andy, Rotor and Jacob arrived back the night before the funeral. They went to the hospital to see Red.

He was deaf and in a bad way, but he would live. He had just undergone surgery and was under anaesthetic.

They waited as long as they could for him to come round but he didn't.

They went back to the station to arrange further follow-up matters with operations in the field.

Matt left them a short while later.

He found Danielle at the Vans, with Suzanne's parents.

Danielle had done her best to be there to help, to be there when close friends were needed, to be brave, but aside with Matt she was scared and distraught. She wept.

Matt hugged Suzanne's mother, Sarie's grandmother, to him, and crying started anew.

They were all so pleased to see him. Despite their grief they were concerned for him, that he should come back safely.

He shook hands with Suzanne's father, Sarie's grandfather, and was clasped to him. There were tears in the eyes of that hardened farmer too. The grief must have been very deep, for men out there, in war, had long since learnt not to show such emotion.

Matt embraced Tanny and Oom Van.

He said and did all the right supportive things to show them they were not alone in their grief – that in their time of need they could depend on him, just as they had been there for him when part by part his immediate family had been taken from him. They were not to be disappointed in him in this, though even now he felt almost as emotionally battered, for Suzanne's death was the nearest he would come to losing a sister, and Sarie's death was the nearest he would come to losing a niece.

The following morning, Matt picked up Red in a wheelchair from the hospital, weak as he was, and against the surgeon's vociferous advice, and together they went to the funeral.

Just about all the farmers from the valley were there, and many friends besides. James and Alexandra, Andy and Elaine, Rotor and Jacob were there.

Seeing the two coffins, one so small, being committed to the earth side by side, Matt felt how readily God called out names and cancelled them – if there was a God. He felt like gesturing to the heavens with a terse 'stick-it-up-your-arse', but he didn't before the others, only in his mind.

Afterwards they had to take Red back to hospital because he was bleeding badly.

Back at the Vans there were the bravest of faces. The women all got together cooking and all of them took to drinking to celebrate Suzanne's and Sarie's departure into a better world.

Matt felt how both worlds counted the same, that one had to make the best of where one was at the time.

They sang songs to hide how sad they all were at their own loss. For all of them things could never be the same again.

The girls consoled each other. For Danielle, Alexandra and Elaine there had been a nasty twist to the war; while they had been so concerned about their husbands, the war had side-stepped the men and taken a wife and child. It was the women who had suffered the first fatalities. Never for a moment had they realised that their next get-together would have been like this.

Matt got dead drunk.

Danielle found him lying flat on his face out in the garden.

The Sabbath again.

'There are rumours,' said the man.

Matt and Andy waited.

'They are just rumours,' the man advised.

'Then these rumours will have to be tested,' Matt said.

The man grinned.

Matt and Andy found the place where it was rumoured the guerrillas had been.

Matt picked up the spoor.

As he was moving through the bush, he inexplicably thought about what !Kai had once said to him. But then again perhaps not so inexplicably, for thoughts had the habit of being related to events by association – no matter how seemingly obscure.

He had looked across at !Kai as he had squatted down on his haunches in front of him.

!Kai had looked back at him but was unable to suppress his mirth and bowed his head, unable to hold his gaze. His laughter had sounded many times as loud as it might have been in the quiet bush.

Matt had looked at him. 'Well?' he had enquired.

!Kai had looked squarely back at him again, his lips had tightened together, then his eyebrows had risen and he had spluttered into laughter once again. He had tried to control his merriment with his chin pressed against his chest, but with limited effect. A dribble of saliva had worked its way out of his mouth.

Once again !Kai had tried to explain, but another eruption of laughter had rattled him.

Matt had shaken his head, unable to prevent himself from smiling.

At last !Kai had spoken. 'It is why men put their beds up on bricks,' he had chuckled, 'to prevent those familiars of witches who are short in stature from hypnotising them into some dark act as they sleep.'

Matt grinned again now with the memory, then when he thought about it some more, about the ones who come and go as the wind, the ones who arrive but are not seen in arriving, who depart but are not seen in departing, he was no longer grinning. The description seemed to fit him just as much as it did Mumvuri.

His mind returning to the spoor, Matt realised that it was so fresh that he could bump into Mumvuri at any moment. Prickles of coldness ran up and down his spine.

At last, after all he had been through, after all the failure, he was about to come face to face with The Shadow – The Shade – that had caused so much blood to run cold in the valley, that had pressed him to the limit, his body, his mind, his love of the bush.

Matt could see where Mumvuri had walked for some distance in a stream that looped down into the valley. He had swung through trees as he had come away from it.

But Matt was still there, right behind him.

Kraals and crops gave way to rugged *koppies* and dry ravines.

Sight, hearing, touch, smell, taste . . . and that other sense, the bush sense . . . all there . . . concentrated . . . aware of everything around him . . . stones that had been turned over, incomplete prints, broken old seed-bearing pods, winter flowers compressed flat in their night configurations . . . the sounds of birds and four-footed animals . . . the feel of the bush, the grass, the plants, the thorns, the wind . . . the smell and the taste, the acrid dry earth . . .

He was led away from all standing water, through the punishing heat of the valley and out into a land where all rivers had long since drained away into the dry earth, a region where no human willed to be.

Squinting his eyes against the sun, Matt looked at the tired white cumulus sky, clouds that had formed alone evaporated alone. No two clouds came together to procreate.

The further east they went the closer they came to the border.

The spoor on the gulley paths was comprised of full imprints made close together. Then, on flat ground, the spoor was comprised of imprints made by the balls of the feet, long strides apart.

Factors of age, speed and direction trudged through his parched mind. To be on the move was to overcome idleness, idleness that would set him to thinking about anything but Mumvuri.

His was a world of bush-silence, quietness full only of bush sound, not human. Guarding against his own sound and scent was Man's supreme virtue in the bush.

Forever listening, forever watching, Matt followed the spoor at the base of a low ridge, and then it was gone on the scrambled rocky plateau over the border.

Matt stopped.

Andy stopped the required 'safe' distance behind him.

Matt's scrutiny took in the terrain and his expression became deeply suspicious.

'Would you say it was wise to follow Snake into his hole?' asked !Kai's voice from the past.

'No,' said Matt.

He studied the terrain with his eyes. There was no alternative route to be taken.

He continued across the border. It was the nearest he had come to finding out where Mumvuri kept disappearing to.

It was a desolate landscape. There was no vegetation growth, no trees. Loose small stones on the dark of the massive rock looked like seeds that had fallen on ungiving hard ground and petrified, never to germinate in a place that gave nothing of itself. You had to be careful where you trod. The sharp edges of the dark base rock could slice through the soles of a man's boots. Eyes strained to find some life source amongst the dead landscape in which every rock looked like a stunted man in a crouching position.

Then all spoor was lost to him.

Matt cursed. He suspected Mumvuri was 'rock-hopping', and very carefully at that. He could find not even a scuff mark. Mumvuri could do that for several kilometres and in any direction. Where was Matt to start trying to find sign as to where Mumvuri had stopped anti-tracking and moved on normally once again?

He tried to circumvent Mumvuri's cunning in every way possible, but finally in sheer exasperation and disappointment he turned to Andy and threw his arms in the air.

Andy made as if to pull his hair out by the roots and then did a most uncharacteristic thing. He threw his rifle on to the ground and just sat down.

'We've got to keep looking, we can't afford to stop for even one minute,' Matt said to him.

'I'm beginning to think this bastard really is a shadow, a spirit,' said Andy.

Matt looked down at Andy and shook his head, then looked out to the barren rock-strewn land before him. He wanted to go on alone, take on Mumvuri one-to-one, but at the same time he couldn't leave Andy there alone, not across the border in enemy territory.

He turned on the radio he was carrying on his back and contacted James, giving him the co-ordinates where they could be up-lifted at a place back across the border.

'Come on.' Matt turned to Andy somewhat coldly, and they started back for the border to be there in time for the up-lift.

August

Over dinner on Matt's return, Danielle wanted to talk to him as they used to, about things he had helped her to see in nature, things they used to share, how the sting of the early mornings was blunted, how the air, warming up after the winter months, wasped over them, how little buds were peeping from branches, how green blades of grass were shyly poking above the ground for the first time; how the green wheat fields under the irrigation sprinklers with their rainbows, showed a surge of new growth; how there were young antelope and cubs and fieldmice, and little fledglings all-a-feather; how proud she was of overseeing the main calving months of the year; how it was spring, the season of new life.

She tried to get Matt to chat with her but got little response. He just read the entries she had written in the farm journal, without bothering to discuss things with her. So instead of talking about the things she wanted to, she only thought of them.

It was the time of agricultural and fashion shows, beautiful livestock, rosettes, funfairs and toffee apples, but she and Matt were to take no part in them, not that year. They used to go with the Vans. The Vans didn't go either.

Matt kept an eye on floor prices for beef, and as the weather warmed up, supers and prime cattle came from the winter feedlots to go to the abattoir.

While Matt was back Danielle took precious time to prepare vegetable beds and plant seedlings around the house gardens.

Calves were born. Throughout spring and into summer, the cows would give birth out on the *veld*.

204

Those about to calf could be easily recognised. There was a hollow each side of the tail-head, the udder and teats were swollen, and the vulva was enlarged. When it was time the cow could be seen straining with muscle contractions. Three hours of that or so and the 'water-sac' membrane appeared, then, if the delivery was normal, the fore-hooves of the calf would appear followed by the head.

Because the cows had been carefully watched and examined throughout their pregnancies it was possible to tell which cows were likely to have problem deliveries and they had been put in the pasture nearest to the house.

On several occasions, Danielle stayed up all night with Matt and one or other of the concerned farmhands in the barn, catching a few minutes of sleep here, an hour there with a blanket in the straw. They saw several calves into the world that way.

Matt would make sure the membrane was clear of the calf's head. Once one of the calves was not breathing after delivery. Matt simply blew into its nose and its lungs expanded with its first breath, that of Matt's from the farm air.

Before he left the calf, he ensured that it had suckled its mother to benefit from the first yellow-milk which acted like a nutritional booster that the calf needed initially, but the richness of which would rapidly decline so that if the calf did not avail itself of it in the first few hours it would lose out.

He was concerned, compassionate and as a farmer with all manner of farming knowledge in his head, was extremely gifted, but more than anything, what showed through was his love for nature, the animals and the farm.

As for Danielle and Matt? They seemed to be some distance apart.

There had been little new guerrilla infiltration into the country during the winter months because of lack of water, *veldkos* (bush food) and vegetation cover.

Listening to the sounds of the African night, Matt thought how the most recent information from James indicated that there was to be a concentrated build-up of guerrilla insurgents across the border, ready to move in along with the rains.

When he was suddenly aware that Danielle was intently watching him, the glass in his hand moved to his mouth. He took a long swallow. He felt as if Danielle was there to witness his every act, passing silent judgement on it.

Danielle could feel the atmosphere pushing her back, as if he had put a hand against her breast and shoved her away, excluding her, shedding her just as the cattle were shedding hair now winter was over.

Her disillusion rose within her anew like a marsh mist. She wanted him to take her, even if for the wrong reasons. But his eyes were a cold motionless blue.

He got up, leaving his drink unfinished.

As he strode off past her she took hold of his hand.

There was an awkward silence.

'You don't have to go back out into the bush,' she told him.

'Yes,' he sighed beneath his breath, as if he wanted to believe it but couldn't. He pulled his hand from hers. 'Have to see to the cattle,' he said.

He spent much of his time with the cattle. But now, through a kink in the curtains, she saw him outside, checking the farmhouse security fences.

Further interrogation of the captured guerrilla James had saved from the snake pit revealed there was a bush transit camp about twenty kilometres further on across the border from where Matt had last lost track of Mumvuri and Andy had refused to go on.

Although authority to breach the border had still not been given by the Ministry of Defence, Matt felt at last they had the opportunity to find out where Mumvuri kept escaping to, and James was prepared to take the risk.

James got Rotor to drop off Matt and Andy with the captured guerrilla who had shown his willingness to indicate the whereabouts of the guerrilla arms cache.

Matt, not trusting the man, but taking James's word, took him along. He cautiously watched the man's every move, but as it turned out the man informed them well in advance of stumbling on the camp and Matt had ample opportunity to watch, to listen and to check the area.

The transit camp was a crude one, consisting of little more than branch-and-grass shelters near a natural spring in an otherwise waterless wasteland away from the river. It was deserted, but there were signs that it had been visited days before by one man. Considering the time and place he had last tracked Mumvuri to, Matt felt that Mumvuri had to be that one man.

Matt examined the camp thoroughly. He followed footpaths to

and from the camp but found nothing of particular interest. What he expected to find if anything he didn't exactly know, but none the less he expected to find something. The camp was altogether too clean for his liking.

He asked Andy to call James forward to up-lift them.

The trip there seemed to have been a futile exercise. There must have been scores of such transit camps, any one of which could be used by the guerrillas, and nothing new had been learnt about Mumvuri.

Waiting for the helicopter to arrive, Matt continued to wander around. Something about the place still disconcerted him.

It was while continuing to search around that he suddenly stopped. There was a small area of ground that troubled him, but he couldn't make out why. He thought how he must have walked past the spot at least ten to fifteen times before but that now it was different.

He studied the area intently.

Then suddenly he knew what it was that had been troubling him. There was a small subsidence of earth, perhaps no more than a hand in length – natural maybe, except the subsidence was in a perfectly straight line.

Apart from that there was nothing else unusual. Grass was growing naturally over the area, the soil colours and structures were undisturbed and as they should be, nothing else suggested that anything was out of place, and the more he looked from other angles the less certain he felt about there being anything unusual there at all. Why, then, after all the times he had passed the spot had he only felt troubled by it now?

Then he realised. Perhaps it was the angle of the sun that had outlined it to him – pure coincidence.

When he let his shadow fall over the spot there appeared nothing out of the ordinary. When he let the light on it once again the straight line reappeared. He called Andy over.

'Do you see anything unusual?' Matt asked.

'I think you're imagining things,' said Andy.

Matt shook Andy's remark off, choosing instead to approach the spot with extreme caution, treating it as if it were a land mine. He lay flat on the ground, took his jacket off, placed it beside him, and with arms outstretched to the spot in front of him, began to clear the earth away on to his jacket.

As he was clearing the earth away he heard the sound of the approaching helicopter but didn't let it distract his concentration. He heard Andy pull the pin of a grenade, heard it being thrown, and smelt and saw the green smoke of the marker as it blew over him.

He heard the helicopter land.

He examined the soil as he removed it, looking for signs to suggest that it had been tampered with, but it had good binding, grass roots, insects, everything one would have expected of normal soil.

He was beginning to think he was cracking up, that he was getting unnecessarily jumpy about things. Mumvuri was succeeding in destroying his nerve without even being there.

He heard James approach and he heard Andy say, 'Matt's digging a hole, have you anything you'd like planted?'

Matt felt somewhat foolish, but angry at Andy's remark at the same time.

James said nothing to disturb Matt. Instead he backed off a way and lay flat, following Matt's example, and watched.

Matt had dug a hole almost a metre deep when he struck what seemed to be wood – it was a wooden board – a trap door?

Matt saw how well fitted it was, except for a small crack of about a hand's length between the board and what appeared to be a wooden frame. Contraction of the wood in the winter dryness could have caused the wooden board to separate slightly from the frame after it had been placed there, probably in the wet summer.

Matt noticed Andy was now lying down too and watching attentively.

'Get the cord,' Matt told him.

When Andy returned with the cord, Matt tied it to a wooden knob that served as a handle on the board, moved back thirty paces, and pulled – the wooden board came out freely.

Matt approached the hole once again with caution.

He looked in. It was dark. He took his penlight from his shirt pocket, turned it on, shone it into the hole, inspected it carefully for signs of booby-traps, then disappeared inside.

'Jesus!' he heard Andy exclaim.

'Close,' retorted James in reply.

Matt found himself in a wide bunker shored up with timber poles and wooden planks, some two metres beneath the surface. It was crammed with weapons and ammunition of Communist origin in their original 'Export' boxes, or wrapped in old plastic fertiliser bags.

He checked further for wires and other signs of any anti-tampering devices for about twenty minutes, but could find no evidence of anything untoward.

What he did find, apart from the weapons, was a cash box – full of local currency and money from back home.

He popped his head up through the hole momentarily to pass the cash box to James and to say to a shamefaced Andy, 'I could do with some help.'

He disappeared once again and started passing weapons and boxes of ammunition to the surface.

'There's about twice as much down here as the previous arms cache we found,' Matt let James know.

'Fucking hell,' exclaimed Andy.

'See if you can't get Rotor to bring his chopper as close as possible, and we'll start loading this stuff,' said James to Andy.

Meanwhile, James took the opportunity to question the captive as to the arms cache. The man, looking on with obvious amazement, said he knew nothing about it, that only the Sectoral Operations Commander knew where the arms caches were located as he liked to establish them personally with no onlookers.

James, Andy, the captive and Rotor formed a human chain, passing the weapons and other military equipment across to the helicopter, with Jacob loading them aboard in a most meticulous manner to distribute their weight equally.

Rotor watched the helicopter gradually sink on its wheels.

'I wish we had the sling net. We'll be lucky if we get off the ground,' he said.

Jacob grunted.

'Only joking,' Rotor told him. Then turning to the others, he said, 'He's tuned this crate to the peak of an orgasm,' but all the same, he had an expression of doubt on his face.

By the time they were finished, the helicopter was loaded fore and aft, around Rotor's and Jacob's seats, practically to the 'rafters'.

'Where exactly are Matt, James, Andy and our fine trustworthy friend supposed to sit?' Rotor asked Jacob, gesturing to the captive.

Jacob answered by clinging to one of the horizontals of the airframe.

'You better be the one to tell them,' Rotor said.

'Now it's my turn to say Oh Jesus!' said James.

Rotor laughed.

Back down in the hole Matt had left the original front row of armaments aside, and now he replaced them to make it look as if the bunker had never been disturbed.

To a land mine on the top layer he replaced an anti-lift device, and was in the process of arming it when he heard James say to him, leaning into the hole, 'Matt, there's a border patrol visual. About twenty of them. We don't know if they've spotted us so we're sitting tight, although with green smoke and the sound of the chopper to have alerted them I'm not so optimistic.'

'I'm almost done here,' said Matt, 'But there's still the trap door to replace and the hole to fill in. It'll take some time to do properly.' He spoke as he continued to work on the booby-trap.

Matt finished arming the device and came on out, placing the board on its frame behind him to seal the hole. He was replacing the soil when he heard the crack of bullets about them.

'Nobody return fire,' James ordered. 'We're not supposed to be here, so we don't want an international incident. We must just get the hell out of here.'

Rotor and Jacob were the first back to the helicopter, the others in quick pursuit.

Matt was last to grab hold of part of the airframe and place a precarious foot aboard, having had to leave the arms cache hole exposed.

The rifle fire from the neighbouring government's border patrol was more sustained now, and was becoming more accurate as they closed in from their range of about 400 metres.

'For fuck's sake, get moving,' Andy yelled at Rotor.

Rotor didn't so much as bother to secure his shoulder-harnass and lap strap or put on his flight-helmet. He pushed in the igniter circuit breaker, rolled the throttle open on the collective, and hit the starter ignition switch.

The electric motor whined.

The engine seemed to take forever to run up to operation speed . . . then centrifugal force moved the shoes outwards to engage with the steel periphery of the drive disc . . . the turbine caught . . . and the rotor system slowly began to turn.

'Purr, baby, purr . . .' Rotor pleaded.

Slowly, slowly, the rotors turned and then they were spinning so fast they looked like a solid disc, but the helicopter battled to rise more than a couple of feet off the ground.

'She's too heavy,' said Rotor.

Matt started chucking weapons out.

'Nah, Matt, you risked your life for that stuff,' said Rotor, still trying to get airborne. 'You don't want to give it back. Besides, some other time they might shoot at me with it.'

For a few moments they were out of sight of the border patrol as it moved in, obscured by the bush.

'How about getting rid of fuel,' Rotor said to Jacob. 'It's only 32Ks back to the border, we can afford to lose most of it.'

Jacob was immediately under the fuselage with the fuel cock full open, aviation fuel gushing all about him as he frantically tried to drain off most of the fuel load in the tank, to accommodate the excessive weight of passengers and equipment aboard.

The patrol appeared again and their shooting resumed.

'TBFK,' Jacob shouted at last, and, reeking of fuel, climbed back in.

'Try not to light any cigarettes,' Rotor said.

Matt saw how the fuel gauge looked as if it was on zero. If Jacob was wrong in his assessment of how much fuel they could afford to lose, they would go down before they reached the border.

Ground resonance of the helicopter built up alarmingly. 410 kilowatts of turbo-power strained and shuddered to get the over-loaded helicopter off the ground. Rotor demanded the limit of what the helo could give. It screamed in what seemed to be pain. But it would barely leave the ground.

It took several bullet hits.

Rotor nosed the ship forward, picking up speed along the bumpy, rock-strewn ground, through the bush and between trees for some distance, both rotors cutting a thirteen-metre diameter circle about them, threatening to strike the solid trunk of a *munhondo* tree at every revolution.

The tip-path trimmed the grass on the starboard side of the *koppie*.

Rotor pulled in the collective, turning a fistful of throttle. Matt could feel the air pressure build up under the rotors. The disc coned as it marginally pulled the ship out of the bush.

The helicopter flew in the ground cushion where the thrust was augmented due to interference with the downwash, until the minimum forward power speed could be translated to vertical lift.

Bullets from the border patrol guards were ripping into the treeline. Green tracer flashed through the air just behind them, searching them out as Rotor manoeuvred the helicopter through the tree cover.

At the very moment of translational lift, Rotor gave a full foot of right pedal. The resultant power that came off the tail was immediately absorbed overhead, and just enough to make them airborne. He immediately banked almost ninety degrees hard to starboard, refusing to present himself as anything but a quick-silver target if he had to be a target at all, the rotor tips almost furrowing the ground.

Hanging sideways in the air, kept aboard by nothing more than the invisible finger of centrifugal force, Matt's face rushed crazily past the ground. His gut tightened with the abrupt acceleration.

The helicopter ripped across the tree tops at upwards of seventy-five knots.

The rotors chopped young branches in the ship's precarious path out, cracking like 20mm cannon fire, as Rotor tried to evade the tremendous volley of bullets zinging about them from twenty sub-machine-guns on the ground.

The fuselage slipped between the canopies of trees.

Suddenly the trees disappeared from beneath them and they were dropping down the opposite side of the *koppie* into the valley.

Rotor used the speed of the drop for the maximum climb he could get out the other side.

Then they were above and beyond the range of rifle fire and in level flight heading back home.

Rotor suddenly noticed wind whistling through a solitary bullet-hole in the Perspex canopy, and with a smile to Matt made no attempt to check anywhere on his person but between his legs. Then he put a hand to his head, only to remember, as it seemed, that he hadn't put his flight-helmet on.

'I wondered why my little girl was performing so noisily,' he shouted to Matt. 'I'd thought she was about to suffer a seizure but hadn't the heart to tell anyone . . .' He put his flight-helmet on and connected the radio cord. He gestured for Matt to do the same.

Matt heard him say through the earphones, pointing at the bullet hole, 'Jacob isn't going to like that.'

'Like what?' demanded Jacob, banging on the back, unable to see through all the equipment crammed about him, and the bodies hanging on to the airframe.

'His ability to understand English improves remarkably at such moments,' Rotor said.

James clicked the radio to his office's frequency, and requested an armoured troop-carrier with drums of fuel for the helicopter, and with map in hand he turned to Rotor, with a 'Where do you think we'll make it to on home soil?' He noted the position Rotor pointed to on the map, and passed the locstat to the man in the office.

'I thought you were going to try and drive back, bush or no bush,' came Andy's voice to Rotor as soon as James had finished speaking to the detail manning the radio.

'If you only knew how close it came,' Rotor muttered under his breath.

'You won't catch me in this fucking overgrown lawnmower again . . . that is, without a few drinks in me first . . . ever,' came Andy's note of finality.

Rotor just grinned.

'Damn!' Matt said, suddenly recollecting. 'I rigged up a land mine for Mumvuri, to go off as soon as the door was lifted from the arms cache, but I didn't have time to cover it to make it look as if it hadn't been disturbed. One of those border patrol guards is bound to go in and trigger it off.'

'We'll blame it on the gooks,' said James, 'create a little discord between them and their hosts.'

Shortly afterwards they crossed back across the border, and arrived at their rendezvous point.

A little over an hour later the troop-carrier arrived with the fuel. They refuelled, handed over a quantity of the arms haul, and headed on back to town.

'Drinks at the hotel, courtesy of Mumvuri,' said James, waving the wad of notes they had captured along with the weapons.

There was a roar of approval from Andy and Jacob in the back.

'I wouldn't say no either,' said Rotor, as he guided the helicopter to follow the tar road.

Straddled across the warmth-retaining tar was a flock of crowned guinea fowl.

'Food,' said Matt, gesturing.

Rotor brought the helicopter swiftly in above the birds which were scattering in flight. The full downwash of the rotors forced them to the ground unable to fly, their alarmed calls lost in the roar of the turbines. Rifle fire poured out of the helicopter, the air full of explosive sound and the smell of nitro-cellulose.

When they flew off again, eight severely ruptured greyish specked

213

bodies with their blue faces and red crowns dripped blood on the floor.

Rotor flew away from the road to follow the river. They passed the farm nestling in the late afternoon light, looking as snug and as tranquil as could be.

'You want to stop off, Matt?' Rotor asked.

Matt answered with a shake of his head.

The river near the town had eroded the basalt lava of its bed over countless thousands of years, to appear more than 100 metres below its original level. Forced to flow in contrary directions by the rock structure, the river zigzagged, revealing only short stretches of itself at any one time. It seemed they were flying directly into walls of rock when at the last moment a slight touch of the cyclic to the right or the left revealed another passage.

Rotor reduced the collective and the helo dropped to a few metres above the river that charged angrily across the rocks, fuming white water.

At times they were so close to the sides that they could see the fine grain of the dark bluish basalt rock and flecks of crystal. Above them were age-old jungles; palms, liana, and ferns; a tropical paradise; succulent green vegetation that seemed to knit together, closing the top of the gorge. It grew darker and darker. The safety-cord of grey sky frayed above them. It grew colder. Light did not seem to be able to reach them there. Waterfalls burst and exploded from breaches in the rock high above them, pounding the rocks below.

They were bucked and jolted in the turbulent air. Spray formed droplets on the Perspex canopy. Rotor continually corrected the dynamic instability of the helicopter's flight-path with fractional movements of cyclic and pedals.

They were into a cloudy nothingness for unnervingly long seconds. There was no sensation of movement. Matt could learn nothing from the fuselage attitude; it remained the same whether in climb or descent. The way they were facing meant almost nothing; they could be facing the same way whether the flight-path was forward, backwards or sideways.

Then vision slowly returned.

The water below grew sluggish. The waterfalls became weeping rock. The sound of the turbines reverberated loudly.

Then they were between the hills, hills that became wavy hillocks and rises, then the town was before them on the horizon, then the hotel.

'Drink,' said Rotor pointing, but they didn't stop there immediately. They flew on to the police station. Rotor put the helicopter down inside the security fence.

They unloaded the captured weapons they had retained on board, taking them into the armoury, finished James's whisky there, then drove to the hospital.

They intended to smuggle Red out of hospital and take him along for a binge at the hotel like old times, but they found him humped over and empty-eyed. He was almost totally withdrawn.

His fractured bones, lacerations, abrasions and contusions would mend. He was deaf, yes, but he acted as if he couldn't speak either. He had suffered something worse than his physical injuries that didn't look as if it was going to mend without him fighting against it.

'If I hadn't been drunk I might have seen something,' he wrote, and that was all they really got out of him.

Nothing they did or wrote in reply seemed to make any difference.

'The mine didn't hurt you as much as you are hurting yourself,' Matt yelled at Red in sheer desperation, then realising Red could not hear him wrote his words down on a sheet of paper with a blunt pencil and uncontrollably let reign to his anguish. 'It's time for you to stand on your own two feet,' he wrote. 'No longer am I going to let you follow me around like some puppy dog, some overgrown kid. You've got to pull yourself together.'

Red, seeing the words, the way they were written and the hard expression on Matt's face, couldn't but have understood what was happening. Deafness was no retreat for him in that.

Matt wasn't even out of the door when he was wondering what he had done. He was scarcely out of the passage when he was questioning his own character and hardly out of the hospital when he hated what he had become.

He walked to the hotel by himself. James and the others met him at the bar later.

Andy tossed the guinea fowl on to the bar counter. The barman took them without batting an eyelid to have them cooked in the kitchen. They said nothing about Matt's outburst. James just ordered a round of drinks.

'The silence is punishing. Why don't you just tell me that Red's been through perhaps the greatest emotional and physically traumatic experience of his life, that I'm an arsehole.'

'OK, you're an arsehole,' said James. 'That make you feel any better?'

'No.'

James pushed Matt's refilled glass to him.

The bar was filled with cigarette smoke and people talking. There wasn't a woman in the place. Faces; faces Matt didn't know. It made him feel how things had changed in the valley.

Andy lifted his glass, draining its contents in one long thirsty swallow. 'Shit,' he said, letting free a deep burp, 'I needed that. A war's one hell of a damned way to earn a living.' Then he said, 'I'm nervous about going back home to Elaine. We've been bitching at each other quite a lot lately. Week after week it's been getting worse and worse.'

Matt took a deep draught of his beer.

'Comes with the territory,' said James. 'It's rough on Alexandra too, only after twenty years she more or less knows how to handle it.'

'Moving parts in contact require lubrication to avoid excessive wear and possible seizure. Lubrication is needed where people rub together . . .' Andy said, taking a swig of his next drink by way of punctuation.

'Is that biology or vehicle maintenance?' asked James as he cut his whisky with a little water.

'What's the matter, you got an ulcer?' Andy questioned, looking at the diluted whisky.

Matt drank his beer quietly, gazing ahead of him over the bar, seemingly unaware of what was going on around him with respect to others in the bar, but he *was* aware, watching the reflections in the bar mirror.

City types, he observed of the rowdy men in camouflage uniform near to him.

He looked at a big man with a large head, at the face with a weak chin, at the small eyes closely set in folds of pallid skin. No, not big, stodgy, he decided. The forehead was low and flat, suggesting a man who acted without thinking.

The man next to him, though of lesser build, was the one to watch. He had more sway with the group, and had the physiognomy that suggested a choleric temper; his hair was crisp and

216

frizzy, inclined to stand up; the flesh was pallid, the eyes dull and asexual, and his lips, unfirm, caressed his words with obscene suggestiveness.

The others were flick-knife-thin men.

One of the men was playing with a large bullfrog on the bar counter. It bloated its throat to give the appearance of greater size and ferocity. It was a futile defence, for it was the defence that fascinated the man.

'You should have seen Jacob and I when we were first flying together . . .' Rotor was saying. 'One of our first jobs was to fly a couple of Afrikaans nurses cross-country to the mission. We switched seats, and I pretended I was the tech.' Both he and Jacob went into a fit of laughter. 'He was wearing the wings so they thought he was the pilot . . . but he pretended he couldn't fly that day because he had a bad hangover . . . He asked me to fly in his place . . .' Rotor was repeatedly breaking off mid-sentence to join Jacob in rising amusement as the story was related. 'I then swopped places with him and sat back in the pilot's seat, and he sat back in his seat . . . He gave me instructions from the back on how to fly, telling me that as long as I listened to him we stood half a chance of making it. I went through the pre-flight and cockpit check like I didn't know what was what . . . By that time the girls were so nervous they tried to bail out . . . but I had cranked up and was already hopping down the runway like a gorged vulture . . . He was still trying to tell me how to keep the damn thing straight, and I was continually asking him what to do next,' said Rotor. 'Pull in a bit of collective, I'd say, you know, that big handbrake-looking thing between the two front seats . . .'

At this point he cajoled Jacob into giving them a demonstration, and they hopped about on their stools, side by side, tilting them this way and that, Rotor nervously enquiring what to do next, and Jacob in a pretended alcoholic daze, with hand to head and eyes closed, sort of obliging.

' . . . think they're human,' spat the voice of one of the men near to Matt.

'The only good black is a dead black,' said the frizzy-haired one.

For a moment, Matt felt his eyes glow with what seemed the heat of an internal fire, then dim again, watching, listening to the snake-like man, the flickering of his tongue, the sibilant hiss, the slits of the eyes, the sinuous movement of the body.

At the urinal, in front of Matt was a sign cautioning ARE YOU HAVING A SECURITY LEAK?

The big man muttered something about how decent white *volk* shouldn't have to tolerate those 'black apes just down from the trees'.

Matt nodded meekly, and urinated on the man's boots without the man being any the wiser.

When Matt sat back down at the bar, the snake-like man was directly addressing the mirror the length of the wall behind the bar counter:

'Mirror, mirror, on the wall
Who is the fairest of us all?'

he sang out.

'Snow White, you black bitch
And don't you forget it.'

someone else chimed in answer.

Matt gave no hint of interest, made no move, gave no sign of anything, just continued to gaze placidly over the bar counter at the mirror. But he missed nothing.

'Black boy, another round,' shouted the big man to the barman.

Matt could see the humiliation in the barman's face. Matt liked him. He was an honest, hardworking man. Matt used to chat with him every time he came to the bar – had done so for a number of years, ever since the man had been working there.

Whether as a deliberate slight or not, the barman served several other customers before the crass, loud-mouthed individual realised.

When the man did realise he grabbed the barman by the lapels of his jacket with one hand and pulled him forcibly against the bar counter to stare him in the face. 'Think you're funny, black boy?'

Matt didn't move from his bar stool, and still staring into the miror at the back of the bar said, 'Let him go,' his voice flat, cold, brooking no failure to comply.

One of the man's companions tried to step in, but as if accidentally Andy blocked his way. 'Oh sorry,' he said. But by then it was too late for the man's companion to interfere.

'What was that?' the man demanded of Matt threateningly, but without letting go and still staring the barman down.

'Don't you feel unclean being touched by that?' said Matt in English to the barman, so that his tormentor would understand. The big man swivelled round, his punch moving towards the point where moments before Matt's voice had come from. Matt moved marginally to the side, the punch deflecting off the side of his forehead, and a rock-like fist rode deep into the other man's gut, followed by a deft change of stance and lightning jabs to the kidneys.

The man just crumpled. He didn't get up again.

Andy, dead-pan, kneed in the groin the man who had been intent on interfering earlier and now made another move too many.

The snake-like man stood facing Matt with a glint of steel in his left hand.

Matt's manner, his facial expression, didn't so much as twitch. He stared with the rigidity of a shot-gun barrel aimed straight between the slits of those eyes. Matt didn't take his eyes off the man, not once did his eyes leave the man's face, following his every intention, knowing it even before the man translated it into physical action.

The man hesitated. It was a moment of hesitation that he would regret.

When the moment came it showed in the man's eyes. Matt saw it and had the man down on the floor with the knife at his throat, the point of the blade penetrating the skin just deep enough to draw a little blood.

The man did not dare to move.

James never lost his look of benign aristocrat. Somebody took a rifle from the weapons rack, but before he could cock it, James had stuffed the barrel of his pistol down the front of the man's trousers. There was no way the man could shake free. All James had to do was pull the trigger. The man dropped the rifle.

'Can't let you ruin the evening for everyone else now, can we, boys?' said James to them drily as he put a call through to the police station.

A couple of police vans arrived shortly afterwards with the Duty Officer, his burly black sergeant-major and a couple of other country-rugged looking details.

James had a quick word to one side with the officer. 'Just stick them in a cell for the night to cool off. There's no need to advise the Military Police. They tend to frown on this sort of thing, we'll all have extra paperwork and they'll be spending the rest of their tour of duty in detention – no way to win a war is it?' he smiled.

The men were removed from the premises.

'They're in a mad rush to pick a fight with anyone in the country with anything more than a suntan,' said Matt.

'Probably just needed to let off some steam,' said James, slapping Matt heartily on the shoulder.

Their roasted guinea fowl arrived. The hotel manager, an old friend, bought the next round, and well into the early hours Matt got blindly drunk, drinking more than enough to make up for the whole group that had been evicted.

When Matt woke up it was afternoon, and he found himself in one of the hotel rooms. Somehow he felt the tension had eased. There was a tender area on the side of his forehead. He fingered it gently. He wondered how it had got there. He sat naked on the bed just staring at the wall for some minutes. Then he remembered.

He went through to the shower and ran the water freezing cold. Afterwards he gave himself a rough towelling down and felt invigorated. But his mouth tasted bad. He found a toothbrush there and brushed his teeth vigorously. Looking in the mirror he inspected the grazed skin on his forehead. It was almost hidden by the fall of his hair. Not bad, he thought. He wondered if the graze could be the reason for the 'something' that still beat inside his head, and smiled to himself, knowing that it was a hangover that was making him feel the way he was. His eyes were red-veined like a relief map.

Turned out to be a good night after all, he told himself.

September

After the landmine incident and the deaths of Suzanne and her baby, the four farmers of the Horseshoe Ridge area decided to form a roster system so each only had to travel once a month to town, which meant that mail and newspapers and miscellaneous items could be picked up once a week.

As Matt was away when the system was to start, Danielle was the first to drive into town and she did so nervously, though she was in the mine-proof Land Rover with its sub-machine guns, and joined a police convoy on the tar road.

In town, women were wearing their gay spring dresses and the models on the pages of magazines all looked so glamorous. She met Alexandra and Elaine for lunch at the hotel for the first time since Suzanne's death.

They all felt how a big hole had been left in their group and said how strange it felt without Suzanne. The loss had brought them closer together, but they found it hard to look for fun.

When they parted, Danielle felt more alone than ever.

She postponed going back to the farm for as long as possible. It would be a month before she could get out again.

But once back on the farm, the vegetables were doing well and the seedlings in the garden were coming out in flower. The trees, too, wore their new colourful apparel. The deciduous fruit trees were in delicate scented blossom, tinged white and pink; the jacaranda and poinsettia trees that lined the driveway were in magnificent mauve and red show; and even the common *musasa* trees flamed in the colours of a new glory, coming out with buds and young leaves, not all at once but in ones and twos with the last fall of old leaves of each individual tree. There were as many shades as there were leaves, in golds, bronzes, coppers, greens. There was syringa on the *koppies* with their pale greenish-white flowers; *muzeze* in striking yellow; *mufufu* in rose, violet and purple; and the thorny *muunze* acacia in raging red.

The increasing temperatures brought on the ripening of the wheat. Kudu broke through the fences to feed on the seed. Lambs were born. Calves were born. The cows had been well cared for with supplementary feed throughout the winter to supply good milk, and their calves were welcomed with the promise of the feast of summer grazing to come.

Danielle was not pregnant, and living things continued to die. There were two still-born calves.

She had to spray against smut in the wheat with fungicide.

The fields for the maize were harrowed to get rid of weeds and to break up the clods of earth from the ploughing, levelling the soil. Danielle tried to remember everything she had learnt from Matt. She thought how the moisture content of the soil had to be just right. If it was too moist it hampered working, if too dry it became powdery or too hard.

She got off the tractor to make an adjustment to the harrow. She felt small alongside the head-high rear tyres. She made the necessary adjustment, and got back on the tractor, putting its powerful engine into gear once more, trundling across the field with the farmhand riding shot-gun, looking all around as they went.

As she drove along, she wondered how things were going to work out between Matt and her. She wondered if they would survive. She wondered what would happen to the farm if she were to take a weekend off in the city – go to an art exhibition, go to a charity ball, go to restaurants or perhaps a nightclub cabaret like she used to. She felt trapped. She couldn't go anywhere, speak to anyone, felt guilty taking time off to speak to friends on the phone. She seemed so far away from everyone and everything.

In her loneliness she felt she had let Matt down by having miscarried his son, when he had already lost so much, grandparents, parents and brother, and how he had so desperately wanted sons, how ecstatic he had been when she was pregnant, how he pandered to her every need, concerned that the least thing should discomfort her or disturb the baby in her womb.

She mourned the loss. It had left her empty.

She mourned Suzanne's parting, wept over nightmares of Sarie lying mutilated and dead in the road.

Back at the house that evening, Danielle remembered the first time she and Matt had ever made love, almost reliving it.

'Do you know what I feel like doing?' she asked excitedly. She smiled and kittenishly ran her tongue curled slightly upwards along her front teeth. She spun out of his arms, unbuttoned her blouse, shrugging out of it as she unzipped her denims and stepped out of her panties. Nude, she waded out into the dam.

He remained on the bank, watching.

She completely submerged herself, then came to the surface brushing aside the wet hair that had strayed across her face. She turned over on her back, floating, the moonlight playing on her, and stretched out her arms to him. 'What are you waiting for?' she called, and when he instantly dived out into the water, clothes and all, she gave a little startled scream and hastily splashed further away. But he grasped hold of her legs and she found herself swimming furiously on the spot. He altered his hold to her waist. She struggled playfully in his embrace. The dogs on the bank barked excitedly, as if uncertain whether they should do so in pleasure or aggression. Matt and she laughed together, then losing all interest in mock resistance she repeatedly kissed his wet face.

She wanted to love him and was caught up in the strength of her emotion.

The dam reflected the pale moon in its shadowy night sky.

Her hands interlocked behind his neck, she rose on to the tips of her toes and reached for his mouth with her own, her tongue searching. And as she kissed him she murmured, against his mouth, 'I want you.' Her voice was strained as if the desperation of her need had muted her.

Their breathing came harder and faster. The steamy spring heat of the river valley seemed to bring about the same condition in all things.

He lifted her up in his arms and laid her down in the grass of the bank, dripping with water.

She watched as he removed his clothes.

She arched her back as he came down on her, her legs parting to receive him, and guided him into her. Her tongue was in his mouth. She felt his hands exploring her body. His hands stroked through her wet hair. He smelt coolly scented of the river and the earth. She tasted the water as it dripped down over his face.

Naked unashamed passion, warm wet movements, her thighs smoothed against the firm muscle of his body, wrapping around him, tightening as she reacted to his attentions.

She felt him rise and fall like the lapping of the water on the bank, felt the warmth of his breath like the breeze. He took each hard nipple in turn into the warmness of his mouth.

Her quick hands were searching, feeling, softly grasping.

The burning fluidity of love burst within her, the breaking of a sexual fever. He was wet with it. She moaned with agonised pleasure. Flowing weightlessness. Then back to the world, held close in his arms. The glow of the moon was once again on the waters.

They went to the farmhouse.

He awoke before dawn. As he moved to get out of bed she stretched out an arm sleepily, giving that innocent smile of hers that she knew he found so captivatingly typical. She yawned. He kissed her full on the mouth. She delighted in the texture of his lips, his sleep-warm taste. Like a sleepy child she snuggled against him. The man-smell of his body and his warmth propositioned her once more.

Afterwards, they lay unmoving, apart from the occasional caress, watching the dawn sky gradually lighten, pushing aside the last remnants of night.

He reached for his cigarettes. She lit one for him and placed it between his lips. He took a long draw and slowly allowed the smoke to escape over his teeth.

'I love you,' he said.

On one of his returns to the farm Matt had another nightmare. He had to pace about the room to calm down, sucking constantly on cigarette after cigarette, each quickly burning down to the filter.

In the nightmare, he was taking a tame gook (converted guerrilla) out on an arms cache indication. James warned him against it, saying the guerrilla was not to be trusted, that the guerrilla's change of heart was only a bluff.

Matt told him not to be such a jumpy old man.

The arms cache site was there all right, but it was empty.

As Matt came out of the bunker, he stopped dead. The tame gook was pointing the AK James had issued him, directly at Matt's heart from less than ten paces. The gook could not miss. Matt heard the click of the firing-pin as it was triggered, incredibly loud in the quiet bush where all breathing had ceased.

But the rifle didn't fire!

The man's face went pale, his finger frantically pulling the trigger again and again.

Afterwards, standing over the man's body, Matt picked up the weapon that hadn't fired on numerous attempts to make it do so.

He saw James Creasely smile from the shadows in the bush, wagging a metal file in the air.

Matt inspected the weapon – James had filed the firing-pin down, not so that anyone would have noticed until they had attempted to fire the weapon. The pin stopped just short of striking the percussion cap of the bullet in the breech.

James Creasely had saved his life. James had known that the man was not to be believed, but had let Matt find out for himself.

Matt's grandfather, father and brother were applauding from the shadows.

One would learn. But the more mistakes one made the less likely one would live to learn by them.

Matt was deeply troubled by the nightmare. It was what had taken place in reality the month before – but distorted; the captured guerrilla who had indicated the transit camp had not been armed, hadn't known about the arms cache and Matt hadn't trusted him at all while James had. And the danger had not come from the man but from the neighbouring country's border patrol.

He was shivering, shaking.

Danielle held on to him. But he moved away to the edge of the bed with his back to her.

Matt felt how his dependency on Danielle had become a vulnerability that offended him – and a danger for what he had to do. In facing Mumvuri he couldn't allow the slightest softness.

Come first light he went out along the river with the dogs. It was tranquil. The river valley seemed to be draining away the mists.

Sitting down on the trunk of a fallen tree at the river's edge, picking thumb-nail blue ticks off the dogs whose tongues lolled from their mouths between hard enamel-white teeth, dripping saliva in time with their panting. He looked at them and they looked back lovingly, licked his hand, and he wondered if animals could be subject to such a vulnerable feeling of love.

Over the rest of the month there was no further news of Mumvuri.

On the Mumvuri file in James's office, Andy drew a mushroom. It had become their new logo, symbolising the way Mumvuri kept them in the dark and fed them on shit.

October

One season had passed into another, to come back on itself like a snake swallowing its tail.

It was the hottest month of the year.

Routine things like the weekly dipping of the cattle went on as usual.

Calves were de-horned. Caustic ash was placed on their horn buds, preventing the horns from growing, or injuries in bull fights would result later, and horns would get caught in the crushes, weigh scales and dips.

Those male cattle not wanted for breeding were castrated, the spermatic cord crushed. There was no bleeding. If the castrations weren't done there would be unwanted progeny, deformities, and the meat would be tainted by a strong flavour that reduced the quality of the meat.

For Danielle there were the usual routine things to do too. There was the clinic, the vegetables, the dairy, butter to make, cooked meats to prepare with Maruva, the weekly get-togethers with the women folk on the farm, decisions concerning the school to make by herself now that Suzanne was gone, there was the house to keep clean, paperwork in the office to keep up to date, a hundred and one different things to do.

Together Matt and she went into town to select seed for planting the maize crop when the rains came. The maize seed had to be selected new each season as the hybrid varieties Matt used didn't always breed true from year to year like the wheat.

Matt didn't arrange to meet anyone for lunch at the hotel, and he barely paused to reply to greetings from people he hadn't seen for months.

As for herself, she called in on Alexandra but couldn't stay long as Matt wanted to get back to the farm. She couldn't call on Elaine who had gone to the city for two weeks, combining business with pleasure.

Back on the farm, when the wheat was dead-ripe and the grain sufficiently dry, Matt commenced harvesting, hoping to get the crop in before the rains.

Danielle thought how summer was there, but she just wasn't as delighted as she felt she should have been. She felt the strain in her relationship with Matt accounted for that. She no longer felt the same pleasure in things, not even the bright warm weather now that winter was over.

She thought that even between Maruva and Matt there was no longer anything more than wary politeness.

She strolled down the driveway on the carpet of mauve-violet jacaranda petals, for no other reason than it used to feel good to do so, and tried to put her thoughts in order. But all she could think of were trivial things like it was the time for summer frocks in the city.

She went once again to help with the harvesting, driving tractors, working late into the night with the records.

She thought how in the old days she and Matt used to have friends round to the farm almost every weekend, how her friends from her student-nurse days used to come to the farm at least three or four times a year, but that there was just no time for her to entertain as she used to. She didn't invite them, and she made excuses when they phoned. She was so busy during the day and so tired at night that all she wanted to do then was sleep. Her meals, when alone, were coming to be no more than a boiled egg and toast, or salad and fruit.

They had the usual beer-drink after the harvest.

Matt got aggressively drunk. Danielle didn't know quite how she had managed to get him back to the house without him making too much of a spectacle of himself before the farmhands who respected him.

The morning after, Matt didn't remember much about the beer-drink.

No sooner was the wheat out of the fields than the tractors were into others, to be ready for the maize seeding and the summer rains.

Danielle drove one of the tractors, to be with him, but he did no more than adjust this or that and then was off somewhere else yet again.

How the fire on Matiziro *Koppie* had started no one knew. Perhaps a dewdrop, delicately hanging on a blade of grass, had focused the intense sunlight like a magnifying glass on to dead dry foliage. Perhaps a spark had flickered, grasped towards a mere wisp, almost immediately burst into convulsive life, from twig to twig, a crumpled leaf to a dry root, hesitant, then on, devouring years of priceless growth.

It had grown and grown, taking on the fury of a rampaging hot-blooded monster, unstoppable, insatiable.

Zebra, blue wildebeest, impala, kudu, tsessebe, rodents fled. Young were burnt to death.

In flight, fork-tailed drongos and lilac-breasted rollers gorged themselves on insects fleeing from the flames.

All the occupants of Horseshoe Ridge, every man, woman and child who could handle a branch or a wet sack were there – even Red, whom Danielle had been to hospital to fetch with Oom and Tanny Van only a few days before. But it was clear things between Red and Matt had changed. Danielle didn't know what had happened. If Spitskop hadn't been endangered too it didn't seem that Red would have desired to be there at all.

!Kai too was there, old as he was. More than anyone, the bush around Martiziro *Koppie* was his home.

They burnt controlled firebreaks in the fire's path. Eyes smarted with smoke, clothes and bodies were encrusted with sweat and ash, blistered and burnt. Bodies wearied, muscles ached. Soaked blackened sacks soon dried out in the flames, and had once more to be soaked. The water bowser trundled to and from the river all afternoon.

Matt led his farmhands and neighbours in the fight against the fire. The bush of Matiziro was being destroyed, and the whole of Horseshoe Ridge was endangered because of a strong wind.

Amidst it all, Matt became aware of the competent manner in which Danielle helped direct the farmhands, and even though she was a woman the respect was there for her. He knew he had missed something important in the development of her relationship with them, for those men did not give their respect casually to just any employer. It had to be earned through a hard demanding process. They would work, yes, they had to earn a livelihood, but to give their loyalty and respect, that was something else.

Suddenly Danielle turned and saw him staring at her.

He quickly averted his eyes.

The sun set.

The fire continued to rage.

Tongues of crimson heat spat glowing sparks deep into the solitude of the night. Clouds of choking smoke tossed and turned, as if the whole of the black sky was tossing and turning. It was heavy over the *koppie* and drifted over the farmhouse and towards Spits-kop.

A dangerous wind change suddenly blew burning embers over the heads of a small group of the farmhands, threatening to engulf them.

Suzanne's father tried to help but his trouser legs caught alight.

Matt was the next one there. He dived on top of the man to get him to the ground and smother the flames with earth. Suzanne's father was fortunate to escape with his legs only singed. Danielle was quickly there to attend to him.

Matt couldn't see a way through the flames to get to the trapped farmhands. Suddenly he realised Red was beside him. They looked at each other. Matt gestured to the tractor and ran to the water bowser behind it. Red, still not properly recovered, hobbled after him.

Matt opened the outlet valve fully, dived on the ground beneath it and soaked himself thoroughly, and soaked a sack, putting it around his head, before he turned the valve off.

By then, Red had climbed on to the tractor and started it up.

Meanwhile, the farmhands trapped by the flames were screaming for help.

The other farmers and farmhands were frantically beating at the flames but the heat was too overpowering and they were barely helping at all, perhaps even fanning the flames more.

Red drove the tractor, towing the bowser with Matt on the back as fast as he could, to where the pandemonium was.

Matt gestured for him to reverse the bowser through the flames. He turned the outlet valve full on again as they entered the fire and disappeared in the resultant steam. The bowser was only partially full, but it would have to do.

Through the wall of fire, a narrow path had been opened before the bowser emptied. Matt carried the smoke-choked and suffocating farmhands out on his shoulders one by one.

After a couple of trips, panting with the exertion, he found he couldn't hold his breath long enough on each subsequent trip. Carrying the last of the endangered farmhands he felt his clothes and the sack about his head were singed, having dried out completely in the unbearable heat. Then he was coughing and spluttering on the smoke. He felt he was suffocating. His eyes seemed to bulge from his head. He couldn't breathe, could no longer stay on his feet. He fought against it but he knew it was no good, his legs buckled beneath him.

The next thing he knew was that he was lying in the foetal recovery position on his side well away from the fire, with a couple of the recovering farmhands smiling and thanking him, and Danielle resuscitating him with oxygen from her first-aid kit.

'Red pulled you out of there,' Danielle told him. 'You're OK.'

'How are the others?' he asked.

'Everybody's safe.'

It took Matt another ten minutes to recover enough to join the fire-fight once more.

He found Red, who was limping more than before. Matt presumed it was because he had over-exerted himself in the rescue.

He thanked him. 'I owe you one,' he said.

Red just shrugged it off.

For the next couple of hours, Matt wheedled, cajoled and threatened once more . . . and then the fire was under control. It died soon after.

They gathered at the house, exhausted but relieved, with ice-cold beers with dew on the bottles.

When everybody had gone back home, having earned a good sleep, Danielle washed and went exhausted to bed. Matt opened another bottle of beer and drained half of it on his way to the shower after her. He threw off his clothes and took the bottle in with him. He turned up the cold water so that the needle spray stung his body. He finished the beer and hurled the bottle hard out of the window. He finished by rubbing himself down with a coarse towel so that he could feel every square centimetre of his skin tingle with life.

Towel wrapped round his waist, he pulled a pack of beer dumpies from the fridge, turned off the lights and slumped down on the verandah floor, leaning against the wall, and stared out to Matiziro *Koppie*.

He just sat there drinking, and staring out into the dark. He couldn't help feeling the pain of years, of something irreplaceable having been lost.

He was there for the sunrise, and winced as he saw that the *koppie* had been transformed to a bald black pile of rocks. He didn't want to think of how many animals, birds and insects, apart from plants and trees, had been consumed in the fire. The raw earth was sloughed of its bush cover. The ash would act as fertiliser, but nitrogen had been leached from the soil. Trees were withered.

Smoke! It was still there all about him, as evil in the bush as the odour of Man. Yet fire had been part of bush life long before the coming of Man.

If Matt hadn't known better than to think so, he would have sworn that *he*, Mumvuri, had been there.

The dark hole of Matt's thoughts had taken on a greater depth than before.

There was an eclipse of the moon the following night. It turned a dull copper-red as it passed through the earth's shadow.

Danielle thought how Matt had once told her what !Kai had told him, that the moon was like a hunter, that when it could not be seen it was away hunting – and now? the hunter was bleeding.

Danielle felt that war had quickened Matt's senses. She felt it was something like the elevated state of awareness induced by drugs. War could be just as addictive perhaps, she thought. It made whatever else life offered, in the way of delight or torment, pedestrian by comparison.

A few days later, Matt and Andy were scouting across the border trying to follow up further information on guerrilla transit camps obtained via James's office.

They had taken enough water and food rations for three days, had eked them out to five days and found themselves remaining there for seven – the last two days without food and with very little water.

They found nothing of intrinsic value, but Matt decided to stay in there as long as possible – hoping. Nevertheless, apart from enabling

James to classify his sources, they had ascertained nothing they could act on.

Weary with heat fatigue, dizzy with lack of water, Matt retraced his steps to the dry riverbed he and Andy had passed several hours earlier.

By the lowest bank in a rocky bend, he prodded the river bed with a stick, looking for water. When he was on the verge of giving up he thought of his childhood days with !Kai. The thought compelled him to keep prodding, and then his stick glistened with the tell-tale signs of water below the surface. He dug a hole almost hip deep before the sand felt wet, and digging deeper still water slowly filtered into it.

'You look like a warthog,' Andy said with a laugh, looking at Matt, on his knees digging into the earth as if with his snout.

Matt felt himself wince at Andy's lapse of bush sense by talking out there, and in enemy-controlled territory too!

He perforated the pithy inner divisions of a couple of long dry reeds with a thin younger reed. After they had all drunk as much as they could, he shored up the walls of the well with stones and placed a large tight-rolled ball of grass in the centre to prevent sand filling it again. The two hollowed reeds protruding through the surface when the hole was covered were all that could be seen of his workings once the sun dried the wet sand once more; unless known for what it was, it appeared nothing more than other reeds in the river bed. They would have water until up-lifted.

When Matt had taken a back-bearing from two prominent land features, accounted for magnetic variation and worked out their position on the map, he passed the co-ordinates to James.

James said he might not be able to get there until the following evening as Rotor and Jacob were having nagging problems with the helicopter since it was last shot-up, and there was no replacement available as all other helicopters were involved in military actions elsewhere in the country.

Matt felt the most serious possible problem, that of lack of water, had been solved but they were still weak with hunger from exertion in the heat.

Now they waited in the semi-shade of *musasa* and *munhondo* trees, beside the glaring tawny sand of the river-bed. But still the soporific heat found them. Heat blunted the mind and constricted around the lungs.

Matt could sense !Kai sitting beside him from a past occasion in the bush, remembered his nostrils inflate. Something, someone had been close by then; Matt felt something, someone close by now. He scrutinised the thick bush and the long dry reeds.

It was a while before he saw a little suni antelope, smelling of musk, cautiously step from the reeds and stare at him. He stared back. Neither moved. And then it darted off into the reeds once more.

He would have shot it if it wasn't for the noise that might have attracted unwelcome visitors; recollecting his previous encounter with the border guards, he preferred not to be acquainted with them again.

Sun spiders dashed about erratically on the cracked and blistered ground, as if the ground was too hot to stand still on. A rock lizard appeared from a crevice in front of them, its belly pulsing softly. It moved from the hollow of shade on to the sun-baked granite, its head characteristically bobbing up and down.

'Good looking *chidhambakura*,' !Kai would have grunted with satisfaction.

Matt thought how he and Andy would need to eat if they were not up-lifted. They had to keep their energy up in order to survive if they came under attack by a border patrol.

Matt placed a carefully selected stone, smooth and of acceptable weight, into an impromptu sling, whirled it around his head for it to gain velocity, and released one end, allowing the stone to fly free. It struck the lizard's yielding side and knocked it off the rock into the bush. He rose from his sitting position, walked over to where the lizard had fallen, and picked it up.

!Kai would have praised the once-living lizard, humbly apologetic that he, !Kai, a mere other creature should have deemed it necessary to take its life. But if one was to live one had to eat, and all living things ate other living things.

Matt tucked the lizard into his pocket, and sat down to await the appearance of another.

'Let's hope James arrives before I'm forced to watch you eat the bloody thing,' Andy said.

James arrived by helicopter the following morning.

On returning to the office, Matt and Andy were immediately debriefed by James. At the end of it, James agreed to Matt's request to see if he could get the airforce to do an aerial reconnaissance further across the border.

Before going back to the farm, Matt gave himself a precursory wash with soap and water in a basin of the toilet room adjoining James's office – for immediate appearance's sake rather than cleanliness, only attending to those parts of his body that weren't covered by his clothes – face, hands and back of neck. He didn't want to be too conspicuous driving through town. But even then, without mineral turpentine, camouflage cream remained beneath nails, in the hair, ears, and in the lines and pores of the skin.

He telephoned Danielle from James's office advising her that he had returned and to expect him home shortly.

He didn't always do that, so he wondered why he had done it now, especially since things had changed between them. In the beginning he liked to surprise her by just arriving back home.

He was about eleven kilometres from the farm when he slammed on brakes and skidded on to the earth verge of the tarred road. He pulled the steering wheel round full-lock and with the rear wheels spinning up dust behind, did a U-turn and went back the way he had come.

He had decided at that precise moment, with no forethought, that he would go to the big city, civilisation, yet another world. It was Friday afternoon. He remembered the Friday nights out with the boys in the old days. He wanted to find a piece of that action again.

He pulled into the parking area of the hotel. He went to the bar, ordered a beer and then went to the telephone. He made another call to Danielle.

'I won't be back until Monday,' he told her.

'You're going out again, already?' The voice came across to him through the receiver, sounding thin.

'No.' He could have lied. He wasn't sure why he hadn't. 'I'm going away for a while.'

'Where are you going?' The voice sounded hurt.

''Way.' He realised how much a part of his speech monosyllabic statements had become. He felt he should say something more. 'I need to get away. Just for a weekend,' he offered in consolation.

There was an awkward silence.

He remembered the reasons for his never having taken a break away with her. But now he thought he'd have to take the chance and be damned, or be damned anyway, for he felt that if he didn't follow his instincts now he might crack up under further stress.

He could visualise Danielle sitting there, with that 'what have I done?' expression that never failed to find the guilty part of him so that he would comfort her. But somehow he did not feel that way now. He was conscious of fighting against any vulnerability of emotion.

'I'll see you,' he said.

'Yes,' she said. Her voice was weak.

Matt drained his glass of beer in a few seconds, paid the barman, and walked out of the hotel.

He couldn't wait to get out of town.

Outside, the heat struck him after the cool air-conditioned comfort of the bar. It was heavy to breathe.

Over 300 kilometres of wide tar lay before him, but it wouldn't be long before the sun set and driving would be cooler.

Crossing the road and railway junction with its sign CROSSING WITH BOOMS, he found himself grinning almost hysterically, wondering what would happen if Mumvuri ever came to see the sign – a couple of command-detonated explosions perhaps, he thought.

He took the road joining the low and high *velds*, on to the watershed.

He came to thinking how nothing was the same any more, how things had changed.

The bituminous surface of the road looked sticky in the heat. It shimmered with mirages of water in each dip, but it was dry, all dry, no water anywhere.

Wisps of vapour, like phantoms in the sky, vanished almost as soon as they had formed.

Danielle had changed.

Everything had changed. Nothing was the same any more.

> *Aiva madziva ave mazambuko*
> *Aiva mazambuko ave madziva*
> What used to be pools are now crossings
> What used to be crossings are now pools.

Night padded on like a dark cat, and was soon lying across the road.

There, up ahead, a pride of lions that had strayed from a nearby game reserve and were warming themselves on the sun-saturated tar, which had absorbed the day's heat, appeared in the beam of the headlights. A sleek lioness, her body fixed, muscles tense, compressed, ready to spring, firm in her shanks, stared, motionless, into the headlamps. He edged the Land Rover on slowly. A lion with a heavy tousled mane heaved himself lazily to his feet, stood motionless, stared into the headlamps like the lioness, and then padded off the road into the dark bush, lioness and four cubs following, walking away from Man and manmade machine as if in disdain.

Matt checked the mileometer. Less than 100 kilometres to go.

The occasional military vehicle approached from the opposite direction, passing with a dazzle of lights.

Alone in the Land Rover Matt's mind wandered. He thought of Danielle. There were things beyond his control. If he allowed himself to think about them they worried him. Worry was debilitating. He had to stop thinking about them, about her. How better to do that than to go away? Where better to go to do that than the big city? He could go there and find himself not concerned about those things that the city found cause to be concerned about. It would be as if he were immune. It seemed logical to him. He laughed aloud to himself, alone in the Land Rover. Then the whine of the tyres on the tarmac, and the constant reverberating growl of the engine filled the silence that followed. Another oncoming troop-carrier's headlights flashed past. He was left in the dark once again, and he was aware of it.

The band of black road, parted by the white dashes of the central demarcation line, came on at him.

In the distance was the glow of the neon-lit city against the base of low cloud cover.

The city!

There too was one big killing ground, where clawing and biting, the greater civilised ate up the lesser civilised.

Twenty minutes later he passed through the outer suburbs, dual carriageways lined with streetlights, traffic islands and robots, and rows and rows of fenced houses crowded one upon the other; houses, with fragile glass windows, and burglar bars that could be snapped off in a second with a pair of bolt-cutters; houses, with doors, doors with locks that would break apart with one well-placed strike of a five-kilogram hammer; doors with safety-chains secured by a couple of screws that would snap from the wooden door frame with one kick of a booted foot.

Civilisation in Africa, a sore which in time would heal, a fugitive interruption of the darkness.

A neon light flickered and went out.

He hadn't really thought about it, about dying that is. Never really at the time, only afterwards. It was at times like now, now that he was away from it, that the war came to him in all its unvarnished reality. To escape it he fixed his mind on the blocks of flats, garages, shops, high-rise office blocks, blocks, blocks . . . blocks. Claustrophobic blocks leaning in on him. Streets lined with jacaranda. He thought of the farm's driveway.

He drove through the city, its sound hollow inside his head. Night traffic had turned the streets into rivers of artificial light. Where the city stood, was once bush.

People were rushing, just like those he had remembered seeing the last time he was there. But they had seemed different then. Perhaps it was because they *had* been different then, were different now, but he thought it was more that he had been different then, was different now. People rushing, rushing from block to block, back behind their pitiful fences, barricaded against the invasion of the 'outside', prisoners behind walls they had made with their own hands. They shielded themselves from the ultimate truth; that the world they strove so hard to construct was doomed to degeneration and decay.

What were they all rushing for? Flat soufflé, scratch on the Mercedes, to theatres of illusion, to cinemas of celluloid life? Rushing, rushing, so many mechanical people, all engrossed in their own inconsequentialities, their own trivialness. They could not know what it was to live unless they knew daily what it was to die. Most were going through the mannerisms of riskless half-living simply to preserve life, its length but not its quality.

Housewives there had been buying pre-slaughtered animals, even pre-cooked animals, for so long that they had become out of touch with death in perhaps its most important form – as food, in that everything fed on something else. In the process the flesh of animals had come to be labelled as naturally non-living pre-packaged meat with names like venison, beef and pork, and dead-man in his protective coffin was artificially prevented from his constituents returning back to the soil to contribute to the natural cycle of life – even in death he was detaching himself from it.

Matt made his way through the suffocating, pushing, hooting, screeching of brakes, revving of engines, exhaust fumes, prohibitions and commandments of white words and lines on narrow tracts of black tar, controlled by ambers, reds and greens, authoritarian lifeless robots.

The city's five-star hotel appeared before him, its many floors overlooking the central park on one side and the city centre on the other. 'Clays', as they called it in military slang, its distinctive shape that of the prominent convex bulge of the Claymore anti-personnel mine. It stood there, a symbol in southern Africa; like the Claymore, it carried within it the seeds of its own destruction.

The sound of the Land Rover engine reverberated hollowly in the basement parking. Everything about cities seemed hollow. And it was that hollowness which had brought him there – an artificiality that you could not injure in any real sense of the word; not deeply, for it had no depth.

He booked into a suite at the top and on the end, nearer to space and the stars, away from the milling, passing to and fro of the lower floors, not boxed in by the sound of screwing above and below and behind, radios and TVs blaring loudly through paper-thin walls that divided the press of humanity, the personal lives of people.

'No luggage?' the receptionist enquired with the quizzical lift of a delicately plucked eyebrow.

He shook his head.

'Any firearms?'

'No,' he lied.

Cities unnerved him.

Not going up to his suite, he went straight to one of the hotel's bars; the posher one.

Matt suddenly remembered he hadn't washed apart from his face and hands and back of the neck for over a week, that he must have smelt like something that had died long ago.

The barman gave him a questioning look.

The man in the black bow tie with the pearl stud and dinner tails, standing to the right of him looked down at Matt's foot propped on the bar footrail as he leant against the bar counter drinking his beer. The leg of his trouser had risen up to reveal a sockless foot in a *velskoen* and a bare leg a shade of grey-brown, a crust of camo-cream, sweat and dirt. He grinned to himself and did not withdraw the foot. The man in the black bow tie with pearl stud, and dinner tails, pulled a face and moved away.

Matt ordered another beer. He needed to get drunk.

On the other side of him, on his left, a voice whined plaintively.

Matt turned sharply on the man attached to the voice. The man had an anaemic look about him, a little boy's face buffed with a powder puff, effeminate hands leaping to his delicate gold frame glasses that persistently slipped from his upturned nose, and hips too small. To Matt, there was something obscene about the man's femininity.

One of James's adages came to mind – 'Never underestimate a man, particularly when he's a fool or a jerk' – and he laughed out loud, alone.

He drank the other beer slowly, looking round him at the other people in the bar. There were a few men in full military uniform. Others in collar, tie and jacket. He realised that he wasn't wearing any rank or insignia and no belt. The Team didn't have any ranks, insignia or stable belt. Partially dressed, the military police would love to remind him of the fact that he should have been properly dressed, no questions, no excuses, a night in the stocks, he knew. He noticed carefully polished shiny shoes, and thought of James.

He looked at the swallow of beer left in the bottom of his glass and pushed the glass aside with an expression of distaste. He knew that what he needed only a woman could give, the softness of a woman's touch to bring him back from a hard non-resilient world.

Danielle was over 300 kilometres away.

He swore the situation and the drinking off for the night, but when he left the bar he felt that he had abandoned his only friend.

He went up to his room and was asleep almost immediately.

The next morning Matt was up early and had breakfast. He turned down the customary offer of coffee or tea and asked for a beer.

He finished eating in time for the opening of the banks.

With a little surprise, he remembered it was Saturday. Saturdays were only half-working days in the city, and then there were Sundays which were no working days at all.

He found himself avoiding stepping on the joints of the pavements as if each one was a trip-wire.

Matt left the bank with a couple of thousand in notes stuffed in his pockets, divided in terms of their number against thieves or muggers, and headed through the shopping mall, ducking in and out of shops.

In the next hour he had purchased a couple of casual jackets, a couple of pairs of shiny shoes, a few shirts, a couple of ties, a couple of pairs of trousers, a couple of leather belts, underpants, socks, razor, toothbrush, a strong carbolic soap and a bottle of turpentine, all the necessities to become just another face in the city.

Back on the street, he saw a young black boy, shabbily dressed, pass directly between two white businessmen dressed in pinstripe suits and speaking to one another animatedly outside the entrance to a building society. They swore at the boy, calling him an 'impolite kaffir bastard'. Matt could tell by his manner and the way that he was dressed that he was a rural boy plainly unaccustomed to city life. In his home environment, which was no doubt ravaged by war and hence his exodus to the city, he would have passed between two elders in the same way he had done those white men, to show that he harboured no harmful intentions, as if voluntarily passing through a gauntlet.

Further on, Matt saw a black boy avert his eyes respectfully when addressed by his employer. The employer slapped him about his head, misreading the boy's failure to hold his gaze, a sign of respect and a declaration that the boy felt he was not of equal social status, as a certain indication of the boy's 'shifty character' and thus that he had been the one who was responsible for a theft. The man told him as much. Ignorance, thought Matt. Ignorance that would lead to fear and fear to hate. Europeanisation had imposed itself upon Africa with no regard for her own particular conditions of being. To his anguish the black man found that every white man, no matter how coarse his tongue, no matter how base his ways, no matter how low his purpose, was regarded above him.

Matt found himself remembering !Kai's sons' aspirations to become white. Po and Kut were somewhere in that city. Somehow the black man had been made to feel inferior and that his only way out of such a condition was to become white. Matt felt the answer was not to become white but for them to become more black, to get back in touch with their own ways and traditions, and to do it well, to become the best of what they were.

On the pavements, people were still rushing about in different directions, as if they still had matters of dire importance to attend to.

A man hurried past him with a bottle of single malt showing out of a brown paper packet. Matt found himself accosted by an image of water swirling into an empty water-bottle dipped in a stream. He wondered if the man knew how good water could be.

241

He thought how, irrespective of the world out there, the city went about its own code of existence.

He watched his feet stepping along the pavement, and was jostled by faceless people all competing for the next footstep of concrete. Concrete had claimed them, partitioned them, defined the parameters of their existence, laid down a law of confines. It was lived-in-concrete, like a vast tomb, a memorial to a society that lived only to construct its burial chamber, and hide from the knowledge of it.

Scurrying people breathed in the carbonised air that had formed them. Depilatory-clean girls, smooth-limbed, wore skimpy skirts and see-through blouses . . .

He went back to the hotel, showered and scrubbed himself with mineral turps and carbolic soap, shaved and changed.

He looked at himself in the mirror. He was a different man – on the surface.

He ate a leisurely lunch, an enormous almost-raw T-bone steak that left little room on the plate for potatoes in their jackets and a simple salad, out on the patio, in the shade of a bright yellow sun umbrella. The sky was an empty blue. The aroma of the charcoal grill and grilled meat, women at other tables in clean-flowing light summer dresses that accentuated lithe bodies, and everything, the relatively tender rump steak, succulent with a little marbled fat, Super A, the meat of cattle four teeth or younger was not as good as on the farm but good enough. He seldom seemed to get a straightforward steak on the farm. The potatoes, the salad, the smell of grilled meat, the picture, he washed down with pints of draught and an after-lunch toasted cigarette, plain not filtered.

That afternoon naked in the sweating heat, he lay on his bed, the windows well open to allow the wafting breeze from the park in, scarcely able to cool the suite. He knew that if he looked out the window he would see the pool deck far below with all the semi-naked bodies of women in bikinis.

He didn't look out of the window, he just lay there. He slept.

When he woke it was almost dark. He stared out the wide open windows at the sky. The curtains on either side hung motionless. There was not so much as a breath of a breeze to disturb them. He got up and walked over to the window. Outside, there in the city, the dim glow of the streetlamps, the neon sidewalks, car lights and the filtered light from behind closed curtains glowed brighter with the falling of dusk. Down on the pool deck there were fewer semi-naked women.

He had a cold shower against the afternoon's sweaty sleep, dressed, donned a jacket, and went down to dinner at the hotel's most salubrious restaurant. He sat at a corner table; he always sat at a corner table. It meant that no one was behind and that he had a clear view to the front; and none was so vicious as a wild animal if cornered.

Without bothering to consult the menu, he ordered the inevitable almost-raw steak, potatoes in their jackets, a salad and a beer.

Waiting for his steak and drinking quietly, he looked around him at the others in the restaurant. There were families and there were couples in evening dress, couples smiling at each other, hands interlocked across tables, couples conversing affectionately. At the very next table sat a plastically beautiful woman, her face painted on precisely, her hair coiffured. She sat, not a fold of her dress hung out of place, *dernier cri*, not a fingernail showing cracked or chipped nail varnish. Her tan looked as if it followed the sun from summer in one country to summer in another; but when Matt studied her more intently he noticed that it was a little too carrot-like, the sort of tan that came out of a capsule, a tube or a sunlamp. She had a gold, diamond and Sandawana emerald dress ring, that even though it was lifeless rock put the green of her eyes to shame; her watch was gold with a diamond digited face. A diamond pendant on a delicate gold chain nestled in the cleavage of what looked like, to all intents and purposes, young and firm breasts. Matt decided that her face and figure were too perfect, the sort of 'perfection' in a human being that you couldn't trust for fear of it being manufactured, engineered in a technical world where any deception was possible.

She sat with a man who comfortably fitted the stereotype of a wealthy international business executive, a whizz at manipulating the stock markets – paper gains and paper losses; well-tailored clothes, manicured appearance, carefully trimmed moustache (hair by hair?), and grooomed head, not a wave out of place. A force ten wind couldn't have unsettled it. Poor woman, no tidal waves there, Matt grinned. And the man too was tanned in a similar fashion to that of the woman; not so much tanned as shit-coloured, Matt smiled again to himself. At the table a chef expertly attended to a flaming crêpe Suzette. Matt could smell the brandy.

He thought how, as far as he had come to be concerned, food fell into two categories, edible or non-edible. There were no degrees, although he was capable of appreciating cordon bleu cookery he found no necessity for it. Desire for certain tastes went no further than a physiological need for sugar or salt, not determined by a fastidious palate. Fancy cuisine generally pandered to the senses, merely creating the illusion of nutrition, not nutrition itself; and in the city people placed so much importance on it, while in the country people ate what they could. A sick body was sick no matter how much the surface was painted with cosmetics. An invalid would not get better simply on what made him appear better, but on what actually made him feel better.

Civilisation had created many absurdities, he thought. The bush, bloated with meaning, was of as great significance as Truth, as Good or Evil, and it waited with the patience of Time itself for the passing away of the sorry invasion that was civilisation.

Danielle had fallen into the habit of pampering him with 'something special' whenever he returned from the bush. How could he tell her that food just didn't mean anything to him any more?

After dinner he commenced a pub and nightclub-crawl. It was after midnight when he arrived at yet another nightclub. On the dancefloor, close couples shuffled body to body, and some mouth to mouth. Matt glanced in the mirror behind the bar. There was always a mirror behind a bar! Sitting at a table away from the band was a woman dressed in a red evening gown, low-cut back, plunging neckline. It clothed her like the soft skin of a cling-peach. He turned and faced her directly. His glance dropped from her face, over her body, over her legs showing through the provacative slit of her dress, to her feet, and rose up over her again, to meet her eyes once more. He saw them momentarily flicker. She was aware that he was not just looking but inspecting, touching. He did not withdraw his gaze. Those eyes of hers were inviting him over, he felt sure of it. He went over. He looked at the two whisky glasses on the table in front of her, one empty with lipstick around the rim, the other half full with no signs of lipstick. She noticed the direction of his observation.

'He's gone,' she said.

Matt ordered her a drink and sat down.

He noticed the band of pale skin on her wedding-ring finger. Involuntarily his mind recalled the sister at the mission whose wedding ring had been removed from her hand, with the finger. He thrust the recollection forcefully aside, but only after it had registered; there was nothing he could do to prevent it.

They talked, but the attention of neither of them was primarily on what they were saying, and both were aware of the fact. As she reached for her drink her hand moved almost accidentally across the cloth of his jacket sleeve, as if she had momentarily stroked his arm, but he couldn't be sure.

The band were playing slow, after-midnight stuff.

'Come,' said Matt, taking her by the arm and leading her towards the dancefloor. She resisted. But only long enough to kick off her shoes. Matt thought how it was the sort of thing Danielle would have done. On the dancefloor, he could feel her sway towards him, the tips of her breasts just touching his shirt front where his jacket hung open. The floor vibrated under his feet with the base tone of the music. He abandoned himself to it, to the effects of alcohol and the perfume that filled his nostrils, pungent and warm from the body of the woman he held. Looking down at her, he found it hard to keep his expression fixed as he noticed her nipples harden, showing clearly through the flimsy material of her dress. He raised his eyes to hers and saw at once that she knew what had been going through his mind. She moved closer against him. He felt the engorging in his trousers. She did not pull back, rather moved against the hardness there. He felt her leg, bare from the fall of the slit dress, against his own. He felt he could endure no more without throwing her on her back and mounting her there and then. He pushed a hand into a trouser pocket. She saw him do it and he could see that she knew why.

'Let's go,' she said.

They went back to the hotel, to his suite. Their mouths found each other's even before they were through the door. He kicked the door to. Her fingers unzipped his trousers. He unhooked the back of her dress and it slid to the floor. Her breasts naked, he caressed them with his lips, tasted her body, flavours of urgency.

In bed, he thought of her as something wild, like a wild cat, though not exactly dangerous. She had a cat's eyes. He suddenly felt he had identified their quiet fiery assurance, wary, watchful. She knew what she wanted and she took it. Nut brown eyes, with a kernel of fire, he thought, and he thought of Danielle's warm gentleness, not a wild idolatrous fire, warmth not a burning destructive heat that would consume others along with itself, would not endure.

She lay back on the bed, the dark triangle marking her vulva luring him irresistibly, her golden skin like the soft buff belly of a leopard exposed invitingly to a pack of wild dogs. Her eyes held his. Her strong, supple limbs and sharp claws were ready to rip him apart and toss him aside. The leopard, a nocturnal hunter, growled when hungry, and she was growling then. He looked at the glorious body with regions of light skin where a bikini covered them. Was she one of the semi-naked women in bikinis he had seen at the pool? He saw Danielle with her all-over tan after skinny-dipping in the river. Always recollections, so inopportune, he couldn't escape them. Her insurrectionist tongue was in his mouth again and all over his body. She was under him, over him, beside him, coming on and on, relentlessly.

When he woke with a strange woman in his bed he couldn't immediately remember how she had got there. The only clear sensation was the need to empty his bladder.

When he came back into the room he saw her sitting up in bed, smoke trickling from her nostrils. Danielle didn't smoke.

He couldn't remember the woman's name. Had she even told him?

'Pass the cigarettes,' he said.

Instead, she lit him one and passed that to him.

'Good morning,' she said.

He couldn't recall having heard her voice the night before, only a purring, growling; moans, groans of sexual conflagration. He looked at her, studying her. She returned his gaze undaunted. First thing in the morning she looked faded, make-up smudged, nothing like he had imagined the night before. The sheet came to her waist, the upper part of her body bare, propped up against the headboard. Her dark, long hair, dull, not bouncy, not sleek and shiny like Danielle's hung limp over her shoulders. Breasts not firm and pointed with dark areola and hard cherry nipples, as he had remembered, taken into his mouth, they sagged a little, from how much pounding?

He took his eyes off her, and out of the need to occupy them with an alternative focus of observation, looked around the room. The ashtrays were full of cigarette butts. There was an almost empty bottle of Black & White. There was an ice bucket that now contained only stale water. And there were glasses, made opaque with the fingerprints of frequent use. There was lipstick on the rims of both glasses. He remembered how much they had drunk, both of them, she as much as he.

The cigarette smoke tasted foul in his mouth. He stubbed the cigarette out.

The night before? The only way he could think of describing it was to equate it to a cat fight, yeah that's right, a cat fight.

He took her again.

Afterwards, he phoned room service and ordered a huge breakfast, everything they had on the menu, and a Bloody Mary. He lifted his eyebrows towards her.

'The same,' she said.

'Do you know what I've ordered?' he asked in disbelief.

'Just about the whole kitchen it seemed to me,' she answered him. 'I'm famished. You're responsible for that.'

He ordered for two. A while later there was a knock at the door.

'Come in,' he called out.

She entered, but only far enough to see what she had stumbled on and then withdrew with a startled 'Sorry!' She wasn't room service.

Absolutely unprepared, it took Matt a few seconds to register who it was. As soon as he did, he bounced up naked out of bed, snatching up a sheet around him, and without pausing to think, darted down the passage. She was nowhere to be seen. He found himself by the elevators. They were in use, going down. He pushed the elevator button anyway and stood there aimlessly. There were the surprised faces of an elderly couple staring at his sheet-clad form as the lift eventually arrived back up and the doors opened.

'Wrong button,' he mumbled, and turned back to the room.

If he had caught up with her he had no idea what he would have said. He searched around in his mind for an explanation, and found that he didn't have one. People change but their propensity to read wrong into any given situation they do not understand does not, he said to himself. He needed someone, she needed someone, that was all.

When he got back to the suite he found that the woman had gone, clothes and all. She was smart enough to get the hell out of there, not wishing to get involved in any marital or lover fracas, for that is how it must have seemed, and what she must have thought.

He was angry. Suddenly Elaine had caused him to be alone. And with two breakfasts, he thought wryly. There they were, parked on a trolley in the centre of the room. Suddenly all the taste had gone out of the weekend.

That afternoon he booked out of the hotel. When he went down to his Land Rover in the basement parking, he felt empty.

With a quiet melancholy he beheld the raging letters BASTARD written on the windscreen in lipstick. He knew the lipstick to be Elaine's 'capricious red'.

He arrived back early in the morning.

He was walking along the passage to James's office when he bumped into Elaine walking towards him on her way out. The word 'bastard' stuck in his mind like a burr in the fur of a dog.

She glared at him and made as if to walk straight by without so much as a word, disdainful.

He took hold of her by an arm.

'I'm sorry,' he said.

The glare did not leave her eyes when she spoke. 'The one you should apologise to is your wife,' she said cuttingly, and then, 'But don't you dare say anything about it to her. You bear the guilt, she's my best friend and I wouldn't like to see her hurt. It would maim her.'

There was a pause in which neither said anything, just looked at each other.

'Besides,' she said, breaking the deadlock, drawing in a breath, 'I don't suppose you'll be going back to the farm now. Andy just asked me to bring his shaving-kit and toothbrush. James wants you here.'

Matt nodded, indicating that he had heard her, but that was all. There wasn't really anything he could say to her to rectify matters, and anyway, he didn't feel that he even wanted to.

'I saw you drive out of the hotel basement on Saturday night. I waved but you obviously didn't see me. I was staying at the hotel for a business convention that same evening. Anyway, I got your suite number from the reception. The following morning after breakfast I saw your key wasn't on its hook so I presumed you'd still be in the hotel. I went up to your suite to say hello and goodbye before flying back home.' She stopped and looked at him. 'What am I excusing myself for, as if I'm some sort of voyeur? If you ever do that to Danielle again I'll tear your eyes out,' she spat and strode past him down the passage and out of the building.

Matt continued up the passage and stepped into Andy's office.

'Thank heavens you're back. James's been insisting that I contact HQ and have all the fuzz in the big city out looking for you – or, as he said, to arrest you.'

Matt stood there.

'We'd better go and see the Old Man together, there's safety in numbers,' Andy said. 'I called Danielle, she said you weren't at the farm, said something about you needing to get away for a while. Then Elaine said something about "surprising" you in the big city.'

They went through to James.

James glared at him, then quite calmly said, 'The aerial reconnaissance crew is waiting for cloud over the valley to clear. We must all be on hand over the next few days to help interpret the photographs, and to act on whatever we find as soon as possible.'

Afternoon.

Still waiting.

They were ready to act, eager to act, but nothing was taking place. The radios were quiet, the phone didn't ring, intelligence reports were mundane, almost banal.

In the air-conditioned operations bunker they were only aware of the weather through technical meteorological reports from the teleprinter.

Andy scrutinised every scrap of information, from every met. report, the routine monitoring of the radio net across the border, to every contact report, before and after they had been through James's in tray . . .

Matt pined for news, any news. He was prepared for anything but that incessant wait. He felt that a ten-tonne truckload of bricks was being dropped on him – one at a time.

He was drinking yet another cup of strong black coffee when the phone rang. James's hand was on it before it had finished its first trill.

It was his wife, Alexandra.

'What the hell are you phoning me on this number for?' he snapped.

'This is the number I've been phoning you on for the past three years,' she placidly informed him.

James looked at the phone, it was the black one not the red. The red one was the secrephone for all top-security calls.

'I was going to ask you how you are but I think I already know.'

Matt heard Alexandra's voice coming from the receiver before he heard it go 'click'. She had hung up.

James looked sheepish.

'You haven't been home for several days,' Andy told him.

James looked at him without saying anything. He turned to his chess set.

Matt looked at him there, surrounded by the walls of his office, lined with shelves of books, indigenous wood furniture, the original Africana paintings on the wall by a renowned local artist, and he felt how James was, in his own way, perhaps as committed to the valley as he was.

James was staring at the pieces on his chess board when Matt picked up the phone, dialled James's home number, and handed the receiver to him.

James looked at him questioningly.

Matt didn't want to see the other wives being rebuffed in the way he had Danielle. But still he couldn't bring himself to phone Danielle himself.

Alexandra's voice could be heard from the other end of the line.

'Will you have breakfast with me in the morning?' James asked.

'Sure,' she said. 'In bed or in the hotel?'

'I'll come over to the house first thing,' he said.

'See you.'

'See you,' said James. He replaced the handset.

He looked at Matt. 'I think it's my turn now to dial your number.'

The red phone rang.

Matt shook off all the bricks in one go.

November

For the next two weeks, with high-powered magnifying glasses, together with the airforce photographic experts, Matt, James and Andy scrutinised every square centimetre of the aerial photographs for 150 kilometres of the valley across the border.

There appeared to be nothing of obvious military interest there. But then again it was easy to overlook the tiny tell-tale signs of a well-camouflaged guerrilla camp catering for at least sixty guerrillas, which they knew had to be there somewhere for information indicated as much. But where?

Mumvuri was known to keep on changing his camp's position and layout.

They accessed all the computer files of guerrilla interrogations and information acquired from other sources, and together they tried to determine where the base camp was most likely to be.

Captured guerrillas who had been commanded by Mumvuri were re-questioned.

At the end of it all there was much conflicting information. The most they could come up with were several possibilities for the new site for Mumvuri's base, at points that showed up on the map as nothing more than collections of *kraals* in otherwise uninhabited untamed parts of the valley to a distance of 120 kilometres across the border.

'There's nothing left for it but a ground reconnaissance. Would you be prepared to go?' James asked Matt and Andy.

'Yes,' said Andy.

'Bearing in mind that the first step you make across that

border your country will be forced to disown you if you should be captured.'

'If I go, I go alone,' said Matt.

'For Christ's sake, Matt, what exactly are you saying?' exclaimed Andy.

Matt felt there was no easy way to tell Andy, so he told him straight out. 'With all due respect, Andy, you have one helluva understanding of intelligence matters, but survival that far into enemy territory requires more than that.'

'Don't cut me out now, Matt, not for the big one. I've been through all kinds of hell with you.'

Matt stared coldly.

James tried to intervene. 'What if you get injured or fall sick? How will you sleep without having someone to watch over you?'

'Out there no one is to carry your weight except yourself. You either live or you die, there's no in-between.'

'I can't believe this is happening,' spat Andy.

Matt was unyielding.

Andy pleaded.

Matt inwardly cringed, and started to leave. It was sickening to see a grown man act the way Andy was.

James put a hand on Matt's shoulder, restraining him.

'The success of this operation is all that counts,' James said, turning to Andy. 'Do you think you can lead a successful mission on your own?'

Andy too was halted in his tracks.

After looking disconsolately around the room, he angrily sat behind the typewriter and typed out something in triplicate. Finally he turned to James and handed him the original and a copy. 'My resignation,' he said.

James didn't even look at it. 'Matt will need all the back-up he can get. Who better to give it to him than someone who has worked out in the field with him? Who better to understand the problems he'll be going through and who other than you would work your butt off to ensure that the information he sends back receives the attention that it should?'

'There's you,' Andy said, turned and walked out.

No sooner was Andy through the steel door of the ops bunker than James put the resignation letter through the paper shredder.

Later that evening, Matt and James were putting together

information that might prove pertinent for the reconnaissance, when Andy came back in.

'I'd like to withdraw my resignation,' he said to James.

'That's five hours off your pay. Don't let it happen again,' James said.

Matt said nothing.

'Information's worth fuck-all unless it's put to good use. If it's big James won't be able to cope with it by himself. It'd better be big,' Andy said, and sat down, picking up where he had left off, as if the past few hours hadn't existed, but he sat now with a face like thunder.

As Matt travelled to the border in the troop-carrier, smoking a final cigarette, he was aware how the *musasa* and *munhondo* trees of the higher altitudes gave way to *mupfuti* and finally *mupani* trees which could best survive in the hot lower reaches away from water. They were a forewarning of the great dryness and heat he could expect anywhere there but at the river, and he would be travelling through the surounding hills above the jungle of the valley floor, well away from the river and water but where movement was easier until he got nearer to each of the possible target areas.

Along the heavy black soils of the valley floor he was then travelling through, he was aware of the impala lilies which alone had flowered during the winter and had been browsed almost to the ground, looking like bonzai baobabs with their bulbous leafless trunks.

Finally the vehicle pulled to a stop at his intended departure point on the border. He looked out across the fences. The fences had been cut in a couple of places, and the land on the opposite side had been burnt by poachers or guerrillas since he had last been there. Tender shoots of blue buffalo grass were rising from the ashes, inviting game to stray across through the breaches in the fences. Both the poachers and the guerrillas killed game for meat; but the guerrillas alone had a further use for their strategy, the game acted as 'pathfinders' through the border minefields. A couple of anti-personnel mines had been detonated, there were two holes and two corpses picked clean by vultures where the mines had been.

Matt picked his way across the border minefield, armed with his AKM folding butt assault rifle, less than a mere three kilograms in weight, five 30-round magazines of ammunition, a 35mm SLR camera with high-power zoom lens, ten reels of fast-grain colour film, radio for transmitting morse messages, and ten days of high concentration rations in a small back-pack.

When he was through, Matt waved once, without stopping, to the anxious faces back across the border, then they were out of sight and he was on his own.

Mukarati (wild syringa) and *muhacha* (mbola plum) had been blackened by fire though they seemed resistant to it. Matt thought water might be found a metre or two beneath the surface of the dry sandy soil, somewhere within the radius of the tree's root system.

Several kilometres later, he sank slowly and silently to the ground and shook out a three-horned devil-thorn that had worked its way into one of his *velskoene* and was worrying the flesh between two of his toes.

He looked like a guerrilla, everything he was wearing and carrying was guerrilla issue.

He thought over the last words that had been spoken before he had crossed over the border.

'You stand a bloody good chance of getting your arse blown off,' James had said. It was his way of saying good luck. 'If you can't survive out there no one can. Is that why you cut Andy out?'

Matt hadn't answered.

'I guess I'll never be sure, will I?' James had said.

Since then there had been nothing but the silence of the bush. Even the most discreet self-made noise sounded vulgar in his ears.

Matt moved on once again, dust and ash blotchy on the horizon. The naked heat pressed down on him, pounded against him. The sun started to dry the sweat on his body the moment it filtered through the pores of his skin; there was a band of green cloth around his forehead preventing the sweat from running into his eyes. Dust had gelled with the sweat on his face. He felt his jaws tire from chewing a piece of sweet tasting *mukute* bark that served to create saliva in his mouth and so stave off thirst. He spat it out into the palm of his upheld hand and put it into a pocket. He felt himself wishing he was like a weevil which never had to drink even though it ate only dry foods, sustaining itself on the metabolic water from its respiratory process. He felt so damned thirsty!

The flow of the major river, seen periodically far below in the valley, could be followed almost as a compass point, but the low gradient of the land elsewhere made for irregular courses of the lesser waterways which had the habit of changing with each new rain, and with each new rain new waterways had the habit of forming.

It was hot, dry and inhospitable. The temperature was perhaps thirty-five to forty degrees centigrade in the shade. The acrid smell of parched earth was strong in his nostrils. Here human life held no tenure. The land seemed to call out to him: 'Bring me not guns or votes. If you are so clever, Man, bring rain.'

From a blushing sky the fire of sunset seeped like blood through a bandage that wrapped the hills.

As he pushed on and on, he was continually taking note of the terrain, deciding where the best use could be made out of it, in case of being engaged in a firefight; broken ground, good cover, he would think to himself at one point; silhouetted on the shoulder of the ridge, stay well clear, he would think at another; the aperture on the boulder there, 'A boy scout with a strong sphincter muscle could stall an entire detachment there for hours' he would say to himself at yet another.

The shallow dry ravine that stretched out before him, filling with night's gutting shadows, deepened.

He made his way through the frail skeletons of stunted *mutengeni* (sour plum) with their thorny branches and their young leaves and twigs bristling with reddish-brown hair, just like Red's. He plucked the miniature egg-shaped fruit as he walked, squeezing the inner fleshy pulp from its red skin into his mouth, spitting out the stone and dropping it with the skin into a pocket. He thought how !Kai had taught him an infusion of the roots would help rid the liver of the bilharzia worm.

Before night gripped the land as tight as it could, he reached an expansive grove of *mutiti* (fever) and *mukute* (waterberry) trees that had been clearly visible for the last few hundred paces, with their dark green leathery leaves. He was counting on the fact that the water table would be high there.

He followed a game trail that wound through the grove to a natural spring that bubbled at its heart, subterranean water forced to the surface by the crystalline rock formation, forming a small pool, flecked in parts with stray shafts of dying light. After a brief respite above the ground the water followed its course below once more. The water was sweet and cold. He drank freely, several times returning to the water's edge, and picking fruit, from the *mukute* trees and from a solitary *mukuyu* (fig tree) invaded by ants. He had a vision of !Kai carefully picking out or dusting off the ants before eating the fruit; not out of fastidiousness.

He rested there as the darkness bonded the gaps between the surrounding tree trunks. The spring was an unexpected relief in a land that was showing more and more of its hostile face. He had expected that nothing would change, not the heat, not the dryness; not the lack of water. And suddenly out of nowhere, when he least expected it, there was a spring, crystal clear, pure and sweet, so much was its unexpectedness, so much was the quality of its water that a single malt could go to hell, he thought. He ate from his ten-day ration supply.

He filled his water bottles and grabbed a couple of handfuls of the blotchy plum-like *mutengeni* fruit from the overhanging branches, soft and pleasant in his mouth. He moved silently, cautiously, like an eland there.

Sweat that had formed in armpits and in the groin, congealed uncomfortably with the increasing coolness of the settling night.

He left the spring to wait out the night away from the chill ground mist that would develop at the spring in the early morning.

The clear night sky was starred with cold, white splinters. With the aid of the constellation of Orion, clearly visible as always when the sky was free of cloud, he worked out his north-south bearing and the celestial equator. With those he was able to verify which direction he was moving in and in relation to what.

He moved on for a couple of hours, but the terrain was hazardous in the dark. He stopped beneath a copse of young *mupani* with leafy heads that would shield him from the formation of dew. Humidity during the day must have been upwards of seventy per cent, and the dewpoint would be perhaps two degrees centigrade; it would be colder than that come early morning, meaning there would definitely be dew.

The darkness was heavy upon his sweating body. But in a few long still hours, dawn would haemorrhage like the fresh opening of an old wound. He closed his eyes and slept, mindless of the hard ground.

He awoke.

Moisture that had formed during the night had collected on the grass about him. He raised himself into a sitting position and with his back propped up against the trunk, he faced the horizon where the early morning sun would soon show itself.

Even before full dawn he went on.

When the sun was above the horizon he felt its primeval warmth begin to seep into his body, and he partook desirously of its energy.

He searched the first of the possible sites for Mumvuri's base camp but found nothing but long-abandoned huts.

Come noon, Matt came across an oozing scar of a ravine. It consisted of stagnant pools in shaded bends where the water that ran beneath the sunbleached sands was driven infrequently to the surface by rock formations below the river bed.

His throat was dry and raw from the acrid dust.

He dug a hole a pace away from the murky water's edge, and let the water filter through into it. He swilled his mouth out with the water. Despite having filtered through the sand, it tasted of acidic grit, of animal urine. He drank regardless. He could feel the warm water almost immediately seep through the pores of his skin, turning to hot, oily sweat.

For some time he had heard a shrill high-pitched whine, not unlike thousands upon thousands of cicadas, but he knew the sound that filled the air was not of cicadas.

There was no wind, yet the air didn't seem to be still, the sheer volume of sound seemed to disturb it. The noise increased as he neared its source. It was painful to the ears.

He crossed the wide empty river bed and moved into the long brittle grass of the once marshy ground of the opposite bank. As he came over the rise of the bank a cloud of birds exploded like ack-ack fire in the sky. They were *chimokoto* (quelea), several hundred thousand, a million, perhaps even more of them.

The air was dense and damp down in the gulley, not unlike the heavy stench of an overcrowded and soiled chicken run in the rainy season. The pestilent small red-billed finch-like birds had formed vast clans, each overlapping the next to form an enormous colony taking up residence in the trees along the river banks. There was a large basin of water there, trapped at the surface, surrounded by round-seeded grasses that had been stripped of their seed and flattened. The light appeared mottled above it. Birds moving in flight obscured the sun, almost eclipsing it.

Countless grass nests weighed down the ends of every twig on every branch of every tree. So great were their numbers that branches had snapped under their weight. The bushes and grass below the trees were encrusted with ammoniac droppings, as blindingly white as salt.

Matt thought how just north of them were tribal villages where the average size of a family's holding with some ten to fifteen dependants each was perhaps little more than two to three hectares, good arable land being the exception rather than the rule. He worked out that the colony of *chimokoto* before him, eating its own weight of small grain a day, could eat five families out of their entire season's cereal crop between a single sunrise and sunset. And it was in a community barter system where one bag of the small seeded *mhunga* (bullrush millet), or *rukweza* (finger millet) fetched two bags of the larger grained maize.

Within a couple of months, when the breeding season would commence in earnest, the colony would consume two to three times as much seed. Towards the end of the season, the summer crops would have attained young maturity, the milky seeds, not yet hard, as if preferred by God specifically for the feeding of young birds.

When the birds descended to drink, they did so in flocks. Some were forced under the water by the pressing mass of little bodies and the simultaneous beating of countless thousands of pairs of little wings. With saturated feathers, unable to break free of the water, they drowned.

Inevitably the colony attracted predators. The birds that drowned, caught up with the river debris on the banks, along with young birds that fell from their nests, would be eaten. That was the law of Africa. What hyenas, jackal, vultures and the other carrion-eaters left, grubs, ants and the weather would attend to. Africa was horrifyingly proficient in her ablutions.

Matt could make out the excited moving shapes of two spotted hyena, their dull tawny colour, their sloping backs, their short manes of hair at the base of their heads. They would eat the birds, skeleton, skull and all . . .

In leaving the area, Matt was watchful for signs of the larger wild cats which would have been attracted by those smaller animals attracted by the birds. Man, after all, it should not be forgotten, was far more of a meal than a morsel that was little other than bones and feathers.

He looked up at the sky. In the past few hours, clouds had formed. An intent breeze was clustering them to the border from which he had just come. Central African air, drawn in by a cool, moist low-pressure zone, was being displaced by north-east winds. The first of the long rains would come before the next dawn.

The clouds trudged across the sky, leaden and brooding.

He craved for the rain, the taste, the feel of it, the sound of it on the ground and in the leaves of the trees. But worse than the sweaty heat would be the torrential cold, the wet that would swamp the land for days to come. The breaking of the waters, after the shy virginity of the dry months that had held back for so long, would soon be upon him. On he went, on and on.

A guerrilla base always had to be constructed at a permanent water-source, guerrillas needed water too, and it was one of the factors that went into the choice of possible sites to be checked by Matt. He surveyed the second of them now.

Rifle cradled in his arms, Matt came down from the hills to the river's edge for the second time since he had crossed the border. Several more tributaries had fed the river in the valley by then and it had grown in size. He squatted in the undergrowth there. The land on either side was riven by gullies. The river followed its rocky course dead-centre between its crusty banks. Elsewhere, there were numerous stagnant pools. He lowered himself into one of them, amongst the debris attracted to the edges. It clutched at him coolly, but stiff with bilharzia. He plucked a water snail from a reed as he left the bank, the small snail that was host to the liver-destroying larva. The cercariae that developed in the liver would pair in the veins and swim against the blood flow to the bladder or the gut where the female would lay her eggs. He squashed the snail between two fingers, and moved through the unmoving pool to the agile river. There he disappeared beneath the water only his rifle held above it. When he surfaced he blew a spray from his lips. The relief from the heat was felt throughout his body.

The river writhed and twisted over its rocky bed, limiting his view to short stretches between the bends ahead and behind. *Murara* palms, their tall slender trunks swollen in the middle as if pregnant, lined the banks, watching him pass. The trees grew best in soils subject to seasonal flooding. He could see the flood-soil rim far out on the banks.

His vision swept the ridges on either side, then returned once more to the river.

Step after step, bend after bend, he moved on, inspecting, trying to determine if there was any guerrilla presence there. He could stumble upon heavily armed guerrillas at any moment if he wasn't careful enough to observe the signs of their presence before they saw signs of his. But there was nothing except the wash of the river and the sun beating down, reflecting off the water and radiating off the rocks.

Clouds continued to bank in the sky, momentarily shielding the sun's heat. The wind that brought the clouds was also beginning to relieve the heat.

He felt his trouser legs chafing the skin of his crotch where sand had collected in the weave of the fabric.

A few hundred paces further he noticed a cigarette box on the left bank nearest to which he was travelling. It was a brand that was only available back home. Whoever had thrown it away was accustomed to crossing the border. It was nothing surprising. The border divided tribal families; they would often make illegal visits to one another, but he didn't think that was the case here, not so far back. He climbed out and inspected it. He noticed that it was between the water level and the upper flood rim level of the last season. Immediately he knew it had been dropped there since then. The cardboard box was not weathered, the red colour had not yet had a chance to fade in the sun, and the grains of tobacco inside had not yet lost all their moisture or their smell. The box had been left there only recently, he finally decided.

He examined the ground and there was the spoor of six men. If it was a patrol it meant there was a military encampment nearby.

Once again he slid back into the water. This time it felt cold. And once again he slid back into his earlier rhythm of silence, as if his thoughts had been loud verbal interruptions.

A gully widened. The bush jungle about the river thickened. There was the sound of a waterfall in the gulley. Certain information received had revealed that Mumvuri's latest camp was near to a waterfall . . . Matt's expectation increased.

He pulled himself out of the river into the undergrowth. His saturated guerrilla battle-dress hung heavily. Sodden boots squelched distressingly loud as he walked, an unnerving extraneous sound to his ears, all out of proportion to its actual volume absorbed in the swirl and splash of the river and the growing sound of the waterfall as he approached it.

He suddenly stopped and sank down low amongst the vegetation.

The parched ground thirstily absorbed the water dripping from him as he crouched there.

Before him, through the trees, white water trickled over an abrupt verge of naked rock, a drop of several seconds into a great natural pool. It was where the gulley met the main river. It was an aesthetic sight, with no roar or aggression, just a graceful soft cascade, pleasing to the eyes and the ears.

He felt the drying effect of the wind evaporating the water on his face, tightening the skin there. The sodden fabric of his clothing began to feel more uncomfortable.

He studied the area for some time but saw nothing that detracted from the natural order of the bush.

He began thinking that perhaps he was wrong about his earlier interpretation of the spoor as a six-man patrol, thought that he was perhaps at the wrong waterfall, how there must have been many waterfalls on the river.

Matt relaxed a little once more, looked up at the sky where clouds were brewing for a storm. He got up and was moving on when he saw it. Its effect on him after telling himself that there was no danger, and having exposed himself to view, was like an electric shock.

Almost completely concealed by a hut-like construction of *daga*, branches and thatch below tree cover, and at the top of a sheer face of rock, seemingly inaccessible from where he was on the other side of the river, was a slight showing of gun-barrel blue metal. Careful to remain under cover, he moved position to get a better view around the rocks and through the trees. It was an anti-aircraft battery, partly dug into the floor of the hut. It stood high above the lower stretch of valley, overlooking it, guarding it. There was a ZPU 14.5mm heavy machine-gun configuration – four barrels – covering a considerable sweep of the sky above the valley.

It was just a single anti-aircraft emplacement, the only one he could immediately see, but to Matt it was evidence of the where-abouts of a guerrilla base camp in the valley. His heart beat faster with a surge of adrenalin that the knowledge had brought. It had to be Mumvuri's. He couldn't help feeling how after a year of being toyed with by Mumvuri, he was there in the lair of Mumvuri himself; Mumvuri's weak spots, the guerrilla breeding ground for the valley.

The guerrilla incidents of the past year flashed through his mind. After the death and destruction, the dissolution of his marriage and friendships, having been made so terrifyingly aware of his

261

inadequacies, having been outwitted again and again it had taken more and more effort, more and more willpower, just to keep going, called on everything he had ever learnt from !Kai, everything he had ever learnt about the need to persevere in life and now at last he was there – Mumvuri's refuge and nerve centre.

He couldn't prevent a feeling of triumph overwhelming him. He couldn't help feeling that no matter how many Mumvuri's victories had been, they amounted to nothing in comparison to the blow that Matt could deliver in return.

Just as the feeling had warmed him, it suddenly left him cold. It was one thing to be there thinking thoughts, another thing entirely to turn those thoughts into action. There were guerrillas there waiting for him to make a mistake, although they didn't know it, when they would pounce on him and tear him apart like wild dogs at a hare.

He could just make out, after searching further, an A-frame *basha* down there in the valley. There was a fire burning.

He took out the camera from his small canvas back-pack, unwrapped the telescopic zoom lens from its oilskin, fitted it to the camera, and balanced it in the forked branch of a bush for stability.

The fire was a cooking fire beneath a lean-to shelter. Four armed, camouflaged forms hustled up to it. The flames played shadows beneath the branches of the trees, seeming to grow brighter as the sun retreated and the storm built up.

A moving barrage of rain-heavy clouds, pushed on by the north-easterly monsoon airflows, screened the sun which threw its intermittent light on the rock face.

Suddenly self-conscious, he checked that the sun was behind him. It was.

When he was in shadow, there could be no reflection from the lens. He assured himself that he was no more than a shadow amongst shadows.

The clouds, driving and binding together were darker now, if that could be possible, or perhaps it was because there was less light.

Once again, he started moving up on to the hill-line above the valley. He checked for spoor as he moved, keeping well clear of common game paths. Barbed branches tore at him, finding flesh through the tough cotton camouflage uniform. He shivered as the wind cooled and strengthened, penetrating the cold wet layers of cloth.

The sky, dark-rimmed, curling grey and black, was illuminated by soundless flickers of lightning, still some way towards the black sky of the border he had left three days before.

He leopard-crawled painfully slowly along one of the lower slopes, in and out of rock cover, straightening parted grass behind him. Then he watched the activity in the valley, lying flat against the earth, as if part of it.

He had a good view into the valley – a view Rotor, used to the perspective from his helicopter, would have called a 'worm's-eye' one. He could see only a few branch-and-grass shelters scattered beneath the trees, a few wood fires, and a few well camouflaged gun emplacements disguised as huts along the high ground either side of the river.

Nothing to get excited about one might think, but the volume of guerrillas moving in and out of the huts suggested that as information from captives had revealed, there was a warren of underground bunkers there, with a complement of up to sixty guerrillas at any one time.

No wonder an aerial recce hadn't been able to pick up clear evidence of the camp, Matt thought.

Apart from not being discernible from the air, Matt thought how the covered trenches, in the event of an attack, would offer good protection from bombing, mortar and small-arms fire.

He had been there only a few hours and already he knew that his task of supplying detailed information of the camp structure and strength was going to be more difficult than he had anticipated.

He thought if his presence there was to be discovered, even so much as tell-tale spoor, he would not only be in grave danger, but, more seriously, Mumvuri would escape yet again.

Time passed slowly as he examined the valley, when suddenly he winced, slightly, but it was like the exaggerated mannerism of an actor on a stage to his sharpened sensibilities. He saw a small black insect crawl off his arm. It looked just like an ant, a velvet black ant with white spots. But he knew it for what it was, a wingless wasp. It was a sting more painful than a yellow-jacket hornet, many times more painful than a bee.

The silence was strained, as if the seams containing it were about to split. But no sound came from him. He fought against the need to cry out in pain. With the sharp edge of his knife he scraped the sting site clean. If there was to be an adverse reaction he would soon know.

There was considerable swelling and much throbbing, but nothing worse.

Time still continued to pass.

He noticed how the sky and earth were becoming overpoweringly dark. Then there was a streak of silent lightning and with its disappearance it seemed to be suddenly night.

The wind lulled briefly but then was up stronger than before, driving the storm on with a vengeance. The trees tossed and thrashed their heads. The scything wind stripped the thatch from the crudely made *musasa bashas*. It cut coldly through his wet apparel. His body cringed against it.

The clouds were severed by another buckled blade of light. He could see the nicks of battle on the whetted cutting edge. Thunder shook the bruised and swollen heavens.

'Nature talking to us,' !Kai would have said.

'The whore is swearing,' Andy would have said.

Another streak of lightning illuminated the dark bush.

Matt started counting in his mind . . . one thousand and one . . . one thousand and two . . . one thousand and three . . . one thousand and four . . . one thousand and . . . thunder shook the heavens once more . . . five. Five seconds. So, judging by the windspeed, he calculated that the storm was only three or so kilometres away. It would soon be upon him.

He saw the camp fires' hot ash blown about by the wind.

The sky overhead sank lower and lower.

He felt cramp set into his limbs from remaining in one position in wet clothes for too long.

The impending weight of rain sagged heavily downwards, pressing closer and closer.

The electric discharges in the mounting storm made his first radio transmission difficult, and he had to repeat it several times between lightning flashes, but eventually he got through via a mountain relay station on the border, to James who was sitting in the comfort of his office. Matt didn't envy his position there, waiting, not knowing, not being in control. Then he thought how he had deliberately tried to shield Danielle from what he was involved in, so she would not have to bear the burden of fear along with him; her fear would have weakened her and it would have weakened him. He needed her to be strong.

The only way Danielle could explain Matt's change in behaviour towards her was to blame it on the war.

She never knew where he was from one moment to the next any more, only periodically finding out that he was even still alive.

James had told her that Matt was unable to get in touch with her for a while. She wanted to know more, but James couldn't tell her. He told her that if she should need anything she shouldn't hesitate to get in touch with him.

She needed the relationship she had once had with Matt. James was the last person who could help her on that score.

Danielle hated the not knowing. She hated the war taking her place as Matt's wife. She hated knowing that there was nothing she could do but wait. There was nothing she could do to help him if he needed help, nothing she could do if he was dying at that very moment.

She felt helpless, and terribly alone.

In the absence of knowing, she filled her mind with thoughts and fears of events that were in all probability far more horrific than could ever happen to a single man in a single life, and the worry that went with it was exacerbated likewise.

To escape it she tried to think over her day.

In the morning she had gone to see the Vans.

It was difficult for all of them to accept what had happened, and the change it had brought about in Red. He didn't trust himself to speak. He was almost totally withdrawn. His wife and daughter had died and he blamed himself. He hated himself.

Alexandra and Elaine had braved the roads and come over for lunch. It was the first time they had come to the farm since the land mine. The roads were still unsafe, but they said they didn't want fear to rule their lives.

'Danielle, there's something I have to tell you,' Elaine had said almost at once.

There was an awkward silence. Danielle feared the worst.

'What, Elaine? Is it about Matt?'

Elaine suddenly seemed to realise the panic she might have caused. 'Yes, but not what you're thinking – he's fine.'

'Then what?'

'It's just that when I was last in the city, I saw Matt there without you.'

'Oh, so that's where he went. He phoned me before he went.'

'It's not you he was trying to escape from,' said Elaine, 'but the war. Andy's been doing strange things as well. What I wanted you to know is that it's not just happening to you, it's happening to me as well.'

All the men were involved in something again, and as usual the women didn't know what, though they questioned each other to find out what they could piece together from what each had found out individually.

Both Alexandra and Elaine said James and Andy had taken to sleeping at the police station, which, from past experience, meant that something of importance was happening.

For Danielle, it meant that Matt was out somewhere alone.

They tried to comfort her by getting her into a light mood but the weight of the discovery and the uncertainty of things hung heavy on her.

Although they had to leave early, while there was still plenty of light and so that they could catch the convoy on the tar road, they promised to stay in touch, and told her they were there for her at any hour if she should need them.

Danielle looked out the window to the storm growing out there.

She saw a *chongololo*, a millipede. She watched its many legs moving in ordered rhythmic unison across the ground outside. Superstition had it that if someone trod on a *chongololo* there would be rain.

She thought how the farm could do with the rain, but that it could do without it if Matt was out in it.

The rain came out of the darkness in the early hours of dawn.

First the light pre-wetting rain, and then the heavy soaking storm. It came in cutting diagonal volleys, with such hissing force that each drop stung like an assegai. It came in such quantity that it seemed to displace all air and Matt choked and gasped on it. The slope seemed to slide away from him. Brown water swept down into the valley.

The valley swallowed the rain until it could swallow no more, and it too choked on it.

He shivered in soaked clothes that plastered his body. The light jacket, made from the cloth of an old parachute, second to none in excluding cold wind, was useless against the rain. Those heavy assegai raindrops found him even when crouched behind rocks and trees. They stabbed andd sliced. He cursed the rain, and then knowing that it acted as a defensive shield against detection, praised it in the same breath. He tasted the November salt on his lips and it was good. He thought how the rain that fell within the farm's catchment area would flow into the farm's river, and into the valley across the border.

Later that night Matt saw lights moving from hills to the east and down into the valley through the bush and the rain. He didn't know for certain what the lights were but thought that they might be vehicles. It took him half an hour to get to the point where he had seen them.

He came across a track made by heavy transport vehicles through the bush. He walked along the edge of it in the direction the lights had been moving. He observed that during the day the track would be almost entirely concealed from the air by the overlapping canopies of the trees. It didn't appear to have been used for some time. Vegetation had grown on the track since it had last been used, effectively camouflaging it. From the aerial photographs only game trails and footpaths had been observed.

After some distance he heard the high revving of heavy duty vehicles ahead, and after another couple of bends in the track he saw the light from their headlamps.

Making his way carefully on his belly through the rain, mud and bush, Matt got to a position where he could clearly see the vehicles themselves.

Two trucks were trying to tow a third from where it had got stuck in the mud. By the look of a multitude of mud tracks, and the other deep holes that the vehicles' rear wheels had churned, it appeared that one or other of the vehicles now towing had got stuck earlier.

Whatever had happened, Matt was thankful for it, for it had allowed him ample time to catch up with them on foot – over an hour.

He got in closer. The stench of muddy water scalded on exhausts, and of burning clutch plates, was strong in his nostrils.

The two vehicles buffeted through thigh-deep puddles, splashing great bow-waves behind them, revving high to prevent engines stalling and the subsequent decompression sucking water through the exhaust to seize engine blocks. Windscreen-wipers slapped furiously.

In the light of headlights from behind the stranded vehicle, Matt could see through the raised flaps of the canvas canopy into its back.

There were weapons and armament supplies, and he could clearly see several land mines and recoilless rifle shells of the type that had killed Suzanne and Sarie, and deafened Red.

Apart from a driver in each of the three vehicles, there were about twenty others in full guerrilla garb. They were splattered with mud from trying to manhandle the loaded vehicle onto firm ground.

They were all armed, but their weapons had been propped up against a tree as they chopped down branches to place under the wheels of the vehicles to give them traction in the mud. From time to time they were crowded together.

Matt thought how easy it would be for him to open fire on them, killing several, then set the vehicles alight, destroying their cargo. But it could not be. Fate had decreed otherwise. He was only there as an observer. Under no circumstances could he let himself get involved. He would let those truckfuls of guerrillas and armaments go. By a twist of fate Mumvuri himself was no longer the direct target.

He couldn't help but think how it had shades of his first operation with the Team, how he had allowed a single Mumvuri to live in order that a greater number of guerrillas should die, and how he had rued that decision ever since.

He couldn't help thinking how close to possible death those guerrillas were without knowing it. And he thought that perhaps it was that way for all people everywhere, never knowing how close they were to the end.

The guerrillas started to lighten the stranded vehicle's burden, removing armaments from the back. Matt made an inventory of all that he saw – some seven to eight tonnes of weapons and armaments, many land mines and recoilless rifle shells.

It was another hour before the vehicle had been unloaded, towed on to firmer ground, reloaded, and the guerrillas had continued into the valley, with shouts of jubilation and one-fisted black-power salutes, leaving Matt alone in the bush, the rain and the night.

He tried to contact James but weather conditions were against him. There must have been electrical storms on the border mountain range.

The following morning it was still raining.

There was plenty of water, albeit gritty, but one tended not to want to drink what one was swimming in!

Matt had eaten his rations each day since he had left the border, and his pack had become lighter, though, soaked with rain and the more tired he got, it seemed to have become heavier. He ate a little something now.

Where there had been watch-fires in the camp the night before there were now only muddy black puddles of ash.

He saw over fifty guerrillas training there.

Once again he transmitted his report. If his transmissions were being monitored by the enemy in the camp he was not perturbed, since his transmission signal was powerful enough to have been coming just as easily from across the border, and not just from that part of the valley. Intelligence had confirmed that at no time had the guerrilla army been supplied with the sophisticated detection equipment necessary to have pinpointed his actual transmission position.

He saw the three transport vehicles leave later that morning, but he thought the rain must have made the rivers impassable. They returned shortly afterwards, still empty. They were camouflaged by branches and thatch screens where they were parked under heavy tree cover.

The waterfall in the gully, which had been no more than a ponderous trickle the day before, hurtled in a reckless arching leap into the void, frothing and pulling at the air in its perilous drop. The ringing fury of water churned with water and crashing on rock pounded in his ears. With the rain it overpowered all other sound.

How the hell, Matt thought, was a man on sentry duty up there supposed to hear anything?

The incredible volume of falling water struck the rocks and was broken into countless pieces. The pool below it was a graveyard, so full of shattered remains that it could not contain them.

He sat under an overhang of rock that offered some shelter from the rain on the lee of the Mapfupa 'Skeleton' Hills; less wet there. It was raining as much as ten centimetres an hour on the lee; hell, if that was the case he didn't want to be on the windward side. Once drenched, how much wetter could you get? You would need a snorkel!

As he was looking out into the flooded valley, watching the guerrilla activity there, night once again collapsed about him.

Still there was no change in the weather.

His body shivered in sympathetic response to keep warm. But his body was deceived; it had been too cold for too long.

Matt sat in the dark; there was no hope of a fire, not even a cigarette. And there was no sleep.

He felt himself mesmerised by the steady dripping of rain from the overhang. It left a drip-line of small holes under the impact of each drop in the soil. He counted the drips until numbers stormed uncomfortably in his head with unstoppable momentum. He remembered himself as a young boy counting flying-ants as the winged termites broke from the mound of hardened clay that was their nest. He knew by its size that the nest was older than he was. If it were a relatively new nest of a year or two it would have been no bigger than his foot. !Kai had told him. From deep below the earth the flying-ants drove their wings for the light of the gas-lamp hung above the top of the mound high on the branch of a tree, instinctively brought from their nest by the change in climatic conditions; the warm sultry evening, the coming of the storm, luring them on. They came simultaneously from all the mounds around. And then the rains would come, and those that were only then leaving the nest would be beaten to the ground in their nuptial flight by heavy raindrops, losing their cumbersome transparent wings some distance away from the nest, stuck waterbound to the soil. But there too, new colonies would be founded.

He would catch them in the air with !Kai, pull their wings off and scorch a pan of the bulbous thoraxes over a fire. Rich in fatty-protein, they tasted like slightly rancid butter melting in the mouth.

It seemed that night would never end.

Towards the following dawn it stopped raining.

Matt saw an assembly of some 120–130 guerrillas in the valley. A couple of men in civilian clothes seemed to be addressing them. It was apparent that more guerrillas had arrived there since he had. Matt thought how they had arrived unobserved, probably on foot, as the vehicles had not yet been able to leave the camp.

He noted down the date, the time the assembly had commenced and that it was Saturday.

Shortly after sunrise the guerrillas disbanded. He noted down the time.

He couldn't explain the sudden increases in the guerrillas' strength. They were mind-boggling. He could only guess that it was through Mumvuri's camp and through the valley that the guerrillas' wet-season infiltration into the country was to come. He radioed the information through to James.

He continued to shiver in uncontrollable spasms until the sun soaked into him. His clothes steamed.

The earth looked fresh, recovering from its bedraggled wash. Muddy earth began to dry. Wind-blown soil and seeds that had been trapped in hollows and crevices of rock would now begin to germinate, starting life in seemingly the most barren of places. Green grass was already showing itself right across the land as far as the eye could see. Game would begin to scatter far and wide, no longer confined to small patches of greenery beside a few remaining high-saline waterholes away from the river.

He managed to sleep a few short hours as he dried in the sun.

Later that day he continued his observations of the valley.

The guerrillas had spread out in small concentrated satellite groups over several kilometres, dug in and protected at every turn by rocky ground and fully leafed tree cover. Almost every point of high ground he came to was defended, not only by a covered trench system but more threateningly by anti- aircraft gun configurations disguised as huts with thatch roofs that could quickly be removed and walls that could be pushed over in the event of an attack.

He recorded everything he saw and frequently transmitted his findings back across the border.

The earlier the crop was planted the sooner it would be ready for sale and the higher price it would fetch. The problems of pests and disease that came as the rainy season progressed would be reduced the sooner the plants were established, growing strongly.

So, as soon as the rains broke, Danielle consulted with the farm's senior farmhands and commenced the maize planting.

Back and forth the tractor-drawn planters went across the fields, opening furrows, releasing fertiliser, just the right amount in just the right places and seeds just the right distance apart, then lightly closing the furrows and fertilising the surface.

Last thing each day, before anyone could rest, the tractors were cleaned and refuelled, the planters greased and oiled.

That was all there was to Danielle's day – farmwork. Everything that didn't contribute directly to the survival of the farm had to be done away with. In her life there was no longer romance, recreation, not even small talk. Everything had been clipped down to pure physical practicality.

Having no one else to talk to most of the time but the farmhands, never before had she been so aware of her own thoughts. A feeling of powerlessness engrossed her. The bush war was in her back yard, and on her front doorstep.

She phoned her mother. It was a link to life as it used to be for her – a link with civilisation and normality.

By the time she put the phone down again she felt better. But then a helicopter passed overhead. The beating of the helicopter rotor blades in the sky drew her eyes mechanically upwards, even though she was inside beneath a roof.

From time to time helicopters passed through the valley towards the hospital, from the war. She had come to dread their sound, to fear what they might bring. Matt could one day come in that way – a name handed on a clip-board to a nurse, an identity disc around a neck, a shattered bloody form excreted from a bird of prey. She dreaded the day that it might happen, and she hated her fear as if the mere thinking of it might make it happen.

Every day it was not Matt being casevaced in that helicopter she felt as if another spin of the revolver's cylinder in the absurd Russian roulette that was life had come to rest on another empty chamber.

Then, realising the way she was thinking she felt guilty immediately, for though it might not be Matt it had to be someone. She could visualise the face of some other battle-torn young man, the nurse holding his hand, soothingly wiping away two embarrassed but uncontrollable tears of relief from glazed terror-stricken eyes.

She looked out the window. The helicopter was not flying in the direction of the hospital. She released her held breath.

For five days Matt followed the lines of least resistance through the Mapfupa Hills that enclosed the valley, taking photographs and notes of everything he saw: guerrilla strengths, defences, camp layout, and incorporating the slightest detail no matter how seemingly trivial at the time.

Daily he made his transmissions to supply as full a picture as possible of all developments in the valley. If anything should happen to him, James having at least received daily transmissions, would have the necessary up-to-date information to mount a follow-up reconnaissance without the operative or operatives concerned going in there blind.

What he knew now more than anything was that where they had expected there to be one small bush camp there were many small bush camps adjoining one another through several kilometres of the valley and he hadn't seen more than a part of it.

He counted the paces of guerrillas as they walked about different camp structures in the valley, determining distances between the huts, the straw-and-branch *bashas*, cooking shelters, shell-scrapes, ammunition bunkers and gun emplacements. Often he cursed to himself when he was in the process of counting and the man he was using as a measuring rod suddenly altered his course before completing the entire route he had wanted to measure.

On two more occasions, vehicles of troops and weapons arrived in the valley. But what intrigued Matt more than this was that the vehicles arrived by different routes – meaning that each path could be rested for a while, allowing fast-growing weeds, at least, to establish themselves. From the air the tracks would appear now and again through the trees as no more than game trails, or at worst, footpaths.

He saw a vehicle driven sump first on to a nearby rock used in the absence of a jack to have its punctured tyre changed.

Once again he had the opportunity of observing what weaponry was being brought into the valley. He calculated that there were twenty to thirty tonnes more weapons in the valley than the week before.

Almost daily, more guerrillas had arrived. Matt estimated that there were four times the number now than they had initially expected.

Something big has to be going down, Matt told himself.

He logged all comings and goings, even to the extent of recording vehicle registration numbers. There were only a few obvious departures from the camp, and then again only in section strength of eight to ten men. He could not work out whether they were infiltration groups to cross the border, or whether they were merely patrols to safeguard the camp, for he never saw them return; and just because he didn't see them return didn't mean that they were not patrols, for they could have returned without him having seen them.

He finished his rations. He filled his bottles from rainwater pools on the ground, in rock depressions and holes in the forks of trees.

Without more rain to replenish his water points, they were fast drying up.

He photographed everything he could of interest, and now like his food, he had used the last of the film.

On several occasions he had had to avoid detection. One night he was almost trodden on by a member of a patrol. Another night he badly skinned a shin on a tree stump hidden in the grass, and had cried out in pain, unable to stop himself, with a hut only about thirty paces from him. He felt that his conscious discipline over himself must be diminishing with his strength, due to lack of proper food, water and sleep.

He decided that it was time he started thinking of his departure, but the camp was growing so fast before his eyes that he felt it was important that he stayed. Invaluable information would be lost every day he wasn't there.

In the dark of the next morning he made his way into a shallow *donga* that ran like an old prospecting trench, overgrown with bush and grass, almost concealed, close to a group of huts, which camouflaged four 14.5mm heavy machine-guns in anti-aircraft configuration. There was also access to a bunker system.

By mid-morning the sun was like a raging abscess in the sky. Its heat clamped about him, sapping his energy. The earth baked.

As he rolled over, ever so slowly, to relieve cramped muscles, a trouser leg caught on a thorn bush — just the rasping of cloth but it sounded like a fire alarm to his ears. He suddenly felt like stone, unmoving, expectant, but there was no reaction from the huts.

That was at least twice he should have been observed, he told himself. He felt that kind of luck couldn't hold. Once more he thought about departing. He felt his continued presence there was like letting one's life savings ride on consecutive spins of a roulette wheel.

He pocketed his notes and reference map. It had taken on more and more comprehensive a form. He had noted everything: what they wore, habits and customs, even where the latrines were, what they ate and didn't eat.

As he withdrew from there, he heard the distinctive slapping together of wings in groups of three far above his head. He could not see it but he knew that up there in the sky was a flappet-lark intent on courtship. He thought of Danielle. And he thought that he could not have hoped for a clearer omen suggesting that now was the time for him to withdraw.

Dom Van, wearing his old felt bush hat with its broad rim and leopard-skin band, together with Tanny, came around to the farm once again to see how Danielle was coping by herself. It was good of them. They could ill afford the time.

They had grown older, tireder. The vitality that had clung on for so long seemed to be leaving them; even so, they walked with the dignity that was conferred on those who had suffered a lifetime of physical and emotional punishment in their labour on the land.

When she asked how Red was, Dom Van intoned with a motion of his hand, as if to say, 'What can be expected?'

'He's alone in his own world and doesn't like his own company,' said Tanny.

'Tell him I said hello, please,' Danielle said.

'Of course,' Tanny smiled at her. 'He's been getting back to doing the farming, you know.'

'I'm pleased,' Danielle said.

'We're learning sign language.'

'With Red's times of non-talking with Matt in the bush he seems to have a natural way with it,' Dom Van said.

'I'd like to learn as well,' she told them.

'It's difficult to get a fulltime teacher for Red,' said Tanny Van, 'what with the war and everything. But we have some good books. Next time we see you I'll lend you whichever ones you'd like.'

'Thanks,' said Danielle.

'We've invited for Christmas the teacher from the school for the deaf, and some of the other deaf people he met whilst in hospital. There is one young man who also lost his hearing in an explosion.'

'It'll be marvellous to have them around, for us as well as Red,' Danielle said.

They chatted about other things as they drove around the farm buildings with her, offering help wherever they could, but otherwise just enjoying each other's company.

Danielle didn't let on how lonely she felt, how scared she felt, though Dom and Tanny Van seemed to know without having to be told, and it seemed that was one of the reasons for them having come round, despite their own problems.

When they drove back to Spitskop, Danielle was left alone in the big farmhouse and her life felt empty. Her mind seemed full of the mounting tragedy that had befallen the once peaceful and happy valley.

That night corded heavy black rain clouds charged across the heavens back into the valley.

James phoned her to tell her that Matt was still fine. Despite that she felt particularly uneasy, that there was something he was not telling her. She felt how that condition-report on Matt could change by the very next phone-call. What was Matt doing, why couldn't he get in touch with her himself? The not knowing was of the same order as the darkness outside. In it she was frightened, and the fear whittled at her nerves.

She thought how the bush made people seem so insignificant in contrast; but with Matt's refusal to be insignificant, what was going to happen to him?

The bush was effortless yet all-powerful, non-purposeful yet flourishing, birth-giving yet it took life.

Matt loved the bush. No. He'd abandoned himself to it. Was there a difference? She wasn't sure.

She tried to read, tried to engage her mind on something that would exclude the worry, but she found that she just couldn't focus her attention, and kept reading the same line again and again. She gave it up.

She felt helplessly weak and vulnerable. She went through to the comfort of her bed.

She thought over what had been done and what still needed to be done on the farm. The maize seeding had been completed at last. It had taken longer than normal, she knew, but at least it had been done. Another season of insurance concerns, price fluctuations, fears of storm damage, spiralling fuel costs, unavailability of spare machine and vehicle parts, had somehow commenced without any apparent transition from the last.

Over the radio she heard that a nearby farm in the valley had had a number of its cattle hamstrung by guerrilla sympathisers.

She turned off the light.

Darkness came into the room.

She felt snug and warm in bed, but she was thinking of Matt

276

and knew it would be a long time before she would be able to go to sleep.

Outside, the storm came.

Just before dawn, Matt saw the guerrillas assemble once again despite the rain. He noted that once again it was Saturday, the same day as the last assembly, and when he looked at his watch he noticed that the meeting had started at the same time as the previous week. The only thing that had changed was the number of guerrillas. There were perhaps three to four hundred of them.

Matt finally felt that, for him, the area had become grossly overcrowded. He didn't fancy his chances of going unobserved for much longer. He was scared. He was without food. He had used up all his camera film. He was cold, tired and weak, and he didn't want to put what he had already discovered in any further jeopardy.

He felt that what with another rain storm approaching to hinder the visibility of pursuers and to cover his tracks, and with the majority of guerrillas assembled where he could see them and not spread out in patrols throughout the valley for him to bump into, it was an opportune time for him to withdraw.

He moved away, back into the lower gradient land away from the valley, back towards the border, armed with enough photographic evidence to convince the politicians of the necessity for a full-scale cross-border raid, and for the army and airforce commanders to engage in proper planning.

The storm was upon him.

December

Danielle hadn't immediately noticed that it had stopped raining. It had been another grey sky that had rained and stopped raining, and then rained again. The heavy cloud had sunk so low that it had seemed to be just above her head. The rain enveloped everything with a veil. It shrouded Horseshoe Ridge. The clouds would thin to show a clear touch of blue, and just as you started believing that the sun was coming through, the clouds closed and it started raining again.

Danielle felt that the weather mirrored her feelings only too horribly. Alone in the farmhouse, she felt prey to her memories. Past events appeared in her thoughts like flashes of blue, while her present and the future were like dark cloud.

She went into the study, knowing full well that she was deliberately looking for something from her past to cling to. She wanted to observe things as they used to be, to escape the present. Almost lovingly, she stroked the richly grained solid stinkwood desk, the leather chairs, the crystal brandy decanter, the calfskin-bound books, and the cigars in their silver box.

She picked up the Bush Lore manual Matt had been working on, and paged through it. It was so engrossing she sat down in one of the big leather chairs and read for a couple of hours. She was enraptured by the power and simplicity of what was said. What she read was written by a man with a great love and understanding of Nature, of the bush and all living things. He had great perception and compassion. But what disturbed her was that for him, horror and beauty, good and bad, life and death were seen as composites, not

278

opposites. For him the bush was blameless in all things, it was without malevolence. It simply was.

Matt had included a solitary note in the margin, the last time he had been home. 'Nature Has No Heart . . . yet I love her just the same,' was what the note said.

When she paused, looking out the window, Danielle found that it had stopped raining and that she was not so much aware of the outside as she was of her reflection in the window-pane. She was aghast at the drawn apparition that stared back at her. The wide-awake levity of youth had been replaced by a tired oppression. She always used to make sure she looked her best, even when Matt wasn't there, as much for herself as in case he arrived unannounced, but at some particular point she had let herself slide, she thought.

She took one more fleeting look at the face in the window and strode off spritely to their bedroom. She sat down at the dressing-table. Perhaps that's part of the reason why he's lost interest in me, she thought.

She found that it took her longer to look her best now. Before, it was a flick of the hairbrush, some light eye-shadow, now she was using quantities of make-up like a tart.

She felt she was caught up in a no-win situation. Her complexion looked sallow, noticeably older, but Matt didn't like a lot of make-up; he thought it wasn't natural.

How funny it was that you only notice such things suddenly when they must have been happening gradually all the time, she thought.

It had stopped raining by the time Matt reached the same point on the border he had crossed almost two weeks before.

'Anything to declare?' Andy shouted to him as he came through the breach in the fence.

James, Andy, Rotor and Jacob were there to welcome him back. They were all in high spirits, congratulating him from all sides.

'Well done,' said James, shaking his hand vigorously, not wasting words.

'We've finally found our super-gook's hidey-hole,' said Andy amiably thumping Matt on the back.

'Have a smoke,' said Rotor, carefully offering him a single cigarette rather than passing a pack. 'I especially bought them for the occasion.'

'TBFK,' said Jacob.

On the way to the debriefing, flying over the town, James tapped Rotor on the shoulder and gestured to the main street below. Rotor landed the helicopter in the middle of it. James jumped out and bought a bunch of roses from the old woman flower vendor on the street corner. Climbing back in, he tossed the roses to Matt. 'For Danielle,' he said. 'I'll buy you a hangover.'

'The heat and sweat are shrinking the tie around my neck,' said Andy. 'Matt, you don't know how much I've been going mad here.'

Matt couldn't help noticing that the roses were of a hybrid tea variety, lemon that would change to cream then almost white, from the colour of cowardice to the colour of purity in the process of maturation. They were known as 'Peace'.

He thought how one moment he was out there alone in the bush, every second his life in the balance, and the next he was in his home town where attractive girls shopped unconcernedly in shops before closing time.

Matt spent the next two days being debriefed by James and Andy.

During the days that followed, Matt worked with them in correlating all the information to hand, and helping drum up support for the operation.

They had no trouble in getting the commanders of the army and airforce on side. In fact, troops and pilots were immediately put under training for just such a possibility.

Winning the approval of the politicians proved decisively more difficult. For almost three weeks the politicians hummed and hahed about what the international repercussions would be.

Although the team had their tasks cut out for them in the meanwhile, waiting for the final verdict was almost unbearable at times.

James and Andy had been able to use the aerial photographs to best advantage. Since the photographs had been taken so that they overlapped one another, it was possible to view them stereoscopically, and since all exposure parameters were known – flying altitude, distance between exposures, and focal length of the camera – exact proportions of each ground feature were able to be measured and a scale papier mâché model was able to be made of the target section of the valley.

The model had been meticulously added to in accordance with the information on the guerrilla camp structures Matt had passed on. All other details Matt could possibly recall were now added.

Over and over again, the model was checked for accuracy.

Finally, the model was just as Matt could remember the real thing. The river, over countless millenia, had worn its way through high hills to form a densely wooded valley. The guerrilla camp was spread out over six and a half kilometres. Its centre was where a tributary met the main river via a waterfall. Numerous small satellite guerrilla groups radiated out from the central assembly point. Few constructions were above ground level. Almost every point of high ground was defended by a system of branch- and grass-covered trenches, and heavy weapons, particulary anti-aircraft configurations, disguised as huts. The ground cover was extremely good, with much rocky ground and overlapping tree branches. Each open end of the valley was heavily defended.

Every time more guerrillas and weaponry had arrived new satellite groups had been entrenched, reinforcing the overall camp structure.

Because of the dispersed nature of the camp, with its many small concentrations of heavily armed guerrillas in their camouflaged and well dug-in positions, any attack on it was likely to be a costly exercise in terms of manpower and equipment. Even saturation bombing would have a limited effect, since the rocky ground and tree cover would dissipate much of the explosive power.

The only weakness was the weekly politicisation assembly when most of the guerrillas, those not involved in defence or cross-border operations, were concentrated together.

Matt felt that this weakness was hardly in keeping with the errless traits of Mumvuri that he had come to know so well. He felt that more than likely it was because Mumvuri had been overruled by one of the over-zealous political leaders in civilian clothes who conducted the weekly meetings.

His suspicions were confirmed by information James had to hand.

Information from sources within the guerrillas' administration across the border revealed that Mumvuri had been promoted by the High Command to Provincial Commander. No longer was he just in control of guerrilla infiltration of the district via the valley, but of the whole province. Sections were to be infiltrated throughout the rainy season via numerous valley routes when water, bush food and cover were good, and whilst movement of security force vehicles and weapon hardware was hindered by soft ground.

Exact numbers of guerrillas to be involved in the push were not known, but figures between 500 and 1,000 were mentioned. What it meant was that if the first figure was correct, the camp in the valley had almost reached its full complement by the time Matt had left there; if the second figure was correct, the camp in the valley had not even reached half.

In conjunction with the model, detailed blue-prints were made of the layout of guerrilla defences and positions in the valley.

A composite intelligence report was drawn up.

Towards the end of the third week of canvassing for support, James managed to get the Minister of Defence, the Director of National Intelligence and the commanders of the army and airforce to give their support in principle, and to agree to a full-scale briefing at Operations Headquarters. When they found out that James considered the matter of enough urgency to warrant requesting a meeting that could keep them away from their families on Christmas Day, each to a man said in his own way, 'This had better be good.' James was fully aware of the implications for his career.

'Finally, the Minister of Defence has hinted that the government will be prepared to endure the international political repercussions that are inevitably going to be felt after a raid across our border, only if the raid is a total success. A statement of particular political deviancy that suits him, for we would have to make the raid before we know what its outcome is going to be,' James said, and paused before continuing, 'I'm not happy to suggest that you put your life on the line again, Matt, but I believe the only way the Minister will be convinced of the chances of a raid's success will be if you are prepared to go back out there.'

Matt could see him looking for the nature of his reaction.

Matt didn't so much as blink. 'I had a feeling you'd ask,' he said.

James pursed his lips, nodded and continued.

'The two points I'll be able to sell the plan on are as follows: firstly, that you are out there to supply up-to-the-minute information regarding the latest developments, qualifying and amending information where necessary; secondly, that you are there to determine whether the pattern of the weekly politicisation assemblies holds firm, and if so, to call in the strike immediately the guerrillas are seen to have assembled on Saturday 6 January. I doubt I will be able to hold up the necessary security forces, aircraft and equipment much longer than that. That gives us eleven days.' He looked at Matt for approval.

Matt nodded.

The model was checked over once more for authenticity to detail, and packed in a security crate.

James, armed with the model of the camp, maps and intelligence reports, flew directly to the city.

Matt went back to the farm.

'Good God!' Danielle exclaimed when she saw him. 'What's happened to you?' Although he was washed, shaved and wearing clean clothes, his eyes looked glazed, he was much thinner than she last remembered, and his cheeks looked hollow.

Danielle was haunted by the feeling that part of his spirit was snagged behind him on some thorny branch of the bush. He had pulled at it and pulled at it, eventually it had torn, and he had come on home.

How long would it be before his spirit was fused with the bush's spirit when to pull away would only serve to tear himself?

When she spoke to him he replied but it was as if he was staring into the distance. She knew that he didn't really see her.

'Are you all right?' she asked, and immediately recognised the inadequacy of her question.

He acknowledged with a nod of his head.

He was distracted by the slightest sound outside.

Then their eyes met. She saw his glance drop from her face, quickly over her body, and lose itself on the floor.

She saw that he was chain smoking, lighting the next cigarette with the dying stub of the last.

Even there in the room before her, he was alone, apart from her, subdued and remote.

War was void of feeling. The bush was void of feeling. Matt was void of feeling.

Later that afternoon Matt felt he couldn't stay there. He prepared to leave once again.

He was scared of what lay ahead for him, and he could not allow himself to reveal that fear to Danielle, for he knew that she was the one who could weaken his resolve to go ahead with what was expected of him, regardless of how scared he was. Anyone would be scared, he told himself. If he didn't do it someone else equally as scared would have to. And some other relationship would suffer because of it.

He chucked a few things into the Land Rover.

Danielle followed him.

'What about tomorrow?' she asked him.

'What about tomorrow?' he asked.

'Matt, it's Christmas.'

'I'm sorry, I won't be here,' he said.

She was taken aback. She found it awkward even talking to him.

'Well, when will you be here again?'

'I don't know,' he said. 'James will keep you in touch.'

Unable to control her sudden rage at events, at what had happened to their relationship, Danielle started kicking the Land Rover, hammering angrily at it with her fists.

Matt made no attempt to restrain her. Instead he joined in.

But no words passed between them.

Finally Danielle dropped to the ground, sobbing, and sat there with her back against the front wheel, one of her knuckles bleeding.

He handed her his handkerchief, and slumped down beside her.

Her reaction was more one of anger than sadness, he realised, anger at the sadness. He knew that same feeling of his own only too well.

'Spit,' he said after a while of just sitting there not knowing what to say.

'What?' she exclaimed.

'Spit,' he said again, 'like this.' And he spat on to the ground.

A smile crept over her face.

'Spit,' he said. 'The custom, "the blowing of water", all the anger comes out with the spit, remember?' And he spat again.

Danielle, smiling now through her tears, started spitting as well.

For a couple of minutes they tried to outdo each other, and laughed together.

The situation was ludicrous, and each realised it.

Danielle turned towards him, and they instinctively knew that each wanted the other to hold them.

He held her in his arms, his hands deliberately soothing in defence against her tired sad fury. But it went no further. A vast distance still separated them.

'The next time I come home it will be for good,' he told her, giving her something to hold on to. One way or the other, he thought to himself, in a coffin or because his task would have been finished.

He went back into the house to get his rifle, took a six-pack of beers from the fridge, came back out and climbed into the Land Rover.

It was mid-afternoon when Matt drove into town. The steering wheel and the seats were scalding to the touch. He tilted a beer bottle to his lips, steered with one hand, and squinted ahead through the sun's glare. The steering wheel bucked in his hands with the bumps of the road.

Matt felt how he had experiences in his life now that nobody else had shared. He was alone in coping with them. Again, as when his father and brother had been killed, he felt that there was nobody he could rely on any longer but himself.

Back in civilisation, Matt looked around him at the faces of the people – Danielle, James, Rotor, Andy, Jacob, even Red – and there was the nagging suspicion that he was no longer one of them, that he didn't belong, that he was part of something else.

He went to the hotel bar.

It looked as if half the army was there.

Several insects were attracted to a light bulb in uncoordinated flight. One of the soldiers there idly cupped one in his hands. Matt could sense the flutter of its wings against the man's palms. The man squashed it on the bar top. Oily juices stained the wood. The man wiped his hands off on a trouser leg. Matt looked at the mark on the bar top for a while, the skin around his eyes puckering in thought.

'What'll you have?' asked the barman.

'What've you got?' Matt responded somewhat vacantly, with a question of his own.

'Christmas whisky, Christmas brandy, Christmas gin, Christmas vodka, Christmas cane, Christmas beer . . .' said one of the soldiers.

'That's fine,' said Matt.

'What, beer?' asked the barman.

'The whole lot – in one glass,' said Matt.

'Sort of a Christmas punch, right?' asked the soldier.

'Kick of a Christmas giraffe.'

The man laughed, and the barman gave him his usual beer. From where Matt stood the night looked long and he had to get through it.

'They've cut the training of new recruits in the army in order to put more men in the field as quickly as possible,' one of the soldiers said.

'Yeah, *in* the field' another retorted.

'Pass me another one of them little brown bottles,' called Matt to the barman.

The night soon gained momentum.

'I didn't know what had hit me, until the surgeons practically reassembled a 75mm recoilless rifle shell from the pieces they pulled out of my butt,' came another voice.

'Dead soldiers', Matt's empty beer bottles, went a good way to filling an empty crate behind the bar.

At some point later, Matt couldn't remember exactly when, he climbed up on to the bar, pulled his trousers down and with his rifle in one hand and dick in the other, recited over and over again the old army adage:

> This is my rifle, this is my gun,
> This is for shooting, this is for fun,

and waggled both about. There was much applause and one of the soldiers bought him a beer.

Before the night was out he had won an argument that one could re-utilise one's body's waste fluid when confronted by a lack of water. He urinated into a glass and drank it.

Just before the bar closed, Matt bought a couple of bottles of whisky and drove to the nurses' home.

He noticed that the roses James had bought him to give to Danielle were still in the Land Rover. He had forgotten them. Now the petals had withered and fallen off. He picked up the bunch of stems and threw them out of the window as he drove.

Somehow he ended up stark naked with two new nurses in the town fountain when the police arrived.

A vehicle chase followed. He drove down the pavements, drove into the shopping arcade to escape.

He and the girls swilled whisky and laughed as the police cars went speeding past, first one way then the other.

He and the girls were naked in the car, having had to leave their clothes at the fountain in their hasty retreat.

The police eventually found them.

It was 4.30 a.m. Christmas Day when James rattled his keys on the bars of the cage at the police station.

Matt opened his eyes and looked around him at the reinforced concrete cell with the steel bars. He had a bone-splitting headache and didn't seem to be able to think through it.

'Good morning,' said James. 'Sleep well?'

Then Matt rememberd, and the remembering seemed to make his headache worse.

'You planning on staying here all day?' James asked.

Matt ignored the question. Instead he looked at James for an answer to the unsaid question of his own which had been troubling him all night.

'It's go,' James confirmed. 'They agreed five minutes before Christmas.'

'Your timing is immaculate,' Matt said.

James smiled.

Matt didn't smile. The fear in him was too much for that, the fear that he had tried to escape with drink, the fear of having to go out there again, the fear that he had lost his nerve.

Back at the office, and still with a bad hangover, Matt put himself on a Ringers Lactate drip to hasten his sobering up, as they set about arranging things necessary for his next reconnaissance.

Matt decided he would parachute in thirty kilometres from the target that time. As he knew where the camp was there was no longer the need to scour the length of the valley on foot.

For the rest of the morning he prepared the equipment he would take with him. James and Andy helped him, checking everything again and again.

For the entire afternoon he practised HALO-ing, High Altitude Low Opening freefall jumps. When he was up there, for the first jump, hesitating before he threw himself out into the sky, he imagined something fluttering above him, above his eyelids. !Kai, with his pixyish look, his high cheekbones that gave him the appearance of always smiling, flapping around up there as naturally as if he had been born with wings. 'The birds are in the sky, therefore I have already been there. When I have seen the birds flying, I too have been flying.' Matt remembered what !Kai had once told him. No sooner was he on the ground each time than he had repacked his parachute and was flown back up in the air again. The last time he had done any parachuting was when he had earned his wings during his military training several years before.

Back at the office he went over the equipment again, and went over with James and Andy all information that could prove pertinent once back across the border.

He ensured that the will and testament he had drawn up on his marriage to Danielle was re-validated, signed and witnessed as of that date, and that all insurance was in order. He didn't want there to be any problems for Danielle and the farm if he didn't make it back.

That evening, there being nothing else to do but wait, his nerves scraped raw, Matt passed the time in the operations bunker below James's office, by stripping several different communist weapons used in the camp, muddling the parts up on the floor and then reassembling them, again and again.

He should have slept, but he couldn't.

Andy sat with his chair tilted back against the wall, feet up on the desk, with coffee mug in hand, rocking backwards and forwards.

Bugs were flying crazily around the bare light bulb, clanging against it. Andy reached back and flicked the light-switch off, not losing his rocking rhythm. The clanging stopped.

Matt continued stripping and assembling the weapons regardless of the dark.

A bottle of beer stood on the desk, flat. He had not even drunk a toast. James had come in with a beer for each of them. 'Merry Christmas,' he had said. 'Sorry I'm not in my top-of-the-Christmas-tree-angel outfit.'

If not for that, the Christmas day festivities might have gone by without observance.

While the expectation of Matt's homecoming, at least for Christmas, had buoyed her up, now Danielle felt depressed.

She was worn out. A calf had been born in the early hours of morning to one of the dairy cows, and she had been up with it all night.

It had only taken until lunchtime for the town's grapevine to have informed her, isolated on the farm as she was, of Matt's dalliance in town – naked with two of the nurses she knew there.

At the same time she worried about cultivating the maize and cowpeas and oats and how they would need fertiliser soon, and how grazing in the pastures and on the *veld* had to be controlled or there would be danger to erosion . . . there was the weekly dipping to do to protect the cattle against ticks, particularly during the summer with the rains and hot days, and the long grass. The cattle had to be counted, weighed, dosed against worms . . . perhaps needed injections for disease and illness . . . Birds were pecking at the young maize seedlings. Many birds were helpful as they fed on insects and soil organisms but others were destructive to the crop.

Danielle felt she was so busy struggling to keep the farm going she had no time for herself, couldn't go out – besides, where could she go, where Matt hadn't preceded her? How could she face the people? There was only the hotel in the small farming town, and that was crowded with raucous soldiers nowadays. She felt guilty even thinking about going to the Vans for Christmas dinner.

Oom Van came to pick her up. She didn't feel like being with other people, didn't feel like celebrating; she just wanted to be alone. But despite herself she was smiling at him dressed in the bright red Father Christmas outfit he had worn for as many Christmases 'as he couldn't remember', and his 'Ho, ho, ho,' of greeting.

'No need for a cotton-wool white beard or a pillow-paunch any more,' he smiled, tugging at his beard and rubbing his pot-belly.

Although they were laughing the same as any other Christmas, it was not the same, could never be the same again. Too much had changed, too much had been lost. Suzanne and Sarie weren't there and never would be again. It was the second Christmas that Matt wasn't there. It was as if Red was only half there – with seemingly as little desire to get involved as he had. Her parents weren't there that year, because they'd gone overseas to be with her grandmother who was getting on and might not last out the year. She should have gone too, but she couldn't.

Matt's close colleagues, James, Andy, Rotor and Jacob, weren't there either.

But Alexandra was there with her two daughters, and Elaine was there, deprived children and other members of the School for the Deaf were there, laughing, thoroughly enjoying themselves – laughter that they couldn't hear themselves but which did so much for those who could.

That was Christmas for Danielle that year.

Three a.m. the following morning, seventy-five kilometres across the border, Matt launched himself out of the aircraft into the night sky, the womb of the cosmos, the Grandmother-of-all-things, as !Kai knew it. Immediately he went into the stable arch freefall position.

The slipstream caught him. The wind was horrific, an intimidating force. At twenty knots, Matt had already been informed that it carried with it a risk-injury factor of twenty-five per cent once he hit the ground. A one in four chance of fucking himself up, he thought, Ks from anywhere on enemy soil, so that either the wild animals would get him, or the gooks. There was a difference? There was no turning back. The aircraft was already out of sight, continuing its zigzag flight-path, navigator and cabin lights off, inaudible at the altitude of commercial airliners, high above the people of the night bush.

The ground would be down there, but he couldn't even see it, not really.

Stable-arch and falling, falling, but there was no real sensation of falling, only suspension, clap . . . clap . . . clap . . . clap . . . the flutter of his jump-suit billowing out. He seemed twice the size he was, yet infinitesimally small there in the night . . . the rush of air . . . down . . . down . . . down . . . continually checking the illuminated altimeter, only it, an inanimate object, reminded him he was falling, it would be so easy just to turn off the mind and go with the sensation all the way down . . . 5,000 metres above the ground . . . 4,000 . . . 3,000 looking for the supply box to follow it down . . . 2,000 . . . where was the parachute of the supply box? . . . It should have deployed by now . . . 1,000 . . . tracking all over the sky . . . closer and closer . . . to what? He grabbed a fistful of rip-cord handle and pulled. He continued falling without cessation, then the snapping open of the parachute, the abrupt check in downward motion. He looked up, no candle, no streamer. It was as if he was hanging there in the night sky. A flash of intense light burnt scars on the retinas of his eyes . . . an incredible explosive sound shook his head, shattering the quiet of the dark early morning . . . He immediately thought a rocket or something had been fired at him. But then no further commotion followed, and the realisation that the parachute of the supply box hadn't deployed came into his head. Christ! . . . That's all he needed . . . fuck . . . they would have heard that all over the Communist bloc . . . Bastard! Damn! Furiously he worked at the toggles that controlled the flow of air through the vents of the high-performance canopy, tracking through the night sky, a safe distance away from the supply box's point of impact. He thought wryly that he had been wondering if anyone had been below and if they had heard the snapping open of his parachute. Now he wondered whether he had been seen in the few seconds he was visible in the darkness before he would hit the earth. With his peripheral vision he could make out the contour of the ground, and . . . trees . . . a whole wood of them . . . trees . . . Goddam it. He brought his legs tightly together, knees slightly bent, prepared for impact. The wind was a force unto itself. At the optimum moment above ground level he turned into the wind, but even then knew it was going to be one hell of a ride. He was crashing through the branches. They broke easily beneath the impact of his falling weight, but the wind was tearing him through them sideways and his entire lower body was receiving blows. He hit the ground with what felt like bone-snapping impact, giving him no chance of rolling out of it. The wind dragged him across the rough earth for several seconds before he managed to flick the quick-release catches, detaching the parachute from his harness, letting it blow on.

At last it was over. He lay there, unmoving, throbbing with pain.

God! he thought.

God! he said to himself again.

When he got up he saw that the parachute had snagged in a copse of trees further on. He buried it.

Then he sat there, with compass and map, trying to orientate himself. Bearing in mind the wind's speed and direction, and the time he would have been descending, he estimated that he was about two kilometers from where his container of supplies had gone down. He went back cautiously to have a look.

The container was spread out over a dry ravine. The munitions inside it had exploded on impact, destroying spare ammunition, grenades, explosives, food, medical kit, even matches . . . everything.

He buried what he could. Then he tried desperately to think of what course of action he should take from then on. He could start walking back. Within three days he could be safely back across the border.

He slung his AKM folding butt rifle over a shoulder, and started walking on towards the camp. So long as he had the radio, he had the means to fulfil his purpose for being there, he told himself.

'Hang in there,' James had said.

He hadn't replied then; now he did. There's as good as any place to hang in!

He had two full water bottles, rifle, three 30-magazines of

ammunition, radio with morse key on his back with two spare batteries, and there were a couple of plastic-sealed sterilised bandage pads, a packet of salt, as well as a smaller sachet of pepper in his trouser pocket – that was all, but it would have to be enough to survive.

Morning was already on the horizon.

A grey lowrie was there to meet him.

Kuwe . . . kuwe . . . go 'way . . . go 'way . . .

The bush was pitiless to human frailty.

All extraneous information reflected on the screen of his mind had to be excluded. Home no longer existed. The bush was all that mattered now. Emotions and codes of existence from the outside world, with rules of law, codes of ethics, and cans of processed foods for the asking – all at their price – had to be forgotten, they had no place there.

His whole body was tender, bruised, but no bones broken.

He heard the resonant call of a ground-hornbill and he thought of !Kai. The call was a method of signalling !Kai had taught him as a boy, the direction and distance difficult to pinpoint, but the sound easily audible.

He remembered how early one morning in the bush of Matiziro, !Kai had badly sprained an ankle.

'I'll have to carry you,' Matt had said.

'Only when I am dead,' !Kai had told him curtly.

'I'll go for help,' Matt had said.

'If you need it,' !Kai had replied, 'but a man must help himself.'

!Kai had made it back on his own, and in his life had never missed a day of work.

Matt nodded now at the memory. A man must help himself.

He thought how a couple of hundred soldiers and pilots rehearsing arduously back home were counting on him, without knowing it. Accuracy and validity of information was the most invaluable thing right then against the guerrillas in the valley – so much so that he had been prepared to risk his life more than once for it, as it was on that that others would live or die.

He thought how every innocent person killed in the valley from then on, he, Matthew Nel, would be guilty for, in not having prevented it while he had had the chance. If he failed Mumvuri would have won yet again.

He thought carefully over what he had to do. The first thing he had to do while still able to do so, away from the concentration of guerrilla movement about the camp, was to satisfy the two most immediate and basic needs of mankind – thirst and hunger. Without water and food he stood no hope in hell.

He made his way through the surrounding *mutusa* trees, their leaves as silvery in reality by day as they had seemed by moonlight. He breathed in the early morning freshness; familiar with the bush, content in his familiarity.

Camouflage was to defeat observation, to break down the shape of everything that was of uniform shape, easily identifiable; body, equipment, rifle. He looked through or around cover, never over it. He never disrupted a continuous surface shape with his body, no matter how well camouflaged he believed himself to be. Such disruptions were always obvious to an onlooker. He avoided isolated cover, it was the first place that the enemy would disturb with heavy searching rifle fire if suspicious of intruders; and why wouldn't they be, with bits of fucking supply box scattered over the ravine behind him?

Everything alien to the growth of animal and plant was an advertisement to the presence of Man.

He found the spoor of eight men. The edges of the footprints had been eroded, and sand had been blown into the impressions. Matt knew instantly that the shortest time ago that the spoor could have been made was before the previous night's wind which had died down several hours ago.

When he followed the tracks to ensure they were old enough not to be of any immediate threat, his supposition was verified by the spoor of a galago night-ape superimposed over the human spoor.

He moved on through the day, always careful that his body should not appear as a silhouette, marking itself for observation in the magnificent sunlight, on a ridge against the horizon, walking across the light expanse of grass in a clearing. Beautiful aspects of nature took a man and turned him into a target!

The heat of mid-afternoon came, and in the shade he slept, able to do so almost as soon as he closed his eyes, and able to wake by instinct as soon as required to do so.

Late afternoon he heard the bellow of a kudu in thick acacia bush, but it had moved off in the opposite direction before he could get to it.

He moved on through the tree-covered grassland, the canopies far enough apart to allow sunlight to penetrate and an undergrowth of grasses, shrubs and herbs to grow.

He searched for edible bulbs and tubers, for moisture and nutrition. The bush was a veritable supermarket, and like any supermarket there were the specials, if one only knew where to look. Fleshy grubs, found under the bark in the rotting pulp of an old dead tree trunk. A scorpion, its poisonous sting plucked off and the soft innards deshelled like a small lobster. (When Matt was a boy, !Kai had taken him to see the baboons on Matiziro doing just that.) African wild potatoes, advertised by yellow flowers on their bare stems. He ate them raw.

All the time he was looking for a suitable LZ for helicopters to refuel and re-arm in safety when they attacked the valley.

He was walking along now, eating berries as he went. He thought how !Kai, with the bush discipline born to him, would momentarily stoop down to push a seed of the fruit he was eating into the earth and cover it.

Towards evening, there came the anxious snorting of a wart hog and the growls of lion.

With night, lying on his back, his hands behind his head and propped up on a rock for a pillow, he heard the crunching of bones, and the feeding snorts and groans of appeasement of a pride of lions, in their feeding pattern, elder male first, female, and then cubs.

Once the pride had eaten it would make its way to water. The waterhole must have been close by, for he could hear the lion roar loudly several times, then grunt and cough as was the habit after drinking. Another one of Africa's cruel and bloody dramas had evolved out there in the bush which night had quickly covered up.

Matt thought how cruel yet beautiful the bush was. No matter what happened to him he knew he wouldn't blame her. Nature didn't have a heart, she was simply all that was living and dying. A man had to know that and persist regardless.

He thought of the farm and he thought of his grandfather, father and brother and knew that no matter how hard things became they would have continued uncomplainingly – would have done what had to be done.

He wondered how the farm was doing, and he thought of Danielle. He wondered how she was doing. He thought how she was the one person he had come to need in his life – really need. At a time when he had lost all those closest to him, he had grown to learn increasingly not to need anyone at all – never to have anyone he would care about losing.

But he did care. One thing he had never learnt to do was not to care. He had forced himself to become more psychologically able to hunt Mumvuri, growing further apart from Danielle and the others in his life who were important to him, but it had not been painless.

Right now, though, the past had no place in his life. The present was all that mattered. He was far from everything and everyone who could offer him any assistance, he only had himself to rely on. He alone was responsible for whether he lived or died.

He transmitted a coded radio message to James, advising his predicament, and that in order to save batteries he would not be transmitting again until further information on the camp was to hand.

Mid-morning, the presence of a kill was marked by vultures circling overhead.

When he arrived, a large lappet-faced vulture was driving a number of quarrelling white-headed and white-backed vultures off their find. He in turn drove the lappet-faced vulture off its find. It was the remains of an old wart hog. There were the wart-like tubercles on the side of its face and the procumbent lower incisors. Sections of skin left were almost hairless apart from a few bristles. The eyes and mouth had been pecked clean, entrails and stomach had been pulled through holes in the skin.

There was the recent spoor of a pride of lions all about.

He could see where the lioness, downwind of the quarry, had lain in wait, flattened against the ground, unmoving, so as to seem part of it; where the wart-hog had come out of the dense bush nearby at a trot; where the lion, lazily stirring himself from his place in the afternoon shade had alerted the wart-hog of his presence, and the wart-hog, fleeing, had run straight into the ambush of the lioness. Matt could visualise the lioness clawing on to the wart-hog's flank, swiping across its face, claws across the eyes, dragging it down, biting through the vertebrae of the neck and severing the spinal cord.

Slightly decomposed food aided digestion! But there was next to nothing left, skin, teeth and bones. Even the tough shin joints were gone. Hyena, no doubt near, would crunch and swallow even what was left of the bones – all but teeth and hair would be digested. What was left was alive with the frenzied flight of flies, squat and glistening green-tinged, that seemed to be coloured with decay themselves. But there wasn't even enough flesh left for the remains soon to be crawling with the bloated pussy-white maggots.

He followed the spoor the lions had left the night before. It would take him to water.

At the waterhole, just as the sun was setting, a pair of immense lion foreleg pug marks was displayed in the soil near the water's edge. The soil had been dampened then by splashes, since dried by the tremendous heat of the sun during the day.

Now it was the cool of the evening, a time when a man could be alone with his thoughts, think of his cattle, look in pride over fields of maize in summer, every stalk heavy with a pearled cob, and in the winter watch the wheat gild the land with living gold, and know that he could quietly relax after a long hard day's work.

Matt drank his fill, replenished his water bottles, and moved off once again, anti-tracking as he went.

He stopped when it was as dark as it would get with the quarter moon, which would set only a few minutes into the new day.

He couldn't help thinking how, left to cook slowly in the diminishing heat of the ashes of a trench fire, the shin joints could have been made as tender as the choicest fillet steak.

Cooked meat. Cooked!

Home!

Danielle!

After the thrills and the excitement the love and respect seem to die and only bitterness is left, he thought, the bitterness of failure. Nothing rhymed for them anymore.

You can only know yourself in relation to the things out there, he said to himself, and looked out into the bush.

There was nothing in the bush that wasn't food for something else; that which moved of its own accord before it was killed being more concentratedly nutritious than that which didn't.

The following day, Matt took finicky care in making and placing snares of tree bark and traps made out of branches and heavy stones. He checked for obvious feeding and watering places, nests, holes and game paths. He made use of natural hazards, where game was forced to pass along one particular route, restricted by rocks and dense thorn bush. He brushed the ground at these places with a swale of grass in order to make his task of identifying where and what game passed that much easier.

He made a basket-like trap out of thin young branches and placed it over what looked like a rat burrow. It was a trap easy to get into, but not so easy to get out of 'unless the rat had a map', as his brother had once said.

He went through a day in the heat, without replenishing his water and without food and that night returned to the traps. He found he had trapped nothing.

He examined his places of clean swept ground for likely looking spoor and in one of them was not disappointed. He placed snares there.

He moved the plaited basket trap to another burrow where a root near the entrance had been recently gnawed through.

Come dawn again, Matt's mind dwelt on the fact that it was Saturday, that it was the time for him to have confirmed whether or not the weekly guerrilla assembly in the valley had again taken place, but he was still about twenty kilometres away.

He defended his decision of not having gone on ahead by telling himself that he still had another week to stay alive, and if he had moved on without water or food, in all probability he would sooner or later have made a careless mistake, resulting in far-reaching adverse consequences, fatality. There was no underestimating the power of the stomach over the mind to weaken it.

After another day of thirst and hunger, he found that one of his traps had been triggered. After a careful examination of the ground he suspected he had been close to snaring a francolin; there were many clearly discernible prints of a game bird, but more revealing, the bird had lost one of its feathers in the trap.

On the third evening, feeling weak and defeated, he found that he had caught a klip-springer. Immediately he felt all sense of defeat leave him.

But equally, he mysteriously felt how his victory meant defeat for the klip-springer. He recognised it as the sort of sentiment !Kai would have felt.

He was aware that the little antelope was close to full size, perhaps fifteen kilograms. He was aware that it had no horns – that it was female, in milk, pregnant.

His knife-point pierced the throat of the tiredly kicking and bleeding animal, draining the blood away from the carcass.

He drank off the little milk afforded by the teats, and pocketed the snare. Grabbing hold of the hooves, fore and rear, he carried it around his neck, and over his shoulders, away from the place where its cries and the scent of fresh blood might have attracted predators, both two-legged and four. The grey-brown coat, flecked with yellow, was coarse against his neck.

Once well within the shelter of woodland half an hour from there, he laid the little animal down on the ground. Once again he removed his knife from its sheath. He was thankful now that he had spent careful attention to honing the blade before he had come out with it. He skinned the carcass easily, leaving it on the skin to prevent it getting covered in grit; he didn't hanker after crunching on grains of sand embedded in the meat.

He cut into the abdomen carefully so as to leave its inner organs intact. He removed the stomach and put it to one side. He cut out the uterus and the foetus, a delicacy in the wild. The remaining offal, *matumbu* (entrails), heart, windpipe and rectum he discarded along with the head; predators would soon take care of them; it was his contribution to the other inhabitants of the bush. Everything interacted with everything else.

He jointed the rest of the carcass, slicing the haunches and all other available meat into thin strips, making the cuts following the grain, cleanly so as to avoid rough nesting areas for bacteria and blowfly. Within hours the outside tissue would form an airtight skin, to postpone the internal growth of putrefactive bacteria.

As he worked, he thought of making soup out of the bones, but even as he thought about it he discarded the bones about him as well. He imagined stewing the brisket in its own juices, with fresh *veldkos* relish and herbs. It seemed he could smell the fillets grilling, and a roast basted with spitting melted fat. But he could not risk a fire, so it did not warrant thinking about.

He hand-rubbed the strips of meat with salt, and wrapped them all together in the skin to cure for a day and sweat off some of the water content before hanging. He rolled the skin tight and tied it with bark.

When he had finished he took a handful of the pulped contents of the little stomach, and with his thumb extended like a teat, squeezed the pulp so that its liquid content ran down his thumb and dripped into his mouth. It smelt just like liquid excrement – as could be expected – but it served ideally to relieve his parched mouth and go some way to quench his incredible thirst. He favoured the gut content to the blood. The high salt content of the blood would only have served to increase his thirst rather than diminish it.

He put the stomach, tied with bark so it would not leak, beside the skin bundle. !Kai would have enjoyed it, he knew.

He concealed all man-made spoor as best he could, and then picking up his two bundles, moved on to recover his other snares, and to find somewhere to spend the night.

At the top of his skin bundle, between two folds, he placed the liver. He cut some of it off and chewed it raw as he walked. It was fresh and warm. !Kai would have liked that too, he thought.

That night, Matt squeezed the remainder of the liquid from the contents of the klip-springer's stomach into one of his water-bottles and drank a little, before burying the stomach and moving on to find a place of good cover to sleep.

January

One sidereal year went straight into another one.

The sun rose early on the first day of the New Year, and Matt rose with it.

He used a little of his precious salt supply to clean his teeth and disinfect his mouth which tasted foul. He used a piece of cotton from his jacket as dental floss.

He felt how he would have preferred to stay on there in the hills well away from the camp, but none the less picked up his skin bundle of salted sliced meat and moved on.

He was less than a kilometre from the Mapfupa Hills of the valley above the camp when he was suddenly made to halt in his tracks. The peace of the bush was abruptly disturbed by the repeated thudding clatter of what he made out to be 14.5mm heavy machine-gun-fire from over the ridge in the valley.

He strained to hear the sound of aircraft engines but didn't hear any either. He scanned the sky for aircraft but didn't see any.

He realised his heart was racing. He breathed deeply, trying to calm himself down. He had thought that the forces back home had jumped the gun and had already initiated the attack, but now he knew how unfounded such a thought was, for without him there was to be no attack. Without his up-to-the-minute verification of the exact guerrilla strength, firepower and whereabouts of every one of the anti-aircraft defences of the camp spread over several kilometres of the valley, any attacking force was sure to suffer severe casualties. First-hand, exact information together with proper planning and rehearsal were the be-all and end-all of military success. There were no short cuts.

He moved on to the ridge and looked down into the valley. There were the scattered huts, like conventional *kraals* when sighted from the air, but containing heavy weapons, and concealed trench and bunker systems. There were also hundreds of men in camouflage dress, doing weapon exercises beneath the trees, and there was the practice firing of an anti-aircraft battery. Only it was not men firing it.

A new development in African history was occurring down there. The traditional subservience of the African female was undergoing a radical change. No longer simply accepting the role of bearer, baby- and breakfast-maker, women were being versed in the operation of the anti-aircraft heavy machine-guns.

Matt thought how the participation of women in combat roles had perhaps been deliberately initiated to cause men who had avoided guerrilla recruitment to lose face in their society, a society in which it was customary for the man to protect his woman.

Danielle.

It was not the time or place to think of Danielle, of what things had been, or what they might have been, only what they were now, but by association he found himself unable to avoid thinking of her. Just over a year ago they had been one of the closest couples he knew. Everything they did had been in harmony, even their thoughts were meshed, they would instinctively know what the other was thinking. But the bush war had come between them. It was a part of his life she could not share – and right then it was the only part. He couldn't tell her about Mumvuri and his involvement in the bush war because of security reasons, and because he had no intention of involving her in the horror that he was living through. All that mattered now for him was to survive. There was no room for gentility, etiquette, niceties.

He dropped the subject of his relationship with her almost as soon as he had taken it up, as if the voices in his head were used to much bigger things, that there was no real conversation value in a relationship between a man and a woman – not when all that mattered right then was to survive.

After a while in the bush, one's sense of time became instinctive. There was a change from linear time to cyclic. Events were swallowed up. Trying to fix them in time became valueless; on their own they had no value. There was no need to look at his watch. If he did he'd be forced to think of Danielle. It was she who had given it to him. He didn't look at it.

That evening, he strung his radio's aerial up in a tree and transmitted his latest report across the border.

He spent the following day surveying the changes that had taken place in the camp since he had last been there. What he saw thrilled and unnerved him at one and the same time. The camp had once again grown significantly in size, by exactly how much he had yet to find out. Nevertheless, he immediately knew that once again he had his task cut out for him. He would need every hour of every day of the coming week before the following Saturday to obtain the necessary information for a successful raid to take place. He estimated that the camp had perhaps doubled in size once again since his last visit.

As it was growing dark, he peppered the strips of meat he was carrying, as a precaution against flies laying their eggs on them before they properly dried, and placed them in a lattice-work basket made of strong reeds.

He thought how if he walked about with the meat, flies would follow him like a cloud and the danger of predators would be increased, so he hung the basket in the leafy crop of a tree in woodland, away from predators and human eyes, but where the wind could get to it. Day by day the meat would progressively dry. It was something to look forward to.

Danielle laboured in the fields along with the farmhands, cultivating the weeds while they were still young. If the weeds were allowed to establish themselves, attempts to remove them then inevitably damaged the shallow and deeply spreading roots of the maize plants.

She worked in the heat of the day like Matt used to, when the maize plants were limp and not turgid with moisture, so that they were least likely to be damaged by the tractors passing overhead.

There were more weeds than last season. The ground hadn't been harrowed as often to cause weed seeds to germinate so they could again be harrowed under. Danielle thought how Matt always used to pay so much attention to preparation during those times which were normally slack for other farmers, that he was just as busy at any one time of the year as any other, but during the busy times he was at least able to spare time to concentrate on quality. Soon the maize plants were going to be too tall to cultivate with the tractors.

Danielle worried about cut-worm feeding on the young plants, cutting them off at the ground. Dom Van came round and helped her oversee the putting down of poisonous bait. As with his dislike of weedkiller chemicals that didn't break down in the soil and water, Matt preferred to use organic solutions to fight insects that were harmful to the crops.

Even when the cut-worm were taken care of, Danielle worried in case stalk-borer fed on the inner growing part of the stalk, or rust ruined the leaves.

What had made her pass through the farm's workshop on the way back, she didn't know. She didn't have to be there. Why she was suddenly aware of the signs of neglect she didn't know either; they had obviously been happening for some time. It was Matt's domain, and he preferred to take care of everything there. But now, in the office, vehicle log books, machinery records and manuals were out of their correct places. The pencils in the mug on the desk were blunt, and pens had run dry. A tractor was on a pit, stripped down. Spare parts were not available to put it together again. Single-furrow ploughs and hoes that should have been hanging from the tie beams out of the way, were piled up in a corner. The repairs, service and lubricating section was dusty. The wood planings in the bottom of the vehicle pits hadn't been changed for several weeks and were blotched with used oil. The red fire extinguishers hadn't been serviced. Two of the fluorescent tubes in the roof weren't working. The smithy was smokey. There was a distinct absence of spare parts and accessories on their respective shelves. The screw-top fruit-preserve jars containing nuts and bolts, nails and screws, washers and ball-bearings were not all attached to their respective lids on the under surfaces of the shelves. Sizes were mixed up in some of the jars. A number of tools were in the wrong places, not matching the respective outlines painted on the hanging boards but left lying around on the work benches.

Danielle suddenly felt particularly depressed. Matt had left everything to go to neglect.

The farm could run on its own, yes, but at the expense of many things that Matt usually performed instinctively from a close interaction throughout his life.

Danielle felt that no matter how hard she tried, for every step she took forward the farm took two steps backwards. Whilst she had one enterprise under control, others slipped away from her. She didn't know how Matt had achieved what he had without constantly supervising. The farmhands just didn't seem to have the same sense of cleanliness and material order that she did.

She started tidying up.

First thing in the morning Matt started surveying the latest additions to the camp, and did so for several hours, sketching down every new defence emplacement, noting the types of weapon, numbers of guerrillas, newly arrived vehicles observed, and once again, that evening, he silently transmitted his findings – by one-way communication. He would have liked to have had someone to talk to.

Afterwards, looking for water-containing roots near to his previous night's sleeping place, he came across the spoor of running impala. They had been disturbed by something.

Still searching for food, he found a few *muhacha*, mbola plums.

A short while later he found the fresh ground spoor of Man, a partial boot print. Then again there was fresh aerial spoor, damaged vegetation, the bleeding relatively recent.

As darkness slunk on, he found evidence of the resting place of several men. It was an unsuitable place to rest during the heat of the day, so he believed the men had been there the previous night – no more than fifty or sixty paces from where he had been. If he had made one sound too obvious, it would have been his last.

It was hard enough moving about the hills of the valley not being observed, every movement deliberate and exhaustive in the heat so as not to leave obvious spoor while making careful observations, without having to water and feed himself too.

If his presence there was discovered, the guerrillas could come after him in force, but worse still, they could surreptitiously reorganise their numbers in the valley, leaving some areas as decoys while they strengthened defences elsewhere, allowing an attack to take place which would inevitably prove counter-productive due to heavy casualties of manpower and aircraft for the attacking force. If he was captured and interrogated, perhaps they could even lead the attacking force into a trap to annihilate them. In both cases, the propaganda value alone would outweigh the military victories themselves.

Matt often thought of these possibilities. They were very real, serving as a constant reminder to what he had to do, for him to be extremely careful at all times, yet at the same time to take the calculated risks necessary for him to fulfil his reconnaissance role.

His gravest problems, however, remained lack of water and food. He could find little water in the hills, although the abundance of it that was the river was often in sight. The difficulty was getting to it without compromising his presence. As for food, he had to forage, and with the heat and the energy-sapping nature of his activities requiring intense concentration at all times, he was always hungry.

He felt that he couldn't wait longer for the meat to dry properly, so the day after he had hung it in the tree, he removed it. The strips had dried a little black on the outside, but still had a blood-red core. He took them with him.

Before the meat, since he had been there, he had eaten nothing but berries, roots, and some kidney-shaped tubers. But in the morning he found some yellow-staining mushrooms for breakfast. They were growing near to the deceptively delicious tasting but often fatal death-cup. For a hungry man who didn't know the bush, collecting all the mushrooms would have been disastrous.

In a grass-lined hollow in the ground, he discovered a clutch of creamy coloured eggs, speckled and spotted with deep sepia, umber and burnt sienna. Kurrichane, 'button-quail'. The equivalent of a couple of chicken eggs for breakfast. He cracked open each egg and felt the little lump in his throat as he swallowed the embryonic contents of each one.

He ground some of the shell and swallowed it with a little tepid gut-liquid from his water bottle to boost his calcium intake.

Altogether a satisfying breakfast, he thought, but for afters how he wished there was *mutukutu* (monkey-bread), the dry pulp of the pod just like Tanny Van's best rusks, except without the raisins, but the trees were only in flower, there was no fruit.

Then, as fate would have it, he saw a *mugaragunguwo* (tar berry) tree, and found himself with 'raisins' without the rusks!

In thick bush on his way back to view the camp, he saw a bulky black rhino grazing peacefully. An aggressive son of a bitch if bothered, he thought. On the rhino's back were the tickbirds, so small in contrast, that would alert it to any intruding presence with their warning cries and sudden flight. It was an admirable reciprocal relationship they had. The birds' picking of ticks off the rhinos was beneficial to both. The one had better eyesight, the other better smell. Each served its warning purpose. The tickbirds were so much more able to detect movement than the poor-sighted rhino, but since they required movement to attract their attention Matt deprived them of it. When animal life moved, it was against a background of unmoving plant life and mineral that it did so, inevitably drawing attention to itself.

When the rhino and birds moved out of sight, Matt backed away. Moving downwind so the rhino's acute sense of smell could not detect him, he took a laborious but none the less necessary detour to a new observation point.

He thought how the rhino would be no match for a machine-gun, and if the guerrillas came across it it was likely to lose its life along with its main horn.

Wisps of cirrus cloud were high in the sky, pretty but they told him nothing of the weather to be.

The rest of the day was uneventful.

The whole of the next day he spent in reconnaissance.

That evening he settled down once again to radio James with his revised estimate that there were over a thousand guerrillas now congregated in the valley, with more arriving daily.

But he paused, thinking long and hard about the fact that dawn of Saturday 6 January, the date originally set for the planned attack was not even thirty-six hours away, and he felt that because the camp was growing so fast he had not even recced half of it. Despite the recollection of his first encounter with Mumvuri, risking quality, or now risking everything for a greater number, and despite his desire to get the hell out of there, he felt that so long as he was there he had to do the job properly. He had lost the first five days due to unforeseen circumstances, and he needed that time back. He struggled with himself over this for it was clearly against common-sense regard for his own safety. He couldn't believe that, of his own volition, he was actually putting his head on the line for yet another week. But he was.

When he transmitted his report he said simply that he needed more time, leaving the final decision on that basis up to the powers that be, a greater force than himself. He requested an immediate reply.

To prevent compromising him, James or Andy would only ever transmit when requested, and only then it would be for a matter of the utmost importance – which this was.

Matt had a vision of his coded information reaching the relay station in the highlands on the border, being taped by some bored signals operator, not having a notion what the coded message was all about, and just passing it on.

He had a vision of that same message arriving in the operations bunker with James and Andy, waiting on tenterhooks for every dot and dash, and the consternation that it would have caused.

He envisaged them plotting the information on the papier mâché model. He thought how James had to rely for the most part on *his* information alone now, as few cross-references were possible with the camp growing daily before Matt's very eyes. Not even a black operative who may have been able to infiltrate the camp and who had since managed to cross back across the border would be able to recreate the up-to-the-minute picture; and it was likely that such a man would only know in detail the part of the camp he was directly involved in. No single guerrilla would know the entire layout of the camp – except Mumvuri.

Matt envisaged James and Andy immediately liaising with the commanders of the army and airforce whose responsibility it was to formulate the attack strategy, the logistics of the operation, and to ensure the correct training and rehearsing of the men under their command without revealing the exact target, as there were spies on both sides.

Much to their credit, but a mixed blessing for Matt, they came back almost immediately with an 'affirmative', and a no-nonsense personal addendum tacked on – Good Luck!

On his part, there was now the possibility that the task force could be disbanded for deployment elsewhere before the week was out. It was up to James and Andy to ensure that didn't happen. He realised how difficult that was going to be, he didn't envy them. He could see James having to call in and give out quite a few markers in the process.

The following night, after a full day's reconnaissance, Matt approached the valley by a new route. It was one of his standing rules never to use the same route often enough both coming and going to establish any pattern.

Ironically, it was then that he stumbled across a covered trench system he hadn't known to be there. He could hear the sound of snoring men.

He had somehow made his way right past whichever out of them had been on guard without being challenged. He supposed that either the man was asleep, or he had merely dismissed any sound and movement he had observed as that of one or other of his comrades, hardly expecting the enemy to be wandering around in their midst over 100 kilometres from the war zone.

Matt thought how he could eliminate several of them if it came to a fire-fight, but what were several of them when he could have several hundred?

He backed off nervously into the dark bush about him once again – until he heard a voice ahead.

Where exactly the trenches were and where the men were sleeping, scattered as they were, Matt didn't know. Yet another voice, in answer to the first, came from no more than twenty paces to his right. A shadow gradually straightened, detaching itself from the rest of the night.

Very slowly, so as not to draw attention to himself by abrupt movement, Matt crouched down, and remained absolutely motionless, like the bushes and trees around him.

He endeavoured frantically to control his breathing. Perhaps the man would feel warm breath on his face. Matt kept his mouth shut. Perhaps the man would see the whites of his eyes in the dark. Perhaps. Matt held a darkened hand over them, merely peering between his fingers.

He could smell urine as the man emptied his bladder. He was so close. He was so close he could sense the man's eyes dilating wide to gather in the diffuse starlight as he looked about him in the dark. He could sense the man's ears straining to hear extraneous sound.

He could sense the man's lungs inflating, nostrils sniffing the air. But the man would smell nothing out of the ordinary, only the natural scent of the bush would reach him, not toothpaste, not deodorant, not perfumed soap, none of the usual trappings that white soldiers were wont to wear. He would smell nothing that was alien. There were only animals out there – and Matt was one of them.

Matt experienced a cramping coldness of the guts and chest. Was the man so close that he could see the hard amber iris and the white of each eye, discoloured by the usual yellow tinge dominant in the eyes of the black African? Shiny eyes that were touched with green flecks of hatred, not colour.

He saw the *bandria* across the man's chest, each pouch stuffed with a spare loaded AK magazine.

308

The slipping of a safety catch sounded like an alarm bell.

But an animal needed movement to attract its attention, and Matt would deprive that animal, like he had deprived the rhino and the egrets, of the presence of that all-important factor. He could hear !Kai's voice even then, far from the contented past of his childhood. 'Doesn't the painted-snipe, when being hunted, stop all movement rather than fly away and so draw attention to itself? Isn't it the long-claw bird that simply turns its back and seems to disappear amongst the leaves and branches of a tree?'

The animal kingdom knew the best defence in such situations, tried and tested by natural selection. Who was Matthew Nel to doubt it? Yet his fear felt of such intensity that he was convinced it would be his blanched-white face shining through the camouflage cream darkening it, that would finally give him away. It was a strange kind of fear, not for himself, for he felt that no matter what happened he could fight his way out of there. It was the fear of failure. It was the fear of Mumvuri winning yet again, and what horror would follow in the country if over a thousand guerrillas were to infiltrate it through the valley. Ironically, the valley itself would see a drop in guerrilla incidents as the guerrillas would not draw attention to themselves as they passed through it.

Using his peripheral vision rather than direct focus, Matt was able to observe movement in the darkness. If one looked directly at something in such conditions one's vision became confused by conflicting shadows. Hadn't !Kai told him that?

There were many more guerrillas than he expected around him, he could see that now.

A man brushed barely paces past him.

He stayed there without moving, listening, watching, making out the layout of that part of the camp and the whereabouts of sleeping personnel as the moon came up.

He instinctively found himself listening to the crickets, the stopping of their singing had something to do with vibrations of the earth, signifying people moving. He listened and watched expectantly before they started up again.

Once he was certain where the trenches were, and where each man was, he slowly began to feel his way out of their night formation.

Inhospitable sons of bitches, he swore.

*

Morning came once again; so long as he was alive at least he could count on that.

When snakes were about, toppies chattered excitedly in the trees. They were chattering now.

Later, Matt saw a secretary bird standing officiously on a rock above the grass. Along with everything else in the bush, snakes were potential meals.

He remembered when he was a child out with !Kai. !Kai had pointed out to him a small harmless brown snake that was fond of sleeping in the hut of an old friend who had recently died. It would come back again and again.

'Jongwe,' !Kai had said. 'He has returned. See the scar on the right of the head?'

And there was the scar just as Jongwe had had.

'He moves as one moves in one's own home; as if to say welcome, you are my guests.'

Jongwe was always a most hospitable host.

Now, Matt kept a careful look out for snakes.

He remembered how !Kai had once showed his brother and him a python wrapped around a large pile of eggs she was incubating, protecting them from the depredations of predators. How !Kai had taken hold of one of his brothers hands and one of his and placed those hands quite casually on the python's body, twice as long as he was, as if knowing that the snake would not react offensively since it would know it would not be harmed. The flesh had been hot to the touch, the raised body temperature particular to the brooding female.

!Kai could have pulled her away from her young, broken her back with a heavy stick, cut off her head, gutted her, coiled her on the coals of a fire, then skinned her before cutting her into steaks and eaten her. But as !Kai had said, 'If one ate the tree without the seeds already growing, there would be no more fruit, no more seeds, no more trees . . .'

Matt came across many young snakes, entwined one with the other. It was not out of fear or from a fastidious palate that he left them alone.

He found a safe route down to the river. A sooty babbler glided across the rocks as he approached. He lay concealed in the bush on one of the banks for some time, watching and listening before he considered it safe to cross.

There were crocodiles, but once he knew exactly where they were, he swam across.

Once on the other side, he waited in the bush once again, watching and listening, before considering that it was safe to drink.

While drinking, he noticed that there were molluscs near where his lips met the water.

After drinking as much as his belly could hold, and having filled his water bottles, he collected handfuls of the fresh-water mussel-like molluscs.

He laid them out on a rock in the sun, a trick to open them he had learnt from observation of the openbill stork when out with his brother and !Kai.

He moved away, scouting the edges of the river, checking for signs of guerrilla movement, and charting the terrain, before returning cautiously to where he had left the molluscs. By then they were open.

He ate them raw, then rested a while.

Late afternoon, replete and refreshed, Matt moved on down river, following a contour trail made by game, down deeper into the valley, the valley that some called the valley of dreams, of secrets, the valley that others called the valley of shadows, of death.

He reached the river basin with the early morning light, the sky a flamingo pink. The mist came off the open expanse of flat water and he was held close in its intimacy. The Mutoto Basin, he named it, after the dripping sound of the fermented *muzhanje* fruit distilling. The air was pristine clear . . . and intoxicating. You could get drunk on the natural grandeur.

He squatted at the edge, rifle cradled in his arms, looking out over the water.

Dikkops cautiously ran along the ground away from him, but found no cause to take to flight. Jacana trotted across the lilies in the shallows. A dabchick traipsed in semi-flight across the surface, with no need of lilies to support its weight.

The soil of the basin was rich, almost black. Streams from the higher ground kept it marshy. It swirled with a mist of yellow-broom and pink and white flowering weeping lovegrass. There were the delicate violet-blues of winged forget-me-nots, the fragile lavenders with golden stamens, the bright yellows, and the vivid orange tubular florets with the protruding red style of others. !Kai always felt that so long as things were, and you knew them for what they were, names were unimportant.

Back in time he could see !Kai, grinning broadly, mimicking the superb dance of the magnificent golden-crowned crane.

Matt couldn't help smiling at the memory.

A white-breasted cormorant rose from the log it had been perched on, dived into the water, and came out with a fish in its bill.

A veritable paradise, Matt couldn't help thinking, looking out over the basin.

The thought of paradise brought back memories of a young black girl he had once seen washing in a stream. As a young boy, eager to taste the fruits of manhood, watching her he had instantly felt the rushing of blood in his loins, the engorging in his trousers. She had a lithe graceful body with firm little upturned breasts, perfectly circular dark areola, and hard full nipples. Her vulva with its triangle of black hair proclaimed her pouting womanhood. Her skin appeared as smooth as a young bird's magnificent plume. Still, even now, he thought her one of the most beautiful women he had ever seen. That the memory was old and nothing more than thought pained him.

His mind returned to the Mutoto Basin.

Pelican, like a group of African spear fishermen, caught fish they trapped in the shallows.

With the abundance of fish in those waters Matt thought he was bound to feast well that night, and have enough sun-dried to last him for days to come.

Then he saw the hammerkop nest built of reeds, grass, twigs, and everything else obtained from close at hand . . . bits of dark green wool, and camouflage denim material!

And in the water, a short distance from the shore, were fishing-net floats made from the cork-like wood of the *mushamba* ('live long') tree. It meant that he might be fortunate enough to find some of the old nutritious purple-black fruit nearby that such trees gave out, but he doubted it. By that time of year all fruit would have fallen to the ground and rotted. On the other hand, what the presence of those floats definitely did mean was that men could be expected to come to the Basin to check the nets for their catch.

He remembered how !Kai, once standing on the edge of a water-pan on Matiziro, like just another bashful crane on his stick legs, cocked his head and sniffed the air, his ears veritably twitching with the perception of infinitesimal sound.

Something inexplicable alerted Matt now. *Chenjera . . . chenjera*

. . . a voice called out from inside his head . . . look out . . . beware . . .

Birds suddenly took to the sky in their hundreds, as if the sky had exploded into fragments.

Twenty, thirty guerrillas appeared in a long sweep-line.

Although he was certain they were after him, he did not immediately withdraw but watched them.

They were a patrol deliberately looking for spoor, he told himself.

Suddenly there was shooting in his direction. In alarm he made to move off, but then saw a man casually walk towards him, pick something up and hold it above his head victoriously so that the others could see. It was a hare.

Then Matt realised his spoor was behind him, so they could not be on to him, but if they came his way they could well come across evidence of his being there.

A short time later, he made his way through the trees, away from the Mutoto Basin, and he hadn't even replenished his water-bottles. He had drunk their contents in the heat of that day, feeling safe in the knowledge that he would be able to fill them when needed since there was abundant water close by. Now things were different.

He made his way back up into the hills, without water, but at least it wasn't so crowded and dangerous, and he had to get back to serious observations of the camp.

One of his reasons for having come down to the river in the first place. He didn't stop cursing himself for having wasted time admiring the beauty of the scenery instead of having got down to the practicalities of refilling his water-bottles, having drunk and then got the hell out of there.

He didn't know what he was going to do for water now.

He spent an uncomfortable thirsty night.

Early morning, he was as thirsty as hell but didn't wish to risk the gauntlet of the camps and patrols to get to the river again.

As he moved away from his night position to get to view another part of the camp, he noticed webs of *nephilia*, the large black-and-yellow spiders, glistening with jewels of dew in the light.

He thought how Danielle didn't like spiders, she used to ask him to remove them from the bath where they would often trap themselves, unable to climb out because of the deep smooth enamel sides.

He thought how relationships were made of bonds that were built up a thread at a time, eventually into a web.

One of the webs was broken!

It meant that there had been movement through there.

He looked down to the ground. Beneath the broken web there was clear ground spoor, on a section of game trail the soil of which was kept damp at night and early morning by the net root system just below the surface absorbing the dew.

It took some time to decipher the complex spoor pattern. Human tracks were superimposed on those of impala moving down towards the river, and impala tracks moving uphill away from the river were superimposed on those of the human tracks. The impala might well have moved down to the river to drink in the evening, and back into the bush of the hills to shelter and feed before morning. If that was so, then the human spoor had most probably been laid the night before.

Looking down, he was suddenly aware of his feet. The heavily dewed grass had soaked his guerrilla-issue boots.

He looked at the effect of the dew on the spoor. Dew dripping from leaves had marked it, confirming that the human spoor had been laid before the sun had come up.

Once again a guerrilla section had moved by him in the night. He wondered if they knew he was there and were looking for him. All the close shaves he was having seemed to be more than just sheer coincidence. But then, bearing in mind the high concentration of guerrillas in that relatively small stretch of the valley, the probability of a guerrilla coming face to face with him was a lot higher than he would have liked to contemplate.

But more significant to Matt right then than the short distance of bush that had come between him and his discovery by the guerrilla section, was the saturation of his boots.

He opened one of his thick medical dressings and, using it as a sponge, collected dew, squeezing it into one of his water bottles. It was tiring work, and risky because the dew collected on open patches of grassland where he could be detected. He had to work fast to get the dew before the sun dried it up.

After having broken cover, and his sweating and exertion he found he had only about a quarter of a water bottle full.

He had a couple of thirsty mouthfuls.

The rest of the day was incredibly hot and incredibly dry, his body

314

was parched, every drop of life-giving liquid seemed to sweat from him, and he was dizzy with the loss. He sipped from the one water bottle that still had a few drops in it. Each day it had not been filled he drank no more than half of whatever he had. In that way the bottle was never empty. It was a psychological deception he had learnt as a boy from !Kai. But now, the water bottle was as good as empty.

The nearer he got to the river the more dangerous it was. The guerrillas were heavily concentrated for several kilometres along it. He had to travel over twenty kilometres to get to a part of the river that he could consider as even less dangerous. The travel there and back all the time would have been too much for him; there would have been no time to survey the camp. Besides that, the longer he was on the move each day the greater was the possibility that he would be observed. He was safest when he was not moving but observing.

He considered approaching the river at night, but his last experience of wandering into the lair of a guerrilla night position still unnerved him. In the dark he was unable to observe signs of guerrilla movement which increased his chance of walking into an ambush.

All things considered, he remained in the high hills to do what he was there to do – observe the camp. The camp was so vast and spread out that he had not yet come to know it all. He could ill-afford to waste any time of the day on his own needs, so long as there was still so much the task force needed to know to avoid their being routed.

That afternoon, he dug a hole in the earth beside his observation position. The area where he dug was in a mossy depression shadowed by one rock or another throughout the day, indicating that it was a place where run-off water would have settled when it rained, and where it had been protected from the ravages of the sun. The hole was knee-deep when he placed one of his water bottles in its centre, broke up bits of water-containing vegetation around the bottle almost to the top, then covered the hole with the broad sheet of plastic from the dressing pad he had used to soak up the dew the day before. He sealed the edges of the plastic with stones and sand, and placed a small stone in its centre to depress it towards the mouth of the open water bottle. Water that condensed on the plastic sheeting would drip into the bottle.

The water-still in operation the rest of that day and throughout the night, he slept the best he could.

Come morning he had a few mouthfuls of rusty-tasting water, hardly sufficient to sustain a bird.

He moved on through the hills checking all he could about the guerrilla positions from his advantage of high ground. But all the time he was looking for reeds and other flora that would alert him to the presence of a waterhole, or at least to moisture containing fruit, roots and bulbs.

His every sense was aware of the smallest change in his environment. How crowded a place the bush seemed, apart from the guerrillas. The pageantry of animal-Africa went on around him. In the bush he was simply another animal; words, dialectical discussion, pretentious airs and graces had no place there, only raw physical survival. He was just another competitor, destined to live and die. He might not see all his other competitors, but they were there none the less; they were always there, the bush was alive with them, composed of them.

A leopard. A black-backed jackal. A blur of yellow and black as a serval cat hurriedly vacated the antbear hole in which it had no doubt intended to sleep away the heat of the day. Without a wasted hiss or a snarl or any other sound of departure except for a rustle in the bush, it was gone. A pack of wild dogs, which he made a wide detour to avoid. He would not have lasted long with them on his scent.

From time to time he would see unmistakable signs of the activity of other animals: their spoor, the sharpening of claws on the bark of a tree, the pasting of hyenas on the grass or their collective droppings. It was his mind and body against every other living thing.

He came across a *muzhanje* tree. Just one, out there amongst all the other trees. It had female flowers, destined perhaps never to bear fruit for he hadn't seen a male tree anywhere within pollen range. He wondered how it had got there. A couple of leaves had been torn off a branch by the passing of something. The leaves hadn't yet lost their shine so whatever had passed had only done so in the last few hours.

He looked about him. Damn! More ground spoor, and plenty of it. He altered his direction to move other than where the spoor was leading.

To a man familiar with the sounds of the bush, the effect of the wind on the grass and through the branches of trees, the calls of animals, the flutter of wings; the gurgle of water from a water bottle, the clink of a metal mug, the rattle of rifle-stock, cut through the bush like industrial machinery. He immediately went to ground.

316

As he sat concealed in the bush, he could smell woodsmoke and the aroma of roasting meat. It was cruel. His taste buds were instantly salivating with spit he never knew he still had.

Damn, and bloody damn again, the guerrillas seemed to be everywhere.

He could not risk so much as his spoor being identified as anything other than one of the guerrillas, for if they became aware they were being recced they would move in even more heavy weapon defences and the boys in the sky would not thank him for it.

If the guerrillas had not caught him out by sheer numbers they were effectively preventing him from having free and easy access to water and the abundance of food that the river would bring, and perhaps all without even knowing about it.

He withdrew. But as he did so his shirt caught on the thorns of a bush, and as he moved on he inadvertently tugged it so that the bush moved. He immediately rolled quietly from it, and not a moment too soon, for one of the guerrillas must have seen movement. He shouted and fired several rounds into the tree line. Birds flew out of the bush all around, and instantly Matt gave the curious barking call of a green pigeon.

Then he heard the other guerrillas laugh at the man having fired several shots at a green pigeon and missed.

The man turned back to them, and shrugging his shoulders resumed what seemed to been the conversation before his embarrassment.

'We will slaughter them,' he said.

'Words don't wear football boots,' said another.

It was strange to hear guerrillas casually talking about a proposed football match out there in the middle of the bush in hostile territory.

Matt cautiously moved away.

Well clear, Matt thought how, when in danger once of his movement being observed by a group of poachers on Matiziro, !Kai had used the call of that very same bird. Every boy in Africa, having hunted the bird for the pot, would know the distinctive call, and would have known how difficult it was to see the dapple green of its feathers in the bush!

That afternoon, feeling particularly weak, Matt rested in a place of dapple shade. For a long time he just couldn't muster up enough strength or willpower to scratch himself where he itched.

He closed his eyes, but because of his thirst couldn't sleep.

He did not know how much time had passed when he felt a shadow fall upon him. Instinctively rolling away, he flicked the safety catch of his rifle, his eyes flung open.

There was no one there. It was only the shadow of a branch in the wind. The sun had dropped a few more degrees through the earth's heaven, and the shadow had moved with it.

Once again he fought the mounting heat's debilitating and soporific effects. The land of the hills bordering the valley was scorched, the grass was brittle, and the same could be said of him, he thought, his lips cracked, throat so dry that it hurt and rasped when he breathed.

It was then that he noticed the unusually high concentration of *mupani* trees in a shallow depression of ground, a particularly poor drainage area. There had to be standing surface water somewhere in the vicinity, he thought.

The thought gave him illusory spare energy. He got to his feet and continued his search for water.

After searching without pause, during which the sun had dropped considerably nearer to the horizon, Matt realised that the separate game spoor that he had been crossing since he started, had all been converging towards a particular point. Those that had been moving up hill, out of the depression, he had ignored as indicators to water. Now he followed them to where they led.

As he went, he imagined dew condensing on the upper branches of a tree and dripping down into a hole in the fork between branches. He thought of butterflies and bees, thousands of them, in continuous lines, a certain indicator of water. He thought of juicy *muuyu* (baobab) bark, of the sweet wetness of the combretum vine.

A *leguuan* (monitor lizard) lying across a rock, watched him as he past. There was a superstition that *leguuans* stole milk from cows and lactating female antelope.

A *leguuan* would be near to water!

Matt simply had to keep going, hope to find water before he collapsed and dried out completely, became nothing more than a collection of bones strung together with leathery skin to be picked clean by vultures and polished by ants.

Digging for water-containing tubers often meant more energy and sweat loss than he could possibly hope to replenish with what he found.

He just had to keep going. The old man !Kai had survived no

matter the odds, he, Matthew Nel, now had to survive no matter the odds. He knew his brother would never have given in.

If he failed he doubted there was time enough for anyone else to complete the reconnaissance. The guerrillas would have infiltrated the country in their hundreds.

The game spoor converged on a rainwater trap in amongst rocks on the slope. From afar the stagnant water seemed to move sullenly with its own ethereal life.

Then he saw why – mosquitoes. The air was filled with the beating of countless thousands of tiny pairs of wings, each mosquito an integral part of an ominous whole.

He checked for scratches or water and mud splashes on the rocks that would indicate other humans had been there before him. He could find no evidence that anyone had.

The stagnant water hardly looked appetising, but he had to risk drinking it, to hope that he wouldn't be infected by it. And he was only too pleased to have it. It was a case of do or die. He knew for one thing, that despite the off-putting presence of the breeding mosquitoes, malaria was not passed on from them to their larvae so there was little danger of that. He was bitten by many of the mosquitoes, but he knew that if he was to get malaria it would be at least ten days before he suffered the symptoms and by then the raid would have been completed.

One at a time, holding a hand over the mouth of each of his two water bottles, he lowered them into the pool at arm's length below the surface, where there were mosquito larvae together with floating debris, and above the bottom, where there was sediment, and let each bottle fill with the middle water which was relatively clean.

Man has the mating radius of a mosquito, he thought as he filled the bottles. He mates with what he bumps into. If it has a hole and moves, fuck it, was the sentiment.

Danielle!

He had had to keep defending himself against her. It had not been easy to bear seeing Danielle get hurt, but he could bear even less to give up the fight against Mumvuri. So he had withdrawn from her, and had to keep defending himself against her.

So many beautiful women in the world, he told himself, but choice was simply by random contact, a given place, a given time, that was all there was to it.

He drank from the water bottles, slowly at first, intending to see if

319

it had any untoward effect on him, then against his better judgement he found himself gulping down the entire contents of both.

He refilled the bottles then moved a safe distance away before stopping to rest.

He felt a great deal better. He could feel the smile on his face, and feel his manner less tense. He lay on the ground and revelled in the feeling of his bloated belly.

Thinking of the mosquitoes, he remembered his brother offering a couple of quinine tablets to !Kai on one of their early times out in the bush.

'Not that you need them, the mozy that tries to bite you will get a bent proboscis,' his brother had joked.

'The one that bites you will get the sickness,' !Kai had joked in return.

!Kai was somehow naturally immune to malaria, and many other illnesses that plagued later arrivals to the land.

Abdominal pain.

He was caught in its tentacles, alternately cold and sweating. He was flung about in its grappling throes. Cramps seized him. Nightmare images stormed his brain in chaotic profusion, he had difficulty focusing his eyes.

He slept on and off through the following day, between bouts of vomiting and diarrhoea, so intermittently that he no longer knew how much time had passed since last he woke, was no longer able even to be sure of what day it was. He panicked, terrified that he was going to miss the next guerrilla assembly, his last chance.

He felt like weeping. The whole operation seemed lost to him. He felt he had failed.

He was incredibly thirsty. He had lost so much fluid from his body that he was in danger of dehydration. But all he had was the water that had poisoned him.

He closed his eyes.

When he opened them again all he saw was blackness. The blackness seemed to be in his head, his pupils seemed full of it.

He felt he was buried deep within something. He heard things as if he was in the body of some living thing; the process of digestion, the beat of a pulse, the rush of blood, the squish of intestinal juices, went on around him. He felt movement as if something was alive and shivering, and then the shivering stopped. It was as if what he was inside of had suddenly died, and that only in its death was he aware that it had been alive. Rigor mortis was setting in, the stiffening of muscles, sinews, ligaments and joints. He was suddenly intensely aware of the stopping of a heart, the beating of which he had taken for granted, only feeling it now through its absence.

A moan wavered about him, distanced from him, he seemed quite separate from it. His eyes felt heavy, wandering around in their sockets without seeing.

He presumed that he was dead. But then he saw the stars. It was night. The bush was swamped with it.

Throughout the night he felt himself falling, spiralling. Dark hands reached out at him from the darkness. He struck out, kicked, scratched, bit, and must have driven them off for there was light on the horizon.

Morning came, but he felt too weak to get up.

As the sun became hotter, he crawled into the shade and just lay there, hoping that whatever was ailing him would wear off soon enough.

Lying on the ground, he was intensely aware of the busy insect life going on there, whereas before, his perceptions of life had been formed mostly from above the ground. When he scraped the top layer of soil he found worms and bugs and things, and deeper still, more bugs and things dead or alive, deeper, deeper, each grain of soil a home for micro-organisms, smaller and smaller vehicles of life, one upon the other, nothing escaping being food for something else.

When he looked outwards he saw the sun, centre of a solar system, a billionth part of a galaxy, a black hole, bigger and bigger manifestations of existence . . . the deeper he went in, the nearest he came to the furthest point that he could reach if he looked out, there seemed to be no beginning and no end.

His mind concentrated on a rhino-beetle, an amazing insect reproduction of its mammal namesake with horns and all, cousin of the scarab, sacred to the ancients. He watched its every activity, manoeuvring a damp ball of dung. Even through his feverish mind he told himself that such a find meant that game had recently been there.

Then there were stinkbugs. He examined them in the smallest detail, pulled them apart, minutely inspected a leg.

Just because things were small it didn't mean that their existence was any the easier to understand.

How far more grand was the mystery of non-existence!

A stick-insect walked over him.

He felt how he would waste away to its proportions if he didn't exert his will over nature.

Insects crawled in his mind.

With great effort he got to his feet and looked for things to eat.

Even when he found a few berries and a couple of roots, and forced himself to eat them, he couldn't keep them down. His stomach seemed to lurch into his mouth. His teeth clenched and his mouth was filled with bile and partially undigested food pulp. The action jarred his entire system. A streak of hot pain sliced his chest. Nauseating pain squirmed around inside his head, trapped, with no way of escape.

Then, when his stomach had settled down once again, for a while after he seemed to be borne on by a dark river, as thick and as warm as blood.

He was thirsty, hungry, ill and alone, far from home and friends, deep in hostile enemy territory with over a thousand guerrillas all about him.

Out with Alexandra and Elaine in town to get away from the farm and the tension of living under the constant threat of guerrilla attack, and over tea that turned cold in the cup without her bringing it to her lips, Danielle allowed the tears to well up inside her. At last, all the resentments, doubts, disillusions and buried fears she had harboured within her, denying them expression burst to the surface and at once exploded in profusion.

As she talked to them, she twisted the wedding ring around on her finger. She needed someone to confide in, someone to talk to, and Alexandra and Elaine could understand.

Matt was out there alone, and the enormity of what that meant had suddenly come home to her.

She, Suzanne, Alexandra and Elaine had been close from the start. But Suzanne had gone, only Alexandra and Elaine were left. They had found themselves telling each other things in the first few days of their friendship which they had never told to people they had known most of their lives.

When she was with them, no longer did conversation revolve around the culling of the non-productive, the old, the weak or deformed birds in the hen house, pelvic girths measured to see who were the layers; clipping of piglets' needle-like canine and pre-molar teeth to prevent them injuring the nipples and udder of the sow when suckling, and to reduce injuries to each other in piglet fights; the docking of tails of the Ronderib Afrikaaner sheep; or the castrations of those animals not wanted for breeding.

And it was only yesterday that Maruva had been making sausages: polonies, using the large intestines of cattle; pork and beef, using the small intestines of pigs; and viennas, using the small intestines of sheep!

Alexandra and Elaine were from town, one in a beautiful summer dress, the other in her femininely-tailored grey business skirt and jacket. They chatted of fashions, of books, of films, of people in the international news, of ideas, aspirations, and of love . . .

'I don't know whether to blame it on the war, him, me, both of us, or what,' Danielle said.

'The war won't last forever,' Alexandra told her.

'Yes,' she said, in an artificially buoyant voice.

'Now let's be naughty and have some Black Forest gateau,' smiled Elaine.

They ordered the cake, and chatted about little things void of emotive content, while they waited for the waitress to return.

But Danielle could not buoy her feelings up much longer. 'The thought passes my mind that if he was incapacitated, just a little, he would have to come back home.' Immediately she was shocked at having voiced such thoughts. 'God, what am I saying!' she exclaimed.

'It's all right, it's all right,' soothed Alexandra, taking hold of her. 'In the beginning of his operational police days, I had such thoughts about James as well. When he got wounded in the leg and was prevented from doing field work for a long time I felt strangely pleased. But it didn't stop him. He just worked harder, got the use of his leg back and resumed where he had left off.'

There was an awkward pause.

'It was something he felt he had to do, to fulfil himself as the person he was. And oddly enough I found that it was that kind of commitment to the things that he felt mattered, despite the risk to himself, that I admired, and, amongst other things, loved him for.'

'Danielle, I'm so sorry,' said Elaine. 'I overheard Andy arguing with James one night. I heard what Matt did, how he cut Andy out. That it was for Andy's own safety.'

'This time of year Matt usually checks the maize plants to see what additional fertiliser they need, whether more nitrogen, phosphorus or potash. He would almost instinctively know what by the state the plant was in, whether by poor growth and purple patches on the leaves, or by scorched leaf edges and susceptibility to disease. To ensure a good harvest I have to know exactly what is lacking and how much. If too much is added the plants will turn pulpy, ripen too fast or too slow. And less fertiliser is needed for the maize following the cowpeas . . .' Suddenly she stopped. It seemed such an irrelevant stupid thing to say.

But Alexandra and Elaine seemed to understand the stress that Danielle was under and what she was really saying: 'I wish Matt was here. I wish Matt was just left alone to farm.'

Night came as a dead weight above him and he wrestled with it.

Hallucinations bred like reptiles in his mind, cavorted and twisted. Spasms of pain wrapped around him like the muscular constrictions of a python about its prey, tightening as he breathed out, preventing his lungs from re-expanding.

At those times he found himself calling out to Danielle, but the words remained prisoners in his throat.

He found himself thinking of his grandfather, his father and brother, and !Kai, and how he couldn't let them down, how they would have found the strength to carry on. Nothing short of death had ever kept a Nel down for long. A profusion of lessons he had learnt from them all crowded his mind.

In his bed of raw earth, he clutched his memories to him and the poison in his system violently ravaged him.

When the sun rose it was raw and angry.

The temperature shot up thirty degrees Centigrade from the cold dawn to the sweltering mid-afternoon. The heat was painful. It tore at his flesh.

Tired; that a man could be so tired!

Grit scratched his eyes, bloodshot eyes, eyelids swollen almost shut; his vision blurred, watery. The sun was too bright to keep his eyes open; he had to peer through them almost closed.

Matt sat there leaning against a tree, unable to think clearly through the profusion of images in his head. And he couldn't bring himself to move – even when he heard a distant scuffling in the grass coming towards him.

Then he remembered how once he had just sat down on the spoor when out tracking a kudu with !Kai, refusing to go on. !Kai had simply reminded him: 'It's but a short way to go on, but a long way back.' And it was.

Matt rose on loose legs, the razor grass cutting his hands as he pulled on it for support. He turned his face to the sun and forced his feet to move under him. Pain that could not now be isolated to any particular part of his body threw him cowering back down again. But the memory of !Kai, a little man who didn't let even the debilitating effects of old age prevent him from continuing as he always had, made him pull himself instantly back on to his feet.

There was the sound of voices now, nearby, urgent and questioning.

He stumbled on.

He concentrated on the slap-slap of his feet on the earth to keep himself moving.

He found a square of *mutute* bark he had discarded in his jacket pocket some time ago. He took it out and pushed it into his mouth. He chewed on and on, in time with the slap-slap of his feet, his jaws working incessantly, following the rhythm, on and on, slap, slap, slap, slap . . .

Nothing seemed quite real. He was struggling once more to come to terms with his surroundings.

A warning kept wriggling in his thoughts. He flinched at the sounds his feet made. He tried to step more softly, but at the same time he had to get away. Nothing else mattered. He ran as best he could. He ran as if that was his calling in life, as if to run at that particular moment in time was what he had been created for. Trees and bushes loomed up before him, rising at his feet with each step as he ran. To run was the only thing left that was significant.

Sweat trickled away, his brain felt as if it was being shaken to runny jelly, liquefied, dripping from his skull, on and on, empty-headed, running on and on . . . his legs moving faster and faster beneath him, trying to avoid the trees and bushes, tripping and sliding, hopping from rock to rock, swinging his arms madly to keep his balance, frantically trying to keep pace with his feet, on and on . . . slap, slap, slap, slap . . . He was running with his brother and !Kai as a young boy. The kudu he had wounded, failing to kill, had continually frustrated his thinking, it would slow down, even stop but as soon as he got near it would run on again. But it was he who had caused the kudu to suffer, so it was he who had to put out that suffering, no matter how much he suffered himself in the process, no matter how thirsty, hungry, tired, weak. For the body to continue the mind had to hold on no matter what. It had come to the stage where he no longer believed that kudu at all, only that everything it did was a tactic specifically devised to frustrate him. Just one more hill. But no sooner had he run up that hill than there was another one, and another one, and another . . . Even when he saw the kudu standing exhausted with the loss of blood and the exertion, unable to run any further, he could not believe it.

Most would have doubted that !Kai's little legs could have carried him either very fast or very far, but it would not have been the first time men had been deceived by appearances. Those legs, even when old, could still run a wounded antelope to ground. Within that thin ropey form was the knowledge of the African bush itself. Hardened by experience, there was no soft skin on his entire body, every part of him had known fatigue, and overcome it. The skin on the soles of his feet was like rhinoceros hide, and he could run as fast as a rhinoceros too.

Matt ran on now, on and on.

His mind fixed on the next tree, the next rock, the next tree, the next hill, the next rock, the next tree . . . telling himself that that was as far as he had to go, but when he got there it was always the next point he had been meaning.

His bowels, emptied the night before, intestinal glands inflamed, suffered muscle contractions even now as he ran, as if trying to force the bowel itself through. And whatever moisture was left in his body not consumed by fever's heat was sweated out in the running. As he ran he thought of the semi-succulent leaves of the climbing milkweed. He had visions of 'rain trees', frog-hopper nymphs dribbling sap from the tree shoots. All his visions were of water, any water.

His brother, with an arm around his shoulder, helped him on.

His lungs heaved painfully for the thin transparent air.

Sunset.

Now he was shuffling, dragging his feet. Keep moving, whatever you do, no matter how slowly, don't stop, he told himself.

Just over the last ridge, out of sight, he looped back on to his spoor, so as to be overlooking it for pursuers, and burrowed into dense bush, his breath rasping dryly in his throat. He fought to bring his mutinous breathing under control.

He saw no one on his spoor, he didn't even know if they had seen him, or whether in fact they had picked up his trail.

At last, night fell like a comforting blanket.

On cue, believing that once more he was out of immediate danger, Matt collapsed on his back on the ground. He felt that he could move no more, even if absolutely necessary, that he was finished if he should be found there.

So long as he had kept running the sweat had evaporated from the surface of his body with the flow of air cooling him, but now stationary, his sweat soaked him, and as his body cooled he became cold and wet.

Night was no longer a comforting blanket.

He spat out a slug of yellow rheum. Pain jarred through his body. Muscles cramped, particularly his stomach, painful every time he moved.

Now there was no cause to push himself on, no psychological deceptions necessary, no self-promises to keep him moving, no self-accusations, no fixed points of thought to the exclusion of all else. He was delirous with dehydration, with fatigue.

It seemed as if he was transported to a level above it all, above his own physical imperfection. His senses were below him, and what he perceived he perceived through layers of space and time far divorced one from the other.

'Life is painful. Death is not the absence of life, but it is the absence of pain,' he remembered !Kai had once said.

All night he shivered.

It was sheer will to survive against all other imposed wills that brought the dawn.

Now, all day, he sweated beneath the sun. Legs stiff, body sore, breathing difficult, he gathered what meagre berries and roots he could, and once again tried to force himself to eat, for the moisture content if nothing else.

He did his best to disguise his spoor, to conceal his whereabouts.

The temperature dropped noticeably at sundown, as usual, and then went into a steady slow decline, only it did not recover at dawn.

*

Guti cloud rolled in, a maritime wind invasion from the Indian Ocean.

The cold clutched at him and pulled him down to the cold ground. It seeped through his flesh to the bones, chilling the marrow there.

He sniffed mucus from the inflamed membranes of his nose into his throat and swallowed; but a knuckled lump formed there. He swallowed again and again. The sickly precipitate sank at last to the bottom of his stomach. It compacted in bitter gall, and then rose up again into his throat. He had constantly to wipe at sour drops that dribbled from his nostrils down to his mouth.

After excessive change and destruction of body tissue resulting from the body having overheated with the effects of the poisoning, he now sat there with the temperature having dropped around him. He sat shivering, sniffing, coughing and distraughtly fingering the radio. He thought of demanding an immediate casevac, but did no more than think of it, leaving the radio alone once again. Life was painful, death was not the absence of life, but it was the absence of pain.

When he realised that in fact he wasn't going to radio for help, and so could not rely on such knowledge for succour, he breathed with the heavy gasps of an old man overcome by exhaustion and age.

Tink . . . tink . . . tink . . .

Tink . . . tink . . . tink . . . A yellow-fronted tinkerbird, hidden in the white-out.

Tink . . . tink . . . tink . . . tink . . . Perhaps a hundred times without cessation, on and on, like Chinese water torture, the incessant drip-dripping on his forehead driving him crazy . . . tink . . . tink . . . tink . . . tink . . . tink . . .

He once again used his wound-dressing as a sponge to collect moisture, this time from the broad-leafed plants where it collected best, and left his water bottles beneath two such leaves, for moisture to collect and drip into them overnight.

The *guti* did not lift the next morning. It had, if anything, become heavier during the night.

He drank from the small quantity of water that had collected in his water bottles, fervently trying to work things out in his mind. If he just stayed there he would get weaker and weaker, and that would be that.

He eventually decided that he had to risk being observed and get to the river. He would use the *guti*, that wrapped everything in its thick whiteness, as his daytime security. The morning was almost as

328

isolated and personal as a moonlit night, only he would be able to look out for spoor, and watch for any physical sighting. He would not be seen in the dense bush and dense *guti* from more than ten to twenty paces, which ruled out the guerrillas being able to see him from their observation postions on the points of high ground, which under clear conditions had been one of his greatest worries.

'We must look for food or there will be nothing for our stomachs but the scabs on our bodies,' he rememberd !Kai once telling him.

He got up and walked, and as he walked he could not help but breathe the cold vapour into his lungs like an old wheezing asthmatic.

Spoor he came across was not recent. It was made before the ground had softened with the *guti*, and in places was partially obliterated by the dripping of it.

Four hours later, having made his way through almost impenetrable bush, he reached the river and followed its edge for a while before he found a rocky recess. Instinctively he checked a pool there for signs of life before drinking, ensuring it was not contaminated again. Close to the bottom of the pool, out of reach, were the moving shapes of several fish. He filled his water bottles first, as a precaution against having to move on quickly again and missing the opportunity to get water. He then drank, slowly, intent on retaining discipline now; in time he would restore lost body fluid, and flush his body clean of impurities.

Not far from the pool was a *mufonde* (candelabra euphorbia) and not far from the *mufonde* a cave. Here was his water, here was his food, and here was his shelter, he told himself.

He barricaded with branches the small channel where the fish might swim out of the pool, between the rocks into the main flow of the river.

That finished, he stumbled back to where he had seen the *mufonde*.

Having to stop several times to regain his breath, he chopped the entire cactus-like plant down with his knife. Once it was down he threw earth over the stump to hide its whiteness, stabbed his knife into the thick trunk of the plant, and using it as a handle away from the sharp thorns, lifted the plant up, so as not to create any drag marks on the earth, and straining with the effort, carried it to the rock pool.

He clumsily hacked it into chunks on a rock there and set about crushing each chunk with a heavy stone, careful to shield his eyes. In his energy-depleted state it took some time, but eventually the rock ran thick with a white latex. He felt his skin burn where drops of it had splashed on to him. He washed them off with water, then scraped the latex off the rock into the pool. It formed a milky film on the surface. He threw the green residual pulp in after it.

Worn out even further, but the job complete, he went to the cave in amongst the reeds close to the water's edge. From there he could see the ripple rings on the water as fish momentarily surfaced. The latex would congeal on their gills, inhibiting respiration.

He woke up to find himself curled in the mud of the cave like a foetus. Despite being cold and wet, his exhaustion had caused him to sleep. He was inside the drip-line of the cave mouth, but the slope of the ground meant that the floor had been wet.

The low cloud was still all about, lying heavy on the ground. All was still. But on the surface of the pool there were fish of many types and sizes, some floating lifelessly on their sides, some beating their tails from time to time, moving about haphazardly, diving beneath the surface but always drawn back to it by the latex, like a rubber band.

He swept the surface clean of fish with a leafy branch, and strung them, most as big as labourers' hands, on a long strip of bark through gill and mouth.

The *guti* still thick, he decided to risk a fire.

Summoning up the energy he could, he forced himself to break down branches from a standing dead tree. Being off the ground the wood would not be water-logged. He stripped the wet bark off, and splintered the inner wood for better burning.

Before he lit the fire he screened the small entrance to the cave with leafy branches and long grass.

He lit the fire using friction between a stick of hard and a chip of soft wood, boring a hole until it was red-hot then sprinkling it with the contents from a cartridge case and strands of dry grass from where they had been blown to the back of the cave. Soon flames danced like enchanting priestesses, bringing light and warmth and mystery to the dank rock chamber.

He de-gilled and gutted the fish, placing them on sticks in a lattice-work over the fire and around its edge.

Many more fish would die in the pool, but he would have no need for them, and could not prevent the process now. Although he was purposefully downriver of the camp, he could not break down the branch barricade and allow the pool to clear, for dead fish and pulped *mufonde* would drift down-river and alert any of the patrols that ranged far from the camp. They would not have much difficulty finding their source, and as he had no intention of moving, they would find him there.

Holding his hands over the flames, he was all too aware of intense pain as feeling returned to his numbed flesh. He withdrew from the fire. He could not allow himself to become too accustomed to its warmth, not just yet.

I must wash, get rid of the grime of sickness, he told himself.

He made his way a little further up river.

Fully clothed, he settled between two rocks near to the bank sheltered by bush and reeds. The water rushed over his shoulders. He felt so weak he could barely hold his rifle on extended arms above his head out of the water. He put it down on a rock close beside him, and stripped off his filthy clothes. He scrubbed them and himself clean with sand, ridding himself of the oily fever-sweat, the bits of grass and leaf in the unkempt mass of hair on his head, the stubble on his face, and the three weeks of encrusted grime and scabs from wounds inflicted by the bush. His skin tingled; bruised by rocks, scratched by bushes and grass, stung by insects, aggravated by dirt and sweat, and one long purulent laceration on his right leg, torn by a thorn, since infected, now soothed by cleansing water. After a time the water had seemed warm but now felt colder and colder the longer he stayed in it, and when he pulled himself out, picking up his rifle and clothing, the air seemed colder still.

As he ran back along the bank he noticed *bitterwortel* and *cyperus* growing. He stopped to dig up the white carrot-like root of the one, and chop off a length of the running fibrous root of the other. He immediately treated himself to aromatic tonic mouthfuls of them as, shivering uncontrollably, he resumed his way to the fire and the grilling fish.

He hung his clothes across the inside of the branch-and-grass screen to make it more of a light barrier with night advancing, and so they would be close to the fire to dry.

Then, shivering alarmingly, but hunched over the fire, he no longer felt that it was all over for him.

When he had warmed up a little he made a sortie out into the bush again.

When he came back, he placed *mudyamhembwe* (duiker berry) root on the fire. As it burnt it gave off a mild antiseptic smoke, helping to relieve his lungs of congestion. It filled the cave and filtered out through the gaps in the screen and cave walls into the bush already smokey with the *guti*.

Muti was the word for both medicine and the tree – they were one and the same to the natural people of Africa.

As the fish cooked he nibbled at them, then set about tending to the open gash on his leg that had turned septic.

After another sortie outside, he came back with leaves of the white-spotted aloe he had found, sliced them open and applied them to the inflamed wound. A mucilage of a plant of the pelargonium family, acting like carbolic acid, helped kill germs. Mallow leaves, acting as a styptic, finally sealed the wound from the air to combat festering and inflammation.

'Are not such things used in circumcision?' !Kai had once asked him, tending to a wound. 'Without them there is always nettle. Without nettle there is always goose-foot weed. The bush takes life, but the bush also gives it.'

He bound the gash on his leg with the second dressing from his pocket, being careful to keep the plastic wrapper.

As fish became ready, he gorged himself unabashed. He smiled to himself, delighting in the good flavour and abundance of his meal.

He remembered laughing at !Kai once, who looked like a gambia rat taking food to its burrow, as he stuffed the pouches of his cheeks in a like manner with the fish.

Then, by association, he was thinking that to bite like a rat in the night, so skilfully as not even to wake those bitten was the task he still had to perform, and he was a long way from being ready for it.

It was a terrible feeling being responsible for the lives of so many people, the lives of friends back home if he failed in his quest against terrorism, the lives of foes if he succeeded. It was strange how the outcome of his mission there would determine the fate of Danielle back home, and all the others across the border, perhaps without them ever knowing about it.

The next day for the guerrillas' weekly politicisation assembly was fast approaching. He had to be there for that one, or he would have failed. Even now, he didn't know if the pattern of meetings still held firm. He could only hope so.

He would not have another chance. The task force of men and machinery could not be tied up for any longer, waiting for something that might never happen, while guerrillas were enjoying a free season in the country, committing their crimes unmolested. As it was, the country was in dire need of utilising every man it could at all times. Having élite forces and aircraft tied up non-productively was proving a costly experience in undefended lives and money.

Besides all that, he didn't look forward to pussy-footing around guerrilla-infested countryside for another week even if he did have the extra opportunity.

Before dawn the *guti* had lifted.

While it was still dark, Matt blackened the parts of his skin that showed with burnt tree-cork, put on his sand- and water-cleaned clothes, dry and warm, and stuffed as many of the cooked fish into his pockets as he could together with the rest of the *bitterwortel* and *cyperus*. He stamped out the fire and cleared all startlingly obvious signs of his habitation of the cave. The black of the smoke would still be on the walls, and it would be easily apparent to a trained eye that someone had been there, but it was the best he could do.

'I owe you my life,' he thought, to !Kai.

For him, his stomach was no longer cramped with pain and the fever brought on by the poison had broken. He was through.

'Two men of the same spirit share the same life and they share the same death.' The words of !Kai came to him.

Before leaving, Matt cleared the river pool of the *mufonde* debris and dead fish, burying them in the mud of the river bank where digging was easy and it was easy enough to conceal signs of a hole dug there.

A little upriver of the poisoned pool he drank all his stomach could hold, made sure his water bottles were full, and then continued on his way from the cave, up towards the high ground of the Mapfupa Hills to overlook the guerrilla camp once more, just as dawn was beginning to touch the horizon.

The sun was soon high in the sky. Its heat filled him with a sense of well-being.

He stopped for a lunch of fish at midday.

After eating a little, he lay spreadeagled on his back in the bush part of the way up the hillside, with the great expanse of the valley beginning to reveal itself before him. It was a beautiful valley, and he let the sun have its way with him.

When Danielle went into town to sort out farm business, pick up the mail, newspapers and provisions for the other farmers' wives on Horseshoe Ridge, she thought how she could be seen walking along a pavement, the ungainly Uzi slung over a shoulder and banging against her waist; her face set, tired, wearing a lot of make-up, her eyes wary, and when a car backfired how she sought cover, a heavy breath being drawn from her lips and then released as she tried to avoid the gaze of others on the pavement in embarrassment.

The atmosphere of town had changed. The war was in every shop window; on her last visit she saw a Father Christmas, but instead of wearing a red suit, he was wearing a camouflage one. Now, there was a poster in a toyshop declaring: BIG EARS IS A TERRORIST: a poster in the Tea Shoppe cautioning: WHAT YOU ARE ABOUT TO SAY COULD BLOW UP A TRUCK; there were half-price haircuts for troopies at the barbers; there were handbag searches in the department store.

There were always pretty materials in the department store, and women, still wearing beautiful flowing colourful summer frocks, already talked about winter fashions. Danielle looked down at her self-tailored khaki shirt and khaki trousers with thick leather belt. It had become a summer fashion in the city, and had even caught on overseas, she had heard; but not for someone who had to wear it out of necessity practically all year round.

The war was in the newsstands, on the pages of papers, on the glossy covers of magazines, on the radio and on the TV; not analyses of events, but communiqués of enemy forces 'killed' and own forces 'murdered', of commercials directed at those in uniform.

Military vehicles forever seemed to trundle through the streets, packed with several times more soldiers than she had ever seen there before, going to who-knows-where from who-knows-where. And once in a while, instead of being taken through the town at night as was customary by standing orders, vehicles written off by land mines or rockets, with shattered bullet-proof windows, buckled chassis and crumpled bodyworks, were towed downtown in broad daylight.

There were men and women in military uniforms everywhere.

There were amputees.

The war was there, but so also were a people who, despite the horror, still found that they had things to smile and laugh for.

Danielle thought how the war was claiming all their lives whether they were out in the bush fighting or not. She worried about Matt, where he was, what he was doing, whether he was all right.

She worried about the farm, worried about coping with it, worried that guerrillas might attack it. She worried about travelling to town in case there were more land mines on the roads, and she worried when she was in town because of the mass militarisation that had taken away its once sleepy character, and because such a presence meant that the war had escalated beyond all expectation.

When on the farm, she worried that she was a single isolated white woman out there, and when she was in town she worried that she was not on the farm in case something happened to it! It was crazy.

She felt like crying when she thought how dramatically her life had changed in the last fifteen months, how far it had drifted from her first four years of almost idyllic marriage, how even further she was now from her days as a carefree girl on her parents' smallholding just outside the city, when her grandest adventures were to go dancing, to the theatre or cinema, and make a single cup of coffee last into the early hours so that she could stay on chatting with friends at their favourite restaurant, and afterwards go window shopping hand-in-hand with a boyfriend – who would become a doctor or a lawyer.

She thought how the 'good old days' were when she would buy dresses and gowns and silky lingerie, be driven around in big, expensive, fast sports cars with sleek lines, no heavy mine-protective plating and sub-machine-guns.

She recalled her days as a student nurse and longed for them, how the doctors swarmed around her, how she could have had her pick of any of the men – and perhaps have travelled the world, spent her days topless on beaches of the Mediterranean, Caribbean . . . and her evenings at the world's most famous opera houses, theatres, in the most salubrious restaurants and palatial mansions, with butler, chauffeur, cordon bleu chefs . . . children playing in the garden.

At that moment, walking along the pavement towards her, she saw a doctor she knew from the hospital.

He greeted her delightedly. They exchanged small talk. He asked her if she would care to have lunch with him. She declined, saying how she was meeting girlfriends. He said perhaps some other time, and told her to take care. They walked their respective ways.

Danielle didn't know why she hadn't asked him to join her, because she was meeting Alexandra and Elaine for lunch at the hotel.

Neither Alexandra, Elaine nor herself had seen their husbands for at least three weeks now, and they all seemed to feel the same need to get together. All they knew was that something considerably ominous was in the offing that could make the change in their lives irrevocable.

Over lunch, Danielle caught the eye of a man in a suit watching her. He smiled. She hadn't seen him in town before. She thought how good-looking he was, had a warm smile. She smiled back. He resumed his meal and took up the conversation of the others at his table. She ate a little more fish, and rejoined the conversation of Alexandra and Elaine.

High alto-cumulus indicated fine weather to come. Ideal for aircraft.

Matt resumed his journey up to the vantage point of a ridge just below the hillcrests overlooking the camp.

Late that afternoon, he came across a wild beehive. It was in a rock crevice, a location which was particularly favoured by the most aggressive species of wild African bee.

Unperturbed by the fact, he prepared a cigar from wild leaves as !Kai had once showed him to do, lit it, and drawing on the herbal smoke, blew it into the aperture of the hive. That way there was little evidence of smoke to be seen or smelt by the guerrillas.

With a stick, he wheedled the comb through the small entrance aperture, wrapped the pieces in broad leaves and put them in a pocket.

The comb was heavy with brood cells; eggs in nutrient royal jelly, and maturing mild-white grubs like cores of paraffin wax, evidence of the queen's feverish reproductivity from the first opening of the spring flowers. There were also pantry cells, packed so tightly with pollen that they formed solid cartridges of protein; and there were, of course, precious cellfulls of the quickly assimilated, energy-giving, fragrant, almost-black honey.

He continued on his way to the ridge, chewing at a piece of the heavy wax comb dripping with honey and young bee-grubs. A little dribbled down the side of his mouth. He felt that it was as near to ecstasy as you could come.

Near the top of the ridge he suddenly stopped. A scrap of paper was caught on a thornbush. It was the sort of paper used as a seal on a

336

new battery. His immediate thought was that there was a booby-trap somewhere nearby. But where?

He hadn't gone more than a few paces further when he tripped over something drawn tight across the path. Even before he hit the ground, he cried out, 'Oh Christ, no, a trip-wire!'

It was not. He saw that he had tripped over a creeper.

He cursed himself after that, the honeycomb had become crunchy with sand. It had fallen out of his pocket.

That night he was still making his way up to the ridge. He thought how it was Friday night, traditionally his night out with the boys, when they would go into town, have a few beers at the hotel bar, or, once in a while go to the city, do a little bit of hell-raising – but that was before Mumvuri.

The following dawn would be the moment of truth. He would know then whether or not the guerrillas were still assembling.

Nervousness at what he might find, or rather, what he would not find, ate at him.

Bearing in mind the lateness of the moon's rising, he considered that there would be three-quarters of an hour or so more darkness that night, but anxiously fearing that he would miss his last oportunity of confirming that the assembly had taken place, he did not stop to wait for the moon to come out and make his going easier.

He was almost too anxious to want to reach the ridge, look down into the valley and see that no assembly was taking place.

By the time the moon eventually peeped through a gap in the scattered grey cloud overhead, he had already reached the ridge, and what he saw made his anxiety dissipate. In its place he was filled with awe and at the same time such an overwhelming feeling of triumph that he trembled with it. Down there in the valley had congregated fifteen hundred, perhaps two thousand, guerrillas.

He took the radio off his back and sat it down beside him.

He ached, was tired, but was so pumped up full of intense emotion that there was no danger of him falling asleep. Nevertheless, he worried about it.

The end of his mission was in sight.

Down in the valley, an hour before dawn, in the light of countless watchfires, he could see such a mass of guerrillas had converged on Mumvuri's camp as he had never seen in his life before. At one and the same time it was chilling and awe-inspiring.

In the half-hour before dawn, there were now some 2,500 heavily armed guerrillas down at the assembly point, with perhaps another 500 on guard.

He turned the radio on, and hesitated before finally sending the codeword in morse via the relay station in the border mountains to James and Andy in the office some 190 kilometres away as the bird flies.

He listened to the pounding of the guerrillas' feet, listened to their *chimurenga* slogans of the uprising, and listened to their singing. His mind had no difficulty in slipping back a hundred years to before the white man was in the bush interior of southern Africa, conjuring up hordes of warriors striking the shafts of assegais on rawhide shields as the raiding *madzviti* stormed the valley . . . but here were men of a military force armed and trained with sophisticated automatic rifles and machine-guns, here were the descendants of Africa who had inherited the most base yet most advanced of all civilisation's achievements, the knowledge of how to kill more men more easily more quickly . . .

Pambere nechimurenga . . . pambere nehondo . . . Forward with the revolution . . . forward with the war . . . no mercy for the white settlers . . . they're digging their own graves . . . not a day without the struggle . . . not an hour without the movement . . . not a minute without the people . . . destroy the enemy by all means and any means . . . the only fitting way to speak to the white racists, the running dogs and their black puppets, is with more bullets . . .

Their singing was in the close earthy harmony that alone could be found in these people:

> *Vakomanaenda madzi baba ano fora*
> *Vadzoka madzimai vanochema*
> > *Apa yandibaya*
> > *Apa yandibaya*
> *Phururu yandibaya . . .*

> When the boys go, fathers are happy
> When they return, mothers cry
> > Here the bullet
> > Here the bullet
> The bullet has pierced me . . .

Matt found himself tapping along with the beat of those feet – he was caught up in the rhythm.

When he heard the many voices start singing the black nationalist anthem *Ishe Komberera Afrika* – God Bless Africa – he was so deeply moved, humming along, then singing the words to himself, that he felt tears form in his eyes.

There were armed guerrillas down there like *kapenta* fish in a shoal, in their breeding grounds, not in ones and twos spread throughout the valley back home, when ten minutes after dawn the bombers were overhead, barely specks in the clear blue sky at 13,000 metres.

450-kilogram bombs flowered hot and screaming. The sky turned to deep purple, then it burst into flame. It was so bright Matt could no longer see. It was so loud he could no longer hear. A shock wave of jarring light was followed by a shock wave of jarring sound, of such intensity that they caused pain. There was a hot slap of air. Even on the ridge, high above the floor of the valley, he gasped for air as the explosions exhausted the valley of oxygen. The belly of the valley ruptured, heaving up in a horrendous change of form.

Barely seconds separated the devastating thuds of exploding bombs from the ear-perforating screams of the single-seater fighters, moving ahead of their sound, low under radar cover, their approach path along the length of the valley right past him to the primary anti-aircraft batteries at the top and bottom ends of the camp. When he heard them it was already too late, each had struck with rockets streaking, cannons spitting 30mm rounds each with a frag-spread of an offensive grenade, and the anti-aircraft battery he had seen at the waterfall when he had first been there was gone, and each fighter was already pulling maybe as much as 5gs as it climbed up through the sky out of the valley at the far end.

More fighters were quick to follow, carrying bombs in place of their drop-tanks, plummeting down from their perch points, too fast for the anti-aircraft gunners to take a bead on them. They loosed their lethal droppings in stacks of ten, each bouncing off the ground and exploding at head height.

The smoke and dust hadn't even settled when helicopters seemed to occupy the whole sky in an encirclement of the assembly area. They alighted in one place and then another. It looked absolutely chaotic; but he knew they would be working to a strict plan, making false drops, giving the appearance of an inflated number of the strike force, confusing the enemy as to where ambush parties were actually being placed, and having the effect of channelling those that attempted to escape from the assembly area through designated killing grounds. Battle-psyched troops jumped out a couple of metres or so above the ground in whirlwinds of dust kicked up by the downwash of the rotors, the technicians disturbing the bush around them with brutal spurts of their twin MAGs. The helicopters paused momentarily, long enough for their complements to disembark, then lunged upwards straining for speed and altitude to escape the flurry of bullets that sought them out, from surviving guerrillas who had been regrouped into some sort of defensive order.

Matt couldn't tell how many troops were now down in the bush of the valley floor, but estimating the number of helicopters and their troop-carrying capacities, he guessed there were perhaps 120 to 180.

The valley was an eruption of violent sound.

Within minutes, the heliborne 'Crusader' shock troops were sweeping in. They could be discerned by the sound of their rifle fire rather than seen. The unity of their movement was like the marriage of cells in a body; the automation of a drill instilled in them by many arduous hours of rehearsal so that they could perform without having to think about its consequences, its social and moral implications.

Transporters poured out paratroopers; too many canopies to count accurately, deployed in the blue – perhaps a hundred, a hundred and twenty. In the twenty seconds or so before they were on the ground they were subjected to heavy rifle fire. Tracers riddled the sky. It looked as if a few parachute canopies were hit, but none of the paratroopers.

The paratroopers formed stop groups, picking off survivors who got past the heliborne ambush positions, preventing them fleeing from the bombed assembly area.

Gunships prowled overhead, blasting guerrilla escape routes with their 20mm cannons. Gunship 'eggs', expended 20mm cartridge cases overfilling their recovery boxes, rained from the sky.

Spotter aircraft blasted with frag rockets anything that moved within their battle cordon.

In orderly procession the bombers and fighters returned home.

The helicopters came and went, refuelling and rearming at the LZ Matt had selected for them twelve kilometres north of the assembly point.

GAC ground to air comms, and ground to ground, were frantically taking place on just about every frequency he tuned into. But for Matt, events were no longer under his direction. He had done all his transmitting. He had passed the codeword for the attack to commence. Now there was no further need for him to say anything. It was no longer his responsibility. So he just watched his very own command performance.

Action was taking place everywhere. The task force was raking down anything in their line of fire that breathed. They killed the guerrillas as they pushed forward, they killed them as they pulled back, killed them as they halted, killed them, and killed them some more.

The heat haze and smoke became so thick Matt could no longer see the bottom of the valley. On the perimeter the stop groups were faced with the driving violence of those who had seen death more than once and who no longer cared whether they lived or died so long as they took as many of their attackers with them as they could, for the only option was to be consumed in the giant incinerator that was now Mumvuri's camp.

'. . . We have you visual . . . bank left . . . roll out now . . . half way . . . overhead now.' A member of the ground force was talking in an aircraft to yet another enclave of the enemy. There was the constant sound of rifle fire in the background as the ground forces put down as much ground fire as possible, in an attempt to lessen the 'heat' on the aircraft. '. . . Roger . . . fireball . . .,' the pilot responded, and Matt could see the aircraft swoop in. 250-litre Frantan bombs branded the valley with 150-metre long burning scars. The overpowering stench of burning concentrated petroleum jelly came to Matt on the wind and stung his nostrils.

A pall of smoke now hung over the valley just as the early morning mist had done. Surviving anti-aircraft batteries scattered grey airbursts, fracturing the sky above them.

The constant thud of rockets, the mortar belches of earth and smoke, and the incessant pop-popping of small-arms fire. High velocity bullets, their shock waves through flesh as injurious as their solid lead, tore the air at ground level in angry rents.

The explosive sounds echoed between the Mapfupa Hills, until they were just a constant rumbling of unbroken solid sound.

From the air continued to come 20mm and 30mm cannon fire, and the ripping of twin MAGs through guerrillas who clustered as they retreated, presenting themselves as block targets. The helicopters streaked this way and that through the entire length of the camp, in and out of the smoke. Red and green tracers of anti-aircraft fire chased one another up from the ground through the smoke to meet the metal birds there.

'*Dzu*,' Matt heard !Kai's voice from back in time. It was !Kai's word for vultures, and it was also his word for aeroplanes.

Urgent voices drifted through to him across the static of the radio reception. It seemed that few aircraft, other than the helicopters, were taking hits; the main anti-aircraft batteries having been made inoperable, the faster aircraft were into the valley and were almost gone before the remaining enemy gunners positioned elsewhere on the edges of the hills could take a bead on them.

Midday Matt helped himself to a little water from one of his water bottles, his throat dry, and he ate a little more of the smokey grilled fish.

Then mysteriously the valley cleared of all aircraft.

A disturbing quiet pervaded, punctuated only intermittently by the pop-popping sound of small-arms fire.

Well, that's that, it's over, he said to himself.

Then over the radio he heard 'Bombs gone.'

Refuelled and bombed up, the bombers had returned.

Matt pressed against the earth behind a large rock, covering his ears with his hands in expectation of what was to follow. Once again he gulped for air in the horrendous combustion.

Then the bombers were gone.

Back came the fighters, spitting their own kind of death from the air.

Small-arms fire, rockets and mortars resumed at ground level. Pomz II and M-966 'Jumping Jacks' that booby-trapped probable escape paths detonated as guerrillas attempting to flee the renewed conflagration stumbled across the pull-release trip-wires.

The smoke thickened and the noise continued.

Matt lay back; picked his teeth with a straw.

Once again, for what had to be the last time that day because it was almost dark, the bombers and fighters returned. The sun seemed to weep on the hills – with blood.

Matt was looking on at the general scene of the battle when he saw a strela surface-to-air missile streak from the bush and across the sky from the far side of the valley. In the few seconds of its flight, he saw a fully laden helicopter flying in its path, seemingly unaware, then suddenly bank tight to starboard and plummet down to treetop level trying frantically to evade the missile by winding in and out of the trees. The rocket failed to detonate against the branches. The helicopter pilot, though performing an incredible feat of flying, ran short of time by a second or two. The helicopter exploded, seemed to hang stationary in the air, then fell amongst the trees, swallowed whole by the immortal, insatiable bush.

The incident was like part of a nightmare. He saw it but could isolate no particular sounds relating to it from the din of noise that had taken up residence in the valley. All Matt could think was that there was only one helicopter pilot he knew who could fly like that, in coming so close to escaping what in any event was certain death. He looked to the far hillside from where the missile had come – but there was nothing to see there but bush. He held up a hand before his face and noticed that he wasn't trembling, not even with the vibration of a normal hand. He was numb.

The fighting continued regardless.

Then it was night.

Matt stared blankly into the dark.

The artillery and anti-aircraft guns that had once defended the valley had been captured and turned round upon it. They drummed all night, a continual barrage of dull *carump* . . . *carump* . . . a sound which could not be heard without thinking of pulverised bone and ruptured flesh. The light of the exploding shells gently touched the rims of the hills.

Every now and again a section of the night on the valley floor would be illuminated. Icarus parachute flares! Just as a flare popped, another flare went up and another. They hung briefly as balls of light in the black sky then started to float lazily down on their little parachutes, swinging from side to side.

He could visualise in his mind's eye what was happening down there, a task force sweep-line moving forward in sections, one section watching for movement and engaging the enemy in the translucent light while the other section shielded their eyes, faces pressed against the earth to prevent being dazzled by the light. And as soon as the parachute flares had died, upon the signal given by the first section, the second section moved forward, overrunning any of the guerrillas who had survived the first assault, those whose wide eyes still had to adjust to the darkness once again. The task force were using grenades in the darkness, giving no indication of where they were, not allowing so much as the muzzle flash of a single rifle to give away their positions to the enemy.

Danielle closed her eyes and listened to the sounds of night falling across the valley. It seemed as though something of great significance was coming across to her, a part of her life returning, wrapped in its sentimental melody, the time when Matt had asked her to spend the rest of her life with him.

It was a shock the last time she had looked into Matt's eyes. She saw an age unrelated to his own; fifty-year-old eyes had looked at her from a twenty-five-year-old head.

Then, looking out at the farmhouse security fences with their spotlights, she found herself thinking about her first childhood sweetheart. She had thought there would be no one else in her life but that boy. She wondered where he was now. They were both only fourteen, when her thoughts of marriage were of settling down with a nice man with a nice stable job, in a nice little cottage with a nice little white picket fence . . . with nice little children . . .

Matt tried to raise James on the radio but couldn't, the batteries were now only transmitting infrequently.

Looking down at himself, dressed as a guerrilla, armed like a guerrilla, with cork-ash blackened face, arms and legs like a guerrilla, he was suddenly aware that he was not in a particularly enviable predicament. He wondered how he was going to hitch a flight back home. He didn't fancy walking and he didn't fancy braving the border without clearance.

The task force killed anything that moved without permission as soon as look at it, so he didn't fancy waltzing down into the valley unannounced. With machine-guns to talk for them they didn't much go in for asking questions.

Then James came through. Although Matt could no longer transmit, he could still receive.

James suspected what had happened so instructed him to make his position obvious, and he would come and get him.

Matt lit a fire on a large exposed rock on the ridge overlooking the valley and covered it with green leaves then moved well away from it, preferring not to give anyone who didn't know what was going on an unnecessary target.

One or other helicopter would occasionally detach itself from the valley floor so he did not really know that one was heading towards him until, while still far away, the pilot waggled its tail.

It was a typical gesture he knew only too well.

'Rotor, you fucking cowboy,' he said to himself, 'I thought you'd had it.' He found himself smiling.

He threw his rifle into a bush, ripped off his battle jacket and shirt, exposing white skin, not wanting any failures of recognition, and stepped out into the open.

After a short while as the helicopter drew closer, he saw James aboard point in his direction. The helicopter nosed towards him in the clearing he had chosen for it.

James leapt out even before the helicopter touched down, and ran towards him.

James looked as immaculate as ever, dressed in camo garb along with the rest of the task force, but his was superbly tailored, carefully laundered and pressed, and he was wearing a cravat of conservative subdued colour.

James shook his hand vigorously and was unable to prevent himself from embracing him.

'God, Matt, am I pleased to see you.'

Then, for the first time, Matt saw who it was who had come up behind James.

James saw him observing Red.

'He sat in the ops bunker at the office following your every transmission as it was written down. He even slept so close to the radio he was practically on it. He knew it was receiving even before Andy or I did, by the vibration of the table. Once he had found out you were away he guessed the rest. We couldn't have kept him out even if we had wanted to.'

Matt saw how Red looked a skeleton of his former self.

He saw Red's eyes film over.

They hugged each other strongly, crushingly. But Matt quickly broke off – it was too much, too soon.

Red grinned. 'Sonofabitch,' he said.

Matt smiled back.

He looked over Red's shoulder to the helicopter, and saw that the pilot was not Rotor, that the technician was not Jacob.

Suddenly he was no longer smiling.

'Rotor and Jacob were hit,' said James in a subdued voice. 'Surface-to-air missile – strela.'

'They always did joke about themselves being strela magnets,' Matt said.

He felt he could do nothing but stare through clouded eyes into the horror of the valley. He had never thought that Rotor and Jacob would not be seen alive again, he had always thought that it was him that it would happen to.

'Andy still down there?' he asked, retrieving his rifle, shirt and jacket.

James placed a hand across his shoulders and guided him towards the helicopter. As they flew back down to the assembly point in the valley, he told Matt about Andy.

Andy had apparently brought 'doctored' batches of the previously captured guerrilla arms caches – rounds that would explode in the breech, grenades that had a zero-second fuse delay, rockets and mortars that would detonate before propulsion.

It was expected that Andy wouldn't sit still and mope, making up instead for not having been included in the recce with Matt. He wasn't the type of person who would allow himself to be left out without a parting shot.

As the task force commander considered it an impossibility to take back or destroy all the arms caches in the camp in the time available, Andy's 'doctored' supplies were left behind with those intact. If those arms caches were then utilised later by the guerrillas there would be those who, when they next squeezed a trigger or pulled the pin of a grenade, would disappear – Andy's magic . . . pouf . . . gone.

Another task force wouldn't have to hunt down all the survivors. Some of them would kill themselves as soon as they resorted to the use of their own weapons.

It would be difficult, if not impossible, for the surviving guerrilla hierarchy to recall all arms and ammunition later issued from the camp in the valley after the task force had withdrawn and the guerrilla survivors had regrouped, for many would immediately infiltrate the border.

Whether they did recall ammunition issued from the valley or not, it would make no difference as far as consternation amongst guerrillas in the field would be concerned. It would come to the stage where they would be scared to use their weapons.

Any caches overlooked in future raids, whether in the country or outside it, would almost certainly not be trusted by the guerrillas, and would in all probability be destroyed by them.

Andy had dreamed of the day they would have the gooks destroying all their own ammunition. He had visions of every new Communist bloc arms shipment being thrown overboard as soon as it docked, ending up at the bottom of the harbour.

As for the security forces? Any captured arms could be checked quickly under ultra-violet light for particular identification marks. Those doctored arms recovered could always be re-deployed, while safe ammunition could always be used by special forces, such as the Team, for their own purposes.

While Andy had been planting his 'parting gifts', he had been advised that a bunker containing documents had been discovered.

Andy was gone.

The documents had been booby-trapped with an incendiary bomb backed up by a delayed charge of high explosive.

Matt wanted to see for himself that it was just the way he had been told it was, that it was in fact real.

Back on the ground, he saw the remains of Rotor and Jacob in the 'hearse' helicopter, and those of Andy wrapped up in James's jacket, along with four troopers who had died in the fighting.

James, meanwhile, fussed about him protectively, intent on ensuring that after his ordeal he wanted for nothing. But Matt wanted nothing.

James was needed elsewhere but he wouldn't leave Matt alone until Matt had convinced him that he was all right.

Constructions of pole, thatch and *daga* were now just burnt-out shells of constructions. The task force had fired at the valley and the valley had fired back, and the firing back had come less and less.

Like crushed insects, severely wounded guerrillas wriggled feebly on the ground. The air was alive with their cries, moans, screams . . . *maiwe . . . maiwe . . . ndiyamura . . . ndiyamura . . .* help me . . . help me . . . *ndiponesa . . .* save me . . .

Matt unconsciously flicked the safety catch of his rifle on and off, before he was aware of it and left it off, taking his finger slowly from the trigger. Those that screamed were finished off by those that were alive but didn't scream.

A troopie raked the ground directly at the base of a bush behind which a wounded guerrilla had sought refuge, taking in the circumference within which he believed the man to be. The bullets tumbled from the ground, increasing their area of impact and kicked up sand with their ricochets, tearing skin from the face, blinding. Then the man stepped forward, shot the guerrilla once through the temple, picked up a full AK magazine from the webbing of the guerrilla he had just killed, evidently with his last bullet, threw aside his empty magazine and clipped on the full one.

In a foxhole, the corpse of yet another guerrilla stiffened in his scarlet mud. Behind him a guerrilla cowered. One of the troopers saw the rise of the chest as the guerrilla inhaled having tried to hold his breath long enough to escape detection. The troopie fired two shots straight through the corpse the man was using as a shield, and the man did not finish his breath.

Open-lipped wounds mouthed at Matt as he passed.

Every once in a while the bush sang with a bullet or two, from a very brave or a very foolish sniper who persisted in worrying the task force to the bitter end. The fact that Matt had heard the bullets, he told himself, meant that he was still alive.

Two members of the sweep-line got up and ran forward to draw out the sniper. The sniper fired at them, hitting one of them in the leg. The rest of the sweep-line opened up on the tree where they had seen the muzzle flash of the sniper's rifle. Under the incredible volume of fire the tree suddenly lost most of its leaves and branches. The sniper dropped out of it like a tsetse fly sprayed with insecticide.

The sweep-line stepped cautiously over dead body after dead body. Every once in a while a shot or two was fired where they still saw life.

A grenade went off, the base-plug chewing viciously back past Matt's head.

Every time they came across a covered trench a demolition expert came forward and said exactly the same thing: 'Knock knock . . .' someone would laugh, and the man would drop a one-kilogram bunker bomb down one or more of the air vents. They inevitably blew the roof of yet another part of the maze of zigzagging underground bunkers and trenches.

Come afternoon, there was a change. Nothing moved in the paralysed air. Silence, louder than the explosions, filled the valley.

Bodies were in different places, different poses, but they all had one thing in common: they were all dead. Bodies floated in the river.

348

There were still others, disintegrated in the bombing runs; they were in the trees and he was walking on them. They were the *magandanga* – guerrillas, the savage men!

The valley was a red river in a black wasteland. The only things that were standing apart from the task force were leafless, branchless, charred stumps at unnatural angles.

There were monstrous craters everywhere, and the crackling and smouldering of fires.

Moto usingaperi – everlasting fire? No, just Man-made hell.

The fetid stench of seared flesh and burnt hair clung to the air.

People upon people, dead people, killed people, no-more people were everywhere no matter in which direction you took your next step.

Under the front of a chopper, out of the sun, as there was no shade to be found now that the camp was treeless, some troopies were casually listening to pop music on a 'big-means' radio. They had tuned into one of the commercial radio stations back across the border. They had ignited a small makeshift stove, AVTUR and sand in a can, and were making coffee. One of them was shielding the flame with his hands. The coffee was barely steaming when the troopies shared it.

Matt looked at himself in the broken mirror of one of the now bombed-out and charred vehicles he had seen hauling guerrillas and military hardware into the valley. His face had the pale greenish hue of a freshly exhumed corpse.

A rough-hewn branch table stood undisturbed in the middle of a bombed clearing, craters all around it, but miraculously it was untouched. On it was a teased wood-fibre wick immersed in solidified animal fat. And there was a jar lid containing a solution of powdered milk sprinkled with a yellow powder. Fly agaric, he told himself. There were a number of flies dead in it. Everything was absolutely still. It didn't seem possible that it was real.

He could see a couple of troopies a little further on from the table, moving amongst the dead. Something glinted in their hands. Steel. Knife blades. They were cutting ears off the corpses of the guerrillas and stringing them on to gut lines around their waists to sun dry as souvenirs. Matt had heard of it being done before but had never seen it.

A Dak flew up and down the valley. The war was continuing, psychological war, a leaflet drop aimed at the survivors. Survivors?

Amidst all that devastation it was difficult to believe that any of them had survived, but they had.

Pambere negore re gukurahundi
Pambili ngo myaka wembasama-hlanga

'Why die for nothing
and leave your family spirits unappeased?
Come home in safety', proclaimed the leaflets.

The bush whimpered; some may have said that it was the wind.

Numbed, expressionless, holding his rifle by its barrel and trailing its butt along the ground behind him, Matt wandered aimlessly about the killing ground.

He had never seen Mumvuri's face, so he could not have known if he was among the bodies there. And yet he knew him better than any man. He had spent over a year thinking about no one else. On the faces that he saw there were no stigmata, no weals, nothing to suggest any inhumanity, no red eyes, no devil horns, no spear-ended tail. The faces were almost kindly.

Mumvuri's presence was still there, he could feel it, not concentrated as in the form of a man's person, but all around, permeating every man and everything, the centre of its source could not be pointed at.

His rifle dropped from his hand as he walked. He looked back at it, but didn't stop to pick it up. Instead, he pushed his hands into his trouser pockets.

Danielle stopped reflecting upon her past. It wouldn't help the present, and it was the present she had to deal with.

Outside she heard the high-pitched 'peeps' of the striped reed frogs, the croaking of toads, the chirrup of cicadas, the churring of fiery-necked night jars, punctuated occasionally by the hoots of a barn owl. She remembered when late one night Matt had excitedly woken her up and taken her to the barn to see the owl with a rodent it had killed, and a clutch of young owlets. If there was a shortage of food only the eldest would be fed. But here there was plenty of food. 'One of the few birds that actually profits because of Man,' he had said.

James suddenly appeared beside him again.

'There's something else I must tell you,' said James.

350

Matt awaited news of another loss, numb enough to take it without any display of emotion.

'It's about Mumvuri,' James said. 'He's dead. Well, at least I think the guerrilla we set out to get.'

Matt turned to him.

'Information we've just uncovered reveals that he died apparently of bullet wounds after the mission massacre follow-up. The guerrilla who disposed of the body, assumed his name, took his weapon, his clothes, his boots, everything, moved in areas where Mumvuri had not previously been seen, only heard of by reputation, and kept the name alive.'

Matt looked, without seeing.

'The one who assumed the name may be dead out there too, but I don't know. In time information will filter back to us, unless someone else assumes the role, keeping him alive.'

Matt felt too dazed to say anything in reply. What could be said to follow that?

'What happened to your rifle?' James asked.

'Lost it,' said Matt.

James sucked at his pipe for a few seconds, although it was empty, staring at him as if he didn't quite know what to say to that in turn either.

Last light was approaching.

James whirled his hand as the helicopter crank-up signal, and said, 'Let's go home.'

The task force, with captured prisoners, tons of war material and war documents departed.

A fresh recce stick – reconnaissance group – was left in the Mapfupa Hills to monitor activity, to disrupt logistics and communication lines that would attempt to reform.

None of them had known it before the raid, but they all knew it now. Mumvuri's last given orders were that in the event of a raid on the camp, as soon as the surviving occupants regrouped, they were to cross the border and conduct a concerted parcel-bombing campaign against soft targets in the high-traffic areas of the towns and cities – shopping centres, hotels, hospitals . . .

Back on home soil, in town, along with the other multitude of things that had to be done, James arranged to see the relatives of Andy, Rotor and Jacob.

Matt felt it strange that he had got to know Rotor and Jacob so well but didn't know any of their families. He did know Elaine, though, and he offered to be the one to see her.

He found himself at her door, but now that he was there he had no idea what to say. How was he going to tell her? No matter how he worded it there was no escaping the fact.

'He's dead isn't he?' she said.

He nodded.

She was surprisingly calm.

He didn't know whether he was expected to go or to stay.

He had not come with pity. It would have done no good to have come with pity, pity couldn't heal a body that had been blown apart by high explosive.

Elaine stared vacantly out of the window.

'The most beautiful things that developed between us seemed to grow when we were apart,' she said. 'Life is strange.'

Matt saw the pain enter her body, but not leave it. He could see it rebounding back upon itself there in the darkness that had suddenly filled her, to become a yelling soundless agony within her, mounting, mounting . . .

She could not keep up the composure, collapsed into a chair, and started crying with vocal cords that seemed cut, sliced by reality.

He held her comfortingly in his arms.

She sobbed and sobbed until it appeared that she would choke with the grief. Then it was over, the first wave had broken over her and she had borne the rush and weight of it.

But Matt knew that the seventh wave was always the biggest, and the waves would never stop, there was always one more wave after the last.

She clung to him, her forehead pressed against his chest.

'I don't want to be alone tonight,' she said.

Matt held her tightly.

'Matt, make love to me,' she pleaded.

Matt knew that she needed someone to cling to.

He comforted her through the night.

She talked and talked, about Andy and about her; she asked Matt to tell her about Andy and him.

Matt remembered how he had first met Andy in the pursuit of the murderers of his father and brother, and how, since then, he and

Andy had been through all kinds of hell together in their efforts to rid the valley of guerrilla tyranny. How Andy had taken the ultimate step, sacrificing his life that others might live in peace.

He thought how cruel life was, that he had shunned Andy before the cross-border reconnaissance, because he hadn't fancied their chances of returning, but that he had returned and Andy hadn't. He felt that perhaps when it was your time to go, there was no stopping you.

With Elaine in his arms, he thought of Danielle, how he had tried to protect her, prevent her from being subjected to the war's horror, how Red had done the same with Suzanne and then lost her, and how he had lost Danielle in another way.

Although Matt was thinking these things, he told Elaine about the good times, and how in a valley where all things were born to die, Andy couldn't have done more for the things he believed in and the people he loved. He told her how honoured he was to have been able to say he had had a friend like Andy, a man's man if ever there was one, who thought of others before himself, a man who, though scared, took the risks anyway. Matt thought these things, he believed them and he was distraught that at the end he had said things that made Andy think that he had felt otherwise.

'I'm carrying his baby,' Elaine said finally.

When daylight came she slept.

Driving along the dirt road to the farmhouse, Matt longingly breathed the air coming off the *veld*, saw the cattle in the shade of the trees by the fence, was happy to feel every bump on the dirt road, and when the *koppie* came into view with the farmhouse at the top, and the farm buildings clustered around its base, he stopped the Land Rover and turned off the engine.

There was a part deep inside that hurt with the emotion at seeing that sight again.

The quiet came to him and then the sounds of the birds in the *veld*. It was as tranquil as he had ever known.

Past the *koppie*, past the dam, he could see where the farm's river joined the main river of the valley and he could see way down into the valley as it stretched towards the border.

But it wasn't because of the emotional effect of seeing the farm alone that he had stopped. He was unsure how Danielle would receive him, and he wasn't sure whether what he had to tell her was best coming from him.

Looking into the valley, he was looking into the past, to a time a little over fifteen months ago when one Sunday, shirking responsibility of the farm, he and Danielle with a back-pack lunch had left the house with the morning mist still on the river and how they had come back with the sunset. That is what seemed to have happened to their relationship since then.

The momentum of the war had simply taken them downhill. Who could have known what lay ahead of them, and if he could have known would he have decided to do any different?

What he felt was best to do was to turn around and go, perhaps speak to her on the phone first, but instead he started up the engine again and continued on up to the farmhouse.

He greeted the armed militia as they enthusiastically let him through the gate.

The geese scurried from the vehicle's path, the dogs barked excitedly, chasing geese and each other and jumping into the doorless cab as he drove along the rest of the driveway. He acknowledged them fondly, stroking them and shaking them playfully by the ruffs of their collar in the manner they liked.

He went tentatively into the house.

He met Maruva in the passage, and she greeted him fondly enough, but with a trace of uncertainty as to what to expect.

When he greeted her by hugging her playfully like he used to, she nudged him gently away.

'Silly boy,' she accused, but with a smile.

The dogs following, Matt went into the kitchen with its aroma of freshly baked bread, then into the adjoining rooms of the passage, each in turn.

'Miss Danielle's in the bedroom,' Maruva said.

Matt went to the bedroom, stopped at the door, knocked, waited, then walked in.

'Oh! It's you.' It was an expression of polite awareness.

'I knocked, there was no answer, I came in,' Matt said.

'Yes, I can see,' Danielle said, at the dressing-table.

She had retreated to the furthest end of the house, and now realised what an inappropriate place it was to see him again after all that had happened between them. And the fact that he had knocked on his own bedroom door had taken her aback.

354

He stood meekly before her, awkwardly.

When he thought she would turn him away, a shadow of concern fell across his face.

It immediately softened her a little towards him. She suddenly felt the need for a cigarette and lit one.

'I didn't know you smoked,' said Matt.

She coughed on the smoke, her eyes watered.

He gave a hint of a smile. Between them the situation was understood, words could only damage it further.

He found himself reaching out to reassure her. 'Do you think it's worth trying again?'

They stood a respectful distance apart from each other.

'I don't know,' she said. 'I want to, so much, but I couldn't take being so hurt again, I couldn't take any more worry, any more emotional strain, any more responsibility for trying to hold the farm together if you were to go away again.'

'It's over,' he said.

'For how long? How long until the next time?'

'I love you,' he said, in the typical manner she had first known, but now somewhat to her astonishment.

And she noticed there was no black mamba vertebrae choker around his neck.

She came closer to him.

He held out his arms and she came into them.

Chastely, they hugged.

After a while in which time had seemed to stand still, she looked up at him, her eyes moist. 'I'll try,' she said.

Gently, softly, they kissed.

They had changed, both of them. The war had changed them day by day. They were not the same man and woman who had met, fallen in love and married. Both accepted the meeting as if it was their first. It remained to be seen if the two people they had become could find the same love as the two people they had once been.

'I didn't want to tell you this before, in case it influenced how you'd feel about us,' he said, 'so I've left it till now.'

She stared up at him, the concern wide in her eyes.

'Andy, Rotor and Jacob are dead.'

'Oh God!' she exclaimed, closing her eyes.

'James is arranging to see Rotor's and Jacob's relatives. You know, it suddenly occurred to me that we never even met them. However, we do know Elaine and I was with her last night.'

'How is she?'

'When I left her she was asleep.'

'I'll be there for her when she wakes up.'

'We'll be there together.'

The earth was still in orbit. There were eclipses of moon and sun. There were times when the earth was furthest from the sun and times when it was closest. The bush stayed the same as it had always been. And out there in the vast unrelenting continent of Africa, !Kai, a little old weather-brown man, son-of-the-soil, listened to the stars singing.

THE SNOW BEES
Peter Cunningham

Patrick Drake is ambitious. He's a high flyer who wants to get to the top of the corporate ladder – fast. And a business trip to sort out a fiasco of a French vineyard looks just like the fast track to promotion.

It isn't. He reports back to head office and then he's fired.

From muck-raking in a molehill of missing money, he steps on a minefield of murderous activity. In a tightening web of terrorism and violence he finds himself facing the naked savagery of the international cocaine trade. Fighting to clear his name – and to save his life – he unravels a threat of fear and fanaticism that runs from South Africa to Spain, from Ireland to the United States. And at any moment he may feel the fatal sting . . .

'Ripping' *Oxford Times*

'Gripping' *Standard*

FUTURA PUBLICATIONS
THRILLER
0 7474 0137 3

THE SAMURAI STRATEGY

THOMAS HOOVER

IT BEGINS WITH THE MYSTERIOUS
THEFT OF A PRICELESS SAMURAI
SWORD. BEFORE IT IS OVER, ONE
NATION WILL STAND ON THE BRINK
OF RUIN . . .

Powerful Japanese industrialist Matsuo Noda has
set in motion a chilling plan, an ingenious strategy
that involves hiring Wall Street wizard Matthew
Walton to head up a secret investment project. But
Walton soon realizes he is a pawn in a takeover
plot of astonishing proportions. With time running
out and death at his heels, Walton desperately tries
to scupper the high-tech coup and prevent the
ultimate goal of Noda's frightening scheme: to
destroy US financial markets and break the back of
the country's economy. For when America stands
naked before the world, Noda will emerge as a
powerful modern-day Shogun – ready for his next
explosive move . . .

Also by Thomas Hoover in Sphere Books:
The Moghul
Caribbee

0 7474 0068 7   GENERAL FICTION

POSSESSION

PETER JAMES

Fabian Hightower was killed in a car crash. That's what
the police told his mother. She didn't believe them –
she'd seen him that morning. Fabian, the police insist,
is dead. But Alex's imagination keeps playing painful
tricks on her. It haunts her days; it breaks her nights
and it is turning her grief into terror. It drives her, in
desperation, to a medium. And it freezes the medium
into petrified silence. Because it isn't her imagination. It
is Fabian. He wants to come back . . .

'A psychothriller that eschews shock-horror tactics,
offering instead a more cerebral, more plausible
investigation of the paranormal'
Publishing News

0 7474 0336 8   GENERAL FICTION

All Sphere Books are available at your bookshop or newsagent, or can be ordered from the following address: Sphere Books, Cash Sales Department, P.O. Box 11, Falmouth, Cornwall TR10 9EN.

Please send cheque or postal order (no currency), and allow 60p for postage and packing for the first book plus 25p for the second book and 15p for each additional book ordered up to a maximum charge of £1.90 in U.K.

B.F.P.O. customers please allow 60p for the first book, 25p for the second book plus 15p per copy for the next 7 books, thereafter 9p per book.

Overseas customers, including Eire, please allow £1.25 for postage and packing for the first book, 75p for the second book and 28p for each subsequent title ordered.